Keitas

By Evan R. Meyer

Keitas

Copyright © 2020, Evan R. Meyer

Illustration © 2020, Evan R. Meyer

Table of Contents

Prologue

Fell clouds swirled about in a deadly vortex around Thundercrest Mountain, with an ominous calm in the center of the storm. Not-so-distant thunder cracked and rumbled several times a minute, giving the imposing peak meaning to its namesake.

The whipping snow and howling winds which had so thrashed Lynad and Grandma upon their ascent ceased with little notice, as if stepping into a weather-less barrier. The difficult terrain, from steep rocky outcroppings to walls of conifer trees made the trek difficult on foot, much less the idea of bringing forth a horse to carry them. As a result, they had little choice but to leave the fortunate horse in an inn's stable near the foot of the mountain.

Grandma thus far had been a quiet, intimidating companion. She rarely spoke, and when she did, it was in curt sentences, usually giving advice or orders on their course. Little seemed to faze the old woman, as the occasional report of distant Kuru splinter forces was met with indifference, and even the very weather itself failed to slow her. In fact, Lynad recalled that upon their first bit of drudgery through the snowstorm that he swore the snow never even touched her body, nor did the wind. She had walked upright and unflappable throughout the brunt of the mountain's wrath as if it were no more than a leisurely summer stroll through the countryside.

By the time they had crossed into the eye of the storm, roughly halfway up the mountain, Lynad was shivering and soaked while Grandma walked on with little sign she had even been touched by a single snowflake. However, it was difficult to tell, given that the evening sun had long since waned past the distant horizon.

Lynad shook the clumps of snow and ice from his overcoat. "Don't make this look too easy or you'll make us lowly rangers look bad."

She smirked from under her hood. "In my experience, young man, rangers have never taken great pride in their 'looks'."

"It defeats the purpose of looking road-savvy."

"Ah yes. If attraction to customers is what rangers crave, then perhaps a bath from time to time might be suitable?" she asked rhetorically.

It was the most she had said for several days. *Maybe she does have a personality under all of that mystique. One with a bit of pretentiousness to be sure, but a personality nonetheless.*

As they neared the upper quarter of the mountain, similarly to his last encounter the trees did not thin as they proceeded upward. His insides felt strange as if they were being wrestled over and he knew that soon they would be enduring the terrifying experience of falling into the sky.

That is, until Grandma simply waved a hand, her expression neutral.

Immediately his insides ceased their tumult, and the world blurred about him for a second until many of the trees thinned out and they stood on snow again. Looking up, Lynad saw the stone archway above, cloaked in shadow. *She...somehow stopped it. If it was an illusion, she cut right through it!*

A shift in his vision revealed the whisking robes of a figure standing beneath the arch, and he knew it was the witch. Her hood was down and her frazzled white hair lent to her witchly appearance. Clearly she had sensed something very wrong, as the flecks of her face he could see were in wide-eyed anger.

"You treacherous ranger!" her shrill voice pierced the night, "I ordered you to kill her and return to me with her head! By bringing her here, you have surrendered your daughter to me forever!"

Lynad's heart pumped with an uncertain anxiety. If Grandma failed to come through on her promise, he very well may never see his Sera again.

"You and I both know that if you had retained the capacity to kill, you would not have had need to swindle a sellsword into your service. You would have sought me out yourself," Grandma's voice responded calmly.

"My capacity is not in question. But his daughter's life is."

"It does not befit you to continue making empty threats, as you always have. It would seem to my recollection that there once existed a woman named Miria who faced the brunt of her own problems, deigning to treat others with respect rather than to use them for her own twisted ends."

She flinched angrily. "Do not speak that name to me! It bears no relevance to who I am and has not for hundreds of years! I am no longer Miria, but the Witch of Thundercrest Mountain!"

"So you tell yourself. I see your bad habit of kidnapping children hasn't changed, 'witch'."

Lynad watched between them, keeping a vigilant eye out for his daughter. "Who is this woman to you?"

Grandma's eyes narrowed into a look of casual disdain, hands akimbo. "Merely a very lost child of mine, calloused and jaded with age."

"And this *woman* you have spared is nothing more than my self-righteous, power-hungry mother. Tell me mother, how many husbands have you gone through this decade? Did you tell them before they died you would not be joining them in the afterlife?" Miria the witch spat.

"Wait, this old woman is your *daughter*? How is that possible?" Lynad asked incredulously.

"She was my daughter once, yes. Once she had purpose. She had conviction, a beauteous sight to behold for men and her doting mother alike. Now you see what she has become – nothing more than a bitter hermit, a dealer in petty magic and an enforcer of her own contrived image. Miria is dangerous in her own way, to be certain, but the most critical danger she poses is to herself."

"My mother is a *liar!*" Miria barked furiously, "It would be wise to disbelieve anything she has ever told you, for *she* deals in the ways of deception and she cares little for others. Everything she does serves the purpose of sacrificing others for her own gain. You should not trust her!"

"I'm having difficulty with taking that from a woman who wants to steal my daughter from me," Lynad growled, "She had better be alive."

"Your daughter still lives, and you still have time to rectify your mistake. Help me kill her and I will return your healthy daughter to you. Help me now!" the woman demanded, gritting her teeth and leering at her mother with fire in her eyes.

"That will be quite enough." Grandma stepped slowly closer to the witch, the rich timbre of her voice curdling into an ominous growl. "You bear no more ability to kill me than he does, and I have grown weary of your idle threats. You are doing what you have done for many centuries – hiding in your vapid seclusion, fancying yourself a dangerous witch when in reality you are a spoiled child desperate for the very meaning and purpose you were so quick to cast away."

The witch shrieked in anger, striking out with her hand. For a brief moment Lynad lost all bearings on the scene playing out in front of him. The world trembled and his entire sense of equilibrium spun like a compass, and he fell to a knee, filled with nausea. When it suddenly stopped, his gaze returned to see the witch pinned against the ground by an unseen force, and Grandma's arm outstretched, her fingers curled inward.

A low thrum vibrated the earth. "No more will I permit you to live this way," Grandma hissed, "Do not make the mistake of believing the world barren of love for you. There are others who can help you, make you whole again. Old friends with which your acquaintance has been sorely missed. Return this man's daughter to him as you promised, and we shall go our separate ways in peace."

Miria the witch trembled terribly as she fought the force which held her. Anger still burst forth in her words, "I will never go with you!"

Grandma sighed before closing her fist. With hardly a sound the old witch's body contorted and her head pounded back against the stone. Lynad was agape.

"Did you...is she dead?" he exclaimed.

"Of course not," Grandma responded cavalierly, "she is merely unconscious. Less likely to argue that way. Your daughter should be inside. Go to her."

Relief flooded over him, and he wasted no time. Bounding over the snow-covered rock steppes, he threw open the door to the hut. Inside it was small – scarcely large enough to house a single person comfortably. Furs of a plethora of animals lined the walls and covered the ground, with a traditionally Lärimite-style fireplace burning in the corner, crackling softly. Next to an idle loom on one side of the room, he saw Sera.

She was like an angel, sleeping quietly, slumped against the wall. Her middle had been re-wrapped in bandages and the color of her skin was much warmer than it had been upon their last meeting. With slightly longer, washed hair, his daughter was looking every bit as healthy as a young girl should be – if not better than usual.

"Oh, my Sera," he said gently, holding a hand to her cheek, "It's father. I've come to bring you home."

Her eyes slowly flitted open, comprehension returning to her. "Father?"

"I am here. How do you feel?"

"I am...I am better. The old witch helped me. She put some kind of salve on my skin and poured some stinging water on my wound. She talked to me – told me about her life. It was so...sad," Sera recounted.

"I would like to hear all about it on our way back. For now, we must leave this place," Lynad said firmly, easing her to her feet.

"Father, did you…" she trailed off, her trusting eyes darting between him and the door.

He smiled warmly. "No, my flower, there was no need. Grandma came to help. Come, I will tell you more on the way down the mountain." She nodded and took his hand, following him into the crisp winter air and the smell of pine trees.

Returning to the clearing, the witch was gone, but Grandma remained, her hood concealing her features in the darkness. She was still, watching them approach.

"I trust she is in good health?" Grandma asked as if she already knew the answer.

"It is a miracle to see her alive and in such good spirits. You have my everlasting gratitude, and I will make it up to you some day. I promise," Lynad said.

She chuckled. "Be careful to whom you make promises, dear ranger. You never know what they will bid you to do for them."

The point had been kindly administered. "Yes, I…I owe you an apology for what I did."

"Save it – you are already forgiven. Though if I may offer counsel, perhaps you may find it beneficial to keep your daughter out of harm's way in the coming days? Next time you will not be so fortunate."

"I will. I don't know what has happened between you and your daughter, and I doubt you would tell me. Frankly it's none of my business. However, I must ask: if she knew I could not best you, then why did she agree to our terms? Why did she heal Sera?"

Lynad could only see her lips, which evenly showed no emotion. "Because either way she wins. In the absurd event that you are able to kill me, she is rid of her pesky, caring mother. If you cannot… she gains a daughter. She has always wanted daughters."

"This has happened before?" Lynad cocked his head.

"Oh yes. Miria has become remarkably skilled at her façade. Having lived for many hundreds of years, she has sought the company of many children to sate her maternal instinct and drive for companionship." Grandma spoke as if it were a banal fact of life.

"What happened to them all?"

It was her turn to cock her head. "Why, my dear ranger, how long would you last alone atop a mountain?"

He nodded mournfully. "It is time for us to go. I promise we will return home where we belong. Out of respect, I will not ask where next you go."

At that she smiled. "It is for the best that you do not know."

Chapter I

Dark water lapped at the caravel's hull as the oppressive fog began to roll in. Distant echoes of seabirds could be heard through the haze, but none of the crew nor did any passengers see them for the length of the voyage.

Reldon and Alira found the Sea of Whispers utterly disquieting. Whereas the eastern or southern seas were bright and had a feeling of strength and life to them, this sea could only be described as sullen, unfeeling even. Words called out by the crew echoed for miles ahead over the completely still waters. There was no choppiness, no waves, and certainly no evidence of life. The deathlike waters were like a glassy graveyard, unwelcoming to outsiders who would dare to enter its domain. Even in the first fifteen minutes past the wall of fog, Reldon spotted at least three broken masts jutting from the distant waters.

Standing at the raised bow of the ship, Reldon, now nearly fifteen years old, kept a wary vigil on their bearing. *It is certainly difficult to believe the Lärimites find this route safe. Nothing feels safe about the Sea of Whispers.*

He kept hearing wispy noises floating about the cold air, and he could not attribute it to the wind, for there simply wasn't any. In fact, at least fifty men had been recruited to push the ship along using oars below decks. Apparently, according to Alira, this was standard procedure.

I don't like it, Reldon said to her through their mental connection, *These waters give me chills, and it's much more than just the wintery air.*

She answered from the mid-deck. *You're starting to see why they call it the Sea of Whispers,* her melodious thoughts chimed back, *If you believe the sailors, the whole sea is haunted. Spirits of battles long past still come out to sink ships and drag sailors to their doom. Of course, if you believe the legends.*

I think I would be stupid not to. These sailors come this way all the time, so if they believe it, there must be something to the legends, Reldon responded, shivering.

"Excuse me, milord. I shall need at those ropes," a sailor's voice came from behind Reldon.

"Of course," Reldon said, clearing the way. He paused as the man worked, before thinking good of asking his opinion. "Do you believe the Sea of Whispers is haunted, good sailor?"

The grizzled man, bearing a scar across his left cheek, stopped what he was doing momentarily and peered at Reldon, assessing him briefly.

How different I must seem, dressed in such rich, dark attire. While the sailor was dressed in a simple long woolen coat, Reldon was dressed in black Spellsword short-robes, a black-and-gold chest plate, and matching gauntlets and pauldrons. After all, it was no common event they headed to.

"You seem concerned, milord. Don't worry – you're aboard the largest caravel in the fleet, accompanied by a small convoy of ships and hundreds of sailors. Kingsmen are our highest priority," he answered, resuming his rope-loosening.

Reldon grinned. "You didn't answer my question."

There was a small amount of hesitation. "Aye. I believe it. If it weren't for the gray waters below, you would see this place has been a bloodbath. Came from all o' them wars between Lärim, Errum, and them Kuru to the west. Dozens of wars, hundreds of battles, and any of them which took place on water are right here in the Sea o' Whispers. Famous ships, proud as any ship could be, have met their demise on these accursed waters. The *Star Crown*, the *Sovereign*, the *Vona Aelianus*... all gone, and for what?"

"It's terrible to think they all died so suddenly that their ghosts still remain," Reldon mused, "So many of them."

"This is a solemn place to sail. Out of respect, we keep our voices down and do not disturb any o' these gravesites. They deserve to be left in peace."

Reldon nodded. "I promise to respect their wishes."

A crash sounded from the stairs leading to the mid-deck and the always-boisterous King Obrim from Atheria lifted himself onto the deck shouting, "An' don' you think to stop me, ye' great eel! Ghosts don' scare ol' King Obrim, no they don't!"

Reldon and the sailor collectively sighed. "I can't vouch for him, however," Reldon said.

"Oi, your lordiness!" he shouted at Reldon, nearly shoving a cabin boy over the edge of the ship, "I take it you've been our crow on lookout. How far is our destination as you fly?"

The sailor cleared his throat. "We should arrive within the hour, Your Grace."

"Eh? Ah, so you must be the crow then. Shouldn't you be in your nest? I can hear the wee chicks chirpin' from here! Off you go!"

The sailor grumbled as he went astern. Obrim stomped up next to Reldon, peering out at the foggy sea. "Strange times we're in, lad. Strange times."

"You really ought to keep your voice down," Reldon asserted, "It really wouldn't do to run afoul of any spirits."

The king of Atheria was dumbfounded. "First off, *every* man should hope at the end of the day to run afoul of spirits. Simple as that. If you want to know where old King Obrim will be at the end of this sordid affair, that's your best bet. Spirits. Lots of them. And second-of-it-all, there are no terrifying ghosties about to leap out and frighten anyone. Except for maybe that lad over there. The wee kitten keeps following me about the ship like he's waiting for his mother tabby to lean over and give him his evening milk! I think *he* may actually be the ghost! Come here, you! Time to throw you in the sea and find out if you float!"

Reldon only managed to say, "Your Grace, he's your servant aboard this-" before the king took chase after the now-terrified child.

"Master, why must I come to Errum? I wanted to stay with Kex," Elly whined.

The lurching of the ship, on top of the rotten-wood smell which seemed to accompany sea-travel, did little to assuage Alira's stomach, but focusing on braiding Elly's long blond hair seemed to help keep her mind off of it. "We all must make an appearance at the Remdas-Kuwis court. It is a sign of respect," she responded gently.

"Besides, don't you want to get away from Lärim for a little while?" Kiera asked with her raspy voice, "I know I do. I'm tired of Lärimite politics for one lifetime." She had also been echoing Alira's seasickness complaints and sought to prop herself against the hull for support, with limited success.

None of it seemed to placate the young Golden Magician. She screwed up her face. "I hate smelly ships even more."

Sillida was sitting cross-legged atop a massive wooden crate. "Errum isn't so bad. It's where Bryle, Reldon, and I grew up. Maybe you'll like it more than Lärim."

There was a pause as Elly was considering, but the obstinate expression on her face told Alira she was not convinced.

"This means a lot to Reldon," Alira said to her simply.

Her eyes flitted about for a moment before settling on the planks below. "I understand, master."

"Sillida, tell us about Errum. None of us have been there before," Kiera said.

"It's…ah…it's not that special. I haven't seen much of it, other than a few port cities with lots of sailors and the plains with a lot of grass," she stammered.

"Have you been to Remdas-Kuwis – the capital city?" Alira asked.

"For a little while I was there, not very long. It's a big city and there were too many people when I was there. I didn't get to see much other than the refugee camps." An uneasiness had come over the shy girl and Alira cocked her head.

"Where did you come from in Errum? Where did you live?" Kiera asked.

"In…in Freiad Castle."

"You're from a castle too?" Kiera noted excitedly, "Tell me about your castle. How many pig-headed knights live there?"

Sillida's jaw set and her eyes kept returning to the floor. "I…I don't want to talk about it."

Alarms went off in Alira's head, but before she could say anything, Kiera pressed again. "Oh. Well, I was only asking-"

Sillida leapt from the crate. "I said I don't want to talk about it!" she screamed before dashing to the stairs and to the lowest deck.

"Sillida!" Kiera shouted after her, shocked. Turning to Alira, she was nonplussed. "What did I say? I don't understand."

Alira's empathy urged her to go to Sillida's side. "Hadn't you heard about Freiad Castle? That was why Reldon and I were in Korraine to begin with. It was destroyed! She lost her mother!"

"I thought that was just a rumor! Korrainians don't believe rumors spread by kingsmen. I didn't know it was true!" She took a hard step to take after Sillida, but Alira stood and took her leave instead.

"I think it would be best if you stayed here," was all she said before disappearing below.

Kiera pinched her lips together as her regret made her shoulders slump. Sliding down against the hull of the ship, she shook her head and thought aloud, "Well done, Kiera, you ruined any chance of friendship."

Elly was silent, looking on as Kiera buried her face in her knees. Slowly she rose, her feet hardly making a noise as she stepped over to the hurting sixteen-year-old huntress. Her violet, tear-reddened eyes emerged from within her arms to appraise the young magician, who only looked down at her with those huge green eyes.

"It's all right, Kiera. I will be your friend."

She plopped down next to Kiera, imitating her posture with a smile.

Kiera returned the sentiment, sunlight shining through the dark storms of her mind. "I would like that, Elly."

Time was drawing close for Bryle to make his triumphant return to Errum, and his nerves made sure to remind him every few minutes that upon his departure from this land, he had been tasked with returning Reldon home at once. *And now it may be too late. Deciding to fight alongside Reldon and taking care of Sillida were both choices I would make again, but at what cost? Who knows, they could even banish me for refusing to obey the king's orders!*

He had been astern, watching the other ships tear across the silent seascape, but his otherwise nervous disposition forced his feet into pacing about the vessel. *Reldon would never let anything like that happen. Not after everything I've done to help him and Alira. Besides, Errum can't risk angering the Xanem Master, especially given the fact –*

"You're thinking aloud again, Bryle," came Reldon's voice, which had been gradually deepening in recent months. "It's gotten rather creepy."

He had forgotten that Reldon was also above decks, just as pensive as he had been. "Sorry, Reldon, I just can't think straight these days."

"We both know why that is," Reldon said cryptically, leaving Bryle waiting for a punchline.

"And what would that be?"

"Your relationship with Sillida has been the worst-kept secret in Lärim since the battle. We all see the way she looks at you, and how you won't look at her. I would never say it to her face, lest she try to stab me on the spot, but she has fallen for you terribly," Reldon recounted.

"I-I know that," Bryle stated stubbornly, "I just…I don't know how to…Oh boy." Bryle scratched furiously through his sandy hair, leaning against the railings that lined the bow. "I don't even know how to speak the words in my heart." In that moment, he couldn't have possibly felt any more like a fifteen-year-old boy.

"If you fancy her, you shouldn't be avoiding her, Bryle. I'm sure she would like to spend time with you."

"That's not all it is, Reldon. I need some time to think about everything – from her, to Errum, to what I'm going to be doing next. I would very much like to speak with my parents while we're in Remdas-

Kuwis so they may help me figure all of this out," Bryle mused, not meeting Reldon's gray eyes.

Reldon sighed heavily. "That makes two of us. How is it that we went from bashing each other with sticks in Freiad Castle all the way to attending royal ceremonies over the course of less than a year? If next year is to be as tumultuous as this one, I think the world will simply have to accept that their Xanem Master is going to a warm, far-off island for a while to rest."

Bryle punched Reldon's arm. "You love all this attention and you know it. Besides, all that's changed since Freiad is that now we're bashing each other with real swords rather than pretend ones."

Reldon scoffed with a wry smile. "I wouldn't even let you get close."

With a confident laugh, Bryle postured further. "Phyrim isn't everything. Need I remind you of what I did to Gihan? Completely without your special abilities, I might add."

"Just with some help," Reldon grinned back, "Speaking of which, you should probably thank her. If I were as bad at fighting as you, I would need to be pulled from the fire too."

"Says the person who does everything as a pair. If I harmed even one of those four little hairs on your chin, she would be up here roasting me alive before I could even get a word in edge-wise."

They leered at each other for a moment before shaking their heads and laughing.

"This is the point at which we desperately need someone like Lendir to shake us up and tell us to 'stop fooling around' and to 'face the seriousness of the occasion'," Reldon remarked, feeling the weight of his master's Xanem in his breast pocket beneath his armor.

Bryle nodded. "Without him I suppose we all feel a bit lost."

His sentence hung in the air for a moment, the mood suddenly darkening.

"Sorry, I never intended to be so –."

Reldon waved a hand. "Worry not. I miss him terribly, but I think his spirit – if it's somewhere among this pool of ghosts – would want us to remember him kindly and for the ways in which he helped us all grow. If he were still alive and saw me moping or crying all the time, I believe firmly that he would slap me upside the head and tell me to snap out of it."

A distant dinging of a bell rang out from another ship, echoed shortly thereafter by the others. The sailors aboard the ship were suddenly lively, reigning in the sails and preparing to drop anchor.

"Errum awaits. I hope you're ready to set foot back home again," Bryle said to his old friend.

"We will see if it's still home by the moment I leave."

A splash and a chorus of gasps echoed over the top deck. King Obrim's jubilant voice thundered over the rest, trumpeting loudly. "I told you he was a ghost! Farewell, ye' wee kitten ghostie!

Reldon and Bryle collectively rolled their eyes, dashing astern to clean up yet another of the king's messes.

Chapter II

Black petals had fluttered down from the parapets above long since Reldon and the other guests had arrived, contrasting the intermingled snowfall as they increasingly dotted the ground. Reldon knew not how they had managed to cultivate such flowers so they would produce petals dark as night, or how they had kept them during the harsh early winter, but they had added a further sense of poignancy to the already somber affair. The rhythm of his Ilewa's crunching footsteps countering his own was the only sound that he heard as they ascended the dark stone stairs to the royal courtroom in Remdas-Kuwis – that, and the bells. Every few seconds a single large bell tolled, its stately ringing uniting all Nuru of the city in the streets, bearing candles and tossing what flowers or fronds they possessed into the path of the armored cavalry.

An honor guard had been positioned to provide the Xanem Master and his Ilewa a most regal welcome, two lines bordering the snow-covered, cobbled streets.

I'll never get used to being saluted, Reldon had thought to himself, *It's an honor which captains, generals, and kings have earned through their deeds. Simply being lucky enough to have been born the Nuru Xanem Master hardly seems like I've earned it.*

The initial procession had been somewhat of a blur – the official capacity which had comprised the event had made it all so real and so weighty that Reldon's mind was struggling at first to register it all.

All he could do for the first portion of the speeches was stare blankly at the sarcophagus at the head of the royal hall, wondering with all his might what came next for his home country.

Steward Sallard spoke high over the congregation, his echoing voice filling every inch of the chamber.

"For generations, our benevolent King Dunan ensured the continuing growth of our cities, the prosperity of Nuru trade, and protection from the vile Kuru threat to the north. Many thousands of children sleep soundly in their beds each night in the west knowing that kingsmen stand at their aid and provide for their common good. Today we bid farewell to a king who has stood as an iron-willed advocate for this kingdom and its people for longer than most have lived, and it is our sovereign duty to ensure his legacy not die with him. We must see to it that he look down upon his glorious kingdom evermore with pride as his subjects honor the sacrifices he made in service to this country."

News had reached Reldon shortly after arriving that Arch-Steward Greythorne had been summarily removed from his position after the king's death, the empty seat of arch-steward left vacant for a later appointment. The new king had not been diplomatic about his sacking – Lärimite influence was not welcome within the king's court of Remdas-Kuwis, Greythorne having been directly from Nakisho, the Lärimite capital. As a result, the next most senior steward, Sallard, a forty-odd year-old Nuru man from Anthia, was selected to head the procession. By Reldon's own reckoning, the man was doing a fine job. What bothered him was the underlying lack of diplomacy in the decision.

"...And that is why with a heavy heart and the wept tears of all Nuru at our feet, we bid a final farewell to King Dunan, our beloved father and king. May he go well into the afterlife."

The hall murmured in agreement.

A small contingent of troops marched up to the marble sarcophagus, shaped in the life-like form of the old king, each wrinkle on his aged face visible in ageless stone, and proceeded to lift it onto a reinforced metal cart for transport to the king's catacombs beneath the castle, where he would be interred among Nuru's kings for all of history.

"The court criers are now handing out black roses to those among us with whom King Dunan had final wishes or final messages. If you are given one, please remain following the ceremony to be addressed personally by the court," announced Sallard.

Though at first Reldon had his doubts whether the king had had final wishes for him, it did not surprise him when a bowing crier boy offered a rose to both him and his Ilewa. He also spotted from across the hall that Bryle had also received one.

Without further warning, the steward went on. "And now it is incumbent upon this court to, in the wake of King Dunan's death, crown his successor. As the highest Nuru title passes from one man to the next, we as his people will and should afford him every respect as we had his predecessor, as his word is law. The late king bore a single son in his lifetime, who now must take the throne in his father's place and guide us in all ways spiritual, financial, and if necessary, on the field of battle. Our most sacred vow awaits the crowning of Nuru's next king: Prince Garen!

The heavy doors to the hall swung open with lurch, a brief blast of cold air sweeping through from the foyer. From outside stepped Prince

Garen, garbed in a suit of ceremonial black plate armor, flecked with green textiles; a golden longsword, and matching deep-green cape. Around his shoulders was the pelt of an arctic fox, giving a white backdrop to his dark expression as he strode purposefully, almost angrily, up to the dais with his own honor guard in tow.

Steward Sallard flinched momentarily before continuing. "It is our oldest and most sacred rite to bear witness to the king's ascension to the throne of his forefathers through the recitation of the Oath of Kings. Are you ready now to recite this oath and take your place upon the Nuru throne, sealing your place in eternity?"

"Yes, yes, get on with it," Prince Garen replied callously.

"Very well. I bestow upon you the Writ of the Oath of Kings, an ancient scroll whose contents your kingdom now bids you to read aloud. Proceed when you are ready."

Garen opened the aging yellow scroll with an aggressive pull, fortunate not to tear it.

"I, Garen of Errum, son of the late King Dunan, do swear in all good faith and veritable honesty to uphold the ancient sacred traditions which the Nuru Kingdom of Errum have passed down unto this day. I swear to provide for, and protect, the people which this crown hath burdened me to guide, and I swear in all that this throne stands for to serve none other than Errum's interests. This, in all good and fell spirits' names, I swear. Peace unto Errum."

"Peace unto Errum," the people echoed.

"It is with utmost honor that I take this crown, passed down for many hundreds of years, from the former king..." he said, retrieving with great care the gleaming golden crown from the sarcophagus's lap before it was carried away, "...and bestow upon the current king." Sallard placed the crown atop Garen's graying head to raucous applause. "Hail, King Garen! Long live the king!"

"Long live King Garen!" the crowd cheered.

In the highest form of humility Reldon had yet seen from Garen, the man knelt before his people as they cheered his name – whether he was praying, Reldon did not know, but he did know that beneath the iron façade there must have been some part of Garen which was beholding the weight and importance of his new position.

He stood again before the applause had completely waned away. Stepping up the dais to the throne, he did not sit, but instead addressed his kingdom for the first time.

"My people of Errum – my Nuru brothers and sisters – I am humbled by your devotion to my father, to this kingdom, and now to me. However, I wish for you all to know now that I am not my father. My father may have brought in an age of relative peace and respect for Errum, but there was much he was blind to. He was blind to the concessions which he gave to foreign countries in exchange for mere crumbs in the ways of political treatises. He was blind to the rebellious upstarts in the central plains and surrounding regions which slandered his good name and were not silenced. And he was blind to the real danger which threatens our people day in and day out: our perverse, cowardly cousins to the north who hide behind their wall for their fear of facing us as would real warriors. They posture and lash out at our citadels while they isolate themselves with their dark allies the Churai, ready and willing to fall to their knees and serve their every whim.

"We can no longer appease foreign countries who ignore our plights, nor can we continue to ignore the growing threat from the Kuru, who destroy entire castles without shame or remorse. I will not allow another day to pass where I may look upon the refugees from Freiad Castle and do nothing, nor will I allow Lärim to devalue our friendship with each apathetic treaty and attacked dignitary. I am done, and the Kingdom of Errum is done being a secondary power to be kicked around. It's time we showed our might to the world, to finally demand the respect we deserve on the world stage.

"As of this moment, all emissaries and diplomats are being recalled from Lärim – each and every kingdom. Atheria, Teraxellum, Nakisho, all of them. We are finished with Lärimite policy. In regards to the Kuru, I am declaring a personal war against them for all of the innocent blood they have spilled. I am raising the entire country's military to lead an assault on them once and for all. Siege weapons will bring down their Wall of Isolation, and they will die by Nuru sword. Let it be known that if any should wish to march into battle to free us from Kuru oppression forevermore, enlist and take up a spear. It is time we showed the world what we are made of. Let the Age of the Nuru begin!"

"The High King is not going to be happy," Bryle stated plainly.

Reldon rocked back and forth on his heels as they waited to be called back into the royal hall again to receive the late king's words. Alira had been uncharacteristically quiet since the speech. *It must be hard knowing that yet another kingdom isn't fond of your people.*

21

"We must urge the High King to give some ground to Errum," Reldon reasoned, "Garen is not going to stop with this. If he had his way, there would be a Nuru Empire before long."

"Is that such a bad thing?" Sillida chimed in.

"Surely you don't mean that," Reldon replied.

"Maybe I do! He was right, after all, there hasn't been any justice for Freiad. You both should know that best," Sillida said with a fiery passion behind her words.

"Sillida, creating a Nuru Empire, wiping another culture off of the map, and risking becoming enemies with Lärim isn't justice for Freiad. It certainly isn't going to bring the dead back."

"Then what would you do?" Sillida pushed.

"My job," Reldon narrowed his eyes at her, "It's the Churai that are making this war impossible to win, and I guarantee that the sea-borne armies are because of them as well. So long as they exist, the Kuru cannot be defeated. This is a suicide mission."

"Reldon, I would like to follow you on this," Bryle tried a more reasoned approach, "but if anyone is losing ground, it's the Nuru. At some point we have to push back. I'm not trying to lessen what you did in Nakisho, but that was one Churai among countless others. You simply don't have the power to take them all on, especially not by yourself."

"That's precisely my point, Bryle. If Alira and I struggle to fight the Churai, how do you think the common soldier would fare? It would be slaughter. This invasion will be over before it's begun if they do this. I tried to warn Garen and he wouldn't listen," Reldon explained.

A pause ensued as Sillida glanced at Bryle. The closest emotion Reldon could equate it to was frustration.

Reldon didn't allow the pause to fester. "Alira and I need to find a way to destroy the Churai before this army destroys itself. We have some leads, but they may involve us getting into Drunerakerrum, which would be much simpler if we had Lärim's armies at our back as well."

"But you don't, Reldon. That failed, we couldn't convince them," Bryle reminded him, "We're on our own."

Just then, the door creaked open and a crier motioned for Reldon and Alira to enter.

"We'll talk about this later," Reldon huffed, whirling about and entering the royal hall.

With Alira silently in tow, he walked down the length of a green velvet carpet leading to the dais on which King Garen sat in his newfound regality. There was an uncomfortable silence as each of their footsteps reverberated off of the stone columns flanking the way, the eyes of at least a dozen courtiers fixed upon the young couple.

"Presenting Reldon of Freiad, Xanem Master, and Alira Ayuru of Atheria, Ilewa Master. By his former grace's will," announced the crier before retreating back into the shadows. Only a couple of flickering torches and hearths lit the hall, much of it bathed in darkness. *Glass windows haven't quite reached Errum yet.*

King Garen nodded dispassionately and Steward Sallard stepped forward, the developing wrinkles on his face forming a smile as he addressed Reldon directly.

"Welcome back to Errum, my Lord Xanem Master. And of course, welcome to our esteemed kingdom, Miss Ayuru. It is my hope that after your time in Lärim you may still see our country's splendor," he said kindly.

Alira forced a smile. "It is very beautiful, good Steward."

"It is good of you to say so. Now," he began, retrieving the black roses from them, "you have been presented with the black rose to signify that the late King Dunan had wishes or words to relay to you upon his death. In this scroll he contained his thoughts, and they were marked with a white wax seal, meaning his wishes may be conveyed at court rather than in private. So I shall now read to you his eternal words."

Breaking the seal, he unfurled the fresh parchment and began aloud.

"My dear lords and masters of Phyrim and magic,

I find it to have been one of the greatest regrets of my life not to have experienced what I imagine to be the profound pleasure of having made your acquaintances. Your father Telmar and I shared a manner of kinship which followed many good years which I would never trade, and I bear no doubt you would be happily similar in respect.

A great many rumors graced my ears in my last days, and as I dictate this to my scribe, news has reached Errum that you and your Ilewa have defended the Lärimite capital from an invading Kuru force. Both of your actions may be lauded as admirable, to speak simply, and the news of the death of your master has brought no shortness of sadness to this old king's last days. Though I cannot claim to be the first to say so, let it be said unto you that you and your master made this country very proud, and I have already motioned for the scribe to record his name in the annals of Nuru history as a hero, with yourself naturally included.

I know it brings you no peace to hear such, but he died with honor – a sword in his hand and flame in his heart. There is no shame in this.

Furthermore, as not to ramble, as I am wont to do, I bear no illusions whereupon this splendid country's direction shall be dictated. My son has pressed me for many a year to reclaim Nuru sovereignty on the stage of Rim, to take the fight to Kuru lands, to bring destruction upon their people for a change. All of these I have publicly shown caution, as war on such a scale rarely brings lasting peace.

However, there is no force in this world which will inhibit my son's zeal for war. As of the time of my death, Errum will have declared total war on Drunerakerrum. I doubtlessly share your concerns for this action, but given Garen's conviction, the best course of action would be to rally all necessary resources to ensure the invasion's success – for its failure would be catastrophic. Therefore, it is my hope, my last hope as King of Errum, that you and your Ilewa settle your dispute with Huerogrand and enlist their help in the war effort. They shall have need of your power and influence, and you shall require their knowledge and training. Through their direction and your abilities, I believe that this war may be won, and with the spirits' good graces, this world will be a better place in its conclusion.

Farewell, esteemed warriors of truth and courage. May this day bring new clarity to these dark times.

In his Grace's words,
King Dunan, 56th order of the rulers of Errum."

Reldon's fists were clenched so hard he thought his bones would pop. *For all his talk about peace, all the old king ever wanted for us was to just join the front lines. We were right about him from the start.*

"That concludes the king's message," the steward said, rolling up the parchment and placing it within a small tube and handing it to Reldon.

"There is still time for you to reconsider your position on this war, Xanem Master," Garen's voice echoed through the hall, "Even my senile father recognized your power and the need for it in the days to come. Perhaps it is time for you to fight for your country and leave these notions of Lärimite cooperation back in the centuries in which they last happened."

Alira bristled internally, her narrowed eyes leveling at the king.

Reldon restrained himself from screaming back. "Alira is all the proof I need that Lärim may still turn around. Good exists in all countries, and I will find any who wish to help us make a better world rid of the Churai. I will *not* make up with Huerogrand, and I will *not* fight in your war. You are sentencing thousands of Nuru to death, and I will play *no* part in it."

And with that, Reldon and Alira whirled around angrily, their steps down the long green carpet made quick and muffled.

The last he heard before exiting the accursed hall were Garen's words, unfaltering: "So be it, Xanem Master."

Chapter III

"Do tell me why I'm here, again? I have much to attend to back at the castle, if this little project is at its end," Ethilia dropped into a chair with a huff, removing her white gloves a finger at a time.

"I've already told you that – we're investigating this poor kid's death. I'm terribly sorry if you don't like it, Sunshine, but your 'previous engagements' will have to wait. We owe this poor boy at least the time to find out how he died," Kex replied with a touch of irritability. *I'm starting to see why everyone gets tired of her. She hasn't stopped complaining since I dragged her out of the castle by her frilly neck.*

The young boy Harbin's body lay in the center of the floor of his room at the inn, his skin gray and cold, and his foggy eyes staring at the ceiling. Not a drop of blood stained the wood floor surrounding him, nor did any bruises or cuts find their way onto his body. If indeed a kill, it was an immaculate one.

Ironic that this boy, deceased from this world, has less scars than those of the living, he thought callously, touching the gash across his face. Kex bore no lasting animosity towards Reldon for inflicting such a wound upon him – it had been earned fair and square. The only part of this deal which never seemed to end was the pain, not to mention the strange looks. *Not that I'm not used to those, though,* he smiled, thinking of all the times his new friend and pseudo-younger-sister Kiera had called him 'lobster locks', 'rose n' wrinkles', and 'tomato top', among others.

"And *I've* already told you everything I can. Best I can tell, he died of internal injury, ruptures to several organs including his heart. Obviously you couldn't see any sign of laceration on the outside, but his insides were practically swimming in organ fluid, well contained. If there was anything else, I would most surely – did you just call me *sunshine*?"

Kex snickered as he ran his finger across the door sill, wiping up a small layer of silt. "You do have such a *shining* personality."

It had the desired effect as the pompous little thing screwed up her perfect face. "The nerve! I should leave right now for all the good this is doing me."

"Ah, but then you would never catch the killer. That would simply eat away at you."

"It's obvious that ruffian in the castle's prison did this. Why not interrogate him?"

"Oh I most certainly intend to, but something is not quite right with this scene," Kex mused, tapping the ceiling with the tip of his sword.

"You mean besides the dead adolescent, killed by no normal means?" she quipped.

"'Normal' being the key word, my dear Ms. Shine. You might remember that I used to do this for a living – removing poor sods from the world because they angered some two-bit, petty lord with a penchant for vengeance. The coin was good. I'm sure you know all about that."

She harrumphed again, crossing her arms. "No one I know does such things."

"If you knew even half of my contractors, your guiltless world would turn upside down. Anyway, I have a shred of information you might find useful in this case: This method of killing is not only nearly impossible, but it is inefficient at best."

"How do you mean?"

"Phyrim can be used for very silent kills, for certain. A whole sub-class of Spellswords exist for that exact purpose – hell, our friend in prison is clearly one of them. We can send jolts of force or condensed air through someone's head to send them off with nary a sound, but even that creates disturbances in the Phyrimic fog and occasionally leaves blood behind or more if you're a bit overzealous with the strike."

"His brain was intact and without a scratch. Are you telling me that it was done to his organs instead?" Ethilia asked.

"A Spellsword cannot directly affect organs. We can't poke a hole inside of someone's heart. Only magic can do that, and specific magic at that."

"Golden Magic or Death Magic," she finished his thought, "So you're trying to convince me that either one of my golden sisters or a Churai killed him?"

"No, actually. As I was saying, a Spellsword cannot inflict any such injury without direct contact with the person's abdomen, and that's assuming you're able to generate a large enough force to tear his organs to shreds, and in this case without producing any bruising on the outside. Not only impossible, but to even try would be stupidity. There are so much easier ways to kill someone," Kex explained.

"Your critique of the murder is noted, Mr. Kex, but that doesn't assist in finding the murderer. If it cannot be produced by a Spellsword or magician, then are you implying a Churai did this? If so, we should be warning the guard straight away!" Ethilia said with urgency.

"No no, don't go ruffling your skirts over nothing quite yet. What I'm saying is no one could have done this. No one was here." He paused for a moment. "What would you say is your best guess at when he died?"

"Three days ago, just before the invasion began," she stated, "I'm keeping his body from undergoing *rigor mortis* to the best of my ability to keep it in the same condition as when he died, or at least an hour or two thereafter."

"Precisely. I was guarding the door at the time, and there are no other entrances. Jasper downstairs insists no one came in once the invasion started, so that leaves us with a crime committed by no one directly."

"So…indirectly?"

"It sounds so. I think that should be our line of questioning for our assassin in the prison. Would it be possible for you to sneak me into the castle to have a word with him?"

Ethilia sighed. "Fine, but I will not allow my family name to be besmirched in any way. If you're caught, I'm stunning you and turning you in."

"I knew Sunshine was perfect for you."

All too familiar was the trek down to the most secure wings of the Nakisho Castle prison. Though he hadn't been there terribly long, he learned that one quickly gets to know each patch of fungus, every rat, and all the areas where the light from the grates far above never touches. *As it turns out, when you've been stripped of all else to do, the mind fills in the space. I've picked up far too many memories of mold and cobwebs down here.*

Distant water droplets echoed rhythmically. Occasional coughs from the odd sickly prisoner often interrupted the uneasy silence. Only the crackle of the torch in his hand helped to drown it all out.

Kex stole a glance at the beacon of couture at his side, and her face was of pure determination. It never really seemed to waver.

"You don't seem as perturbed by all this as much as I figured," Kex said to her, waving at their surroundings.

She didn't glance back up on him, her icy blue eyes fixed on the downward-spiraling staircase ahead. "I'm down here more than you think. You've only seen living men down here – try spending time with dead ones in the depths of this misery, and you will quickly grow steel in your spine."

It was the frankest she had ever been with him. *Practically warms my heart.*

"You keep a strange fellowship." He smiled wryly.

"It comes with my job. Court healers don't always have the luxury of practicing on the organs of the living until such a time that the practice would have been necessary prior."

From the moment they had stepped down into the wet, dark confines of the dungeon, Ethilia had changed humors from one of a prissy, self-righteous teenage noble to one of a hardened, brutally-honest young woman. *Dear spirits, what has she seen down here that froze her heart so?*

Kex's smile would not be inhibited. "You're too young to be this jaded, Sunshine."

She scoffed. "You talk like my master."

"Perhaps wisdom can be found in many forms. Who is your master?"

"Kaia Melossi, the Court Magician."

Kex stopped in his tracks briefly before continuing. "She sounds very wise."

"Yes, yes, her wisdom knows no bounds. That much I hear at court daily," she responded, her mood clearly fouling.

"I will take a shot in the dark and assume there is bad blood between you and your master," he chuckled, "surely she's not that bad."

"No, she's perfect! That's the problem. A powerful magician from relative means, beautiful, charismatic, intelligent... There are times her standards are impossible to measure up to," Ethilia ranted.

I couldn't have described her better myself, and this girl has known her a fraction of the time I have.

"She also *refuses* to allow me the freedom to really improve my most prestigious craft," she continued angrily, "With all of this world's diseases, and conditions of the mind and body, one would think it simply *paramount* to pursue the invention of new cures, to bring clarity to the minds of those clouded – to do more than settle the upset tummies and self-inflicted wounds of the nobles! If I have to cure one more case of overeating or drunk-sickness, I'll scream!"

The girl was practically seething. For all of her pomp, somewhere beneath all of the sophistication and fancy clothes was a young teenage girl who was hurting and desperate for a purpose. The poor thing probably never told anyone any of this before, save for her master, and if there was one certainty in this matter, it was that Kaia tended to be a bit too wrapped up in policy and process to notice the small details of harm it all caused.

Kex twisted his lips. *If she didn't already hate me before, she's about to now.*

"Look, Sunshine, I hear that frustration of yours and it reminds me of someone with half of your brain but a similar experience. Did anyone ever tell you about my title as Ravager?"

She shook her head.

"If anyone tells you it's because I grew up sad, poor, and without a master, tell them they can take their pity and – anyway, I had a master. One rather similar to yours as a matter of fact. All of these masters from half an age ago know their craft well, to their credit, but they certainly don't know when to use it. My master drilled me from dawn 'til dusk on how Phyrim was a tool and not a weapon, how it was used for defense, how it should be used to keep chaos and evil in check. Blah blah blah, platitudes and niceties. At the end of the day, I was never allowed to actually protect anyone. People died day in and day out and my master only told me to be patient. Eventually I got tired of waiting and I left, something you're not allowed to do in the Spellsword world. Kex the Ravager is a dark spot in their world-view, and I'm an outlaw everywhere I go. I'm not telling you to be like me – heavens no, I would never wish this on anyone – but I do think eventually you have to take your destiny in your own hands."

For a moment she was silent. It was a silence in which he could practically hear the mechanisms in her brain turning and processing. As they continued to walk along the cold, grimy corridor, her head finally turned to appraise him for the first time all day. Her blue eyes seemed to be watching him for something – sincerity, perhaps? Since he had first begun talking to Ethilia earlier that day, she came across as nothing more than a chatty noble using grandiose words, but she had an air about her – a depth which was only portrayed for a fleeting moment as she searched him for answers.

At last she spoke, and it was so simple a statement, it could only have come from behind her icy wall.

"I...wish I knew what my destiny was meant to be."

The corridor opened to a circular wing of cells, most of them empty. The chamber reminded Kex of the cell in which he had been kept, as it rose to a high dark ceiling which he could not see the top of. One difference, however, was in the scant lighting. All of the light for the entire chamber came from a single torch in the center of the circle, which emitted a dim glow barely enough to light the front half of the cells.

Kex felt a familiar sinking feeling shortly after stepping into the room. It was an otherwise incomparable sensation to anyone without power over Phyrim or magic, but it was similar to a room darkening before your eyes, or your ears deafening, coupled with a feeling of dread as the purple fog of Phyrim thinned to nothing. Somewhere just beyond the cells ahead was a concentration of Antitheorum. The young healer at Kex's side clearly felt its weight as she took a deep breath.

Two cells were occupied, each flanked by a contingent of three uniformed magicians: two fire magicians, a water magician, a shadow magician, and two earth magicians by Kex's count.

Inside of one was a young man almost entirely wrapped in bandages. His nearly black hair clung to his neck and face, the grease practically dripping off of him. Sporadic patches of beard emerged between the visible slices along his chin and parts of his cheeks. As they approached, he leapt to the bars, gripping them feverishly.

"Away from the bars, criminal!" one of the fire magicians snapped at him.

He released the bars cautiously, raising his hands over his head melodramatically. "Peace, I meant no harm. I only wished to greet our honored guests. My, what a big scar that is. Run afoul of any self-entitled heroes of late?"

"You're one to talk," Kex quipped, "I've never seen a talking butcher's block before."

The team of magicians saluted. "Court healer. It is good to see you," the head fire magician spoke from behind her hood, "You come accompanied by a Spellsword?"

"It's a long story. We're investigating a murder, and naturally it is my duty to be involved, whether I like it or not. We must speak with the other prisoner," Ethilia responded authoritatively.

The bandaged young man slumped against the wall again with a faux sigh. "And here I figured you were here to check on me. These bandages are terribly itchy, after all, and could use changing."

Kex could tell the head fire magician was growing testy every time the bastard opened his mouth. Hot air shimmered about her sullenly. "Prisoner Gihan. Your attention is required," she ordered.

"I don't want to speak to either of them. Go away," came his obstinate voice, low and boorish.

Ethilia held a hand up, producing a potent enough glow from her palms to illuminate the criminal's pig-like face. His upturned nose, puffy jowls, and nearly shaved head certainly did little to dispute such a claim.

A spark or two popped from her fingertips, and the light briefly dimmed before returning to strength again. Gihan snickered.

"Even you can't fight the Antitheorum, 'Court Healer'. Come any closer and you'll be just as human as we are," he goaded, "Do come closer."

"Did you murder that boy in the inn?" she demanded, ignoring his intimidation attempts.

"So what if I did or didn't? Why should I tell you?"

"How long would you like to be in here?" Kex asked pointedly, "If you want any chance of seeing sunlight again, I would talk. Unless of course you enjoy eating rat."

"I don't see why I should talk before the masters come to get me. They'll be here soon enough to get me out." He crossed his giant sausage arms.

"They're not coming for you. Trust me on that. You've been used, played like a fiddle. I'm sure they promised you all sorts of accolades for doing their bidding in Lärim, but every word of it was a lie. In my experience, the only time they come after anyone is when they want to kill you. If, by the spirits' good graces, you do see them walking down that corridor, they're not bringing your salvation."

That gave him pause as his eyes darted around.

Dear oh dear, he's slow. I never expected that to completely convince him, but this may be easier than I thought. I'm surprised he doesn't have to crank his ears to keep his brain working.

"I...I need to get out of here," he finally muttered.

"Good, then we finally understand each other. Go ahead, Sunshine."

She shot him a glare before continuing.

"I ask you again: did you kill that boy?" Ethilia repeated.

"No, that wasn't me! I didn't have to. They already did it to him to make sure he wouldn't talk," he responded frantically.

"Who is 'they'?"

"The council back at Huerogrand. The masters, they did it! Had him swallow some kind of device before dragging 'im around Lärim. I think it had something to do with making sure he didn't talk or run away, but it clearly didn't work like it was supposed to. Harbin ran away with

32

Tycheronius's Xanem and the council told me t' follow 'im and make damn certain he didn't give it to Reldon."

Kex was in shock. Providing this was all true, which was admittedly a stretch of logic of colossal proportions, this was not only a conspiracy of murder but also conspiracy to cover something up – something so clearly irreversibly damaging to their image or goal that they had to murder a child to keep it from getting out. They wouldn't murder someone for stealing Tycheronius's Xanem, it was an old trinket from a time long past. *The council has always, at least in my eyes, been a collection of dirty, underhanded hypocrites, but this tops it all.*

Ethilia was having a difficult time putting the pieces together, and she furrowed her brow at him. "Why wouldn't they want Reldon getting the Xanem?"

"I dunno, probably because it's an important artifact or something," the swine sputtered, "Harbin should never have stolen it, I told him not to do anything stupid."

"What did this Harbin have to do with any of this? Why were they traipsing him all around Lärim?" Kex asked.

"Don't you know? Because he's one of Reldon's friends."

Kex growled. "Don't they have any qualms about what they've done? That boy had nothing to do with any of this. If what you're saying is true, they murdered a child!"

Ethilia turned a dead-pan look to him. "You spent weeks tracking down the Nurems so you could kill them for gold."

"Point taken."

"Harbin didn't deserve what he got, but Reldon's got his coming soon," Gihan smirked, "Just you wait. He's got a lot of enemies, and he can't run forever."

"I think I've heard enough," Ethilia said shortly, turning to leave with Kex in tow, "Enjoy the eternal darkness."

"Wait, you've got to get me out of here!" he hollered at them.

"No promises," Ethilia waved back at him dispassionately as they climbed the staircase again.

"There is a good chance that everything he said was complete bollocks, Sunshine. I don't know what you intend to do next, but it's an awfully big accusation to call the entire council of Huerogrand murderers. Even though we all know it's true."

"I know we can't trust him, but there may be enough truth to at least begin the investigation, and it can't be ignored," Ethilia said plaintively.

"Ah, so you *will* be taking on this case fully. I knew you had it in you," he punched her shoulder.

She appraised him with her own equally wry smile before pushing him back. "*Actually*, it's *you* who will be pursuing this case from here. I'm not allowed to leave the city, so if you want justice for the poor boy, it will be up to you. Do try not to get into too much trouble, I would hate to have to fix your slimy organs."

"And here I thought we were getting along so well. Fine, I will see what I can do, but you remember what I said."

He stopped and knelt down to meet her at eye level.

"It's your destiny. Follow it, and don't let anyone stop you."

Chapter IV

Cold wind whipped across the snowscape, turning the loose crystals atop the snowbanks into projectiles, pelting the girl's face with every one of nature's breaths. Distant wolves howled with as much anguish as the high-up torrent of wind, but none could ever hope to best the anguish in her heart on this day.

She trudged through the roughly foot-deep snow to where she had known it to be. The average person, much less the average eleven-year-old girl, would not have been able to make this trek through the storm, and *especially* not without a coat of any kind. She hadn't needed one since the ceremony. Snow which clung to her face sizzled away instantly, leaving it none the colder than before. However, she had found that the wind could cool her temperature after a few hours, so she would need to move again soon.

There had always been a lament for the days when she had been – for lack of a better word – "normal". Once she had been a more typical girl, one who loved playing with her friends, chasing animals around her hometown, and pretending to be on wild adventures. Her hair had once been darker, something like an auburn color, and her skin had once been pale.

Not to claim, of course that her childhood had been perfect – her parents had certainly caused enough tears on their own. They regularly worked her past her breaking-point milling flour, accosting her with beatings if she didn't work hard enough or spent just a few minutes too long out with her friends. She hated them with all of her being, but somehow those days were remembered with a tinge of happiness to offset all of the pain.

The ceremony changed all of that.

As soon as her parents caught wind of her magical abilities, they couldn't have sent her off to the Academy City any faster; in fact, they never even said goodbye.

I thought maybe the Academy could be a new start. But I was only there for a few months. Those stupid masters thought that capturing the Ilewa Nuremil was more important than teaching me magic, or making sure I wasn't still angry. None of that mattered.

They had forced her to take the Keitas ceremony a few months before her eleventh birthday, and she selected fire. She had touched the burning globe of light and magic and felt a connection – as if it spoke to her very soul. It was like meeting an old friend which promised to make everything better again, to make her *strong* again.

From the moment the magic filled her, she had been born anew, bathed in the towering flames which would be her salvation. Or so she thought.

They treated her like some kind of freak. Like an oddity amongst oddities.

I never understood why they treated me that way. What gave them the right to judge me? I was just like all of the rest of them!

Only Netha had been her friend, a water magician of a kinder, softer nature, and roughly the same age. She had also taken the ceremony far too early, and struggled to control her abilities as a result. Week after week she poured effort into her lessons in an attempt to grasp ahold of the raging beast that was her newfound power, but she had made almost no headway by the time they had gotten their letter drafting them into an Eleqorum.

Fate had been kind in managing to include both of them in the same Eleqorum, but the effect was the same. Despite directions given from high command which stated the Ilewa Nuremil was most likely to be found in the south or east, her Eleqorum had been sent southwest into Teraxella, in case for whatever reason the Ilewa Nuremil decided to try to skirt the Academy to the west. So back she went, far too close to her hometown in southern Teraxella.

Her memory had repressed the precise events of how it happened, but she remembered flashes of how her far-too-young Eleqorum had been set upon by some Kuru who managed to slip by the western fortresses and Netha was unable to fend them off with barely a fraction of her training finished. Two members of the Eleqorum were killed in the attack, Netha among them. Her only friend in the entire world was gone, and the last flashes of memory she possessed before lapsing into darkness were those of immense, unbridled anger, of coursing flames and the smell of roasting human flesh.

She knelt into the snow, removing her wool hat to allow her crimson-and-orange hair to blow in the tearing wind. With an ungloved hand, she brushed away the snow from the half-buried stone beneath her, steam cascading wildly about.

Carved into the barely-marked gravestone was Netha's name and age, with a crude facsimile of an angel above it.

Six months it had been since then, and the hurt never went away. That terrible pain in her chest loomed every moment of every day since then.

A lump formed in her throat as she stared at the lifeless words.

"I'm so sorry I couldn't protect you, Netha. My only friend."

Breaking down into sobs, she wrapped her arms around the gravestone as if to embrace her friend one last time, repeating "I'm sorry" until her voice was hoarse.

Gripping two handfuls of snow, they hissed and whined until the snow became water in her hands and then became steam. As her emotions poured out, her magic reacted.

It is all their fault this happened. It was the Academy. It was my parents. It was the Kuru. It was... Alira Ayuru! I hate them all! I'll burn them all to ash!

The hissing became almost deafening as all of the snow in a wide area around her turned from frozen crystals to a fog of steam in a matter of a few seconds.

She lifted herself to one foot, and that foot left a charred burn on the dirt beneath, igniting the long-dead grass into transient flames.

"I promise you, Netha, they will all pay."

It had only been a short walk into the village. Though she wished it would have been her hometown, it was one of the neighboring ones, one of the villages which refused to let her play there after they found out she had magical abilities, telling her that she "was too dangerous" to be allowed to run free.

She would prove how right they were.

Stepping into the center of the small village, all was quiet. It was nighttime, after all, so everyone was sleeping except for a contingent of guards which eyed her warily.

Just a simple village, it bore little to no defensive capabilities other than these guardsmen, though she knew it was not this village which would be her prize.

"Oi, what you doing there?" one of the guards shouted out to her. She did not answer.

He walked closer, his white uniform beneath his coat barely visible. "Are you deaf? You shouldn't be out here, girl. There's a snowstorm going on, and it's only going to get worse. Get inside or-"

He stopped as he looked closer at her features.

"Hey, you're that magician girl we used to keep sending away. Go on home, you don't live here. Or go to the inn or something."

"Are you going to make me?" she snapped back, heat emanating once again from her in waves.

"All right, that's enough, young lady, I'm bringing you in. Come quietly or I'll have to get rough," he ordered, grasping her arm.

Immediately his hand began to sizzle and he screamed out in pain. She clapped her other hand atop his as his flesh burned. With a series of shouts the other guards leapt into action, levying their crossbows at her.

"You let 'im go, you! Let 'im go or we shoot!"

Her heart beat with the rhythm of the flames. Anger was dry tinder to her magic, and she provided all she had to its insatiable appetite.

The distorted air around her became solid walls of flame, and her arms were engulfed. Blazing to a brilliant red light, her Keinume thrummed with magical power.

A whistling sound signaled the release of the crossbow bolts, but she merely had to throw up a blanket of nearly liquid flame to knock them off of their course and leave nothing but a flaming husk upon the snow.

She had never truly mastered her own abilities, but at this point she didn't need to. Destruction was her goal, vengeance was her prize.

Throwing out her arms, the flames soared through the air, meeting the three guards with a terrifying crash of light and heat. They screamed out and rolled around in the snow to put out the fires which threatened to eat them alive.

Without a doubt there was a part of her, deep down, which begged her to stop, but her anger could not be sated so easily. The flames needed to live, to grow, and there was plenty of kindling.

Gathering up all of the roiling flames which now encompassed her entire being, she channeled it all into her Keinume and allowed it to overload completely. The thrumming became a roar until finally, like releasing the cork from a shaken bottle, it exploded.

The explosion lit up the night sky. For a brief moment there was no day and no night, there was only her radiance. Like a volcano, a harbinger of smoke and death, the eruption rained down pockets of flames onto each and every building, making the village into one giant matchstick. Smoke billowed into the frigid air until naught but black snow fell from the heavens.

Her revenge would soon be complete. She had many wrongs to right, and in the end she would put flame to any who had a hand in Netha's death.

Ending with you, Ilewa Nuremil.

Chapter V

Kiera felt lost in the massive castle complex that was Remdas-Kuwis, yet simultaneously at home, and that was what bothered her most. Only due to her active involvement in her dream to be a huntress did she spend roughly equal time outside of castle walls as she did within them. This, naturally, had been despite her father's most ardent warnings.

I really despise feeling comfortable here. It should be rolling green hills and the bray of wild animals calling my name, not the cold, smelly corridors of some castle keep.

She paced about aimlessly, waiting for the follow-up hearings to conclude. No one had bothered to stop her as she explored the dimly lit halls, so she figured – much to her chagrin – that she looked the right type to be moving about without supervision.

Making sure not to stray too far from the throne room, she discovered a small chamber lit with the dancing light of a hearth. It was warm and inviting, with a few wooden chairs and tables forming a "*U*" shape like some sort of gathering place for courtiers. There was a book laid upon the edge of the closest table, and Kiera blew the thin layer of dust off of its cover before scanning its contents. It was in a language she could not read, but she knew she had seen it on many occasions before.

"Excuse me," said a man's voice behind her. She started and shut the book with a *thwap!*

Startled, she whirled around to see Steward Sallard's kind face holding up a hand as if to assuage her fear.

"So sorry to have frightened you," he chuckled.

"That is all right – you have managed to sneak up on a huntress and for that you should be commended," she smiled in return, her accent seeming suddenly out of place in this land of foreigners.

"Would you then happen to be Kiera Itholos of Korraine?"

"Just Kiera, good steward."

"Lovely to meet you, Kiera. That book was the property of Steward Greythorne before he was replaced, brought it over from Lärim. It is written in Old Lärimite, so I know not whether you can make heads nor tails of it, but I believe it to be some manner of prayer book. Would that be accurate?"

"I could not tell you. My people do not speak the old language and rarely do they prefer it when outsiders do so in our presence."

"Oh dear, then I do so apologize."

She laughed. "Do not worry, sometimes I think I have more in common with the animals I hunt than the people who raised me."

"Speaking of your people, the king has requested your illustrious presence at your earliest convenience, My Lady," he said with a bow.

"Was I to receive a rose as well?"

"This summons is not in regards to the wishes of the former king, but rather the current one. I will lead the way unless you are otherwise pre-disposed?"

"By all means, lead on!"

The enormous chamber which housed the throne of Errum was completely empty of its denizens, and as a result every sound was echoed threefold around her. Kiera felt self-conscious entering; after all, she hadn't had time to change out of her mourning dress as of yet and as she entered, the fiery eyes of the king were solely on her. He merely sat upon his throne, nodding to the steward as he left them alone.

"Ah, Lady Itholos," his voice rose, "Thank you for coming."

He seemed different. The fury and callousness that had poisoned his voice before was nowhere to be heard.

"You summoned me, Your Grace?"

"Of course, it is not every day I house within my walls an emissary of such esteem. After all, I must be diligent in my new duty as king to know who my friends are."

He's being far too charming. "You are kind to say so, Your Grace, but I am no emissary of my people."

"Why, it's your birthright to represent your people, proud as they are. And as such, it would do for us to talk of important things," he said, beckoning to a servant girl hidden behind a pillar. She scurried up to the dais, bearing a dark bottle and two iron goblets atop a platter. "Would you care for some wine?"

I do not believe I've been treated this well in my life. Perhaps... I can play along and see where it goes. After all, those etiquette lessons had to pay off some day.

"Yes, thank you, Your Grace," she responded, taking the glass of dark liquid, waiting for the king to drink from his goblet before she partook of hers - Bitter, just like the few times she had drank it for ceremonial purposes in Korraine. And a few times in secret.

"So it is my understanding you are on less than amiable terms with your father at the moment," King Garen wasted no time in broaching the topic.

"To my regret, that is so."

"Do you bear love for your father? For your family?"

Her eyebrows furrowed slightly. "Not terribly. I have little in the ways of family left, Your Grace. I had no fondness for the way my father sought to marry me to someone I did not love, nor had even met."

Garen nodded, his features soft. "You have my sympathies for what happened. I understand it cannot be easy to have your fate decided so irrevocably by another. Even I did not choose to be King of Errum."

"You would be something else, your lordship?"

"I had always been a military-minded man - harsh, calculating, and exacting. I know much more about leading and inspiring soldiers than I do speaking with fair princesses from far-off lands, but we all do our best to do our duty with what birthrights we are afforded, no?"

Kiera was a tad surprised to hear the King of Errum opening up to her. "It is so, Your Grace. I would be a huntress, Kakara willing. Instead I have always been groomed as a political tool to be used by my father, and I will not have it. I did what I had to in order to take my own path."

He paused for a moment. "Does this Kakara have meaning to you?"

She laughed. "Kakara is the Korrainian spirit of protection, guidance, and travel. Do you know of my people's beliefs?"

"They have always been told to me as nothing more than superstitions, but I have not yet been given the freedom to travel to Korraine to experience it myself, so my knowledge is very limited. I do not believe our cultures to be incompatible as others do, Princess Itholos. Whereas my brethren, or even some in Nakisho, believe your people to be regressive and animalistic, I see your people as honorable to the traditions which have guided them for many years."

"Why, thank you. Rarely are such kind words spoken of my people by someone as influential as you." *The question is whether these are simply candied words or if, by some stroke of luck, he's being genuine.*

"Tell me, how do your people view mine? What do they say of us?"

She wriggled a little, biting her lip trying to find the right words.

"My people know little about the Nuru, so some choose to see the similarities in our histories of breaking from Rim as a kind of cousinhood.

However, there are many more who view the partnership with Nakisho as one which…" She visibly struggled to say it.

"Go on. I will not be angry."

"…as one which resembles a dog and its master."

He nodded grimly. "Precisely. Then you can see the logic in what I said in my speech earlier. The Nuru should not be treated as anyone's subordinate, and our relations with those in Nakisho are no longer serving us in the interests we desire. My people are proud, just as yours, and we grow tired of bureaucratic nonsense holding us diplomatically hostage. And more importantly, it may be time for old regimes and ways of thinking to be lost to the past." He stepped over to one of the burning hearths, his goblet swirling in his hand.

Kiera allowed the silence to persist until he spoke again.

"Perhaps it is time for our commitment to new ideas to be embodied, to be personified. The old ways of my father, of your father, are dying. Maybe it is time for our cultures to experience something it has never seen before – a reigning queen."

Kiera was absolutely taken aback. So stunned was she, that for a moment, words would not come from her open mouth. "A-a *queen*, Your Grace?"

"You have said yourself that you wish laws were different, that you, and other women, had the right of self-determination. What better way for the world to imbibe such a concept than by realizing its first female monarch? And who could be more suited to the role than yourself?"

Her thoughts and feelings raced. *He wants* me *to be ruler of Korraine?*

She stammered helplessly. "B-b-but my lord, I have no experience with such things, nor do I even have a claim to the throne of Korraine. If my father were to die before an heir is born, it would-"

"- pass to your uncle. I completely understand the current laws of succession. As it stands, even my own courtiers are begging me to marry and produce an heir, but I have no time for such things when the Kuru threaten our very strongholds. In your case, if the old male primogeniture laws persist in Korraine, you will never see the throne, nor will any of your sex. So the only ways for us to change the world to what you told me you'd like to see would entail either amending the laws, which would be impossible with as many angry old men who would rather simply kill you than give you your day in court, or to usurp the throne."

The blood seemed to leave her trembling fingers. "Y-y-your lordship, are you telling me to-"

King Garen stepped towards her and gently laid his hands on her shoulders. "I am not telling you to do anything, Kiera Itholos. I am only giving you options to allow your world-view to become a reality. From the moment I received word of what you had done in your father's court, I admired your drive for change. It was only my intention to make you aware that there are ways to see the changes you seek, to have the freedom to decide your own destiny."

Blinking several times, she couldn't quite wrap her mind around the idea.

"I know you will need time to think. Just know that in the event you decide to topple this old system, in whatever form that resistance takes, you have my personal vow as King of Errum to support you."

All she could think to say was, "You are exceedingly kind, Your Grace, and I shall not forget what you have said here today."

"It is well, then," he took his hands off her with a broad smile. "Thank you for speaking with me. I have arranged for the chambers you share with the Nurems to be our finest accommodations. Sleep well, Princess Itholos."

Reldon floated around in the nether-sphere of Tycheronius's Xanem, his mind pressed to the limit to clarify his questions so the ancient Spellsword's memory could answer.

"How do you know if you're following the right path?" he asked vaguely, expecting a canned answer.

To his surprise, Tycheronius's silhouette seemed to consider for a moment.

"You cannot know until you are well down the path, beyond the redemption of reconsideration. Let the conviction of your position be your guide and all will learn to respect your decisions. In time, so will you."

He had been spending more time than he probably should have inside the pommel's mystical realm, searching for...something. Was it answers? Clarity? Someone to talk to? *I've just felt so lost these days. Lendir was always there to talk to if I was feeling like I didn't know what to do next.* Some manner of frustration, of resentment, a prickling in the back of his mind wouldn't go away, no matter how many questions he asked.

The specters of the long-since deceased Ilewas watched him without expectation.

"Why did he have to die?" Reldon asked, his voice echoing into silence.

They offered no immediate answer, so he went on, his emotions getting the better of him.

"Tell me, why is it that Lendir was taken away while hundreds – thousands – of Kuru and Churai still get to live?"

Tycheronius's eyes peered back at him, either uncomprehending or impassive.

"Tell me, how can the world be a fair, *just* place when the people wanting peace get stabbed to death and those wanting death and destruction can laugh behind their walls at us?"

He glared angrily into Tycheronius's eyes.

"Why!? I *needed him*! I can't do all of this myself! And why am I shouting all of this at you? You're not even REAL!" Reldon screamed.

He hurled the astral version of his sword through Tycheronius's body. It sailed through him with nary a sound and *thudded* against an invisible barrier on the far side of the sphere. Reldon fell to his knees and punched the membranous floor repeatedly before giving in to his anguish.

Gradually the world came to again and he could feel the cold steel of the flat of his blade against his forehead.

"Reldon, are you...all right?"

Opening his eyes, through the wavy haze of tears he saw Bryle and Sillida's concerned faces. He had been sitting cross-legged on the bed in their illustrious quarters, his sword aloft.

"Just put the furniture down and we can talk about this," Bryle coaxed him.

Reldon's attention darted about as he realized that several tables were lifted clear off of the floor, held aloft by his passive concentration on Phyrim.

As he noticed it, he lost his concentration and they all clattered back down to the ground. An itch on his face also revealed streams of tears.

"What did you see, Reldon? Is there anything we can do to-" Bryle started.

Reldon was simply too emotionally charged. His sword fizzled into nothing but green embers and he stormed from the room.

"What is wrong with him? I don't think going into his sword is doing him any good," Bryle pondered to Alira, who was nearly as perplexed as he was.

Alira merely sat in a cushioned chair, wearing her worried face for so long that she feared it may stay that way. "I really can't say. He has shut me out of our connection and has locked himself in one of the other chambers on the first floor of the castle. Reldon has been terribly sad since Lendir died, but I can't help but wonder if something else is going on."

"Like what?" asked Sillida.

She shook her head with a stressed smile. "I also couldn't say. He keeps going into that sword of his to talk to Tycheronius, but like Bryle says, he never comes out feeling any better."

"Maybe we should take his sword away," Sillida smirked.

"Fair bit of luck you'd need for that, it just disappears when he lets go of it," Bryle remarked.

"Maybe it has something to do with being back in Errum again," Alira mused.

Sillida and Bryle nodded in unison.

"None of us have the best memories before leaving this country," Bryle stated grimly, "and we don't exactly have a home to go back to."

"Oh there must be something I can do to help him. He won't even talk to me at the- Elly!"

Elly had been leaping from chair to chair as if the floor consisted of coiling snakes, avoiding touching even a single toe to it.

At the mention of her name she slid into the chair sheepishly.

"But the floor is-"

"No, Elly, there is to be no jumping between furniture while in the king's castle. Where is your tea? I know I poured you some."

Elly made a face. "I *hate* tea."

"Don't you want to be a proper Lärimite? You can't be a Lärimite if you don't drink your tea."

"I beg to differ," Kiera laughed as she entered the room.

Alira cocked her head. "Do Korrainians not drink tea?"

The Korrainian princess laughed, "Not as much. Drinking tea is such a western custom."

"What have you been up to, Kiera? You look as if you've seen a ghost," Bryle noted.

She waved a hand. "I think I'm just tired. I've been exploring. Where is Reldon?"

There was a silence before Sillida spoke up. "He ran off all out of sorts."

Before she could speak again, Bryle said, "There's no use going after him, he won't speak to anyone."

Kiera crossed her arms.

"We Korrainians have a phrase for times like this: '*Dari ikthos sunamri polimo vurath ta'iin ikthosi polimos*'."

"How inspirational," said Sillida. Bryle snickered.

She huffed. "It *means*, 'for when the fish do not bite, instead bite the fish'. Only action can bring him out of his fog. Do you think he would enjoy hunting?"

"I don't think he'll be given a choice," Bryle laughed, "And that phrase is absolutely terrible."

Her eyes narrowed, but she smiled. "You will see. When we bring back the stag of legend, you will be the one biting the fish." And with that, she turned and left to find Reldon.

As the door slammed, Bryle muttered, "I hope it's a small fish," which put Alira and Sillida in stitches of laughter.

For some time they waited in their quarters for Reldon and Kiera to return, chatting and keeping Elly out of trouble until she fell asleep. However, when a knock did finally come at the door, it was neither of their companions who entered.

Instead it was a woman, around the age of thirty to thirty five. She wore the Adept uniform of an Academy earth magician from years ago, clearly having gone out of style since then. Endless ringlets of black curls fell about her dark complexion. She entered with a curtsy and a smile.

"Sorry to interrupt. A message has arrived for the Ilewa Nuremil from Nakisho. It's urgent." Her voice was a low, full timbre, with a clearly Teraxellan accent.

Alira strode over to her and curtsied in return. "Do you have a letter?"

"No, My Lady, I am a messenger magician. I have been around Errum for many years acting as messenger to the court at Nakisho. My name is Stella, by the way. It's a pleasure to finally meet you," she said, beaming.

"A messenger magician? How do you deliver messages without letters?"

"Through my Ilewa, who is in Nakisho at the moment. If anything drastic happens at court, I am usually the first to know once he does. Easiest way to spread the word or get help."

For delivering such an urgent message, she's so bubbly!

"What a great idea! Does every city have one?"

"No, there are only a few of us. There aren't that many magicians and Spellswords with Ilewas left these days, and not many of them are willing to spend long periods of time away from each other to deliver messages. That doesn't bother me, though. Rallus and I love each other no matter the distance."

"That's beautiful," Alira smiled and felt all warm inside. "Oh right, what was the message?"

"The High King has received word of some destructive force destroying villages in Teraxella, my home country by the way, and he believes you may be the only one to put a peaceful end to it."

"Me?" she stammered, "I'm not that well-trained in magic. Surely there are others who can fight better than I can."

"Not necessarily fight, My Lady. This force…it's a person. A girl, to be specific. A very angry girl who curses your name as she destroys villages. The High King trusts that you can perhaps talk to her and convince her to stand down. Once your business here has concluded, of course."

"I think it just has. Let the High King know we will be on the boats heading to Teraxella tomorrow."

Chapter VI

Chains rattled incessantly as Detryn's most learned cell neighbor continued to fiddle with his bindings in a futile attempt to escape. The great brute had been at it for well over an hour and it was beginning to infringe upon the peace and sanctity of Detryn's daily beauty nap.

"They're not going to come loose, ya' great loon," Detryn said without moving from his hard bed.

"I hate this," came his voice, dim as a dying candle, "When are they gonna come back to get me?"

Detryn let loose an audible sigh. "They're not coming back for you, ye' thick turkey. They're never coming back for either of us. They played you like an oversized pipe organ. One little threat of life inside these iron bars and you sang like a canary in a burning cage."

"What did I have to lose? I thought maybe, just maybe they would come back."

"Well now they have every bit of information they need, and they certainly don't need you anymore," Detryn scoffed, raising his arm over his eyes again.

Gihan groaned to himself before returning to his chain work.

"How many times must I tell you it's no use?"

"Well, what am I supposed to do? I'm not ready to give up my life like you are," Gihan responded, stopping his annoying hobby only briefly.

"I'm not giving up my life, it was taken from me by a couple of would-be heroes looking to save a thankless world for their own self-aggrandizement. Not that I need to tell you about that."

His nod was practically audible. "Reldon will pay."

Detryn twiddled his foot idly. "Yet he and his friends are the ones laughing as we rot in here. As much as I have taken a liking to your most cerebral escape method, I do believe we will need to devise another plan."

He heard a clamping on metal as Gihan grabbed the bars and put his face as close as he could them. "We have to work together if we want to get out. And then we can crush Reldon and his friends."

"Sounds like an excellent plan. Now first…the escape plan," Detryn said, letting the words hang in the air as if expecting feedback. The silence he received was exactly what he anticipated.

The only way I'm going to be able to work with this idiot is if I misdirect him. After all, the guards can hear everything we say.

"That's fine. Let me tell you what to do, since I'm injured and clearly can't do anything," he said, sitting up.

It had obviously caught the guards' attention as the two women were watching them far more intently than before. A whispered word or two later and their eyes were fixed on Gihan. *This might be the only time this will work. The other four have gone on their daily break, but they'll be returning in less than an hour.*

"It's time to fight our way out. This Antitheorum weakens around this time of day, so if you use your Phyrim, you can blast the bars and catch them unawares," he spoke to Gihan, feigning a quiet voice. *If nothing else, this might be entertaining.*

One of the fire magicians stepped towards the cells, saying, "It can't be. It's not poss-"

The other fire magician grabbed her by her arm and pulled her back. "Of course it's not. They're trying to get you to come closer." They both stepped a few feet back, holding a hand out. "Don't even think about trying to escape. We have been given the authority to kill both of you if you even attempt it."

"You won't do it, you're soft. Nothing but soft women with an easy job - watching the caged animals eat vermin. Ooh, if I had your position I'd be simply begging for a chance to kill us," Detryn goaded her.

"I will do it! You shut your mouth!" she barked at him. Hot air roiled about her.

There we go, nice and hot. Good luck, you great stupid animal.

At the top of his lungs, Detryn screamed, "GO GIHAN, DO IT NOW!"

Detryn could hardly believe the dense brute actually did it. As if winding up to throw a ball as far as he could, Gihan reared back and hurled his arm forward, undoubtedly believing that his Phyrim would actually heed his commands and blast him from prison.

However, as any reasonable human being would have known, it was nothing but a ruse. As it turned out, the enraged fire magicians were not in a place to be reasonable human beings.

In all of the noise, confusion, and fury, one issued a shriek of a command to attack. With a fiery glint of light, they both released boiling hot balls of flame, sent hurdling towards Gihan.

In the split second it took for them to reach his cell, Detryn watched the balls of flame lose near half of their strength as they approached the Antitheorum. He then felt the intense heat and shielded his eyes from the miniature explosion it caused. His ears rang, but when the world came roaring back, it took the form of Gihan, slightly singed and angry, but otherwise unscathed.

Detryn's plan had worked and the flames had completely destroyed the front half of Gihan's cell, and luckily he had had enough sense to take cover in the back of his cell to avoid being incinerated with it. And even more successfully, since Gihan had been chained to the floor, the explosion had freed his bindings.

Now Gihan was free, and once he crossed the threshold of the Antitheorum, the battle began.

His first action was to send a Phyrimic pull to try to free Detryn, which of course failed due to the Antitheorum. By then, the two guards sent two more screaming orbs of flame towards him, and he barely dodged one and reflected the other with a hastily generated force-field. Gihan clenched his hand into a fist, and one of the magicians slipped where she stood, the very stones underneath her feet taking on a perfectly smooth, slick sheen. Ripping his short sword out of the Infinity Scabbard, Gihan rushed the fallen woman, only to be met with a solid wall of flame from the other.

Throwing up another force-field with his other hand had saved him from a deathly amount of fire, but he had been burned at least superficially, his skin blistering.

It only served to anger the brutish specimen. With a roar, he shoved his sword in between the stones beneath him and all of the surrounding stones shifted, trembled, and finally came free, sailing towards the magicians in their hundreds.

From then it became impossible for the unfortunate women to concentrate long enough to generate any sort of defense. Their barriers reflected most of the bricks while others battered their bodies.

Gihan then sent a wave of Phyrim at them, pinning them against one of the moss-encrusted walls before sending three bright gems of Phyrimic light into the ceiling over their heads. Three bolts, three explosions, and two fire magicians struck senseless by at least a dozen pieces of rubble.

The shockwaves sent tremors throughout the underpinnings of the castle.

"Well done, you defeated them. Try not to bring the whole damn castle down on our heads next time," Detryn lectured him, "Now let me out of here."

Once he'd been freed, Detryn recoiled at Gihan's face. "You really took a blow or two, didn't you? Actually that might just be your face. I forgot, they're fire magicians, so they only did the burns. You overdid the Phyrim a bit, didn't you?"

Gihan wiped the blood streaming from his nose and a bit from his ears. "No…"

"Don't give me that."

"Look, I did what I had to. They were stronger than I thought." Gihan eyed the partially buried bodies with a wry grin. "Is this the part where we steal their clothes?"

Detryn could only stare at him. "You are as sick as you are simple. First off, that wouldn't even work. We're not magicians, you bell end, and we couldn't disguise ourselves as if we were."

"Well then, how are we to get out of here without being found out?"

"The remaining guards will be back soon, so I suggest we get a move on. Our best strategy is to go with the element of surprise that we have only for the next few minutes. No one knows we've escaped yet," Detryn reasoned, beginning his ascent up the flight of stone steps.

Gihan followed just a few steps behind, every footfall a virtual stomp.

"You'll have to be just a touch more quiet than that when we get to the top," Detryn reminded him irritably.

Luckily there was no one at the top, or at least that they could see. Darkness permeated the upper levels and they did not have a torch.

"You don't like me very much, do you?" Gihan asked.

"On the contrary, I find your obtuseness most endearing. Keep your shoulder to the wall and we'll inch our way up in the darkness."

That seemed to placate him. "So what are we actually going to do when we find Reldon?"

"I would think inflicting on him all of the horrors he inflicted upon us would be a fair place to start," Detryn said, his voice practically dripping with venom.

"Then what?" he whispered back.

Detryn sighed. "What do you mean 'then what'"?

"Are you prepared to kill Reldon?"

That question caught Detryn off-guard. *Honestly I suppose it hadn't crossed my mind. Not for him at least.*

"No. He's not the prize."

"I could do it. After what the masters told me, I could rip him limb from limb."

In light of the approaching zenith of the staircase, the encroaching glimmer of sunlight in the distance, and the inevitable danger of running afoul of the returning magician guards, Detryn wasn't in a particular mood to talk, but that last sentence piqued his interest.

"Oh? And what did they tell you?" he whispered back.

"That he murdered his brothers in Phyrim. Murdered Spellswords. Started wars for no good reason. He's turned into a monster."

Detryn scoffed. "I was there for most of it, and only about half of that is true. You might want to check your sources."

Gihan breathed in sharply as if to respond, but as they reached the open archway exiting the underground dungeon, distant voices echoed off the walls. Most certainly female voices, they were likely the guards returning from their break.

Detryn's mind raced. Any use of Phyrim would get them noticed and most likely killed.

However, as they huddled into the little alcove adjacent to the exit, Gihan must have deigned this fact irrelevant and steadied a hand towards the stairs heading down to the dungeons.

Before Detryn could stop him, he released a small sliver of sparkling energy which jetted down at a rapid speed.

At that point, he was certain they were to be discovered and he would spend the rest of his life eating gruel, making friends with dungeon rats, and listening to Gihan complain.

To his complete surprise, however, he sensed no immediate disturbance in the Phyrimic fog, nothing that would give them away. A silence hung in the air for just a moment until finally the energy struck its target and produced wild amounts of metaphysical waves, nothing more than a pop to those without sorcery, but a tidal wave to those who do.

Immediately the female voices stopped. In a split second they whizzed by and shot down the stairs, not thinking to check the alcove.

Gihan yanked at Detryn's shirt. "Come on, we have to go!"

Detryn raced after him through the exit. "Where in all things sneaky and duplicitous did you learn to do that?"

"In Huerogrand. It's an Infiltrator technique, and they only taught it to a few people when I was there."

"You're going to have to explain the whole 'Infiltrator' thing to me later, but for now, we're in the home stretch if we can sneak out of the castle."

The dungeons emerged into the cold daylight with a corridor ending in an unlocked wooden door. It opened out to the castle grounds in an area tucked away beside the castle keep, largely unwatched.

"This is most definitely not the way they brought us into the dungeons. There must have been another way we missed that leads into the keep," Detryn surmised in a whisper.

"What's the plan now? Leave through the gates?" Gihan guessed.

Detryn struggled to contain his bafflement. "That would be very well guarded and would land us right back there again." He motioned back the way they had come. "Perhaps we can get atop the walls."

"Wouldn't there also be guards up there?"

"There could be sentries, but they would have to be spread thinner to try to cover the entire wall. Methinks if we time it right, we could make it up there," Detryn explained.

"Then what?"

Detryn paused. "That's a very good question. Perhaps we could jump."

"What's at the bottom?"

They heard a shout from below, still far away, but undoubtedly inching closer.

"No time to guess. Let's go."

Their feet pounding beneath them, Detryn and Gihan dashed up one of the outer sets of stone stairs up to the shield-lined walls. At first it seemed as if they had made it up completely unnoticed, but a shout came from the southern rampart from a single sentry.

He's far enough away that we could jump and make it free and away.

Gihan looked between the razor shields. "The river is beneath. Do you think it's deep enough?"

The sentry, garbed in the white military coat of Nakisho, trained his crossbow on them as he approached, ordering them to halt.

In a few seconds he would be on them and they couldn't afford a fight here.

"JUMP!" Detryn exclaimed.

He released a great pulse of Phyrim at his feet, launching himself over the razor shields, over the wall, and plunging down to the icy river below.

Before he hit the water, the only desperate thought he had was that he hoped the river hadn't frozen completely over just yet.

Chapter VII

It had been a rushed journey back to Lärim, their haste necessitated by the news of utter fiery destruction taking place in Teraxella. To Alira it had sounded as if the Teraxellan king was ready and willing to dispatch an Eleqorum to deal with the threat, but everyone involved knew that would end in further bloodshed. Though the girl allegedly cursed her name, Alira knew she may be one of the few who would be able to solve this debacle peacefully.

Reldon had not been difficult to convince of the severity of the threat, but as a result it was more difficult to explain to Kiera, Bryle, and Sillida that the situation was too dangerous for them to get involved. Though reluctantly, they elected to stay at the small port town called Steria located at the mouth of a river on the Teraxellan border with Atheria. From there, Reldon, Alira, and Elly took up horses and traveled northwest. Alira had specifically requested not to have guards accompanying them. If she was to douse the flames of the young girl's anger, strength in numbers would only serve the opposite.

Tracking her wasn't difficult – they needed only follow the smoke.

Massive plumes of black clouds trailed nearly from one end of the horizon to the other, carried by the cold wind high above. Distant eruptions gave them further reason to spur their horses onward, faster and faster.

What could she possibly want to accomplish by doing this? Reldon's thoughts came across with notes of fear.

She's only a child, it doesn't make any sense, Alira responded mournfully, *and how did she get to be this powerful?*

Do you know who she could be? Had you heard of anyone like her at the academy?

No. Someone whose own flames cannot hurt them is very rare, and very dangerous. I had only heard stories of such magicians existing.

Stories... Reldon pondered for a moment. *Do you think she's one of the people mentioned in the prophecy? In that list Darik gave us?*

Why do you say that?

From what you had read, it seems to have some strange types of people in it, maybe those who have abilities more unnatural than just magic or Phyrim. Maybe this girl is one of them? Reldon reasoned.

If that is the case, we absolutely must convince her to stop!

If we can.

His mental words were punctuated with a further set of detonations, closer, more virulent than before. The village within eyesight was already half in flames, with legions of citizens fleeing in all directions into the snowy hillscape. Some who passed by them on the road hadn't even had time to put shoes on before plunging into the cold.

The smell of the smoke was choking. Luckily it did not smell of burning bodies yet.

It only took one person recognizing the riders for their approach to be signaled.

"It's the Silver Rose! Oh thank the Omniscient One! Go and get her, your ladyship!" they cheered her on, tripping over snowbanks in their flight.

Alira, Reldon, and Elly dismounted, apprehension clawing at their stomachs. The cheers helped, but as they stepped closer to the burning buildings, they were drowned out by the roar and thunderous crackling of the inferno, hungry for more kindling.

Elly whined as they proceeded. "Master…" Terror was clear on her face.

"It's going to be all right, Elly. I promise. I'm going to talk to her."

Her words did little to help as the heat grew. Embers soared about the wavy air, distorted by the intense flames. Another explosion from a few streets down jarred their senses. Alira hastily tied back her hair, sweat dripping down her face.

It was a common village, with simple wooden structures, low stone walls, and virtually no defenses. What had remained of the village guard had long since fled. Around two-thirds of the village was now a towering inferno, with the other one-third virtually devoid of its inhabitants.

I'm starting to wonder if she's just blowing up buildings at this point, Reldon mused, *There's no one left.*

She must be very, very angry.

Are you sure you can do this? I believe in you, but this might be too much anger to deal with.

I have to try.

The dirt road (as none of the village had cobbled roads) opened up to a large clearing, which Alira figured was probably the town square before. Where there might have been a statue was now just a smoking pile of rubble. Where there were shops were now open flames reaching up to the blackened sky.

Standing near the middle were three people. Two were around thirty year old peasants, blackened by soot and pleading with the third figure. The third was a girl, maybe ten or eleven years old, her hair a terrifying embodiment of flame, colored crimson red with flecks of orange. It was impossible to tell what clothes she was wearing, as the incredible heat she was producing had long ago caught them on fire and were now smoldering on her body in pieces. Her clenched fists told that their pleas were falling on apathetic ears.

"This is not the way to air your grievances, Ilya! Please stop this madness! You're only going to end up killed!" the man begged her, on his knees.

"Then I'll be with Netha!" she screamed, her shrill child's voice hoarse, "You sent me away so I could die! I hate you!"

White hot flames balled up in her fist, growing with each intense word. It would have been a matter of seconds before she made (presumably) her parents nothing but ash.

"Didn't your parents ever teach you not to play with fire?" Reldon shouted out to her. She whirled around to face him. "Put the fireball down."

Her face contorted into one of pure hatred as she hurled the ball of flames toward them. It was hastily formed and filled with raw malice, and Alira only needed to knock it aside with a shielded hand.

The girl took a step back, clearly shocked. She had expected no resistance.

"Who are you?!" she shrieked.

"My name is Alira. I'm here to help you!" Alira said, taking a single step toward her. Her long-past steam burns were flaring up as the heat grew more intense. *I have to stay focused or this could end badly.*

"Alira…you're the Ilewa Nuremil?"

"That's right, Ilya. I'm here to bring you to safety and-"

She was immediately cut off as the girl sent another torrent of flames whipping towards them. This time she had need to generate a full barrier to ward off the attack. Like waves against a sea wall, the boiling inferno crashed against her silver energy in a shower of sparks and embers. Just when she thought the girl's onslaught was finished, she sent another wave of fresh flames to rebound off of Alira's protective shield. Reldon clutched her hand to provide her all the energy she needed.

After the extended assault, the girl ceased, breathing hard. "I hate you too, Ilewa Nuremil!"

"Ilya, stop! You can't defeat her! She's the most powerful magician in Lärim!" her mother pleaded.

"I don't care! I will make her pay!"

Her energy was waning, but her resolve pushed her to send more towering flames at her perceived enemy. Alira could only wait patiently behind her barrier for the girl to tire and finally listen.

However, she noticed, the girl's power was much higher than even that of a fully trained magician. She couldn't be certain of the girl's age, but typically girls of ten or eleven would be training with only very minor forms of magic and certainly would not have gone through the Keitas ceremony to select their one element yet.

Reldon, I think this girl...I think she was part of Brina's program.

The one where she did the ceremony on young girls and sent them out in Eleqorums to find you?

Exactly. Girls under twelve don't do well with the Keitas ceremony, and I think the fire magic it gave to her was too much for her to handle. Fire is anger. Magicians adjusting to their fire magic are always angry and moody, but it's affecting her so much worse!

Because she's so young?

Maybe. We have to calm her down.

The intense heat subsided once again and the girl dropped to her knees, desperate for breath.

"Why are you doing this, Ilya? Tell me what happened to you!"

Between breaths she gave only clues as to why her hatred ran so deep.

"If it...weren't for you...she would still be alive...my friend...she died...trying to hunt you..."

"Did Brina send you to find me?" she asked.

"She said...you were dangerous... we had to...stop you."

"Ilya, look around you. What you've done here is more dangerous than anything Brina thought I did. Won't you stop this? I can take you away from here and we can be friends!"

"I don't *want* more friends, I want my old one back!" she screamed, leaping to her feet and hurling another ball of white flame at her. Alira reflected it again with minor difficulty.

"This isn't going to bring her back. Nothing can do that. She wouldn't want you to live like this. She would want you to honor her memory with love, not destruction!"

"Shut up, you don't know anything about her!"

"I know that it's time to let go, Ilya. Your parents didn't do anything wrong, your friend never did anything wrong, and I'm trying to right the wrong that you're doing. You could destroy all of Lärim, but your friend won't come back again and it won't bring you peace." Alira held out a hand, taking another step closer.

She sensed instant surprise from Reldon as she lowered her barrier.

It gave the girl pause. Her red eyes gleamed in the surrounding flame as she watched her for treachery.

Alira stopped, extending her hand. "Please. Let me help you."

Reldon, stay back.

Apprehension bled through their bond.

Ilya breathed, her attention flitting from Alira's face to her hand, then finally back to her parents.

"This doesn't have to end in more tears," Alira said softly.

Finally the girl took a step forward, followed by another, until they were just a few feet away. Alira smiled at her.

The girl returned the smile, but it wasn't a sweet smile. It felt forced, but she figured the girl was fighting back tears.

Heat emitted from the small magician's body once more.

Alira, Reldon warned her.

Don't move.

She's going to attack you, Alira.

She won't.

Flames emitted from her skin and her Keinume glowed red.

"Come with me, Illya," Alira continued to hold her hand aloft.

"But you killed her," she said quietly.

Slowly she lifted her hand, her palm facing Alira.

Alira! She's going to-

No she won't! Let me do this!

She heard Elly moaning in fear, "Master!"

"I didn't kill her. The only one responsible for her death is already dead. Brina is dead. You have no more need for revenge. It's time for you to start healing."

Her hand engulfed in flames. "No...no... I won't..."

Alira was fighting back tears herself. "Ilya, think about her. Think about the love you had as friends. She wouldn't want any of this! Just put your hand down."

She's not stopping, Alira!

Her eyes glowed crimson.

"Shut up, you don't know her! You *killed her*! It's YOUR FAULT!"

As she screamed, the flames rising from around her caught the hem of Alira's robes, and she felt intense heat right up against her face.

"NO!" Reldon screamed.

Alira felt an internal wave from the detonation of Phyrim.

There was only a split second as the light crossed the distance. Alira in that moment expected Ilya to throw up a hasty barrier, but she only watched the light approach with widened red eyes.

With a *thud* and cut-off cry, Ilya was knocked from her feet and she tumbled to the ground.

Immediately rushing over to her, the blast of pure Phyrim had burnt straight through her middle.

Her parents cried out in anguish as they scrambled over to her.

"Spirits no! Reldon, what have you done!?" Alira exclaimed.

His voice wavered. "I-I had to! She didn't give me a choice! S-she was going to kill you, Alira!"

"No she *wasn't!*" Tears flowed down her cheeks. The girl's breathing was shallow and she was immediately going pale. "Oh Ilya, why? Why didn't you use a barrier?"

Her answers were terse, wracked with pain. "Didn't…know…how…"

The villagers re-entered the town square, throwing buckets of water onto the flames, which were no longer being sustained. Steam intermixed with the black choking clouds, blotting out any light from above. A few of the townspeople rushed over in jubilance to thank the Nurems for their help, but by the time they saw Alira and Ilya's parents sobbing over the deceased girl's body, they turned mournful.

She had been so close. Ilya was going to change her mind. She was going to come around.

Her wracking guilt and sorrow overcame her.

Why? Why didn't you trust me?

Reldon hadn't moved, his own guilt filling their collective pool.

I always trust you, Alira. It was her I didn't trust. She was going to kill you.

No she wasn't!

I couldn't take the chance! Once those flames reached out towards you, I had to do something.

She was so young… Alira wept. *Why did this have to happen?*

I-I don't know, Alira…

After only a brief moment of her parents' grief, their expressions turned to tear-soaked fury.

"You killed her!" Ilya's mother shouted, "Curse you! You are no saviors! You are murderers!"

Reldon could only sputter in an attempt to calm her down, and in short order the woman and her husband had to be restrained by several townspeople.

"They are the only reason this town isn't ash!"

"Your daughter tried to kill all of us! The Silver Rose protected us!"

The arguing grew to nearly riotous levels until Reldon withdrew his sword in a burst of green light.

"Please, everyone," Reldon exclaimed, "We are terribly sorry that this had to happen. Alira and I will go now to keep the peace, and I hope you are able to rebuild your town." His sword disappeared back into the Infinity Scabbard as they made their leave.

The cacophonous fighting died down in their absence and the townsfolk set about picking up the pieces of their smoldering village.

Elly reached out for her master's hand, and she quietly took it. The seven-year-old peered back to Reldon with concern on her face.

I'm sorry, Alira. I...I did my best.

Chapter VIII

She couldn't believe how stupid he had been.

It had taken a week, a chartered ship, and several horses to get to Huerogrand, and every moment Kaia considered turning back. She had a life to live, courtly duties to attend to, and none of them involved traipsing to Errum to save one wayward Spellsword's sorry rear end from almost certain imprisonment. Again.

Here we are, at war, and I'm still cleaning up his messes. I should've known he would do something like this.

In her typical way, Miss Ethilia Vendimar failed to mention what Kex intended to do until Kaia had brought up the results of their investigation. Her answer had been so casual she might as well have been remarking on the lovely state of the winter blooms.

"He's gone *where?*" Kaia had asked, completely shocked.

"To Huerogrand, master," she had said, sipping her daily tea.

"Why in the world has he gone *there?* He's a Ravager!"

"I would not claim to understand him, master, but I believe he intends to sort out this whole nasty business with the young boy's death. As per our conclusion, only they could have been responsible," Ethilia had said with nary a ruminating thought.

"But of all the fool things to do, what does he expect? To walk in, gather a confession, put them all in chains, and heft them back to Lärim? Or has he gone there to get revenge? Agh, curse your short sighted brain, Kunarus!" At that point she had immediately begun tossing her possessions into a bag.

"Master, do you intend to go after him?" Ethilia asked, the first tinge of concern since starting the conversation.

"I'm afraid so, Miss Vendimar. He's likely to get himself killed the way he's going. Did you try to dissuade him from leaving?"

"Heavens no. I believed it would have been a fruitless endeavor."

Though I wish she would have tried, she was certainly right about that.

Kex had unfortunately been such a headstrong young man when she knew him that there had never truly been any way to change his mind once he had made a decision. Logic, fear, even guilt had little effect on his course of action. Though it might have been an admirable trait once upon a time, it led him to far more trouble than if he had just shut his mouth and followed the leader.

His stubbornness made him a Ravager, his lack of empathy and care for others made him a mercenary, and his lack of remorse lost him his friends. Kex had always been the problem, the one who followed his instincts rather than his head, even if it led him to a path that no one else would dare follow.

Once they had been friends. Once they had all been friends. Four inseparable souls, solving Lärim's problems one day at a time without a care in the world besides justice.

Every young magician and Spellsword has the inkling, the ever-fleeting thought to use their new powers to travel the world, see new places, and save the downtrodden wherever they may live, whatever their problem may be. We just happened to be among the choice few who followed through.

The oldest, most experienced had been Dantus, or "The Hammer" as he had fashioned himself. An accomplished young Spellsword in his own right, he had become a Vanguard Spellsword and took up a war-hammer as his own weapon. Tall, dashing, with eagle eyes, a strong chin, and a singular judicial purpose, he had been the envy of most of his colleagues and the heartthrob of most young women who saw him. *Even I would be lying if I claimed never to have felt for him. He had just been so handsome, so courageous, that one's heart couldn't help but flutter.*

Celia was the next oldest, around twenty four at the time. An air magician, quiet but well-spirited, with raven hair and expressive blue eyes. Like most air magicians, she had always struggled with the idea of actually hurting someone with her magic, aligning more along the pacifist line of reasoning, but she had been fiercely protective of her friends. *If Dantus had been our leader, she would have been the resin binding us all to his leadership, or at least keeping us sane. She had never been one for emotional outbursts, instead proving herself more like a rock to hold onto when we were in distress.*

She chuckled. *I only wish I had been more like her.*

Kaia had the unfortunate pleasure of being the youngest in the group, only nineteen at the time they began their adventures together. *I had been nothing but a child at the time, following the older and wiser among us as we made a difference, or at least we thought we did. In reality, we probably only saved a handful of people when one subtracted the amount of trouble we caused, but it was the best time of our lives and none of us would take it back.*

None except maybe for Kex.

Back then as a twenty-year-old, Kex had been even more idealistic than he was now. He had always been going on about the people he was going to save, and about changing the world to be a fairer, more equal place. It had never been clear what made him so zealous about the whole affair, as he had refused to talk about his past, but it was that zest for justice that brought him to the circle of crusaders that they had been. A decade ago the Academy City and Huerogrand hadn't been quite as strict with what good their older students brought into the world, only so long as it was approved by the councils. Joint operations between magicians and Spellswords were more common, especially among Ilewa couples.

That had placated Kex for a while as they were warranted to travel Errum and Lärim as nigh-mythic figures bringing the judicial banner wherever they went, but eventually the novelty wore off for him.

What Kex had really wanted to was to fight, and not just petty criminals. His goals had routinely been drawn back to western Lärim where relations had broken down between Lärim and Drunerakerrum, and raiding parties continued to strike the countryside. However, ask as he might, the council had a very simple rule – those who had not completed their training could not be sent to open warfare, especially not with the possibility of Churai in the area.

Kex, being the impulsive and stubborn person he had always been, didn't like being told no and left Huerogrand without permission, branding him a Ravager. An obviously unforeseen consequence of that action meant that Dantus, Celia, and Kaia were no longer allowed to travel around with him, and he was to be apprehended if caught.

It had been heartbreaking for everyone. It had had the same effect as killing him outright.

Only once did they come across him again, in the one place they were sure he would be: Teraxella, fighting raiding parties.

We offered to bring him back. We still wanted to be friends, to be together again like before. All he had to do was return to the fold. But he refused, insisted he was doing more good as a Ravager than he ever had done as a student of Huerogrand. Dantus wanted to arrest him and bring him back by force, but I spoke up for him. I told Dantus he would soon enough realize the mistakes he had made and come back.

I was wrong.

Kaia pounded on the old metal door inside one of the abandoned cottages, the ruins of the old Huerogrand. They seemed to change the entrance on a regular basis, but this was the last one she remembered.

A few moments passed before it opened a fraction of an inch.

"Who knocks?"

"Kaia Melossi, court magician of Naiwa-ki-Shokassen. I've been here before."

There was a pause as the dark eye peeking out appraised her, but eventually she heard a metallic click as the door mechanism was released.

"Enter, but you will be guarded. Did you come alone?"

"I left my guards in the nearest town. If I can't handle myself alone, I can scarcely claim to deserve my courtly title, can I?" she smiled.

He gave no response, but waved her in. Inside was the same nearly black corridor she remembered from a few years back, still devoid of almost any light except for the guard's torch.

With a snap of her fingers, she produced a light of incredible luminosity, revealing every square inch of the dark, dirty corridor. The guards flinched.

"I'm a light magician – darkness makes us uncomfortable." *So do ambushes.*

"You're in for a rude surprise, then," one of them chuckled. She cocked her head, perplexed, but didn't inquire.

After a long silent approach, she was let in through a set of double doors, and she strode through with purpose.

Something was very wrong.

The normally brilliant grand chamber was nothing more than a cavern, like staring into the dark gaping maw of a colossal creature. What light existed was provided by small glass orbs affixed to the walls, some type of metal burning inside of them with a white light. As much as it helped illuminate the ground level, the ceiling of Huerogrand could no longer be seen, nor could the far end which led to the catacombs below. It had taken on almost an oppressive feeling.

"What has happened to this place?" she said rhetorically.

"Theft has happened," said a voice.

From one of the corridors stepped a few masters – she knew them well as Master Greff, Master Shindra, and Master Brunai. They appraised her with only a courteous smile – what lay beneath it she did not know.

"My apologies for startling you, illustrious Master Mellosi," Master Brunai said, bowing, "We were not expecting you, else we would have seen to putting up a few more silver flame torches. It has been a task to keep the supply of Therin Metal required to light Huerogrand. What brings you here this day?"

Kaia ignored the niceties and pressed her question. "What has happened to your light?"

"It was stolen, I'm afraid. The young boy who was killed in Nakisho had stolen Tycheronius's Xanem before he made his flight. We are still not entirely sure why he did such a thing, but it has saddened our hearts to hear of his passing. He had been such a bright boy," Brunai said remorsefully.

"It's for that reason that I'm here. My understanding is a former student of yours visited recently to discuss the case," Kaia said directly.

They each flinched very subtly before answering. "In a manner of speaking. That one was a Ravager from many years ago, so though he was peaceful, we had to arrest him and place him in our dungeon. Assuming some peace can be found in the Academy City, both councils will convene at separate times to discuss his fate."

"I may be able to assist in that decision, honored Master," Kaia said coolly, "You see, he was arrested some months ago in Naiwa-ki-Shokassen on a number of charges, including his involvement in the trial of the Nurems, as you may recall."

Master Greff's expression soured, but he uttered, "Go on."

"Therefore with those charges still outstanding, he is to be extradited back to Nakisho to face trial for his crimes. I cannot speak to what the jury or the High King will decide, but their ruling must predate any decision to imprison him elsewhere."

"Master Melossi," Master Shindra started, his voice sounding like a strange mix of patience and condescension, "the individual in question has been designated an outlaw by both Huerogrand and by the Academy City around a decade ago. Reason for his arrest was granted long ago, and with it the right for Huerogrand to pass its own judgment upon him."

"You are correct, but only if an Academy magician or Huerogrand Spellsword apprehended him, which was not the case as he was taken in by royal guard, placing him under the jurisdiction of the reigning lord, which would be the High King. He would like to see his prisoner back in his custody."

She had hoped not to invoke the right of the High King, but they gave her no choice. Once his name was mentioned, they clammed up immediately.

Shindra's response was measured, with a slight stammer. "Do not m-misunderstand us, Lady Melossi-"

"Master Melossi," she corrected him.

"Of course, Master Melossi. We have no quarrel with the High King on this prisoner's fate. It is our hope that the jury's judgment bring him back into our hands again so we may deliver justice by our ancient laws. Until such a time, however, we shall return him to the High King."

"Thank you for understanding," Kaia responded, seizing her victory.

The masters sent a guard to fetch Kex, and in the meantime, Kaia was hoping to probe their knowledge of the boy's death. *Not that I would have the authority to do anything even if they confessed.*

"Whilst we wait, do you have any theories on why the boy passed?" Kaia inquired.

"We really couldn't venture a guess to any certainty, Master Melossi. Perhaps someone knew what he carried and its great value, and murdered him to sell it? Or it is possible that whatever madness possessed him to steal the Xanem was also his undoing?"

"All reasonable hypotheses, Master Shindra. It is my understanding you sent one of your younger students to retrieve the boy."

"That is correct. It was our hope since they knew each other that Gihan could bring the boy safely back to Huerogrand with the Xanem in hand."

"Are you aware that he is currently in our dungeons in Nakisho?"

They were taken aback - whether for show or out of genuine shock, she could not tell. "For what reason?"

"For creating a disturbance and for fighting with a deadly weapon within city limits, if I'm not mistaken."

"What in old King Dunan's name did that boy think he was doing?" he cursed rhetorically, "Master Melossi, I can scarcely imagine what madness took claim of his senses, but his actions are certainly not sanctioned by Huerogrand."

"Of course, I understand. And if *I* had to venture a hypothesis, I imagine the madness which possessed him to be the same which killed the young boy?" she said pointedly.

They only stared at her sullenly for a brief moment before Kex approached, his hands bound behind his back. The young Spellsword twiddled his fingers and the metallic mechanism snapped into place, releasing his hands. Though Kex was not pleased to be in such company, she had spotted the grin he had first appraised her with.

"Thank you for your cooperation. I will be taking this criminal back to Nakisho and you shall hear in the coming weeks what is to become of him. I bid you good day."

"Farewell, Master Melossi. We wish you safe travels back to Lärim." All three masters hastily bowed.

They dared not turn their backs on her, so she obligingly turned hers first to leave, and they immediately followed suit. Though it had most certainly been amongst her concerns that Kex would not leave without causing a scene, she was pleasantly surprised that he was silently following her out. *Maybe he has finally had enough of this whole business. Spirits know I have.*

Kaia and Kex remained in complete silence until the guards left them at the surface, which was cold but still retained some of the sun for the day.

"Kaia, I can-"

She slapped him across the cheek, stopping him in his tracks.

"You listen, Kunarus. I've taken about all I'm going to with your impulsive behavior, your cavalier attitude of acting first and thinking later. Every time you get an inkling in your head that you can fix everything by just barging in and saving the day, *I* have to be the one to rescue you when it all turns sour! This isn't ten years ago, Kun! I'm not even permitted to speak to you, much less spring you from prison the several times I've done it. I want you to tell me something. I want you to tell me what exactly you thought was going to happen by walking right into Huerogrand and demanding answers. Go on."

"They would lock me up," he stated simply.

"They would lock you up," she repeated, "And yet you still went."

"It doesn't matter anymore, Kaia, don't you see? I'm a wanted man across the known world. The very least I can try to do is make any damn difference with the time I have left, and if that means knocking a few heads together to find out why a boy was *murdered*, then I'll do it."

"You haven't changed a bit since I let you out of prison in Nakisho." Kaia crossed her arms. "You still have a death wish."

"No, Kaia, listen-"

"No, *you* listen, Kunarus!" she said, her emotions finally failing her with tears making their way down her cheeks, "I'm finished putting my name on the line so you can find new, inventive ways to kill yourself. If you don't care about what happens to you, then why should I? This is the last time. *This* is the last time I'm going to help you. After this, if you want to go jumping off of cliffs in the hope that it will save a few people, you go right ahead, but I will have no part in it!"

And with that, she whirled around and headed towards her horses.

Her own words stung more than his actions, but she knew it was all she could do. If there was any friendship leftover after that, Kex would have an excessive amount of apologizing to do to bring it back.

Chapter IX

Reldon and Alira sat in relative silence in the opulent solar of the High King, two servants watching them for even the slightest indication that they might need something. They were practically begging to be given an order of some kind.

Finally Reldon gave in. "Mister servant?"

"Yes, my lord?" the elderly man responded excitedly, "What may I fetch for you?"

"Could we have some water, please?"

"Right away!"

The two men made themselves scarce and left the two troubled teenagers alone to each other's thoughts.

It was strange to have been summoned back to the High King's solar once again. Though the last sentiment he wanted to feel was special, there was a particular notoriety in being a regular visitor in the castle at Nakisho, especially after the trial. However, as much as he would have liked to bask in the relative importance, he knew this was to be a more somber meeting. Alira had only stopped crying a day or two back, devastated at the loss of the fiery young girl Ilya. Reldon wasn't completely sure, but he suspected part of the reason her sorrow had lasted so long was because she felt as if she had personally failed the poor girl – as if she had been the one to put her in that situation. No matter how many times he reminded her that she couldn't have done anything differently, she wouldn't listen.

Even the combined efforts of Kiera, Elly, Sillida, and Bryle could not persuade her on their return trip to Nakisho. From Kiera's words of wisdom from Korraine to Bryle's reassurances of the girl's current state of happiness, none could change her mind that it was all her fault. She had been shaken to the core, and Reldon feared she would never break loose of it.

So naturally the rest of the trip had been about as quiet as their current arrangements, one carrying into the other. She had not in any way closed her mind off to his, but she was always lost in thought, swimming in an ocean of self-doubt. There had to be some way to help her, there just had to be.

Do you think if we asked them for caviar that they would fetch it for us? Reldon smiled at her.

It took her a second to look up at him. *Oh. Yes, I'm sure they would.*

He wanted to comfort her, to make her feel better. Nothing he was saying was helping, and he knew if he asked her about it, she would start to cry again. In the end he decided not to press onwards.

The servants returned with two orbs of thick glass with a lip at the top, the water inside appearing twisted by the light.

"Your water, preserved in the most exquisite new glassware, a new feat of those without magic such as your own, My Lord," the servant reported cheerfully.

Interesting. "Thank you."

"Ah, and here he is, announcing the arrival of the High King. Long may he live!" the servant saluted as the High King entered the solar.

His eagle eyes were always the first of his features to catch Reldon's attention. Though his demeanor was kindly enough, his piercing eyes could tell a volume of stories that his expression never could. The orange sunburst surrounding the darks of his eyes lent a vivacity and exoticness to his gaze that only Alira's blue-and-green eyes could hope to match.

This day he was adorned in a navy blue long-coat fastened with gold buttons depicting the Nakisho seal. His long dark curls fell past his shoulders, topped by a flat-crowned wide-brimmed hat of a deep gray with gold stitches, which he removed and handed to the servant. There was little other ruffle or regalia to his wardrobe, no cape nor high-reaching boots. By High King standards, this may have been him at his most casual.

Reldon and Alira stood as he entered, and the High King raised a hand gently to urge them back into their seats.

The old servant pulled the monarch's chair back and forward again as he sat down. High King Julius Xenus Shoka-Dathrim II appraised them for a short moment before speaking in his silky smooth voice.

"Welcome, honored Miss Ayuru and Reldon of Errum. I thank you for returning upon my request, and I am delighted to speak to you both together for the first time."

Reldon spoke first. "It is an honor to be here, Your Grace."

His intense gaze shifted to Alira, not because she had not answered, but because the High King must have noticed her consternation. "Are you well, Ilewa Nuremil?"

"Oh, um, yes. I'm well, Your Grace, thank you," she responded.

There was a slight pause as his lightning mind worked, and Reldon could feel a twinge of anxiety from Alira's mind.

"It was a terrible tragedy what happened in Teraxella with the poor magician girl. However, you must understand that the situation may have been unavoidable. As unfortunate as it sounds, these reports are becoming far too common to ignore, and that is why you have my gratitude for responding to the situation in Teraxella. Hers was a more extreme case, as it was the only report of entire villages being laid to waste, and swift action had to be taken. You have the assurance of the crown that you shall not be summoned in such a way in perpetuity," he said to Alira. Somehow he had managed to adjust his tone in such a way that Reldon could sense her anxiety melting away.

"Thank you, Your Grace," Alira said with the first hint of a smile she had shown in days, "I…just wish I could have done more. I wish I could have saved her."

"Your heart is as admirable as your spirit, Miss Ayuru. I believe it would be remiss of you to blame yourself for what happened. The cold reality of the Academy City civil war has come to bear on a great many lives, but there is little any can do to promote peace and reason in a time of chaos and fury. I, myself, find myself powerless to affect the events which have seen fit to transpire in that so wonderful a city, and it is surely the hope of all that it is resolved before any further bloodshed takes its course."

He leaned back in his velvet chair. What shred of sunlight had peeked through outside the solar waned as the clouds rolled in. As a result, the side of the High King's face that had been illuminated now grew dark.

"We must, however, speak of the consequences, warranted or otherwise, that have resulted from the situation in Teraxella. A swath of the local population are pleased with the kingdom's swift action and feel ingratiated at the dispatch of the Ilewa Nuremil and Xanem Nuremar to their aid, so for many in the area your actions have proven fruitful. As a contrast, the poor girl's parents have been extraordinarily vocal in the last few days as to the alleged callousness of your actions, and word has spread as far as Atheria in just the past few days. There is a grumbling minority in Lärim which finds itself uneasy with being placed under your care." He laced his fingers together as he spoke completely without emotion, as if reading the report to them directly.

"I don't understand," Reldon started, "We've done so much to try to prove ourselves. We stopped Brina from murdering anyone else, we fought to free this very city from the Kuru siege, and we did our best to help Teraxella without hurting anyone. I'm not sure what else we can do!"

"I hardly need convincing, dear Xanem Nuremar, but understand the perspective from which so many of these dissidents find themselves. They see your confrontation with Brina as the catalyst to sparking the civil war in Academy City. For one reason or another, they have chosen to only see slaughter that ensued following the battle at the hands of the Ilewa Nuremil. And now they see the death of the magician girl as another misstep in power. There will always be dissidents, Reldon of Errum, but given your unique positions as almost entirely unregulated sources of immense power, it has at the very least given many pause and at worst given them reason to resent you. One half regards Miss Ayuru affectionately as the Silver Rose, and the other bitterly refer to her as the Black Rose."

I can't believe it, Alira. No matter what we do, people still mistrust us.

Maybe in time they will understand us. It may take us winning a war for them.

I really despise giving him any credit, but Detryn may have had a point.

How?

When he said that people are always going to want more. That they will never be completely satisfied with what we're doing until we're both dead.

He's wrong, though. Detryn's life has been about nothing but himself.

His Grace continued. "Therefore, I believe in the coming days it may be beneficial for the reputation of the Xanem Nuremar and Ilewa Nuremil to be out of the face of the public. Any attempts to overcorrect the situation I fear could have disastrous consequences."

Reldon was taken aback, and he sensed the same from Alira. "You would have us…lay low, Your Grace?"

He sat up just a bit straighter as his cup of steaming tea was set in front of him. "Do not mistake my beliefs for commands. It is not my intention to give orders to the Xanem Nuremar and Ilewa Nuremil. I offer my advice, and my hospitality. Naturally the decision shall reside with both of you, but this may be an opportune time to escape the claws of destiny, if only for a brief time. The Deep Frost approaches, and perhaps not at an inopportune time.

Reldon cocked his head. "What is The Deep Frost?"

"A perennial storm which returns around the same time every year in the continent of Rim," the High King explained, "It has been the bane of many thousand a man and woman over the centuries as it sinks its icy fangs into our country. The terrible storm is a mixed blessing, however. It may bring commerce to a halt and bring undue hardship to many, but it also halts the progress of all wars. None dare venture outdoors during the Deep Frost. At the very least, you can rest assured that during such a time, the Kuru will not dare another invasion."

Reldon peered over at Alira, who looked back at him with her large green-and-blue eyes. "Is there nothing we can do during this storm?"

"We cannot travel," she stated simply, "When I was very young, I spent the Deep Frost with my father in the tavern where they had roaring fires. It was always so crowded, but we didn't freeze."

"How long does this storm last?" Reldon inquired.

"It persists as it pleases. Some years it spans only a few days, while others it lasts for weeks. The longest I've witnessed in my lifetime wrought its vengeance on Lärim for eighteen days," the High King answered.

"That was the year I was born," Alira noted.

"It is well understood that you both bear a destiny which transcends the mandate of lords and kings, and it would be antithetical for the High King to attempt in any way to derail such a calling. That is not my intention. If you should choose to accept my solution, I believe it may be most beneficial for all parties," he went on.

"What is your solution? To lay low here in the castle?" Reldon confirmed.

"During this most trying time, I, High King Julius Xenus Shoka-Dathrim II, invite you both and your friends to join my wife, the High King's Consort, and my two children at my personal residence to the north of Naiwa-ki-Shokassen. There, under guard, you shall all be safe from the most disgruntled and ill-tempered of dissidents as well as the Kuru bandits which still plague our countryside. There you shall also all be shielded from the storm in relative comfort."

Reldon's heart raced. He could scarcely believe it. Alira's mind was also trying to put it all together.

"Why, thank you, Your Grace. What a spectacular invitation. Did you…want anything in return?" Reldon stammered.

"I offer this only on two very simple conditions: First, I ask you to protect my wife and children. And second, you must take my Court Healer with you, Miss Ethilia Vendimar."

"Ethilia, Your Grace? That is not so much a condition, as she is your courtier after all," Reldon said, largely ignoring the cup of tea which had been placed in front of him. Alira sipped hers daintily.

"My family will require her services more than I, but I have come to understand that Ethilia is not the most amenable to certain types. She can be haughty at times, but I require her expertise to attend to my children. I do so hope you understand."

It was less of a rhetorical question and sounded more like a firm requirement. *Not that we have any problems with her. If anyone would, it might be Bryle.*

"That will not be a problem, Your Grace," Reldon said with a smile, "I can't wait to see Bryle's face though."

To his surprise, the High King smiled. Even more to his surprise, *Alira* smiled.

"My wife and children are scheduled to be moved in a mere few hours hence. Will you be able to accompany them on the journey?"

"Absolutely, Your Grace, we will tell our friends."

"Excellent," he said, leaning back in his chair again, his warm smile still gracing his complexion. There was another brief moment of quiet as his orange tinged eyes flitted between them. "Such a peculiar destiny is thine, ye legendary children. I find myself increasingly impressed with your tenacity and ability to handle hardship. Yet do not make the mistake of believing yourselves unflinching and bottomless vessels to be filled with the trepidations of others. You breathe, and want, and live like any other in this world. Take advantage of this time to care for one another." His smile grew wider. "*That* was an order."

Elly patted the horse's muzzle gleefully, repeating to the beast, "That's a good boy! That's a good boy!" The gray mare was most certainly not a boy, but Reldon didn't want to ruin her fun.

The Royal Stables were most definitely the largest they had ever seen, much larger and with many more stalls than had existed in Freiad. Just in one wing, Reldon estimated around one hundred horses, braying and restless, in their stalls. Stable boys in the dozens forked in fresh hay and removed waste while horse trainers would occasionally guide a horse out into the yard for practice and exercise. Each stall bore a name on a bronze plate, some as genial as *"Dung Machine"* or *"Face-Kicker"* to more regal and intimidating names like *"Black Sortie"* or *"Thumdra di Iqusi Tandathra"*, which Alira translated to "Dread Horse of the Void."

It was an impressive display of what modern architecture and military could accomplish. *The only downside is the smell.*

An hour or so had passed since the meeting with the High King, and it was Reldon's understanding that the High King's Consort, her children, and Ethilia were still preparing for the journey. Bryle had not been terribly impacted by the decision to bring the girl whom everyone assumed was his nemesis; in fact, he seemed quite enthusiastic about the decision.

"So when are we leaving?" he asked for the third time, "I think it will be great to leave this city behind us for a few weeks. Times have been a little too hard for everyone here."

"Where exactly are we going again?" Sillida asked, her tone suggesting she may have been somewhat less excited than Bryle.

"To the north-northwest of the city. The High King has his own personal residence there, under heavy guard. We will be safe there during the storm," Reldon explained.

"Let me get this straight, Reldon. Lärimites endure a terrible storm every year that forces them to stay inside for sometimes weeks at a time, and they are perfectly all right with it? We have nothing close to that in Errum," Bryle mused.

"They don't really get a choice in the matter," Reldon stated flatly.

"What do they *do* with all that time?" Bryle asked, the question lingering more towards Alira.

She shrugged. "Adults drink. Children play. It's sort of like a night that never ends."

"Do you not celebrate the storm in Atheria?" Kiera asked, perplexed. However, her confusion was nothing compared to what she received in return for her statement. In fact, the looks she got were of downright shock. She grew slightly red. "Why are you looking at me like that?"

"You *celebrate* a *storm*?" Bryle blurted out.

"Well of course we do!" she responded obstinately, "In Korraine the Deep Frost is an important challenge for my people. Or maybe 'test' would be the better word. When the Spirit of Winter visits our lands, she brings with her the storm to cleanse the land of those with too little ice in their veins. Those who emerge from the snow afterwards are blessed with a growing season as strong as the people are. It is when the Korrainians truly show our strength as a people."

"That's not really a celebration, though, that's just surviving the winter," Bryle commented.

Kiera leered at him. "Is that not enough to celebrate?"

"Stop judging her culture, *Bryle*, they don't have to have festivals in the spring like we do," Sillida snapped.

"I understand celebrating survival, but a lot of people die in the Deep Frost, Kiera. It's just a little hard to imagine celebrating the storm itself," Alira said with a frown.

"Whose side are you on? We are the only Lärimites here, we must band together!" Kiera pivoted.

"What about Elly?" Alira asked.

The seven-year-old peered over from the horses at the mention of her name, though without genuine interest.

"She's Ferrelan," Reldon reminded her.

Elly used a full lung's worth of air to blow a tuft of gold hair out of her face only to have it find its way back in front of her green eyes again.

"I don't know, she doesn't seem very Ferrelan to me," Bryle noted.

"What gives you that impression?" Reldon grinned sarcastically.

"Where do you think she comes from then?" Kiera asked.

"Grandma never knew," Reldon answered, "She said that Elly was placed on her doorstep as a baby with nothing but a name. I suppose the name sounds Lärimite."

"Not a traditional name, though," Kiera stated, "and most certainly not Korrainian. It almost sounds a little Atherian, but the Teraxellans to the west have similar names. How peculiar."

At that moment the doors to the stables swung open noisily to reveal Ethilia Vendimar momentarily glittering in the sunlight before entering. She wore her usual white and gold uniform with a knee-length skirt, but this time it included a hood and white wool leggings.

They could see her breath as she sighed with a huff.

"I'll have you know that I plan to fully cooperate with the will of the High King, but that does not mean I have to enjoy it," she said very generally, her arms crossed.

"Perfect, we have enough Lärimites to even the odds now!" Kiera cheered.

Reldon and the others laughed as Ethilia's shoulders slumped a little.

"What on earth are you talking about?" she asked, completely exasperated.

"We Lärimites were outnumbered before you arrived. Now there are three Nuru and three of us. And one Elly."

Ethilia scanned the young woman with her bright blue eyes, undoubtedly making note of the leather huntress gear and the bead chains around her neck. "You must be Korrainian."

"Right you would be, Miss Vendimar!" Kiera replied with a grin.

"Hmph. Not many families of means out that direction," was all she had to say.

Alira leapt into the conversation before anyone took offense. "But she is very much Lärimite and that's all that matters. Have you heard word of the High King's wife and children?"

"We are to mount our horses and meet them at the northern gate, whereupon we shall depart the city immediately," Ethilia said, her vision shifting to spot Elly tugging at one of the horse's manes. "Ah, good to see you Elliana!"

The girl froze at the voice, her head slowly turning to see her old temporary Golden Magic master. Averting her attention, she walked around the stall until she was concealed by the horse.

Mounting up, everyone had received their own horse, except for Elly who rode with Alira on a horse named "Storm Charger". Reldon's was a dark grey named "Earthstrider", Ethilia's a (naturally) white horse named "Candlestick", Bryle's a dapple-brown-and-white named "Tinder Box", Sillida's a bay horse called "Melian Star", and Kiera's was also a bay horse named "Insect Chewer". All were mares, for good reason.

Riding out into the cold once more, their new equine friends carried them to the north side of the city. There seemed to be some activity going on in the castle as they left, but Reldon gave it little heed.

"What an ungodly name. *'Insect Chewer'!* Who would have the nerve to name such a good girl something so terrible?" Kiera complained as she scratched her horse's mane.

"Maybe it's true and she actually does eat insects," Reldon reasoned.

"That doesn't make it a good name. I regularly spot men doing worse – shall I name them 'Ear Picker' or 'Bum Scratcher'?"

"I'm starting to think you have more regard for animals than you do for humans, Kiera," Bryle commented.

"I had a wonderful horse back in my homeland named Tofty. That horse had more personality and more depth of character than half the people I knew. When every other person in Nevo-Kulan wants nothing but your money or worse, I would rather trust a horse. They're just as happy with a good apple."

"Maybe you should rename your horse, then," suggested Sillida.

"Hm..." Kiera contemplated, "How about 'Ilfi'?"

"How Korrainian," Ethilia remarked snidely.

"What does it mean?" Sillida asked.

"I am not sure what it means in the old tongues, but it was the name of my mother's favorite horse."

Alira nodded approvingly. "It is a pretty name."

Bryle shrugged, a grin on his face. "I like 'Insect Chewer' better."

One of the castle guards had been running to catch up with them as they left, and he finally made it to Ethilia's side to flag her down. Ethilia halted her horse and listened to the man's words as he breathed heavily. Her expression darkened, but for her it could have been anything from the death of a ruler to a minor annoyance.

"What is it, Ethilia?" Alira inquired.

She looked back specifically at Reldon, then at Sillida. "Those two young men jailed during the battle have escaped."

If the immediate pit in Reldon's stomach weren't compromising enough, Sillida and Bryle's visceral reactions were worse. Sillida reared her horse around violently before Bryle stopped her.

"Sillida, stop. There's nothing we can do!" Bryle exclaimed.

"He *can't* be free! I have to put an end to it!" Sillida struggled even to free herself.

"Sillida, listen to me. We have much better things to be doing than to constantly worry about him. It's what he wants!"

"I don't care! He's helping the Kuru by doing this!"

"Don't you think I wish they would go away forever too? The wound isn't even healed over yet, but I know there are more important-"

"I won't let him hurt you again!" she shrieked.

Bryle was stunned into silence.

She breathed hard, her expression fierce, but she made no further attempt to spur her horse back towards the castle. Their eyes were locked in an emotional turmoil Reldon knew all too well.

Kiera's horse clopped next to Sillida's, and she put a hand on the younger girl's back comfortingly. "The black heart of revenge brings sadness to my country every day – do not let it destroy you as well."

Her jaw clenched and unclenched as she hid her face behind her hair.

"Do not stare at her, let us go," Kiera ordered the others, "We must see the High King's Consort."

It took only a few more minutes of painful silence as they crunched through the endless, partially shoveled snow of Naiwa-ki-Shokassen before the royal envoy appeared near the northern gate. There were twelve cavalrymen crowding the gate, each of them dressed in white coats with gold buttons and sashes, with gleaming steel helmets atop their heads bearing gold plumes. As if to match, they all sat atop huge white warhorses.

In the center was a woman, around twenty four or so years old, with silvery hair and blue eyes. She wore a white dress with blue horizontal frills in lines from the top of the bust to the hem of the skirt. Additionally she wore white sleeves and riding gloves along with some very expensive looking white leather shoes with silver laces. Her expression was nothing short of regal – dignified, not pleased nor serious, with her eyes appraising the approaching entourage with nothing exceeding a transient interest.

Ethilia gave a bow, followed suit by the others. "My Lady. I trust we did not keep you waiting too long."

"Not at all, fair healer," she responded, her voice slightly deeper than expected, with an accent indicating she may have lived in Nakisho her entire life. "I am pleased the High King decided to invite you all to his abode. My name is Tavia Shoka-Dathrim, consort to the High King and heir to the Duchy of Umbril. It is very nice to meet you all."

She's so proper! Reldon thought to Alira. *Though I'm not sure what else I expected.*

The High King's Consort turned expectantly towards each of them in turn and Kiera replied first.

"Kiera Itholos, My Lady. Princess of Korraine," she said with as much a curtsy one could give atop a horse.

"Reldon of Errum, Xanem Master. Nice to meet you," Reldon said with a smile.

Alira followed suit. "Alira Ayuru, Ilewa Nuremil. It's an honor."

When she turned to Bryle, he and Sillida smiled pathetically. "Our names are Bryle and Sillida, from Errum. We haven't got any fancy titles."

She returned their benevolence. "That does not detract from your character. Remember that. And who is this?"

"Oh, this is Elly," Alira spoke up, "She's from Ferrela. She is a Golden Magician, and we rescued her. She is my apprentice."

"Oh?" Tavia cooed, her interest piqued, "Miss Vendimar, I trust you have displayed your usual interest in a fellow Golden Magician to this Elly of Ferrela."

"You have no idea," Bryle snickered sarcastically.

Ethilia ignored him. "Naturally, My Lady. Elliana shows great promise, and I believe she would be a stellar addition to the Golden Magician sisterhood."

Elly was only vaguely aware of her name being mentioned as she worked fruitlessly on attempting to braid Storm Charger's mane.

Tavia eyed the girl with a look of bemusement. "I think she would get along well with my children."

Her son and daughter were separated, each sitting atop a horse with one of the dragoons. The boy looked around six years old, with his mother's silver hair and blue eyes. He had been garbed in a russet velvet doublet with a gold collar, a black feathered hat, and boots far too large for his small feet. The girl was almost a miniature, three or four-year-old version of her mother, but with dark, slightly curly hair. She wore a very similar dress, but bore several flowers which Reldon knew were not in season. They both simply watched the group with curious interest.

"Varia is four years old, and High Princess of Lärim. Her elder brother Antixius is High Prince, heir to Nakisho Castle and the future High King. I must express my gratitude that such trusted friends of the High King are to be joining us for the Deep Frost. In such a time, people become desperate and soldiers can only protect so well against assailants of magical training. Before your power we are but humble men and women," she spoke as more of a declaration.

"Has your house been attacked before during the storm?" Reldon asked as their horses walked over the open drawbridge to the north gate.

"It is not without precedent, though none in my experience. To the destitute, a helpless woman and her children are little deterrent when in view of an expensive manor."

"Why would magicians want to break into your mansion? It doesn't make sense," Alira posed rhetorically.

"Not all have shelter during the storm, and therefore not all seek treasure."

"Do you know why His Grace sent Ethilia along?" Reldon inquired.

"I am not privy to the decisions of the High King, but I suspect he worries for our health. His children have struggled at times with problems of the bowels, and he does not wish them to be without care for long," she responded, her lingering gaze on the children ahead of her, bouncing gently on their horses as they rode.

"My Lady, I hope I don't sound too... rude in asking this, but..." Bryle stammered, his inhibitions attempting to stop him, "You speak of the High King as if you don't know him. Isn't he your husband? I don't understand."

Ethilia shot Bryle a death glare, but Tavia held up a hand as if to halt her concerns.

"You are Nuru, didn't you say? Our customs must seem strange to you, especially given that each country within Lärim is just a bit different from the others. Understand that some kingdoms and their laws and customs have changed over time to reflect the changes in culture in those countries. Korrainians for example," she mentioned, directing with a hand towards Kiera, "...are a strong people who desired their own customs many centuries ago and did not wish to capitulate to those of the Crown. To this day their customs regarding queens have been somewhat more permissive than others, and throughout Lärim a woman reigning alongside her husband in the role of an advisor and confidant is not uncommon.

"However, the capital of Naiwa-ki-Shokassen and the role of the High Kings is much older than any of these countries individually. The customs have been tied to the power and credibility of the throne, traditions which would bring instability if any changes occurred. Therefore, my role in the High Kingdom is not a queen, nor am I a monarch of any kind. It would even be a stretch to claim myself an advisor. Our marriage, as all marriages to High Kings have been, was entirely political and for the good of the realm. It brought prestige to my house and it bore his dynasty's children. Beyond that, we are little more than acquaintances."

The explanation was so cold, so sterile, it stirred feelings in Reldon which ranged from pity to anger. It was a similar custom which had threatened Kiera's very independence and happiness, and one from which he had felt honor-bound to release her from.

Reldon struggled to even come up with a question to ask her, but she spoke before he could make the attempt.

"Doubtless you fear for my happiness. Worry not, noble Xanem Nuremar, this is what I was born for, and I would not have it any other way. I see to the growth and health of my children, as any mother would be proud to do, and my needs are seen to by the realm."

These don't sound like her words, Alira. It sounds like she's been drilled into saying them for most of her life.

For nobles in Lärim, there is no greater honor than marrying into royalty, she responded, *So she was probably raised from birth knowing that this would be her entire fate.*

I...dislike that idea.

Why?

Her parents may have planned out every part of her life for her by the time she was even able to talk, but what if she never wanted any of this?

But what if she did?

How would you know? Is it actually what she wanted, or was it because she was told it was what she wanted?

We can never know that, Reldon. If she says she's happy, I believe her.

"You and the High King seem like a good match, My Lady," Alira said at the same time as her conversation with Reldon, "You are both very smart and you speak in similar ways."

"How kind of you to say so, Ilewa Nuremil, but I think that may be a result of our similar education. I have to admit, however, that you are the first to remark on our fitness together as people rather than simply a 'smart' match. It is refreshing."

See? Completely discontent, Reldon poked fun at her.

You're impossible.

"So, how soon is this storm going to be hitting?" Bryle asked generally.

"None know specifically, but it should be here in the next few days. It always hits around the same time each year," Tavia explained.

"How much snow does it usually bring?"

"Many feet of it, but the snow is not as dangerous as the icy winds. It has been said to howl with such intensity that it has driven men mad," Tavia said with a wry smile.

Bryle stopped his horse. "It drives them…mad? How can anyone live in this country?" He flinched suddenly. "I think I just felt a snowflake on my nose."

The High King's Consort turned her head with an evil grin. "Then you had best keep a move on, Bryle of Errum, or you will be left behind in the snow."

Chapter X

The royal residence reminded Reldon a lot of the Vendimar estate, except for another story taller and with grounds stretching as far as he could see. Rolling hills surrounded the estate, topped with beautiful willow and oak trees which still retained their splendor even after having lost all of their leaves. White brick roads circumnavigated the house and led betwixt the gardens, the orchards, and even an orangery near the far east end of the property. *How in the world one grows oranges in this part of the world is beyond me,* Reldon thought to himself.

Shoka-Dathrim Estate was shaped like a square but with one of the sides missing. Three stories tall, it stood as a marvel of modern engineering and architecture with its columns of white granite pilasters across the face and topped with a pediment of the same make over the doorway. Each stretch of wall contained tall, eight-panel windows on each floor, with the longer sides bearing twenty-eight windows. At least a dozen chimneys jutted from the sloped, gold-painted roof.

All of the roads had been immaculately cleared of snow as their horses trotted into the courtyard before the house, coming to rest before a massive dark-stone statue of a man on a rearing horse. Everyone but Ethilia and its residents were in complete awe at the royal estate.

Several men stood in waiting atop the steps which climbed to the front doors. Three looked older, one maybe around thirty, and they all wore the same white jackets and trousers. As King's Consort Tavia approached on her horse, three of the men bowed in reverence while the last man came to aid her in her descent.

"My Lady, it is well you to see you arrive safely. And well before the storm," said the younger man, holding out a hand, "We were unaware to expect guests. Accommodations will be made immediately."

She took his hand and slipped her legs off the horse. "These are guests, offered sanctuary by the High King. The Ilewa Nuremil, Xanem Nuremar, and their companions. See that they are offered every amenity."

"Yes, My Lady, I shall see to it at once," he responded with a nod, rushing off towards the house.

Reldon dismounted and assisted Alira and Elly.

"What a gorgeous house," Reldon remarked incredulously, "It must have taken a decade to build."

"Seven years, but not far off. Once you have all had the chance to settle in, I can commission one of the groundsmen to provide a brief tour of the grounds on the morrow," Tavia declared.

"That sounds like fun," Alira said with one of the most genuine smiles Reldon had seen from her in days.

Unlike usual, the wind had come almost completely to a stop, a portent of an oncoming storm. Reldon had never felt a feeling quite like it before, but he knew that in a day or two they would not be able to be outside for some time.

"Might be the last chance to do so," Bryle said, pulling his pack from his horse and following Tavia towards the front doors.

"At least for a couple of weeks," Reldon clarified.

"Actually we're going to die. This is how it ended, not with fire and steel, but with ice and marble," Bryle said sarcastically.

Reldon nudged his friend where his knife wound had been and the young man flinched and punched him back.

Ethilia sighed. "At least *try* to act like you're in the presence of royalty. And that you're not complete provincials."

The front door opened into the foyer, which was a rectangular room with wooden paneled walls adorned with a series of paintings depicting former rulers, dukes, family members, among many others. A chandelier hung down from above, casting its crystalline light across the ancient faces immortalized in pigment. Tavia guided them through another door directly ahead which led to a grand staircase, flanked by a series of doorways and columns. In the center of the well-lit and thoroughly-tapestried hall was a marble statue of a man in plate armor standing tall, his unseeing gaze fixed on the heavens.

"This is a facsimile of the High King's father, former High King Antixius Xenus Shoka-Dathrim. It was his dream for his family to have a modern residence to grow up in, rather than simply in Nakisho Castle. As a result, much of the current High King's young life was spent here or at an academy. He thought it appropriate to have his father's likeness commissioned in marble here," Tavia explained.

"Did you know the former High King?" Kiera asked.

"Yes, though I was only slightly older than you when he passed away. I could not claim to know him, though I knew I had his blessing in the marriage. I suppose that is all I needed. Elsewise he was a fair king, and largely kept the peace during his thirty year reign."

As they reached the top of the marble staircase, she directed them into another hallway which contained yet another series of doors on either side.

"These are the guest residences. Respectfully, women and girls on the east wing and young men on the west. At the far end of this corridor are lavatories."

Reldon turned the brass doorknob and entered what would be his bedroom. It was much larger than he expected and needed, given the fact that it would just be Bryle and himself. It was another rectangular room with high tin ceilings and gold trim tracing along the corners of the room. Several armoires and cabinets were at their disposal, and two beds on opposite ends of the room were partitioned off by a red-and-gold curtain. Even the beds were over-plush and had far more pillows than Reldon had ever slept on at once.

Tavia graciously showed them around the rest of the house, bringing them into the basement floor which contained the kitchens, the game room, the servants' quarters, and the brandy room. The understory, she told them, contained nothing more than game storage, dry stores, and the wine cellars. The third floor contained more bedrooms, but were not as lavishly furnished due to their lack of use. Anything above that floor were attics, she claimed, which contained little else but perhaps the odd bird.

Leading them all back to the ground floor, she brought them to the dining room, an elongated hall which derived most of its light from a long series of windows on the northern wall, but was supplemented by a number of chandeliers and candelabras of a sterling silver. The table was needlessly long, but Reldon suspected it was used to many more guests in attendance than simply a few hapless heroes. At the very end of the hall was a painting which had to have been twenty feet tall, proudly displaying the current High King, Julius Xenus Shoka-Dathrim II in a thick velvet and white ermine-skin coat, standing before his throne in Nakisho Castle. It looked a few years old, as a few of the monarch's worry lines were missing from his complexion. *Or maybe they wanted him to look younger than he was.*

Every detail, every gold spoon and knife, every embroidered handkerchief was foreign to Reldon. He had never lived in such complete decadent lavishness. It seemed that even one of the paintings in the foyer would have been worth more than Reldon's life before becoming a Spellsword. Reldon could sense it from each of his companions (except maybe Ethilia) as they brought out the first course of food – there was a feeling of having been dropped into a dream which was so precariously hinging on their good behavior that they feared any disrespect would turn it into a nightmare. After all, Reldon and Alira had lived such an eventuality once already, but this felt slightly different. It felt like this was the very height of civilization, a pinnacle of human existence.

This is all making me feel unnerved, Reldon admitted to Alira as she took a sip of her grouse soup.

She nodded subtly. *Same here.*

It just all feels too…what's the word…

Lofty?

That sounds right. This is a completely different lifestyle than any of us have ever lived before. Or at least, I don't think so. I can never truly speak as to Ethilia or Kiera.

"This house is truly a wonder to behold," Kiera said to Tavia, who smiled in return, "You have our thanks for taking us under your roof."

"It is the High King's roof, by all technicalities, but you are most welcome. It will be most endearing having some company during the storm's ravages," she responded. For a moment there was no conversation, and she spoke up again. "You are all so quiet! Is everything quite all right?"

They all shot glances at one another before Reldon decided to speak up. "We mean no offense, My Lady. We are…not used to this. Any of this. I was a blacksmith's son back in Errum."

"Except Kiera, she's probably used to this." Bryle grinned.

She waved a finger at him in return. "I lived in a *castle*, not a palace. They are very different in most ways. This place has no ballistae, and the castle had no clean water. It was an ever so subtle trade-off."

"Still, much nicer than sleeping in the dirt in Ferrela," Bryle commented, skipping the soup and taking a large piece of roast deer.

Tavia's interest had been piqued. "I admit never to having visited Ferrela. What is it like there?"

"It is a country with many problems," Reldon stated simply, "Among them terrible things like corruption, starvation, and disease. It was hard to walk through their cities."

"That is sad to hear. They are such a private country that it is difficult to receive any news to any sufficient reliability. From what you have told me, the rumors are true. My understanding is that they take a deadly serious stance on magic."

Alira's attention flitted to Elly, who was dipping her finger in her soup bowl just to watch the ripples.

"They execute magicians there. We had to save Elly from that fate," Alira told her with sadness in her voice.

"It is most fortunate to have you with us today, Elly. Can you tell me a little about your homeland?"

She withdrew her finger from the soup bowl as if she had been slapped on the wrist. Her face went red as she noticed everyone's attention on her. "It was all right."

"Go on, Elly, tell her about your home. You won't get in trouble this time," Alira whispered to her.

There was an obvious hesitation on Elly's side of the conversation, given the reprimand she had gotten the last time she had been honest at a banquet. Still, Alira's words seemed to give her strength, and she sat up just a bit straighter.

"I lived next to a river. It was pretty and I liked to swim in the summer with my friend Rena. I lived with my Grandma. She's always so nice, and I miss her a lot," she struggled to say.

"Your accent sounds Lärimite, though, dear. Is your grandma from Lärim?"

"I think so, but I don't think she likes this country."

"Why not? Did she ever say?"

Elly shook her head. "Grandma likes to be left alone. Maybe the Lärimites were bothering her."

"Hm," the King's Consort hummed, "What is your grandmother's name?"

The small Golden Magician was perplexed at the question. "Her name is Grandma."

Tavia's attention shifted to Alira as she raised an eyebrow.

"None of us know her name, My Lady. For some reason she likes being called Grandma by everyone," Alira explained.

"Ah, how endearing," Tavia responded, taking dainty bites of her roasted vegetables.

"She's definitely a strange old crone," Sillida commented.

"And very secretive," Alira added. Something caught her peripheral vision and she snatched Elly's hand as she was about to send out a pulse of magic. "Elly, I've already told you to stop using magic on your food."

Bryle and Sillida laughed, but their hostess was intrigued.

"If you would excuse my impertinence, I find myself quite interested in your aptitude for magic, Ilewa Nuremil. All of you, to be frank. My exposure to magic has been extraordinarily limited, so I find it to be somewhat of an artefactual interest."

Is it just me, or is she abnormally interested in very basic things? Reldon shot over to Alira.

She does seem… curious.

"Oh, a large portion of us cannot use magic, Your Ladyship," Kiera said, "Bryle, Sillida, and I are as normal as you are."

"No less important, however." She smiled warmly to them.

"How much *do* you know about magic, My Lady?" Alira asked earnestly.

There was an odd mix of cryptic and humble notes to her voice. "Only what I have needed to."

"Ah, well you see, girls of certain bloodlines manifest magic at a very young age and they are able to use small bits of raw forms of magic. They go to the Academy City to learn more about their abilities and once they are old enough they must choose an element in the Keitas ceremony to use for the rest of their lives. After that, she is a full magician, and can train with masters of that element."

"What is…a Keitas?" Tavia asked, lacing her fingers together.

Has she really never been told anything about magic before? Alira thought to him.

"It is like a little orb that contains elements of magic in it. You have to speak to it…speak an old incantation of some kind in order for it to give you the element you want."

"Does it always give you the element you ask for?"

"Most of the time, but not always. I knew a girl two years older than me who asked for fire but it instead gave her shadow. I don't know why it happens. Maybe the Keitas didn't agree with her decision?"

"What *is* a Keitas, though? Where do they come from?"

"I'm sorry, My Lady, I wish I knew."

For a second there was a touch of annoyance on the High King's Consort's face, but she covered it up with a smile almost immediately. "Oh, quite all right. Not all of this world's mysteries are meant to be understood, I'm sure."

What was that about? Reldon's thoughts became concerned.

She really has been kept in the dark. Maybe she's upset about it?

An awkward silence ensued after that, which had luckily been supplemented by two serving men entering with another course of food.

Lots of greens, along with some figs, cookies, and tea were brought in as a sort of finisher to the meal.

"If you don't mind me asking, Missus Tavia," Bryle started, "In the time we are to stay here, what are we allowed to be doing? I would not wish to enter anywhere we are not welcome."

That seemed to bring the warmth back to Tavia's face. "Worry not about that, Bryle of Errum, there are no forbidden parts of the house. You may wish to avoid the attics or cellars, as they are not the most hospitable or warm parts of the estate. I would also warn you all from venturing outside during the storm, especially if you have not experienced the Deep Frost before. As for any schedule, breakfast and dinner are served the same time of morning and evening, and I respectfully ask you all to attend if you are able. After dinner it is customary for the ladies to retreat to the drawing room while the men attend to matters in the brandy room."

Reldon grinned. "What sorts of matters?"

She returned his look. "More important matters, I am certain. I would not know, however, having been a woman as long as I can remember."

Reldon and Bryle sat in the plush brandy room, certainly amazed at where in the world they had ended up after everything they had been through. There they were, Reldon thought to himself, surrounded by gold, velvet, and hundred-year-old crystalline glasses, while throughout most of his childhood he had been satisfied collecting bits of metal he found around Freiad so he would have something interesting to call his own.

Shortly after they had arrived in the brandy room, the oldest of the white-garbed serving men had entered thereafter and poured two glasses of the amber liquid into some of the most expensive-looking cups Reldon had ever seen. Without a word, he had bowed and left them alone, telling them if they needed anything to simply ring the bell. Reldon never found a bell. *I will definitely have to ask about that later.*

Reldon and his old friend sat across from one another in their lavish chairs as the roaring fire in the marble fireplace bathed them in flickering light and warmth.

"Can you believe all of this, Bryle?" Reldon asked incredulously.

"I've been pinching myself since we got here. Still not convinced I'm not dreaming," Bryle grinned.

"We've come a long way since Freiad. If our parents aren't proud of us at this point, I do not believe it will ever happen."

Reldon brought his glass of brandy up to his lips, and the sheer smell of the stuff could have curled his hair. Sipping the tiniest bit of it nearly brought tears to his eyes.

"Are you going to drink yours?" Bryle asked, his own glass still undisturbed.

"Absolutely not," he responded with a laugh.

"Me neither. They do know how old we are, right?"

"Oh I'm sure they're very aware. When Tavia told those servants Alira and I were the heroes of legend, I swear they thought she was playing a joke on them."

"And what a joke fate has played on us all! Not sure what I did to deserve all of this, but I must be doing something right." He scratched his chin, deep in thought. "Maybe fate appreciates what I did to help Sillida. You know, kidnapping Ethilia and all that."

Reldon chuckled. "I still can't believe you did that."

"She still hasn't forgiven me for it. Every time she looks at me it's with a mix of embarrassment and hatred."

"I don't know about *hatred*, Bryle."

"Just a few hours ago as we entered the estate she stomped on my foot as we climbed the stairs, for no reason. Not a single apology."

"All right, that's not a good sign, I will give that to you. I thought maybe she *did* like you, and that's why she looked at you like that," Reldon poked at him.

"Oh heavens no. I think she understood why I did what I did, but she's one of those highfalutin types that never really got over the embarrassment of being carried around town to the laughter of the locals," Bryle explained without irony.

"Understandably so."

"I did what I had to. She was being stubborn."

"She was born stubborn, methinks."

"She was *born* with an oversized silver spoon in her mouth and no reason why anyone should ever tell her no. *That's* why she's so stubborn – she's used to having her way all the time."

"You sound so finished with her that maybe you would be perfect together someday," Reldon laughed loudly at his shocked reaction.

"No no no, and no again. I prefer my girls a bit closer to the ground we walk on. In the mud with the rest of us."

"Someone like Sillida."

Bryle got very quiet for moment, before saying under his breath, almost imperceptibly, "Maybe."

Reldon responded only with a nod.

"What about you? When are you going to woo Alira? Everyone knows you are already perfect."

"We are not always perfect. Lately she's been moody, even before the incident with the girl in Teraxella. I think she's scared of something, but I can't quite figure out what it is, and she doesn't want to talk about it. Still, I have already... told her."

Bryle about leapt from his seat. "Oh, you have! Well done, mate! And how did she take to it?"

"She stopped slaughtering hundreds of Kuru soldiers."

His friend's enthusiasm appeared to freeze over. "Ah. Well I suppose there are worse ways for her to take it."

"Have *you* told Sillida you fancy her yet?"

He recoiled, shaking his head. "Not yet. I... I can't. Not right now. Not with everything going on."

"You may have a few weeks here without much else happening, Bryle. You have got to do it before we leave, or you may keep putting it off."

"But you *know* her, Reldon. She's all standoffish and whatnot. Hard to approach at times. I'm no good at this kind of thing," Bryle stammered. By the waver in his friend's voice, Reldon could tell this was something he was also not used to even *talking* about.

"You've just got to *do* it. Whatever happens after that is meant to be."

"That's easy for you to say, you're the Xanem Master with all the power in the world. I have no other skills after being a knight-in-training."

Reldon laughed again. "What does that have to do with anything?"

"Girls like men with *skills*, mate. No man ever impressed a girl by being all sappy with her. He sweeps her off of her feet and shows her what he can do!"

Reldon laughed until tears came to his eyes.

"What?" Bryle demanded.

"I don't think you should be sweeping anyone off their feet after that last time!"

Bryle threw a pillow at him and proceeded to assail him with a series of playful punches to Reldon's undying laughter. Elation filled him as he fought with his old friend again, just a remnant of the past which had managed to fit itself back into the puzzle that his life had become.

They were, however, interrupted by a courteous knock at the door, which heralded the entrance of the youngest serving man, whose look of direness brought Reldon back down to the world again.

"My Lord, I apologize for the intrusion, but you have... a visitor. A man waits outside the gates to the grounds who insists on speaking with you and the Ilewa Nuremil. He would not tell me his name."

A cold sweat broke out on Reldon's brow as his heart pumped.

"Maybe it's that ranger... Lynad? Maybe he's found us?" Bryle suggested.

"He would tell us his name. It's not him. I will need to get Alira," Reldon said, pulling on his black coat with gold buttons.

"I have already summoned her. She awaits you in the foyer," the servant replied, leaving at once.

The marble staircase, draped with a red carpet, seemed to go on forever as his feet wheeled in his descent. *Who in the world could be here on the eve of a snowstorm? And after sundown?*

Her thoughts greeted him before he actually saw her waiting among the paintings. *Do you think it could be Detryn? Oh I hope it is not him, I really couldn't bear a fight right now.*

It could even be Gihan. Either way, we can do this, Alira. Stay alert and be ready to fight just in case. We do have soldiers here to help if needed.

He joined her without a spoken word, and they both pushed the doors open into the bitterly cold air together.

A few lanterns, encasing flame in glass cases, stood atop long wrought iron poles around the periphery of the courtyard, lending at least a small amount of light to their path up to the gate. Alira's blond-brown hair whipped about in the wind, which had picked up significantly since just a few hours prior. The youngest serving man, now wrapped in a scarf and hat, strode alongside them.

"Have you ever seen this man here before?" Reldon asked him, raising his voice to be heard over the wind.

"Not in my experience. I have only been here for a few years, but we do not garner many uninvited visitors. The guards are somewhat of a deterrent."

A squad of around twenty five soldiers, their crossbows drawn and ready, awaited them at the imposing black gate. The captain of said guards nodded to them as they approached.

"Good evening, your Lord and Ladyship. This one on the other side of the gate claims he knows you and wishes to speak with you. Merely say the word and we can send him away, with or without new bodily ornaments," he said, shifting his crossbow in his arm.

"Thank you. We shouldn't be long," Reldon responded.

The man standing on the other side of the iron gate was shrouded in darkness, a cloak covering the entirety of his body, with nary a single feature visible beneath it. He stood silently, his weight evenly distributed on both feet, standing at least six feet tall. He did not appear to be carrying any weapons, but Reldon knew better than anyone how little that meant.

Reldon and Alira stood a few feet before the gate, just in case he did intend on attacking through the bars.

"Who are you? How do you know us?" Reldon demanded.

The man took a step forward, reaching up to pull his hood from his head. From what they could see, he looked like a man in the last quarter of his life, his features more gnarled than they had seen from anyone, and yet he stood completely straight, without any sign of weakness. Judging from his powerful build, if magic were taken out of the equation, he could easily beat Reldon in a fist fight.

He bore a full gray beard on his face, with skin nearly as dark as the night around them. There was no smile on his face – only the neutral expression of a man whose eyes conveyed the wisdom and terrors of thousands of moons long past.

"Your names have been heard by more ears and spoken on more tongues than most kings, not to speak of the hundreds of years of prophecy which foretold of your existence in greater apprehension of your birth than you could ever comprehend. *How* I know of your names is of little wonder. Who *I* am is the more operative question, and what I can do to *help* you is of even further import. I am called Sterling, nothing more."

The man's incredible basso voice brought such power and weight that it was difficult to even respond. Reldon stood for a moment completely awestruck and at a loss for words.

"Wh-what do you want from us?" Alira struggled to ask.

"Nothing more than your cooperation and attention. You bear a destiny which would crush the strongest man or woman unto ash, and you have stood so far in capable discernment of this fact. Within you both, you have the singular power to bring an end to this fetid conflict once and for all, but you are like fire – untamed and wild. I am here to complete your training, to bring order to the chaos your small forms bring with you.

95

Without my aid, you cannot hope to withstand the coming storm." His accent was difficult to place, though Reldon thought that it did sound mostly Lärimite, but with a healthy dose of something else – an accent he had not heard before.

"What storm are you talking about? The Deep Frost?" Reldon asked, feeling stupid.

"Not all storms are borne of nature," he responded shortly, his voice sounding like a wild cat's growl.

Reldon shivered from the cold. "What makes you so qualified to be our master?"

Within an instant, before Reldon could even hope to react, every flame in every lantern in the courtyard and on the grounds went out at once, plunging them into hopeless darkness.

Then he felt the sharpest, most potent spike in Phyrimic activity he had ever felt in his entire life, coupled with nothing more than gust of wind and the terrible sound of metal being sheared.

Alira and Reldon turned to see the old man, his cloak rippling in the constant wind, standing atop the statue in the courtyard, cupping two pockets of incredible Phyrimic energy in his palms. So powerful were they, that they created enough white light to bathe the entire estate in a state of near-daylight. From one hand he produced a sword, a wicked curved black blade with white lightning arcing around it. Pointing it towards them, their hearts thumped in unison with abject fear. Twisted metal was left where the gate had been behind them, and the guards could do nothing but watch.

In an amplified voice, his words boomed. "With age, wisdom. With tribulation, strength. With knowledge, control. You know only of destiny and its cruel grip on this world. You are undisciplined, lost, and aimless. I am here to give you focus, direction, and above all else, restraint. Many thousands have died to bring you to this moment. Do not fall unto oblivion."

Reldon slipped into his Phyrimic vision and the man emanated a power which he had never seen before. If staring into Tycheronius's Xanem had been like looking into a bright star, this man was like staring into the sun. An aura of silver Phyrim emanated off of him, reaching out and touching every living being in sight, and it was from this aura they felt the fear and adulation.

In another split second, he flicked out of existence, and reappeared a few feet in front of them, the lanterns having somehow been reignited.

"Am I worthy of your presence, Your Imperialness?" he asked, a touch of humor in its inflection.

Reldon and Alira nodded simultaneously, completely deprived of words.

"Excellent," he said with a small smile, walking past them and right by the terrified soldiers, "Sorry about your gate, I will repair it." And with a snap of his fingers, the metal writhed back into its original shape, with Sterling behind it. "I will see the both of you tomorrow at dawn. Here."

Chapter XI

Reldon tore through the flames, his bare feet pounding the charred cobblestone roads beneath him. His armor and robes were all gone, and he was left with nothing but rags as the flames licked at his exposed skin. Alira stood on the horizon of his vision, wearing perfect white robes. She cried bitterly, echoing into the black, ember-strewn night. So lonely, so stricken was she that her white robes turned to gray and she fell to her knees. He called out to her, but there was no sound.

From out of the flames stepped angry, burned husks of people, completely featureless and carrying pitchforks and torches. They shrieked at him, called him a monster. Reldon had no choice but to stop as they approached, but beyond them he spotted a handful approaching Alira, menacing her with short blades.

"*No!*" he tried to scream. Clamping a hand over one of their faces, he supercharged it with Phyrim until the husk exploded in a shower of flames and screams. Tearing his sword from the Infinity Scabbard, he brought its blade around with a whistle and hew three of them in half, their bodies turning to burning logs as they struck the ground.

"*Alira!*"

The flames moved in and more of them crawled from their depths. The awful stench of burning flesh assaulted his senses. For every two he ripped apart, three more spawned from the inferno.

As they reached out to touch her, Alira's robes turned to black. She stood again and turned to look at him. Holding out a hand, she beckoned to him to come to her.

"Please, come!" she shouted. "Let me save you."

Three pairs of hands grabbed his shoulders and arm, the remnants of his rags sizzling and burning away.

Panic set in.

Reldon flailed about, slicing a few with his sword, but they pulled him to the ground in the dozens.

He screamed and released every emotion he had within him. The flames reached him and the blinding light seared away all of the husks, leaving him standing alone.

Alira still held out her hand, and he rushed to her, stretching his own hand out to join her.

"That's it. Come here," she coaxed him.

"Alira, I was so afraid. I…"

He touched her hand and realized that the hair that hung down into his face had turned red.

Reldon heard the percussion before he felt anything.

A flash of light jolted his vision. He never had a chance to react.

Looking down, where his chest had been was nothing more than a mangled, burned hole. The utter shock brought him to his knees, and the weakness toppled him onto his back.

Alira looked down at him without expression. Another figure approached, standing over him with that same unfeeling look.

Standing above was himself. His own gray eyes appraised him without pity.

"You're not worth saving."

The world suddenly rushed back to into focus. Cold sweat covered Reldon's body, his nightclothes sticking to his skin. The flames were no longer there, but he could feel their heat. His hand immediately went up to his chest, feeling around for the hole, which didn't exist.

A breath of relief escaped his body.

However, he realized that for some reason he was not in his bed. He found himself sitting at the bottom of the marble stairs, feet away from the statue of High King Antixius.

"My Lord?" came a voice.

Reldon leapt to his feet to the sound of the serving man's voice. It was the eldest man who had poured him the brandy the previous night. He wore the same white coat as normal, and he carried a candle.

Are they even allowed to change out of those coats?

"My Lord, are you well? What are you doing here at the bottom of the stairs?" His large white mustache quivered as he spoke.

"I…I don't know. I was just having a nightmare and I ended up here."

"Hm. Sleepwalking, then. Come, I will guide you back to bed."

Reldon sat back down on the bottom step. "What time is it?"

"I would say two hours before sunrise, My Lord."

"Thank you for your assistance, but I don't think I'll be sleeping after that."

The elder set his candle down on the floor and sat beside him on the stair. "If I may ask, what was the nightmare about?"

His interest was certainly a bit peculiar for a serving man, but he answered all the same.

"It was about the…" he started, before hesitating. "I'm sure you heard about the girl in Teraxella."

"The fire magician you stopped, yes I had."

Reldon nodded solemnly. "It was about her. I was in her place."

The old man's expression softened with empathy. "It brings you great pain."

"I've been trying not to think about it. For Alira. Sorry, the Ilewa Nuremil."

"You have not had a chance to grieve. I believe you owe it to yourself to do so, My Lord. Do not hold onto these emotions, or you never know where you will find yourself waking up next."

Nodding, a tear worked its way down his face. "I didn't mean to… to kill her, I had no choice. I've had to kill soldiers before, lots of them. But that was all different. It was war and they were trying to kill me. There was nothing more I could do to save this girl. She…she was going to hurt Alira…"

Arms wrapped around him as the old man pulled him into an embrace. For the first time in what seemed like ages, Reldon was able to cry away the horrible emotions that lay claim to him.

"I didn't want to kill her…" he choked.

"She is much happier now, I promise. I know little of what faith you possess, but whether you believe in the spirits, the Omniscient One, or some other pagan deity, they all agree that those who have passed away, especially young and innocent, do not perish, but live on in the afterlife. A place where everything is built of food and the water is always clean and ready to drink."

Reldon laughed weakly. "I think you made that last part up."

The old man shrugged. "Perhaps it's just time for breakfast. I'm Randolfus, by the way. A pleasure to meet you. Come! Let us go to the kitchens and fetch something to eat. Might make you feel right as rain."

Morning proved no less hostile than the previous day had been. As Alira stepped out into the frigid air, she had to frantically hold tight to the hat atop her head to prevent it from flying away. Tiny bits of ice, swept up from the surface of the sea of snow pelted her exposed face with painful intensity. Finding any remnant of the sun's life-giving rays was proving impossible as the clouds above swirled malignly.

She hugged her middle just as tightly, shivering violently after just a few minutes outside.

This is not weather to be training in. The Deep Frost is very dangerous. What on earth could that Sterling be thinking?

Reldon joined her shortly thereafter, also dressed in several layers of wool and fur clothing. Despite it all, he smiled at her. She tried to smile back, but she just couldn't. Another day, another time she could have, but not now. The emotional strength it took to smile superseded what she could muster these days.

Sure to his word, the imposing man Sterling waited for them at the gate where they had left him the night prior. Though dimmed, the light of even a stormy day revealed more of his figure. His black cloak, made of a thick leather, was ripped in several places and worn in most others. He wore equally weathered black boots that Alira could probably have fit both of her feet into at once. Several scars etched his face, the largest being a deeper cut from under his left eye down to below his left ear.

His dark eyes watched them approach.

"You are good to your word," he said in his deep timbre.

"It is very cold out, mister Sterling," Alira said, her voice wavering from all the tremors of the cold, "Perhaps w-w-we could train ins-s-side?"

His bushy eyebrows pulled together. "Legends are forged in hardship, tempered in fire and ice. If you wish to be warm, then make it happen. We will not be returning indoors until we are finished."

"But how-"

Sterling nodded towards the gate. The heavily layered man standing guard received confirmation from Reldon before unlocking it. Alira and Reldon stepped out to meet the man, who was much taller up close.

"Come. We go to yonder hill," he said gruffly, stepping through the snow towards a fair-sized hill just a few hundred yards from the gates.

Reldon and Alira exchanged looks of concern before following him to the top.

Sterling halted and turned to look at them.

"You say you wish to be warm. Then become warm." His eyes were fixed on Alira, expectation clear in his words.

Alira could only stare back at him, her cheeks stinging out in the open. She expected him to clarify or give her a hint of some kind, but he only watched her.

She felt compelled to respond. "But how, mister Sterling?"

He leaned in close, his words stirring her anxiety. "Are you not a fire magician?"

"W-well, yes, sir. I am an everything magician."

"Then make yourself warm."

Her eyes shot over to Reldon looking for help.

You can do it, Alira.

Taking a deep breath of the nostril-freezing air, she removed her gloves and put them in her pockets before allowing her Keinume to blaze to life. Its beautiful silver rose design was muted in the gray daylight, but as she channeled the angry flames within her, it burned bright red. Cupping her hands together, she charged her latent magical power through her Keinume to bring the fire to life.

A glow emitted from between her palms, not unlike that of torchlight. A small flame grew in the space between, becoming larger with more power input. The warmth of the flame thawed her frozen fingers and they flushed red from the returning blood flow.

"Good. Now generate more heat and sustain it," Sterling ordered.

She nodded. *This shouldn't be too complicated.*

Like a siphon, she released more magical energy into the flame and it grew larger and more vivacious. She could feel the wonderful heat on her face, and she wondered why she had never thought of using her flames in such a way.

But then she realized why.

Before she had any chance to react, the flame grew out of control. It was as if the siphon had broken. The flame expanded by more than double in the course of just a second.

There was a minor explosion right in front of her as the heat expanded exponentially. Fear never even had a chance to grip her.

However, next she was aware, she was surrounded by the shimmering light of a silver force-field.

The burst of flame had melted the snow beneath them and burned some grass, but everyone, including herself, was unharmed. A gnarled hand with massive fingers poked out from Sterling's robes, which withdrew along with the force-field.

"What happened?" he demanded.

"I-I don't know! I just couldn't control it all of a sudden," she almost pleaded with him.

He turned to face the horizon and stretched out his arm, pointing to something in the distance.

"Do you see that boulder? Destroy it with your flames."

Alira still hadn't recovered emotionally from her previous failure, but she tried to focus in spite of it. It wasn't too far away, nothing more than a stone's throw.

Generating a massive amount of magical energy into a nexus of flame, she felt the familiar invigorating hum of the incredible power she was about to unleash.

Throwing out her hand, she tossed the molten ball of flame and let her fury tear through the winter air. As it reached the boulder, the light and energy produced was nothing short of an explosive spectacle. Liquid rock was thrown into the air, along with a continuous stream of thick white smoke. The destruction was almost near-complete, as only the bottom quarter of the boulder remained, smoldering loudly.

The sound rang out for miles. "How was that?" Alira asked with just a hint of smugness.

Sterling had clearly not shared in her confidence.

"Can you explain to me why that was so simple for you, and yet your first attempt was so difficult?" Sterling said.

Alira really had no answer. She searched her knowledge and could not come up with a reason why she couldn't do it the first time.

"May I try again? To hold a large flame?" she asked, avoiding the question.

"No. You will not succeed. And do you know why?"

Alira sighed. "No, I don't. It was just…harder."

"It is not. They are the same power. You are using them in the same way. What was the difference in what I asked you to do?"

She was starting to feel attacked. "One was destructive, and the other was not."

"That may have been one of the differences, but it is not why you failed."

Alira thought about it for a second. "Destroying the rock didn't require any sustaining power."

"Exactly. This is the key difference. I can look at you and I can see you are in no shortage of magical power. Looking at you is like looking at the origin of all magic. You could move mountains and part oceans if you desired, however you cannot even sustain a fire potent enough to keep yourself warm. Tell me, how long has this problem been happening?" Sterling said.

She stammered in her answer. "I…uh…I think as long as I can remember. I tried using a… a tornado on Brina, but it failed because I lost control."

"Have you not been taught to sustain magic?"

Her eyes flitted over to Reldon's inquisitive look before finding her boots. "No. I fled the Academy before they were to teach me."

Sterling crossed his powerful arms as he looked down at her. "This explains why all you are capable of doing is unleashing your power in bursts. You are a vessel of limitless power without any way to control it, and that makes you just as dangerous to yourself as you are your enemies. Today I will teach you to sustain your power, but you must practice every day even after I am gone. Do you understand?"

She nodded. "Yes, sir." *He is absolutely terrifying, but he knows what he is talking about.*

The question is how *he knows all of this. I've never even heard of him,* Reldon answered.

"And you will have to do a better job of concealing when you're using your Ilewa connection. If your eyes were any further away from the here and now, they would cease to be attached to you. Sit."

His rebuke had been sharp and shocking. Alira and Reldon exchanged incredulous looks before sliding to their knees in the snow. Alira was red enough that she swore she was going to start seeing steam from every snowflake that landed on her.

"I am going to have to take you back to when you first started learning how to use magic. You learned to meditate. You learned to recognize the power inside you as something which was a part of you, like another limb or a sixth sense instead of as something foreign that was simply happening to you. I want you to close your eyes and bring yourself into the same oneness with your magic that you have learned since the beginning," his deep voice instructed her.

It wasn't difficult for her to do so. Since she was very young, a fresh student at the Academy City, she had been proficient enough at centering herself and, in a sense, embracing her magical power. It had been like an old friend, always there ready to act if ever she should need it. In only a few breaths, she felt the familiar vibrant sensation coursing through her veins and filling her entire being. It was such an exhilarating experience that she had never found any accurate way to describe it to non-magic users.

"Good. You are skilled in that at least. Now channel fire."

Channeling fire was like remembering old pain, facing old tragedy, and facing it down with nothing more than complete stubborn fury. The refusal to give up. Determination to never die. The dedication to burn those who try to force you to.

Anger radiated within her, her magical power vibrating into an ominous, seething heat. Snowflakes falling near her vaporized instantly.

"Your control of fire is admirable," Sterling commented, "Now I want you to channel just a portion of that energy into your Keinume and allow it to simply boil there."

It seemed like a strange request, but she obeyed.

Her Keinume flared up crimson red again, humming warmly with its new fuel source.

And there it rested. For fifteen seconds. Thirty seconds. Slowly as time went on, her Keinume hummed louder.

"Stop feeding it more power. Hold it steady," he ordered.

When channeling magic, especially when sustaining it, the channeled emotions tended to take over, so whereas normally she would have said something like, "I don't understand, it's not working," instead she snapped, "I'M TRYING!"

For some frustrating reason, she couldn't get her Keinume to stop consuming more energy. Beads of sweat rolled down her face as she tried to retract the siphon of power into it. Once she did, though, it was once again as if she had broken the siphon.

Her Keinume overloaded with her own magical power, and with a flash and an ear-splitting blast of sound, it disappeared and her magical focus with it.

Alira growled to herself and slapped her hand against the snow as the fury subsided.

"I see what the problem is. You have been uncontrolled for too long. You are going to have to work hard to re-teach yourself," Sterling said, "However you have so much energy that you can practice for hours. Unlike other students, you can learn this many times faster if you focus."

She wasn't even breathing hard. Even with her lapse in focus, her magic was ready to go again.

At his instructions, she continued to attempt to control her Keinume's siphoning for at least another hour. Between bouts of complete vengeful anger and recovery she was most surprised that Reldon had been able to sit and watch, completely wordlessly throughout its entirety. He only offered a supportive smile when she looked at him, and her chest swelled each time.

By her fifteenth failure, Sterling looked at her with a small sense of bewilderment.

"Would you allow me to hold your hand while you are attempting this? I wish to understand better what is happening with your flow of magic," he asked politely.

"Of course," she responded, clasping his massive fingers.

"Now pretend I am not here and continue as you were."

She did, producing yet another failure in just a few minutes as her Keinume burst out of existence again. This time she had sensed his presence, not in any way probing, but just observing.

He withdrew his hand. "I believe I understand what is happening, but it is difficult to say for sure. You are a very special case. All I can say for sure to you now is that you are experiencing... a power overflow."

She cocked her head. "How do you mean?"

Gingerly, he lifted himself to his feet, peering off into the horizon again.

"This is going to sound strange, and it will go against what you have been taught, but you must trust me. I want you to unleash as much power as you can possibly muster on that closer hill just there. Burn it. Freeze it. Blast it. I want you to obliterate it with as much power as possible."

Alira only looked at him, her eyes widened. "B-but that's dangerous, Mister Sterling."

"Just do it."

She gulped. Alira was terrified at what she was about to do.

Breathing in deeply, she began to channel. At first she channeled fire, the terrible fury reaching her fingertips and emanating into the world as a cloud of flames spewing from her left hand. In her exhale, she was able to let go of not only the anger but also of even her wants, desires, and simply existed, releasing a rippling current of air to merge with the flames. Cutting off the power, they twisted together to form a twister of flame on the hill, incinerating snow and grass within seconds.

Pulling inwardly, she faced the destruction without fear, channeling earth. Punching the ground, cracks formed up and down the hill, producing an earthquake in that tight vicinity. Allowing herself to think of her mother, her love and loss took grip of every molecule of water around the area, and she pulled them together between the cracks, forcing them apart as they rapidly froze.

Letting herself transition to another emotion, she thought about Elly, and how much she wanted to help and train her. To see her grow and prosper. It was a righteous desire. Electricity coursed around her entire body, flashing between her fingertips. With a shout of exertion, she lashed out with that energy. There was a blinding flash before Alira was knocked backwards. She covered her ears as quickly as she could as the explosion from the lightning turned the hill into nothing more than a fireball of destruction.

The aftermath was nothing short of horrifying. There simply was no hill, but instead a charred hole in the ground with deep cracks in the earth extending outwardly into other hills. Shattered pillars of ice were about all that was left.

"How was that?" Alira asked again, turning back to Sterling and Reldon.

Reldon was in a complete state of shock, having been knocked onto his rump. He stared at her like she was some sort of deity standing before him.

Even Sterling had been lost for words for a moment. "You forgot shadow."

She scowled at him. Shadow had always been difficult for Alira to channel, as it required a level of bitterness that she just didn't possess.

Reaching out, the giant man took her hand again.

"As I thought. That took only a quarter of your power, and it is quickly returning. You do not even look taxed." His words bled of amazement.

"No, I feel fine!" she responded happily.

"You are absolutely terrifying sometimes, Alira," Reldon said aloud.

She smiled at him. "That's right, don't make me mad!"

"I do not think you comprehend how dangerous this makes you," Sterling spoke, "For reasons unbeknownst to me, you contain more power than almost any magician who has ever lived, your body draws in magical energy at an alarming rate, and you cannot control any of it. For the moment, you are nothing more than a walking calamity, a herald of earth-shaking destruction in a blond girl's form. I will attempt to develop a strategy by tomorrow, but until then, do not use your magic. I fear what you might bring to bear if provoked."

"Wouldn't it make more sense not to provoke her then?" Reldon commented.

"Provocation is often outside of our control. So much as lighting a candle could result in burning down the palace. Do *not* use your magic," he told her, pointing a stern finger at her face.

He's afraid of me, Alira's thoughts rang out with a mix of pride and regret.

That makes two of us.

A powerful gust of wind buffeted the three with shards of ice for a long moment, howling loudly in the upper atmosphere.

"I'm afraid there may not be another day for training, Mister Sterling," Alira said, "The storm may strike before then."

"It will not strike in earnest for at least another day," he responded obstinately, "In the meantime we will continue the pace of our work until you have some semblance of control. Tomorrow morning I will have a strategy for you, Alira Ayuru. I am done with you for now. Boy, come."

She felt a pang of annoyance emanating from Reldon's mind at being called 'boy', but he let it pass, standing at attention.

"Mister Sterling, am I allowed to use magic to stay warm? It is rather cold," Alira asked.

"No."

She embraced herself to hold in warmth, pursing her lips in an equal amount of annoyance.

"What would you like me to do?" Reldon inquired.

"Stand up straight. Do not slouch." He placed his hands on Reldon's upper arms and moved his head around as if searching for something on Reldon's face. Reldon's eyes followed him uneasily.

The old master's eyes flicked silver for a second before blinking back to brown.

"What's *your* problem, boy?"

Reldon was taken aback. "Uh, I don't... have a problem, sir."

"Your Phyrimic reservoirs certainly do. You *did* say you're the Xanem Nuremar, did you not?"

Alira wasn't sure if it was meant to try to deduce the problem or rile Reldon up, but if the latter were his objective, it was having limited success as her Ilewa was more confused than anything.

"Last I knew, sir. What is wrong with them?"

"Generate a force field."

"I'm sorry, I-"

"Do it, boy."

He casually held out a hand and a shimmering field of greenish force appeared before him, a rectangular shape about his own height.

"A *real* force field, boy!" Sterling barked.

"I… what are you talking-"

Sterling held out his own massive uncovered hand, touching the force field and, without warning, sent a jolt of Phyrimic energy through it. It was sharpest, most potent punch of danger Alira had felt through their connection since their fight with the Churai. Reldon had not been ready for it, as his force field shattered like a thin piece of glass, knocking him back.

"Did that seem like a well-structured force field to you?" Sterling growled.

"Well I didn't expect you to *attack* it," Reldon growled back.

"What else are force fields for? Now give me a *real* force field!"

Alira felt a powerful draw from Reldon's energy reserves as he generated a force field which looked solid enough to be an actual wall of Phyrimic energy. The air around it seemed to bend in response.

"Better," Sterling said, his eyes turning silver again, "Now hold it."

Reldon did so, his force field humming for at least a minute or two. His face was locked in a look of determination. Alira could sense his irritation with Sterling's instruction helping to feed his desire not to give in.

However after around three minutes, a bead of blood ran down from Reldon's nose and his hands began to shake.

"I've seen enough," Sterling waved at him dismissively.

Reldon released the power, breathing hard and wiping the blood from his face.

"That is what is wrong with you. You have the exact opposite problem as your Ilewa. Whereas she is an eternally overflowing bucket of power, you are a mug that's been half-filled. Rarely have I seen such a strange problem between Ilewas, especially those of your caliber."

Reldon and Alira stared back at him as he crossed his toned arms, his lower jaw jutted fiercely.

"Have you… seen this before, Mister Sterling?" Alira asked from her snowy seat.

"Only once," he muttered pensively. He scratched his greying beard for a long minute as the wind whipped around him. "We will need to change focus today. I will meditate on this later."

For the remainder of the day, which only lasted a few hours with the weather, they practiced a number of drills ranging from basic exercises that Reldon remembered doing in Huerogrand to more strenuous tests which involved them expanding their respective energy reservoirs. It had been exceedingly difficult for Reldon, as Sterling kept forcing him to continue exerting himself well after his Phyrim had run dry. On a number of occasions, the only reason they had stopped was because Reldon's body had given out before his stubborn determination had.

Alira, meanwhile had no such problems. While Reldon had been bleeding from his nose, ears, and mouth, nearing the black maw of unconsciousness, she might as well have been decorating her barriers with flowers and jewels for how little energy it seemed to consume. To her credit, she had insisted numerous times to be allowed to give her Ilewa the power to go on, but Sterling rarely relented.

Dragging himself back downstairs to the dining hall after recovering on his bed for several hours was an ordeal in itself, but he knew that even above the need for food he would not want to slight the High King's Consort. Still, he stumbled into the hall as the bowls of broth were being distributed.

"Reldon, what happened to you, mate?" Bryle asked, "You look like you got into a fight with a ghost. I'm not sure who won."

He pulled out his chair across from Alira and next to Bryle and Kiera, plopping himself down without much attention paid to courtesy.

"Training," was all he could say as he pushed himself up to the table.

"That man must be a particularly harsh teacher," Kiera noted.

Alira nodded, breaking her bread.

"Do you know precisely *who* he is?" Tavia asked, "I daresay I have never heard of him, nor have my servants seen him around these parts in recent days."

"He doesn't really answer questions," Alira said, "When it doesn't have to do with training, he becomes very grumpy."

"Master has a master?" Elly asked.

"For the moment, it would seem, Elly!" Alira responded cheerfully.

"In our profession, learning is a never-ending endeavor, Elliana. In my experience, magicians have masters throughout much of their lives," Ethilia piped in, sipping a spoonful of broth.

"With respect, you're a bit young to have a great wealth of life experience, Miss Vendimar," Tavia poked at her.

"To be honest, when the oldest person in this room is in her twenties, I feel like a conversation about life experience is going to be short at best," Bryle quipped.

Sillida gave him a look. "You are so rude."

"If that's another word for honest, then I'm all right with that."

Elly stuck her tongue out at him. He returned in kind.

Somewhere in Reldon's mind he anticipated Tavia's demeanor to change with such childish behavior in her beautiful palace, but to his surprise she appeared quite happy.

She noticed his gaze. "Is something wrong, Xanem Nuremar?"

He shook his head, blinking the sleep from his eyes. "No, Your Ladyship. You just seem to be enjoying their antics."

Her smile was warm. "It is good to see you all able to relax and be yourselves here. I haven't forgotten the amount of distress you have all been under in the past few months. From the trial to the Battle of Nakisho and thereafter, it was always a wonder to me how you were all coping. If a touch of silliness is how you are handling it, then I am content. You *are* all quite young after all."

"Back to this again," Bryle muttered.

Elly laughed. "You're a child, Bryle!"

"I really don't want to hear that from you."

Kiera leaned over and peered into Reldon's eyes, but it didn't quite register in his brain until she spoke. "Either you are half-asleep or you and Alira are speaking with your minds again."

He snapped to. "Oh, I apologize, I am very drained from training."

"What is it like talking to someone with your mind?" she asked.

Reldon's and Alira's eyes met. She spoke first, "It is very difficult to describe. It is like thinking hard about something, but to him instead of to yourself. Does that make sense?"

"Not very much. Do all magicians have Ilewas? Who is yours, Ethilia?" Kiera inquired.

Ethilia set down her spoon as the entrees were set in front of each of them. "Had I an Ilewa, I would have known of his existence by several years ago. I'm afraid I am likely among the many who simply do not have an Ilewa due to the population of parasitic Churai."

"Do you wish you had one?" Sillida asked. It was an oddly personal question, coming from her.

Ethilia did not answer right away. After having a servant pour her a cup of tea, she appraised the girl with her wintry gaze before softening. "I suppose it would be useful."

It hadn't been the answer Sillida had expected, clearly, as her hopeful demeanor wilted and her attention returned to her food. That was when Reldon caught her shooting a glance across the table at Bryle for no more than a split second. Reldon's heart thumped in sympathy for her.

I don't understand why he lets this continue, he thought to himself, *She is so smitten with him that she can hardly contain herself. He's being selfish by letting her suffer like this.*

Alira stood and excused herself as her entrée was being delivered. Elly, not certain how to proceed, patted after her.

Everything all right, Alira? He asked her.

I am fine. I am too tired to continue tonight.

And that was the last of their ethereal communications for the evening. It seemed strange that she was so tired, given how easy the training had been for her.

Reldon nudged Bryle, speaking in a low voice. "When are you going to tell her?"

"Who?"

"Sillida, you bell end."

He didn't want to respond, instead whispering, "We will talk about it shortly. In the brandy room."

"I'm holding you to it."

Later that night, there came a knock at the High King's Consort's door.

Tavia had not yet retired to bed, so the response was quick. Answering the door, she saw the smaller form of Sillida standing in the low candlelight, dressed in a beige night gown with frill about the hems of the arms, skirt, and neck. She recognized it as one of her own gowns from her youth.

"Ah, young Miss Sillida of Errum, what a pleasant surprise," Tavia greeted her.

"Hello, your…uh…Ladyness," the girl responded nervously, twiddling her fingers. It was a more endearing sight than Tavia's heart could comprehend. "May I…have a word with you?"

Tavia's smile revealed what her heart could not. "You may have several if you wish. Do come in, my dear."

Sillida did not look comfortable with the surroundings, but something else was tugging at her mind which threatened to burst forth from her lips. She quietly took a seat next to the fireplace across from the High King's Consort.

"What's bothering you, dear? You look as if you're about to be sick."

She was practically trembling. "I need... some advice."

Tavia had only heard the young girl speak a few times since their arrival, but her normal brusque attitude and rough words had been replaced by quiet words spoken in complete earnest. It was shocking how much the girl resembled how she remembered herself in her teens – demure in private, proud in public.

"Anything."

"I um...w-what should one do if she has fallen in love?" Her face had gone completely red.

Fighting the urge to simply hug the girl, she posed a question: "And who have you fallen in love with? The other Nuru boy you came here with? The one who is not the Xanem Nuremar?"

She nodded, pinching her eyes shut.

"I sensed as much. There wasn't a moment at dinner you weren't watching him for his reaction to everything that was said. The most casual of observer could tell you fancied him."

Sillida breathed deep. "What do I do, my lady?"

"Well you absolutely must tell him."

"I have. I do not know how he feels. He would not tell me."

"When did this happen, dear?"

She fidgeted. "Before the battle in Nakisho. He saved my life. I kissed him."

"Oh my," Tavia teased, "This is indeed a very serious case."

"I do not know what to do. Every time I am around him, my heart races no matter how much I tell it to stop. He angers me and fills me with joy at the same time. It doesn't make any sense. I wish it would stop."

"What do you like about him, Sillida? Is he dashing? Kind?"

"All of those things. And he's handsome and funny. And completely annoying. I would never tell him he's actually funny. It would only encourage him."

Tavia giggled. "How long would you say you've held affection for him?"

Sillida had to think about that for a moment. "He and I went through a lot after we became refugees out of Freiad after the Kuru attack. We went through even more when we travelled through Ferrela. We were like…partners. And I loved that."

In all of her pomp, Tavia could not help but to allow herself to beam. The air of professional indifference was impossible to maintain under such constant bombardment.

"You are entering your first love. It will fill you, torture you, bring you endless joy, and make you want to scream to the heavens. You will want nothing more than to be with him all the time, to have him protect you and to protect him in kind if you can. The sun will shine and the birds will sing for no other reason than to give him light and music. It is a sort of madness – one which threatens to make you both the happiest and most miserable girl in existence," Tavia explained with all of the passion she could recall. It had, after all, been a long time since her first infatuation as a girl.

Hearing all of that had an impact on Sillida as she sat silently, but still to her there was a piece missing. "But what do I *do*?"

"You must allow yourself to experience either the ultimate victory or the most crushing of defeats. You must tell him for certain. You must tell him what you told me here tonight – what you like about him, and how much you desire to be his partner again."

There were tears in her eyes, undoubtedly from pure fear. "But he should know all of that already."

Tavia shook her head. "That is rarely so. Men are not in tune with our emotions or desires. For one reason or another they require being told directly, for they cannot sense it. They are thinking creatures, but they do not think of abstracts such as affections nor reflect on life's sweet happenings. You shall need to confess directly to him."

"I'm…afraid."

"All are, in your position. Fret not, all will be well."

Sillida moved in for an embrace, and Tavia obliged, stroking the girl's chestnut brown hair. There was something about this Nuru girl which tugged at her heart-strings – perhaps her genuineness? Or maybe it was her mirror-like qualities which brought Tavia back to another time. Or it could have been her willingness to approach this woman, a stranger in most all respects, to ask her advice on a matter most personal and private. There was a sense about her – a loneliness, a longing. It seemed almost as if she was reaching out, filling the empty void of emotional protection and guidance usually provided by...

Oh, poor dear.

Tavia put a cheek against the girl's head. At least for the moment, she was safe within her arms.

Chapter XII

The next morning, Alira was aloof.

No matter how much gentle prodding on their connection Reldon did, she remained stolidly behind the veil she had put up between them. At breakfast, she had sat at one end of the massive table beside Sillida, Ethilia, and Kiera, failing to even once make eye contact with Reldon as he sat further down and ate his bowl of porridge. Reldon found himself at a total loss as to what exactly had changed between the day prior and breakfast the next morning, but it was beginning to worry him.

When it came time to head out into the blinding cold again, she did not wait for him, rather proceeding out on her own. Wordlessly, he slipped on his several layers of additional protective clothing and followed her out to the distant field of practice which he swore would be the death of him if the wind blew any harder.

The weather had certainly worsened, blowing swirling clouds of ice particles into vortexes which could have been produced by Alira herself had he not known any better. The sky high above groaned endlessly, like a wounded creature begging for respite.

Reldon found Alira and Sterling awaiting him when he arrived.

"You're late. That means you will be first today," Sterling said with an evil grin.

Reldon shot a look at Alira, who did not look back.

"Do you have a sword, boy?" he asked loudly.

"Yes, sir." With a crackle of green light, Reldon produced his blade. Its red leather hilt fit his hands perfectly, its gold cross-guard and silvery blade reflecting the sunlight like a beacon. The crystalline pommel housing the Xanem of Tycheronius Niuro gave off a distant hum in his mind, ready when needed.

"Good. A bit standard looking, but it will do."

"Not all swords have to have lightning coursing around them," Reldon responded.

"Just the good ones," he quipped with a wink, "Now it's time for me to find out what kind of swordsman you are. Have you always been apt with a hand-and-a-half sword?"

"Yes, sir. Nothing else felt quite right."

He took a step forward, his eyes flitting silver for a second before narrowing.

"For all its simplicity, there is much complexity in this blade. Much…emotion. And what…is *that* ?"

"This is the Xanem of Tycheronius Niuro. The famous Spellsword."

"I *know* who he was. That is *not* a Xanem. My understanding is that his Xanem's final resting place was at Huerogrand. What has happened for it to be here in your sword? Have you claimed it as a prize?"

"Definitely not. My old friend Harbin stole it from Huerogrand for reasons I still don't understand, bringing it to me in Nakisho just before the battle. When I spell forged my sword with the aid of my father, the Xanem sort of…reacted. It merged with my sword. I think Tycheronius wanted a way to reach through time to speak with me, because I can use it to convene with him and his Ilewa."

"Do you mean to tell me you speak with his spirit?"

"Not exactly. It was a spell he placed on his Xanem during his lifetime, so it only knows how to respond to questions he was able to answer up to that point," Reldon clarified.

"Ah." The giant man nodded in affirmation. "A spell which preserved his memories in an avatar. I have seen it a few times in the past. I cannot imagine he has much insight to provide you."

"Why? He seems quite wise."

"Tycheronius, for all his power and 'wisdom' could rarely bring his head out of the clouds long enough to focus on the dangers directly in front of him. Had it not been for that Ilewa of his, he would have walked headlong off a cliff by the time he was even able to hold a sword."

"You knew him," Reldon said with a stunning lack of astonishment.

"I did not say that."

"How can you be that old?" Reldon almost demanded.

"That does not matter, boy. No more than why you are so young and inexperienced."

"Sterling, why are you here? Why are you doing this?" He knew they were impertinent questions, but he no longer cared. The mysticism had worn out its welcome.

"No. You do not need to know my reasons for why I am here. I am here to help you. To give you focus and strength. Where I come from or how old I am has nothing to do with anything." His words were becoming heated and Reldon was responding in kind.

"You'll have to forgive us for our caution. We've only had half of the people we've met along our way try to kill us at least once."

"Boy, if I wanted you dead, you would not have lived to see this storm."

"You don't want to kill us, you don't want money, and you don't want to control us. You mean to tell me you're just doing this out of the kindness of your heart?"

Sterling's eyes flared open with fury and he looked as if he were about to accost Reldon, but stopped himself, taking a breath instead.

"Fine. I will make you a deal. You train hard. You follow my directions. At the end, I answer your questions. All right?"

Reldon sighed, letting his own anger subside. "Fine."

"Good. Now let me see your sword. I want to look at your Xanem."

There really wasn't any pause from one idea to the next where Sterling was concerned. His thoughts, though pinpoint accurate, seemed all over the place in context. Reldon hefted his sword to eye level, allowing the grizzled old master to see his imbued Xanem.

"Four. Do you know which you have accomplished?" His fierce eyes flicked up to him.

"Are you…talking about the four spearheads that are lit?"

"Yes. Each spearhead represents a task you must complete to become a full Spellsword. To become a warrior. Now you are still an apprentice. You have completed four of the six tasks. Do you know which ones you have completed?" Sterling reiterated without a great deal of patience.

"I do not. I'm not entirely certain what has made them light up. I believe one lit up because I summoned this sword," Reldon surmised.

"That is correct," Sterling said, "The others are different. These first three are always the same tasks. First spearhead will light up the first moment you touch the Xanem. Second will light up after you summon a weapon from the Infinity Scabbard – any weapon. The third you just mentioned. However, you have done this one out of order."

He pointed at the sixth lit spearhead. Its brothers in the fourth and fifth positions were still dark.

"When did this one show up?"

Reldon hesitated, the emotions of it all swirling back to him. "It was…near the end of the Battle of Nakisho. Lendir and I were fighting against the Churai. The Churai hurt him, they hurt him bad. I couldn't…" He struggled to speak further, but Sterling did not stop him. "After I killed the Churai, Lendir was too badly hurt. He was dying and in a lot of pain. He asked me to kill him and...I...I obeyed."

The world disappeared in a sea of tears, and Reldon turned away to hide his shame.

"He meant much to you," Sterling said gently.

Reldon nodded, trying to fight off his emotions.

"To your Xanem, he was your master. That is why the sixth spearhead lit up. The final task can be any noble task which your master deems befits you. Every Spellsword's sixth task is something which may bring meaning to obscurity, safety to the helpless, and a plethora of other meanings, but is always something which between master and apprentice always helps them both grow...or perhaps in Lendir's case... let go."

In the end, Lendir had not asked him to end his life to free him of the pain caused by the Churai. There had always been a pain, a longing to Lendir so much deeper than anyone could have hoped to understand. At the end of his life, Reldon firmly believed that he had not been asking for any desperate respite from the pain his bleeding wounds caused him, but by what scars life had left him to carry long ago.

Reldon touched a finger to Lendir's Xanem in his breast pocket. *I wish with every fiber of my being that he were still here. As much as I wanted to punch him, I needed his every stern word. He slapped me when I needed it.*

"I cannot help you with the fourth task," Sterling continued, "For that will require your real master to be here. Do you know who your master would have reverted to after Lendir's death?"

He nodded. "My father. He is back in Nakisho, healing from an assassination attempt."

"You have a very tragic life, young Nuru boy, but remember your attitude can change how you handle it. Would you be remembered as a poor hero with a terrible life who collapsed each time life struck a blow? Or as a man who let his past make him stronger?"

I know what Lendir did. I have to be like him.

An ambitious flame in his chest shook his entire body, warming his fingers. He nodded, clenching his jaw. "You're right, Sterling. I won't be pitied. I will be strong like Lendir. What do you want me to do?"

"Wipe that smirk off your face first." There was a jovial quality to his jab. "And put that sword of yours away. You're going to hurt someone. Take this instead."

From behind he produced a stick which had had all of its bark widdled off. Reldon caught it and immediately realized it had been

119

Phyrimically altered, as it weighed about as much as a sword and was probably as hard as iron.

Sterling took another stick out of the Infinity Scabbard and pointed it at Reldon.

"Prepare yourself for the most miserable day of swordplay you've ever had."

"Not as miserable as I'm about to make you feel by losing to a fifteen-year-old."

Reldon took the initiative and took a passing step, swirling his weapon in an arc about his middle. Without even a flinch, Sterling's arm came up, bringing his own defense to bear. They clacked loudly.

"You will have to be much faster than that."

With nothing more than a parry and a flourish, he gracefully forced Reldon's stick from his hand and knocked him upside the head with a *thwap!*

It rang his bell worse than he had imagined it would.

"That was just a warning. Follow my directions and you will not be hurt further."

At least two hours had passed and Reldon had counted around fourteen bruises and bumps on various parts of his body which had resulted from Sterling's otherwise forceful form of training. Fighting him had been much worse than fighting Lendir. At least Lendir had given him the opportunity to regain his composure and come at him from a similar angle to teach him methods of how to riposte them in the future. Fighting Sterling was much more akin to fighting a Churai. He was unpredictable and he was relentless. There had certainly been moments where he had stayed his hand or instructed him on a better method of defense, but those moments were arbitrarily strewn in amongst long stretches of vicious, exhaustive combat.

By the end, however, Reldon had failed to strike the old man even once.

"Your forms with the hand-and-a-half sword are firm, strong," Sterling said with his thick accent, "However you are still far too undisciplined to fight in a situation of chaos. One in which everything hangs on your every swing. You panic. You dodge when you should parry. You avoid direct confrontation when it would be to your best advantage. And worst of all you do not use your sword to its greatest advantages. Carrying a Spellsword's blade is not a matter of vanity, young man. It is a tool with abilities no mere man could ever hope to match without our powers, but you instead fight like a commoner with some training. Tell me, what do you know about your sword?"

"I know it cannot be affected by Phyrim," Reldon answered, his hands still shaking.

"It cannot. What else?"

"Alira can use magic to add elements to it in the short-term. I did that during the battle."

"Good. You do know this. Keep going."

He had to think for a moment. "My sword cannot dull nor break."

"Precisely! You can use this. What else do you know?"

Reldon shrugged. "Is there something else I don't know?"

"Clearly. What happens when you drop your weapon?"

"Oh, right. It returns to the Infinity Scabbard."

Sterling nodded emphatically. "Come here. Let me show you something. Try to push against my sword with all your strength."

He did so, his muscles tightening with the effort. Their sticks locked together in the struggle.

Suddenly Sterling's fingers opened up and Reldon felt his entire weight lurch forward, no longer held up by anything. Before he fell to the ground though, he felt a spike in Phyrim behind him, and he received a crack on his back. Reldon was more amazed than hurt.

"You... you just-"

"That's right. In the same breath I dropped my weapon and summoned it into the other. These are the advantages I referred to. There is no such thing as a cheap attack when your life is in danger. Fighting in this way is how the Churai kill so many – their powers over death are their advantage and they feel no regret in using them. It is time for you to be vicious in return."

Reldon nodded with a confident grin. "I will. Thank you."

And without missing even a single beat, he turned to Alira, who had been sitting in the snow shivering. "Now for you, little miss."

She rose to her feet, her face wrapped so tightly with a wool scarf that only her blue and green eyes were visible. Sterling noted her trembling figure. "You may use magic now."

"T-t-t-thank you," she responded, immediately blazing her Keinume to life and producing a bright flame between her hands.

"I have given consideration to your unique condition. I want to test a few theories before I come up with a good solution. First, I will need you to merge your power. Both of you."

Reldon peered over at Alira, who looked at him back. There was a hesitation about her. He could not, for the life of him, figure out what her problem was, and why she was behaving this way. All he could sense when his mind reached out was a strange sense of hurt, of emotional pain. *Could she really still be angry with me over what happened in Teraxella?*

"What is the problem? Go on, take his hand!"

Alira took a deep breath before sidling over next to Reldon, slipping her glove into his without looking at him. Reldon gave a pleading, incredulous look at Sterling.

The huge man stared at them for a moment before closing his eyes in a look of complete agony.

"No. No, no, no, no, no. This cannot be. I have agreed to do much, but I will *not* be put in charge of figuring this out. No, I cannot."

Is he having a tantrum?

"I meditated and contemplated for an entire night, wracking my brain trying to figure out what could possibly be affecting your reservoirs, and I cannot BELIEVE this is what the problem is. This must be a joke."

Reldon and Alira only stared back at him. "W-what is it, Sterling?"

He paced back and forth, biting one of his giant fingers before stopping.

"I should have known when I was dealing with teenagers... Uh..." He scratched his head beneath his hood, clearly uncertain how to proceed. "Look, it is obvious you are both having...a bit of Ilewa disharmony."

Alira's eyes fell to the snow beneath her.

Reldon's mournful expression spoke to his complete inexperience and failure to rectify the situation. "Do you really believe that's what's causing our reservoirs to be so different?"

He took a labored breath. "Yes. Disharmony between Ilewa does not usually cause such marked affects, but you are the exception to every rule. Now, let me tell you something. I am the last person in the world who should be solving relationship problems. I am a warrior. A man of fire, steel, and blood. I could not care less what arguments you are having or what feelings have been hurt. What I care about is how you solve it and bring balance back to yourselves."

Lifting his stick again, he pointed one end at Alira.

"You have problems with him? Then fix them."

Sterling tossed the stick to her and she snatched it out of the air.

"W-what would you like me to do with this, Mister Sterling?"

"If you have a quarrel with him, then show him. Make him feel your pain. And Nuru boy, if you are feeling slighted by her, then let battle be your communication tool."

Reldon stuck one end of his stick into the snow. "Wait, I am not going to fight Alira. She's my Ilewa. We're partners, and I could never-"

There was a loud crack and Reldon was knocked forward as his back suddenly gave out. Shocked, he scrambled back to his feet to see Alira's terrifying expression as she looked furiously at him, stick firmly in both hands.

Sterling howled with laughter. "Not even any hesitation!"

Reldon straightened his back again. "Alira, please, we can talk about-"

THWACK!

She smacked him again with the stick in the stomach and he doubled over, sucking in wind.

He coughed as he stood again, this time lifting his own stick. "All right, Ayuru, you'll have your fight."

Her stick flew at him once again, this time being stopped by a quick parry. With a whistle, she whirled it around and attacked from the opposite side, also being stopped by a simple block. For a third time, she brought it back and down over her head, clacking again against Reldon's defense.

It was only after a few more identical engagements that Reldon realized that Alira really didn't have any form of training or strategy to her attacks – rather, she was just lashing out with a flurry of blows which would undoubtedly leave her exhausted before she ever reached him. *She's not going to be difficult to defeat like this.*

"Alira, tell me what's wrong!" Reldon exclaimed.

She swung at him once more with an audible growl. "I'm...mad at you!"

"I can *see* that!" A low swing rapped against his boot but did not pain him. "About *what* though?"

"About everything!"

How helpful.

Reldon leapt over her next low blow, and before she could strike again, he grabbed the wrist holding her sword. She was not nearly as strong as he was, and she struggled against his grip, using her other hand to punch at his forearm.

However, when it was clear she was not going to be let free, he saw her eyes flicker a deathly red.

"Woah, all right, Alira, let's stop this." Reldon backed off, releasing her wrist. "Before you use magic to burn me alive."

The air around her shimmered from the heat she was giving off.

"Aren't you going to do something?" Reldon pleaded to Sterling.

Sterling shrugged. "We will see how badly she wants to hurt you."

"But I didn't *do* anything! All right, look, I'm setting down my stick. Can we-"

THWACK!

Immediately as he set his stick in the snow, she rushed forward and assailed him once more, whacking him once on the shoulder and another time in the hip while he scrambled to pick up his weapon, after which she conveniently retreated again.

"That was clever, magician girl," Sterling nodded to her with a toothy smile.

"Why are you on her side?!" Reldon asked incredulously.

"I am on no one's side. I am promoting healing. In whatever form that takes. I sense she finds it therapeutic to hit you at the moment. But you are right. Blond girl, you should tell him why you are angry, or else he will stand there with that stupid look."

Alira looked as if fighting back tears as she looked up at Sterling. "He...he doesn't trust me. He doesn't believe in me. And he thinks I'm...selfish!"

"What?! I never said any of those things!" Reldon replied.

"You never believed I could save that girl and so you killed her. And I heard you last night thinking about Bryle. Something about how he was being selfish by not revealing how he feels about Sillida. I heard you."

Reldon had to think for a moment before it hit him. "I was thinking too loudly again, wasn't I?"

Sterling broke into laughter again, holding Alira back from assaulting Reldon again with one hand. He knelt next to her. "What does that have to do with you, girl?"

Her features softened and her puffy blue and green eyes flitted between Reldon and the ground as she bit her lip.

"Oh dear spirits. I'm letting you two deal with this. I will return after noon. Have your affairs sorted by then," he muttered, his monstrous boots crunching on the endless snow as he strode away.

Reldon hadn't broken his gaze at Alira.

"It happened just a few days ago," she started, "Much of what had happened during the end of the Battle of Nakisho came flooding back to me. I had always remembered how much damage I had done…how many people I had killed…but I never could remember specifics. It had all been kind of a blur. Whatever evil magic was inside me was trying its hardest not to let me remember the good parts of my life. Yesterday I remembered, though. I remembered what you said."

His heart could have broken for her, but it was far too busy overworking as his apprehension feared her response.

"Is that why you've been so…flustered lately?" Reldon asked her gently.

She nodded sadly, a stream of tears running down her face.

Reldon stepped towards her and took her gloves into his. Even secured by a layer of wool, he could still feel her trembling terribly.

"I'm scared, Reldon. I'm just afraid…of all of this. I know not even my own feelings, because my heart beats so hard I can hardly hear it!" she wept.

He wrapped his arms around her and pulled her into his warm embrace. For a moment, they simply stood there, two lost souls clinging to each other for answers which neither could provide. Reldon's entire being begged him to hold her tighter, to take away her sadness, to make everything right. Now, however, he had to wrestle with the idea that his very insistence on helping her might be making it worse. In that moment he understood how Sillida had been feeling all this time, and why she had not been demanding answers from Bryle.

"Alira, I may not have ever asked to have an Ilewa, but you were one which I have always been overjoyed to have. You are smart, kind, and much more well-mannered with children than I am." That made her laugh. "I want to tell you that I meant what I said, and I still mean it to this day. But I never meant to scare you, nor would I ever dream of hurting the trust we have for each other. I do not need an answer, and I do not want you losing sleep over it anymore. I would much rather you come to me when you are ready, for you know that I will always be standing by you as your loving Ilewa. Forever."

Dim red coals sifted about in the fireplace as the wood fell apart, its flames recently extinguished. Bryle's snoring was loud enough that Reldon could hear it even over the wailing of the wind just twenty feet above his head. How precisely his friend managed to sleep so soundly with all of this noise was simply beyond Reldon's comprehension. His eyes burned as he opened them, his body desperate for sleep.

Reldon groaned, turning onto his side. *It's amazing how with all of these people and with a connection with someone else's mind that I can feel so alone at times.* Sleep had been evasive for weeks, his mind keen on tormenting him when the struggles of the day left him with the quiet of his own thoughts.

Blame. Doubt. Fear. All of these emotions swirled about, with no rectifying solution in sight. If Lendir was still alive, what would he be saying about all of this? *And if he's still out there somewhere, does he approve of how I'm handling all of this? Would he have saved Alira? Or would he have trusted her and possibly let her die?*

He twisted onto his other side. *Reldon,* he fruitlessly addressed himself, *All of this is pointless. Go to sleep and stop worrying so much. Lendir would want you to be happy and rested.*

A thought occurred to him.

I was able to talk with Alira's mother once, in a dream. I wonder if Lendir could do the same? Maybe there is a way to speak to him one last time. There is so much I would ask him.

The dissenting voice returned. *And why would he give you any useful insight? What makes you think he would give you such great advice? He would be the same as when last he was alive, and you fought him tooth and nail every time he gave you advice. Maybe you don't deserve him anymore. Maybe you –*

There was a *thump* as log crumbled from the heat in the fireplace, snapping his thoughts back to reality. Bryle snored again and again. The tearing wind beckoned to him, rattling the roof over his head. It almost dared him to face it – to leave the mansion and fight.

A twitch gnawed at him. His restless mind begged him to enter Tycheronius's Xanem again. *You could have someone to talk to. Someone who would at least partially listen. Maybe if you phrase the question just right, they could understand and give you exactly what advice you need.*

But he had heard it all before. The same answers, over and over. "*Time brings passing to those who suffer most. Bringing peace to the troubled is one of many facets the gem of death offers us all.*"

And what could those other facets be? It certainly hadn't brought Reldon any peace – that was for sure. Only despair and longing, fear and searching. Though disquieting, his rampant thoughts had more than once posited that perhaps he had been destined to die on that battlefield as well. That perhaps had Alira listened and fled from the onslaught of Kuru that he might be in the silken lands of the afterlife with Lendir at that very moment, watching the world burn from a more golden perch.

These people do not care for us. We saved them all at that battle. I lost my mentor and almost lost my own life, and all they can say is that we're too unpredictable. I could save them a hundred times and they would still comment on how I could have done it faster, or smarter, or with a bit more flair. Maybe Detryn was right. Maybe these people really don't deserve-

Another *thump* was heard from across the room, but this time it didn't sound like wood. Reldon closed his weary eyes once more, until he heard a shifting noise, like stockings across the floor.

Reldon craned his neck ever so slowly to avoid making any alerting noises of his own, his dark-adjusted eyes peering towards the other side of the grand room.

Adrenaline filled his system. His heart raced.

Someone was crouched in the corner of the room. A dark figure, clad in black. It was moving slowly, methodically, attempting to search for something without making any sound.

It's looking through my pack!

He knew it was in his best interest to raise the alarm.

Leaping from his bed, Reldon ripped his sword from the Infinity Scabbard in a flash of green light, pointing it towards the crouching figure. "Who are you? What are you doing here!?"

Bryle's snoring abruptly stopped as he awoke.

The figure whirled around, getting to its feet.

Before Reldon could react, he was slammed by an unseen force and he smashed full-on into the armoire next to his bed, breaking the wooden door in half.

Bryle rolled out of bed with a shout, reaching beneath his bed to retrieve his sword. However, as soon as he pulled it from beneath the bedframe, it was sent hurtling across the room to embed itself in the wall by another blast of force. Reldon struggled to climb out of the damaged pile of wood, and the figure made a dash for the door.

We're going to lose him!

Yanking the door open, the figure tried to flee, but stopped in its tracks, suddenly terrified. It backpedaled, slamming the door once again to block out what it had just seen on the other side of that door, electing instead to make a break for the windows.

Before it could make it even a few steps, the door was thrown off its hinges and a streak of bright light caught up to the figure, grabbing it by the throat and slamming it down onto the floor.

And by the good spirits, this terrifying thing of light was Alira.

At first Reldon thought she was completely engulfed in flames, but they were more like swirling, cascading waves of light. Her hair was white, but her eyes were blood red.

Her Keinume blazed to life on her arm, shining a deadly white light and forming a blade overtop of her forearm and ending with the point over her fist. She jutted it in the figure's face.

"Who are you?! Why did you hurt Reldon?"

The dark-clad figure ripped the black mask from over his face, holding up a hand to shield himself. He looked to be around his late twenties, with curly black hair and a stubbled face. "Please, don't! I don't want any trouble! Don't kill me!"

Bryle ripped his sword from the wall and rushed over to join Alira. "Then you'd best start speaking. Who are you and why are you here?"

"May I stand up first?"

"No. Answer the question," Bryle said, lowering his blade closer to his throat.

"All right, all right, I give! I'm just a mercenary scout. I was told to come here to find something and I couldn't find it. That's all, I swear!"

"What kind of *thing*?" Reldon asked.

"A Xanem of some kind. I-I swear, I don't know nothin' about what it was, they didn't tell me! They just told me I would know it when I saw it."

Reldon extended a hand to the man. He hesitated at first before eagerly taking it. He was a full foot taller than all of them, leaving Reldon incredulous at how Alira had managed to lift the man completely off his feet and slam him to the ground with one arm.

"I know exactly what they wanted you to find. And you would have me believe you're a Spellsword who has never heard of Tycheronius's Xanem?" Reldon inquired.

The man blinked. "*That* is what they wanted me to get? When was it stolen? Did…did you steal it?"

"All Spellswords know of the Xanem, do not try to fool me. It has been gone for some time."

"Reldon, listen to his accent, he's obviously Lärimite," Bryle said.

"I was trained in a compound near the Academy City. I have only heard that Huerogrand houses this relic. Why would you have it?"

"I did not *steal* it, if that's what you're asking. It was brought to me."

"You had best give it back. They will not stop hunting you until they have it returned safely to them in Huerogrand. If you kill me here or I return with nothing, they will only send another. And another."

"I would hate for you to have to return to them empty-handed," Reldon said caustically, "so instead I will send you back with information to give them."

His sword sparked into existence once again and the man flinched.

"See this pommel? This is what has become of Tycheronius's Xanem. It has fused with my sword. I did not intend for it to happen – it simply did. Tell them that their precious Xanem no longer exists, and that sending further men would do them no more good than sending an army. They will never get it back."

"That will not be enough to keep them away."

"Then we will be waiting."

"So…you are letting me go free? Without even a scratch?"

Reldon smirked. "I wouldn't say completely unhurt. I think Alira gave you something to think about."

They shot a glance at Alira, who grinned evilly at the mercenary, her eyes flashing red.

He shuffled quickly towards the doorway, now bereft of its door. "Thank you, your Lord and Ladyship. I will deliver the message. Nothing personal!"

The three watched him leave before Bryle spoke. "Probably should follow him to make sure the guards don't spear him on his way out."

As he scurried off, a concerned Queen Tavia made an appearance followed in tow by a panicked Ethilia, a worried Sillida, and a curious Elly. Before even a word was spoken, her eyes traced the outline of the doorway to the upset door laying amidst the room.

"I would say it was an assassin, but he didn't actually come here to kill anyone," Reldon explained, "A *courier* from Huerogrand followed us here to steal the Xanem of Tycheronius Niuro."

Her incomprehension was fully expected. "Forgive me, but of what item do you speak?"

Reldon was choosing his words very carefully to avoid implicating himself as a thief. "A relic which is fused to my sword. Huerogrand wants it and has been hunting us to get it."

"Where is he? Where did he go?" Ethilia demanded.

"He is just leaving now."

"You let him *go?*" Ethilia exclaimed.

"I needed him to deliver a message back to his masters. Elsewise they will continue to attack us here."

"He will likely die in this storm," Queen Tavia added sullenly, "It is difficult to believe Huerogrand would go to such lengths to obtain this relic. I expect you will tell me the entire situation in the morning, Master Reldon?"

He nodded. "Terribly sorry about this door and the wardrobe inside. He took us by surprise and tossed us around a little before Alira put a stop to him."

The queen nodded proudly to Alira. "Well done, Master Ayuru. And how were you able to confront the danger so quickly?"

She returned the smile. "Whenever Reldon is hurt, it is like feeling a fiery needle in my head. It was unmistakable that he was in danger."

Queen Tavia yawned slightly, clearly trying to suppress such a display. "Then it is well that no one was hurt. I will have one of the serving men set about repairing the door and we will speak again in the morning of this. On the morrow, then."

Chapter XXIII

The next morning brought wind and cold neither Reldon nor Bryle had ever experienced before.

Sitting at the long banquet table eating their porridge, the howling from the gales were growing so loud that conversations in a low voice could no longer be conducted in rooms which bordered the exterior of the house. Several serving men were making their rounds about the mansion to apply a thin layer of some kind of paste to the frames of the windows in order to better seal in the heat, or rather to keep out the cold. It was well that the serving men were so diligent at their jobs, as they were having to keep roaring fires going in virtually every room to keep them from growing too cold. It was Reldon's understanding that they had a store in the cellars beneath the structure of the building which held enough apt firewood to last them through an entire winter without ever leaving.

Though difficult to hear them, rumors had been spreading between the servants that they had seen Sterling outside the walls. However, they claimed, he had not been pacing or even watching. Only two guards had seen it, but they claimed he had been attacking someone – wrestling about with them until the storm grew too intense to see anymore.

At this news, Reldon and Alira at least made the effort to make contact with Sterling. Dressing up with even more layers than they had the previous day, they made it as far as the front gate before the piles of snow simply prevented movement. Alira shouted after him for a time until the ravaging ice drove them to retreat back into the house. She had been dreadfully worried that he was going to freeze to death outside and would much rather have had him safe inside the mansion. It was not to be so, as not another trace was found of Sterling for the entirety of the day.

Queen Tavia's children, little Varia and Antixius were more jubilant about the storm than the others at first, dancing about the foyer as the pelting snow hammered the huge doors.

Perhaps they are excited at the idea of being away from the world for a bit. Even for myself and Alira it's really not a bad thing.

The small joyous children brought much light to the otherwise dark house as the clouds blotted the sun. Alira found that Varia could get quite chatty when she was in a good mood.

"Are you an adult?" she asked Alira.

She giggled in response. "How old do you think I am?"

"Forty-twelve," Varia answered, holding up eight fingers.

"You're very close. I'm fourteen. I think. I might be fifteen. I haven't been keeping track of the days."

"Are you a magician?"

"Why yes I am! How did you know?"

"That's what mother says. Could you show me some magic?" she asked excitedly, bouncing in anticipation.

"Of course, little Varia." Alira held out a hand and decided to make a concentrated effort to impress the girl. Her focus constructed the vision, and the vision entered reality as magic pooled into her palm. Instead of a simple ball of light, she produced a rose, silver and bright.

"Wow! Can I hold it?"

"You may certainly try!" She poured the rose into the girl's cupped hands, and it floated just an inch or so above her skin.

"It's so pretty! Do you think I could be a magician like you?"

No matter how many times she had been asked that question, she found the answer difficult. If she were Elly's age or older, she might have answered 'No, I'm afraid you do not have magical blood as I do', but since the girl would not understand such nuances, she replied only with, "Maybe someday."

The rose slowly faded out of existence before the girl's eyes, but she didn't seem to mind too terribly.

"Is your husband a magician too?"

The question made her heart race.

"U-um, he's not my husband, Varia. He's my *Ilewa*. We can speak to each other's minds. And he's a Spellsword. Boys can be Spellswords and girls can be Magicians."

The girl seemed thoughtful. "Maybe my brother could be my…*Il…ulu.*"

Alira could only smile back at the adorable child.

Ethilia approached from the staircase, calling after the girl. "Varia, where is your brother?"

"I think he is hiding. Just over there." She pointed to the left of the staircase.

"Antixius, that will be enough games, it is time for your nap."

There was enough of a distant annoyance in Ethilia's voice that Alira could tell she had been through this babysitting process countless times before.

The young prince emerged without a fight, much less jubilant than he had been, and quietly took her hand and followed the Golden Magician upstairs.

"I suppose that means it is your nap time as well," Alira said.

Varia shook her head. "I do not take naps when my brother does."

It seemed a bit odd to Alira, but she supposed they had different sleeping schedules or something similar. Eventually the King's Consort did come to retrieve her daughter, but it was several hours later, after they had eaten that evening's dinner.

What astonished Alira the most was the lack of disquiet in the faces of the staff. She could sense all manner of emotions emanating from her companions, as Reldon's stress dripped through their connection, Sillida grew very quiet, Bryle was trying too hard to keep himself occupied on any kind of task, Elly kept casting about worried looks whenever the wind would crescendo, and Kiera had a habit of chattering when she was nervous. Ethilia, being one to hardly ever wear her truer emotions openly, tended to disappear when anxiety pervaded the room. However, the staff never showed any such consternation. The three guards, who had been brought inside, stood in the foyer at attention. The servants carried out their otherwise banal tasks without as much as an upturned look. Even on the rare occasion where a window pane shattered and billowing wind and snow gusted inside, they briskly fetched their tools and replaced the bit of glass with an incredible efficiency.

Alira got about to asking the High King's Consort about them later that evening as the "ladies" sat about the drawing room, attending to their tea.

"They are an elite force in their own right, hand-chosen by the High King as he has paid visits to his vassals and noble houses. Few of such butlers, manservants, ladies-in-waiting, and house guards have had the honor to serve the house of the High King's family, as they are seldom chosen and it is a life appointment. Randolfus, the eldest serving man, has been in service long enough to have brought up High King Julius. In fact, it is my understanding that he and the former High King Antixius were around the same age in their late twenties or so when he was chosen. You would have to ask him if you wish for more details," she explained, nursing a very hot cup of dark tea.

"Is he really that old?" Ethilia asked, "He would have to be seventy years old!"

Tavia produced a grin. "And he hasn't lost his edge yet. I have known him most of my life."

Kiera had a wry look. "That youngest manservant is rather… fetching, is he not?"

Sillida and Alira smiled back at her in a way that said, "I fear what is on your mind."

"That is Kent Symarian. He was introduced to the house a couple of years ago – I believe he had been under the employ of the Dallius family in western Atheria. His skill-set is rather impressive where grounds work and maintenance are concerned. It was he who was able to get the orangery back into working order again after last year's storm," she explained matter-of-factly.

Kiera, who had elected not to partake in the tea and instead had asked for wine, set down her glass and grinned broadly. "Oh you speak about him as if he were some tool, Your Grace. I think I would like to learn more about him by…asking him myself."

"Kiera, you're sixteen," Sillida reminded her with raised eyebrows.
"And?"

Ethilia cut in, "And he probably has at least an extra decade of wisdom and maturity that you lack. Well enough to stay away from the drunk Korrainian girl."

Kiera narrowed her eyes at the court healer, but Alira spoke up before they could start arguing again.

"Your Grace, could you tell us more about the other servants?" It was an obvious attempt to change the subject, but no less appreciated.

She raised her head as if trying to remember each of them. "Tolios is actually Korrainian like you, dear princess. He is the tall, quiet, middle aged one with the dark hair. You might never hear him speak, but he has quite the accent."

Kiera was quick to respond in her own thick accent. "Ooh, which house did he hail from?"

"I struggle to recall. Does the Battalakai house sound familiar?"

"Ah yes, they are just to the west of Deficinas. I met one of their daughters when I was nine and we picked raspberries in the spring. The weather is much nicer in southern Korraine."

Tavia went on. "I know him the least, as I have rarely conversed with him, but he makes up for this in complete and unwavering loyalty and obedience. He would die for any of you without hesitation. The last serving man is Garric Wideford, from King Obrim's court. That man may be in his fifties, but I swear he is as spry and competent as the young man we brought on nearly two decades ago. He has a rather strong Atherian accent as well, and it's endearing to speak with him about nearly anything. I swear if you told him you were from the furthest reaches of the frozen peaks in The Sjard, he would tell you a story about how he had spent a summer in those very mountains and had met some of your friends. He's an incredible man, and he absolutely adores animals and children, and is the perfect caretaker for both."

"It does seem as if the High King favors my fellow Atherians to take care of his house," Alira mentioned.

Tavia shifted and spoke plainly. "Not all are amenable to the High King."

There was a touch of trepidation on Kiera's face as she changed the subject. "So is this what courtly women do in Nakisho? Drink tea and gossip?"

Ethilia shot her a glare, but Tavia spoke before she could get into another confrontation.

"Only the high ladies. What sort of evening entertainment do ladies partake of in Korraine, Princess Kiera?"

Kiera self-consciously swallowed the remainder of her wine. Sillida and Alira laughed.

"I think we have our answer," Alira giggled.

"No no, we do not just drink! Ladies in Korraine have many ways of passing the time. I just… em… don't enjoy most of them."

"Like what?" Sillida pressed.

"Oh, you know, many silly activities like embroidery and singing. I preferred learning language or the beliefs."

"Korrainian beliefs?" Alira asked.

"Yes. We are a very superstitious people. We believe that spirits, both good and bad, inhabit every corner of this world and influence what happens in it. Sometimes they send signs to let you know if you are following the Way."

"I take it the 'Way' is some moral code?" Tavia asked for the room.

"It is the Way of the World. Everything and everyone is meant to follow a path so they might join the good spirits. No one wants to be a bad spirit – they are terrible, tortured entities. We encountered some of them in Korraine when I was with Reldon just before the snowfalls."

"Have you ever seen a…sign? An omen?" Alira inquired.

"Oh many times! The spirits and I have a close relationship. I commune with them regularly, and they send me signs to ensure I still follow the Way."

"What kind of signs?"

She was hesitant to respond. "I understand your question, My Lady, but you must understand that each Korrainian's personal relationship with the spirits is very private. Every man, woman, and child has their own path, and if you pay close attention to the symbols in your life you will see the spirits guiding you. Those who follow them are led to happiness."

"If that is such a commonly held belief in Korraine, then why is there so much crime in Nevo-Kulan?" Ethilia asked pointedly, "Unless of course you are suggesting the spirits are telling them to steal and murder."

"Of course not," Kiera responded calmly, not giving rise to Ethilia's prattling, "These bad men and women do not follow the spirits – they weep as they attempt to help these lost souls, but they are doomed to become evil spirits, forever haunting the world trying to take their fury out on the living."

"Sillida, didn't you mention once that Nuru have similar beliefs?" Alira turned to the quiet girl.

She considered her response carefully before responding. "Some Nuru believe something like that. Not everyone agrees. Some follow the Omniscient One."

"Is that what you believe in? Or the Xanem Nuremar? If you do not mind my asking," Tavia asked.

"I think Reldon believes in the spirits, but not quite like Kiera said. I...don't...don't really believe in anything anymore."

A sort of pall fell over the conversation for a moment. Alira knew it was a collective sense of empathy, as most present were at least somewhat aware of what happened with her parents and the difficult childhood she had endured.

"And there is nothing wrong with that, Sillida," Ethilia offered, giving her a smile, "You are in good company."

"Nothing for you either, Ethilia?" Alira said.

"I believe in medicine. Golden Magic. Real methods of helping people. I try not to deal in the abstract."

Alira laughed. "You can believe in both."

"And what good would that do? Such beliefs would only distract me."

Kiera put a hand on Ethilia's shoulder, producing a flinch.

"I would be happy to help you keep an eye out for the signs. I would not want you to miss them."

"Thanks but no thanks."

Those two really ought to work out their problems. We're supposed to all be friends here.

She knew it would be a highly transparent attempt, but she had to do it anyway.

"Ethilia, would you mind a word?" Alira motioned towards the door.

She seemed confused, but nodded, following Alira to the rest of their piercing stares.

Once a bit down the corridor, Ethilia asked, "What is it, My Lady?"

"Why do you dislike Kiera so much? I thought we all had the same cause here."

"Oh, we do. I would most certainly call her an ally."

"Then why are you so cross with her?"

Ethilia huffed. "She's so…provincial."

"And what do you mean by that?"

The court healer's icy blue eyes couldn't meet Alira's green-and-blue ones. *She doesn't want to say it.*

She took a deep breath. "My Lady, I'm sure you of all people can understand how much bad blood exists between her people and ours, and it seems pointless to me to pretend like it doesn't. Regardless of the disagreements she has had with her family, if ever she were forced to choose between her people and ours, I'm not convinced that her loyalty lies with us."

"Ethilia, she just offered to watch for your spirit signs for you. Whether you believe in the spirits or not, there is no doubting that she cares about what happens to you."

Ethilia scoffed. "I'm sure she says that to everyone. My Lady, the Korrainians have invaded our lands and killed our people for no other reason than because they didn't like the land they were given. And she can proselytize all she wants for the spirits, but she will never be able to convince me that they are a virtuous people who cares about their fellow Lärimites. They can't even stop Korrainians from murdering each other."

"But surely you know that Kiera isn't like that. She has never hurt any of us. She never would!"

"You don't know that. I do not hate the woman, My Lady, and I am more than willing to work with her, but please do not ask me to love her." She turned to head back into the drawing room.

Alira spoke, stopping her. "How long must the cycle continue? Korrainians and kingsmen have hated each other for so long that entire generations probably don't even know why they're fighting, and it's just stupid. Ethilia, we have the chance to be the generation that puts a stop to it – the one that finally says no. Reldon stood in front of the Korrainian king and said to his face that it was time for the old ways to disappear, and he's right. We could live in a future where someone from Nakisho and someone from Nevo-Kulan could be lifelong friends. All we have to do is say no. Just think about it, Ethilia."

Her hand rested on the door handle for a long moment, giving no response. Ethilia's eyes were fixed on the floor as she turned the handle and went inside.

The next morning Alira attended the breakfast table, which for once was completely full instead of just being Reldon, Bryle, and Kiera. As she sat down, she realized that Tavia, Ethilia, and Kiera were all speaking Old Lärimite for some reason.

Tavia was inquiring as to how long Kiera had been studying Old Lärimite, and she responded that it had only been a few years, as Korrainian's were expected to never speak such a language, so she had to learn it in secret.

Reldon, Bryle, Sillida, and Elly all ate their breakfasts in silence, exchanging uncertain looks after each punctuated bit of gibberish.

Alira's Old Lärimite was a bit rusty, but she joined in the conversation as well.

"How many languages can you speak, Kiera?"

"Three. Old Lärimite, Modern Lärimite, and Korrainian."

"And you, Your Grace?" Alira asked Tavia.

She counted them out on her fingers. "Old Lärimite, Modern Lärimite, Korrainian, Ferrelan, some Sjarden, and bits and pieces of the Kuru language."

"That's a lot!"

The High King's Consort grinned. "I am the wife of the High King. If anything ever happened, I would need to be regent to his children, and that would include diplomacy to other nations."

Reldon and Bryle were snickering about something and Alira appraised them both. "What's so funny?"

Reldon turned to his friend and began to speak in another language Alira had never heard. Sillida even chimed in. They smiled and laughed at each other, well to the rest of the table's confusion.

"Why, Reldon, I didn't know you spoke a...Nuru language," Alira said with surprise.

"None such language should exist. Not that I am aware of," Tavia retorted.

"Just shows how much you know about Errum. We keep our own secrets." Bryle winked.

"You made up that language, didn't you?" Ethilia said, taking a bite of bread.

"Yeah we did." Reldon and Sillida roared with laughter.

"Aw, Ethilia, you ruined all the fun." Bryle waved a hand at her.

Ethilia grinned evilly. "Are we just a touch jealous of other languages, Bryle?"

"Not at all," Reldon cut in, "Errum is great enough on its own without needing its own language."

"Ha," Ethilia scoffed smugly, "Like what?"

"Well, Spellswords for one."

"Lärim also has Spellswords."

"But how many of them trained there? Does Lärim even have its own Huerogrand?"

"It has its own secret training grounds, but none like Huerogrand," Alira noted, "They told me that in the Academy City, but they didn't tell me where they were."

"Precisely. Not to mention we have some of the greatest Spellswords in all of history. Like Tycheronius Niuro!"

"He was only trained there, he was not Nuru. His Ilewa was, however." Tavia said softly with a smile.

"I could tell by the accent," Reldon mentioned, eliciting a puzzled reaction from the High King's Consort. "I told you of his Xanem. Tycheronius was powerful and wise enough to sort of embed a past remnant of their memories into his Xanem. It responds to certain questions."

She was taken aback. "How interesting! I would very much like to know what they had to say of this house!"

Reldon leaned forward. "He was…here? That would have been…a very long time ago."

"He was reportedly here, yes. As you know, much of his middle and later life was very well documented as they believed him to be the original Xanem Nuremar, erroneously of course. A preserved document in the High King's possession in Nakisho claimed that he had stayed here for nigh on a week or so around six-hundred-thirty years ago. Back then this was not a house, but a castle – one with some strategic significance as unrest was growing before the Lärimite Civil War. The original castle was much older than that, but I know not when it was constructed.

"Niuro was here with Giavere sometime during the spring, and from what the High King told me, the document read that he was here on a sort of diplomatic mission. Similar to yourselves, the two of them were powerful enough to warrant some level of political clout, and it may have been a way to get closer to the High King at the time."

Tycheronius Niuro was here too? Everywhere I go he seems to have been at one point in his life.

The thought nagged at him as they concluded breakfast and went about their daily goings-on, which wasn't much. There had been a few obscure places Reldon and Alira had been to where Tycheronius had also been – like the Academy in Ferrela or in the exclusive house of the High King. *It is as if he and I have walked similar footsteps over the long horizon of history.*

It just didn't seem like a coincidence. There had been no reason for Tycheronius to be in Ferrela, nor was there reason enough to spend the time and resources to put together an entire realm within his Xanem so he could speak to the future Xanem Nuremar. *It just seems to go beyond wanting to help. He wants to tell me something, I know it.*

The minute he could get to his quarters, he was sitting cross-legged with his sword flat to his forehead. With a rush of magical energy he found himself back in the crystalline realm facing the familiar faces of Tycheronius and Giavere.

They welcomed him as they always did and waited for a question. Reldon had it immediately.

"Tell me of the High King's castle to the north of Nakisho. What had you done there?"

There was a long, considered pause between the question and his eventual answer. Usually if he didn't have an answer, he responded

140

immediately telling him so. However, this time there was measure to his hesitation.

He finally spoke after a moment, his ethereal voice trailing into the endless beyond.

"It was a splendid castle. A perfect place to...get to the bottom of things."

It was the first time he had ever chosen his words so carefully. Long, detailed answers had been characteristic of the old Spellsword, but so far two topics had produced curt answers: the castle and anything regarding Grandma. Why was he being so cryptic? What could he possibly be hiding that he didn't want the Xanem Nuremar, of all people, to know?

"What do you mean 'get to the bottom of things'?" Reldon pressed.

"I'm afraid I don't understand your question," came his default response.

Reldon asked him in a few different ways what he had been doing at the castle, or why he had met with the High King, to which he continued to respond that the castle had been a perfect place to "get to the bottom of things".

He sighed. *Yet another wall. Every time I come close to getting answers from them, there's something else in the way. Why would he not want me to know about the old castle, of all things? It doesn't make sense.*

The world came rushing back as he severed connection with the Xanem, and he was left sitting in silence on his bed. He opened his eyes to see his Ilewa at the foot of his bed, concern clear in her eyes.

"Oh, Alira! Have you been here all this time?" Reldon asked her, returning his sword to the Infinity Scabbard.

"Only a few minutes. Reldon, we're all... well, mostly I'm, getting a little worried about you. You've been spending a lot of time in that Xanem."

"I wished to ask them about the castle that used to be here. I figured maybe he would have some answers for me."

"Answers to what?"

"I...I don't know yet. I feel like I'm getting close to something, Alira, I just know it."

"Close to *what?* What do you think Tycheronius is going to say that will change everything so much?"

"I don't *know* yet, but it can't hurt to ask! Anything he has to say could help us, it just needs to be the right wording, the right question."

Her eyes wavered with uncertainty as she slowly sat down at the end of his bed. Her lips wavered once she spoke.

"Reldon, I hear your thoughts echoing at night sometimes," she said quietly, "I hear how much your mind is torturing you. You can't keep it all bottled up forever. And I know you think talking to Tycheronius will help you through this, but he doesn't have the answers you need. He may still have knowledge we need for other matters, but in your grief he cannot help you."

"In my grief?"

"I know what this is all about, Reldon. I'm always here to listen, you know that."

He rose to his feet and went to the window. "There is nothing to talk about. No amount of talking is going to bring him back."

"Then why keep talking to Tycheronius? He's not a real person, Reldon, not anymore. But *you are* a real person and need to talk to real people about what's going on. Please? I'm your Ilewa."

"That's not fair, casting the Ilewa die."

"It's what I'm here for, you know. You helped me with my mother and my father, so let me help you with this."

He turned to her but did not speak. Eternal turmoil plagued his thoughts. She could help. Maybe she could tell him what he needed to hear, the salve to the festering wound of grief that left a pit in his stomach. But Lendir wouldn't want him to mope about either. He would slap him upside his head and tell him that only blood and toil could move him past this. And on top of it all, Reldon *refused* to feel weak in front of his Ilewa. He respected her, cared for her, and even…loved her…far too much to crumble to nothing every time his feelings were getting out of control.

"I just… need some time, that's all," Reldon stated.

Her words were pleading as she stood to meet him. "You're not telling yourself the truth. This isn't going away until you face it. Tell me, Reldon. Tell me why your heart hurts so."

She already knew the answer, but her attempt to get him to talk worked. He looked into her large blue-and-green eyes, so beautiful in the light, and saw her defiant and compassionate soul reflected back at him.

"I miss him, Alira. I miss him so much."

Those words were all it took. He broke down and sobbed, right there and then, and she held him as tight as her arms could hold him. Nothing more mattered in the world at that time, not the Churai, not the blistering storm outside, not the High King nor even their friends downstairs. For this moment in time, he was where he needed to be, doing what his heart knew all along he needed to be doing.

He wept for Lendir – of what happened that fateful night, the terrible pain his master had endured, and for the guilt he carried having been the one to end his master's life, to plunge his sword into a heart which may once have known love. He wept at what might have been – what lessons the man still might have had for him, the ones he would never hear. As much as they fought, they were more than master and student, they were friends, comrades. Lendir kept him honest and humble while Reldon made him realize he didn't have all the answers.

Reldon wept until he had no tears left, until he was nothing but a sniffling mess, barely putting together words to make meaningful sentences. Through it all, she was there, telling him that all would be well.

Sitting back onto his bed, he cleared the lump in his throat. "I'll…I'll be all right."

She knelt and put her forehead against his. "You are stronger than anyone I know, and though I think it will take some time for you to let go, you took your first step. I'm proud of you, Reldon."

He said nothing, refusing to let her see his distraught face, but she needed no response. There was a momentary spike in their connection as she kissed his hot forehead. If he hadn't been red before, he certainly was after that.

"Thanks, Alira. Thanks for always being here for-"

Before he could finish his sentence, there was a great turbulence. It started as a groaning noise from seemingly high above, and at first Reldon thought it was thunder, but that was impossible in a snowstorm. They exchanged perplexed looks just as they heard a massive crunching noise like snapping logs and pulverized stone. The wood floor beneath them trembled briefly, then stopped.

"What in the world was-" Reldon started. Rapid footfalls approached.

A terrified Bryle swung into the room, frantically waving his arm towards the east side of the house from whence he had come.

"Sorry to, um, interrupt whatever you're doing, but the roof just collapsed over that way! I'm going to get Tavia!"

Though unresolved, Reldon's anxiety had been replaced by fear. Without a single word or thought passed between them, the Ilewas were out the door and down the hall, as quick as lightning. A gust of frigid cold air swept through the eastern corridors, bringing with them flurries of snow.

It took no time at all to find. About a fifteen foot section of the roof above the upper east corridor junction had completely collapsed inward, dumping high piles of snow inside the house and obstructing the hallway in shattered stone columns and wooden beams.

Bryle rejoined them with Sillida in tow.

"How did this…?" Reldon trailed off, unsure of what to say.

"It must have been all the snow. It was just too much for the roof to handle!" Bryle answered.

"That means the rest of the roof could collapse at any time," Sillida said grimly.

Ethilia, Kiera, and Tavia came running next.

"My goodness, what happened here?" Ethilia exclaimed.

Bryle just gave her a look.

"Do you hear that?" Alira said, "I think I can hear the serving men on the other side!"

A very faint shouting begged to be heard, muffled by many feet of solid building material.

Tavia swept away some piled snow and shifted a few broken bricks in an attempt to get a line of sight on them. "Can you hear us? Is anyone hurt?"

It was extremely difficult to pick out the words, but Tavia was sure she had heard them say that everyone was fine, but they couldn't escape.

Elly came padding down the hallway, her curiosity getting the better of her.

"So what do we do, Your Grace?" Ethilia asked.

There was a long pause of hesitation as her eyes darted about. Reldon doubted that the woman had ever truly been in dangerous situations before. He was no expert on the subject either, but Reldon knew that people had a tendency to freeze when presented with a situation they didn't know how to handle.

"We need to work together to free them," Reldon declared.

"Can't you just use your magic to clear the debris?" Bryle inquired.

"Not without taking the whole house down with it. And to use Phyrim to clear rocks one at a time would be just as useful as using my hands."

"There is the matter of the structural integrity of the roof," Tavia pointed out, "We will need someone to get onto the roof and clear off what snow they can."

"But that's impossible. There's got to be tons and tons of it up there," Sillida said.

"I can do it," Alira spoke up, "I can get on the roof and use fire magic to melt the snow so it will just run off."

"Be careful not to set the roof itself on fire," Bryle protested.

She raised an eyebrow. "I'm a professional, Bryle."

"Master?" Elly whined, the fear of the situation getting to her.

Tavia knelt and picked up the child. "There, there, young one. Your master will be well, she simply has a job to do. Come, I will take you to see my children." She craned her neck back at the others. "I will keep them safe. I'm afraid I will otherwise be of little help."

"We understand," Reldon said.

"The eldest among you should go to get help. There is a small outpost about a mile from here, south on the road, that stands ready to assist if we should require it. They will provide men and will relay a message back to the High King of what is happening," Tavia said before heading off to find her children.

"That would be Ethilia and Kiera," Sillida stated.

Ethilia was taken aback, shooting a horrified look at the Korrainian, who grinned widely in return.

"W-w-what?! Why do we have to go?" she sputtered.

"Because you're the oldest," Sillida responded matter-of-factly.

"Come, Miss Vendimar, it will be a stomping good time! The oldest and most beautiful of all, saving the day out in the snowbanks. No offense to you ladies," Kiera hooted, wrapping an arm around Ethilia.

"S-stop it! I really must protest!"

"They don't need a healer or a huntress here – we can put our skills to better use out there. Follow me, we will forge out. Today we test our strength as true Korrainians!"

"But I am not-" Ethilia protested as she was being pulled down the corridor.

Alira sighed and followed after them, preparing for her foray out into the blizzard.

"Bryle, you and Sillida work on freeing as many of these rocks and beams as you can so the serving men can escape."

"Aye. What will you do, Reldon?"

"I'm going to go look for supplies. We will need some way to hold the roof up even temporarily while we're freeing the serving men so we aren't completely buried in snow."

"That is well. We will see you shortly. All right, Sillida, let us find out which of us can clear more debris."

Sillida picked up a rock off the pile and threw it at him. "Shut up and dig."

Reldon practically leapt down the staircase which opened up into the foyer. The marble steps themselves were wide and deep enough that wherever he landed he was confident he would not roll an ankle. When he reached the bottom, though, he realized he didn't know where any of such supplies might be in the labyrinth of a house. *Probably nowhere that would be seen by guests. So perhaps some kind of storage closet... No, that wouldn't have enough of what I need. Didn't one of the serving men mention there was a vast supply of wood in the under-levels?*

It would be a start, at least.

The dark staircase which led to the under-levels was behind a locked set of doors near the kitchens, hidden away in the basement. The tumblers inside the lock were simple enough to click into place with Phyrim, and the chains fell away without issue. Taking up a candle from the kitchens, he plunged into the depths of the understructure, a miserably cold air chilling him to the bone.

It was unchanged from when he had been given his initial tour: a series of connected square rooms made of large stone bricks – the thick kind he had grown to know at Freiad Castle – with meat hooks hanging silently from the ceiling and crisscrossing wooden slats supporting colossal barrels of ale and wine.

The silence made his ears ring. None of the panic from three stories up existed down in the cold underbelly of the house, which remained timelessly inert and unsettling every day without change.

There was another locked door on the easternmost wall, one which Reldon had never been through on the tour. *It must be where the supply of wood is kept.*

Another jet of Phyrim and another muted *click* and he was in. Swinging open the doors, he saw largely what he had expected – a chamber twice the size as the others, filled from floor to ceiling with stacks of firewood in rows from the northern wall to the southern one. Old stone columns carved in elaborate picturesque form supported the structure at each of the four corners.

146

The architecture seemed different down in the under-level. The floor stones had largely been scuffed smooth by countless feet. Doorways were smaller. Stairs were much shallower. Besides from the pillars, everything looked as if it were crudely put together.

It didn't take long to occur to him. *This must be the last remnants of the original castle. It makes sense that they would have built on top of the stone foundation rather than trying to dig it up.*

Reldon inspected the piles of wood, turning over a few of the pieces. It was solid wood, but much too small for what would assist in supporting the ceiling upstairs. He worked his way towards the back half of the chamber but met with an entire network of cobwebs spanning between each of the rows.

"Ugh, I guess they haven't been back here in a while," he said aloud.

Sliding his sword from the Infinity Scabbard, he used the blade to cut his way through. However, the stories in which he had heard of heroes doing this had never mentioned that the webs would stick to the sword *en masse*, which only led to an even stickier problem. *I wish I could burn all of these cobwebs, but in this room that's probably not the smartest idea.*

By the time he had reached the back wall, he had only succeeded in completely covering himself in his own personal cocoon of spider web. There didn't appear to be any larger wooden beams in this section, so he conceded that he would have no choice but to double back around to search the northern row, which meant, of course, more cobwebs.

However, when he turned around, he noticed there was more light in the chamber than before.

His sword's pommel was emitting an intermittent, faint glow. *Tycheronius?*

Holding it aloft, he proceeded back down the row. As he did, the glow faded to nothing.

Reldon frowned and reversed course to the back wall again. Sure enough, the faint glow returned.

What is it reacting to? There's nothing here.

Flipping his sword so the blade faced the floor, he used the pommel as a directional stick, watching as the light waxed and waned in reference to where in the room he was. He discovered that when he approached the center of the chamber, it reacted coldly and went out. Thinking this meant it might become stronger when near the side walls returned mixed results; for example, the north wall yielded nothing but the southern wall was a hotspot.

Soon enough he realized that it had glowed most intensely when near the southeast corner of the room, next to one of the pillars at the corner. He lowered his sword near the floor and it grew so luminescent that it eclipsed even the candle he carried in intensity.

What could possibly be so special about this pillar? What could it have to do with –

It hit him.

'*The bottom of things*'.

He was referring to the under-level. It was the only part of the original castle still left – the only part of the building both Tycheronius and himself would have walked on the same plane.

Reldon ran his hand along the base of the pillar. It was strong, solid, and did not give way in any spot. Still, the light continued to urge him towards it. Every bell in his head rang with the singular thought to simply blast away at the pillar to find out if something was hidden inside, but he feared for the safety of the chamber if he did that.

Instead, he placed a hand against the square base of the pillar, just above where it met the stone floor. His focus sharpened and he felt the very particles that made up the entire structure. He felt what gave it strength, what kept it in place. Finally he injected Phyrim into those particles, influencing them to move.

Faster.

The consistency beneath his hand began to shift.

Change.

What he felt was no longer strong stone.

And fall away.

The previously impervious stone had morphed into something closer to mud. As he took his hand away, the small section melted away into a small pile. Not surprisingly, where one normally would have expected to see more solid stone behind it, instead was a hollow.

Excitement lifted his spirits and he whooped in his elation.

Reaching his hand inside, at first it seemed as if filled with nothing but a layer of sand. Finally, though his fingers found something hard and round.

His jubilation grew to a crescendo as he brought it out.

It was a silver coin, slightly larger than a Nuru silver piece. On one side it was completely blank. However, when he flipped it over he saw there was a single word carved into it: '*Aemerus*'.

It did it! I was right! There was something here all along! It wasn't just my mind torturing me, there was actually something Tycheronius wanted me to find. He has more answers!

But what did it mean? Was it a person? A weapon?

"Woohoo!" Reldon couldn't help but shout as he punched the air. It was an incredible sense of validation. *I'm NOT crazy!*

He felt several detonations of magical energy high above him and knew that Alira was setting to work on the rooftops. *I'll tell her later when she's not liquefying entire tons of snow.*

Pacing about and tapping his chin, he tried to remember if he had ever heard that word before. "Aemerus." It definitely wasn't a common word.

He made his way back up to the second floor though the foyer and found his way to High King's Consort's chambers. The doors were open and Tavia had succeeded in distracting her children and Elly from the outside world by encouraging them to play together. They shouted and darted about the room, wheeling about toy horses and pretending to be magicians.

Tavia addressed him as he entered. "Xanem Nuremar, how fares the repair efforts?"

Reldon stopped in his tracks, realizing that in his excitement he had forgotten all about finding the timbers they needed to prop up the roof. "They fare well so far, Your Grace. I had a question for you before I get back to work."

"What is it?"

"Do you know anything about *Aemerus*? Is it a person? An item?"

She cocked her head in puzzlement. "I hold not such a word in my recollection. Perhaps it is an Ancient Lärimite word, or perhaps as you say it is someone's name. However, I have never known anyone by that name."

His spirits had still not yet wilted. "Thank you anyways, Your Grace. I will keep you appraised of the situation."

Reldon left the room perhaps too abruptly, even a bit rudely. His mind was all over the place.

By the time he reached his quarters, it struck him.

I am so dense. I should be asking Tycheronius.

149

The world around him ceased to matter as he slipped into the pocket dimension. Even the blowing cold air and the grunts of exertion from the end of the corridor from his friends did little to tarry his steel determination to get the answers he desperately needed.

Everything gave way to white again as the blue crystalline world surrounded him and the pleasant faces of the legends of old graced him with a smile.

Reldon was practically trembling by the time he asked the question. "Tycheronius, what is *Aemerus*?"

There was a pause of incredible hope and his heart beat so hard he thought it might burst.

"I'm afraid I don't understand your question."

It was like a punch in the chest.

He retrieved the ethereal version of the coin and held it aloft. "You left this down in the basement. Why?"

"I'm afraid I don't understand your question."

I don't understand either, what am I doing wrong?

"What am I supposed to do with this?" he asked.

Tycheronius returned the same answer for a third time.

Reldon pursed his lips together and paced about silently. *How is it possible that he hid this coin, carved a word in it, and doesn't know anything about it?*

"All right Tycheronius, *who* is *Aemerus*?"

"I'm afraid I don't understand your question."

Let's try something simple instead. "*Aemerus.*"

There wasn't an immediate response. Tycheronius turned his head to look at his valiant Ilewa and she returned his wordless gaze. Finally they punctuated their silence with a smile as they looked back at him.

"Xanem Nuremar," he started, "You have figured out my puzzle. Against all odds, I can confirm without any consternation that you are who you claim to be. Understand that as of our lifetimes, theory does exist which could pry information from the Xanem to which you lay claim to, meaning that when I told you that only the Xanem Nuremar could gain access to this wisdom, it was not entirely truthful. However, I am confident that a combination of the riddle and my Xanem reacting to that coin under the power of a legendary forged sword should have weeded out any pretenders to my message.

"Therefore I shall be free to give you more information than before. I was indeed withholding wisdom from you, and for that I apologize, but it is my hope that you will understand why I did so."

Their expressions darkened, growing somber and serious.

"This message is relayed to the future legend, the one who would seek to save our continent of Rim from the encroaching threats which undoubtedly exist in both of our times. I am here to tell you that those threats are both internal and external. The Churai are a threat to all life. However, there are threats which exist that may be a direct threat to *you and your Ilewa* which exist far closer to your being. We have created this message before our trek to the battlefields where the Kuru and Churai await, and we fear it will be our final battle, but not because we fear the battle will not go as planned.

"Somewhere along the way we have made a mistake. We trusted someone, but we know not who. We have traversed Lärim many times over and come to realize that there has been something very wrong with the official account of history, passed down for generations. Too many passages have been omitted, too many mouths silenced. We are afraid of uncovering the sordid truth of this matter, for fear of our lives, but we simply cannot stop searching. Before anything happens to us, we wish to deliver unto you this dire information."

He stepped forward with purpose until he was a foot away, kneeling so that his clear eyes looked firmly into Reldon's. The line in Reldon's brain between seeing him as an ancient projection and living person was beginning to blur as he could sense the urgency in his words.

"If you are currently working for the High King, I implore you to leave his service immediately. They are a house of snakes. If you are under the tutelage of the council of Huerogrand, I urge you to leave them behind as they cannot be trusted. I suspect they are the head of this plot. They tail us everywhere we go. If you are beholden to the Men of History, the Archaic Guild, or the Chroniclers, I would advise you to wipe all of their propaganda from your memory as it is all false. I would even advise caution as to the Church of the Omniscient One, for they skew their message to push for political change."

He leaned in.

"If you have met a gaggle of older women named Miria, Hanea, or Yapoti, they are bearers of wisdom, but will use it against you, so do not trust them. If you meet a man by the name of Sterling, he is a powerful warrior but has an agenda to which you will never be aware. And if you have met the eldest woman who calls herself Grandma…She is the most terrifying of all."

Reldon's eyes were wide as his blood ran cold.

"She is older than you think she is. She is more powerful than any I have met. And without exception she is the most horrifyingly power-hungry woman that has ever lived. I beg you, *do not trust her.* Do not listen to a word she says. Every utterance she has made has served to heighten her own power. She knows the truth. She knows why entire volumes of the histories have been destroyed or changed, for she was there to witness it. Ultimately she knows this monumental secret which we have spent years searching for, but I refuse to trust her enough to ask her.

"So the simple truth of your future is a dilemma. I tell you all of this, because I know sooner or later you will need to know what the secret is, and you will have no choice but to go to her to get it. She is waiting for it. She has always been waiting. For countless lifetimes she has been patiently biding her time for the day in which you demand from her the secret. Once you do, there will be no going back. I only wish to warn you that she will attempt to use you. For reasons unknown to us, she needs you and your Ilewa. I fear that once she has finished what she has started, she will have no further use for you."

Reldon sputtered in his attempt to respond. "I…I don't understand, Tycheronius. What more power could she possibly hope to have?"

"All of the power. I know not what she would do with it, but I would not put it past her to devise some grand scheme to remake the world in some idealistic image. She is a cynic, a nihilist. She views this world as corrupt and undeserving, its people nothing more than damned souls waiting to be cleansed."

"But how do you know this? How do you know Grandma so well?"

"She was once my master. It is not a coincidence that we have become powerful enough in the ways of Phyrim and magic to surpass most others. But where she excels in raw magical power, she lacks in basic compassion and has a fearful outlook on the future. If you would use her to gain the strength to defeat the Churai, then do so with caution. Understand, though, that you will most likely need to kill her."

"Do you know what magic she wields? I have never seen anything like it before."

"It is an ancient magic. One which no longer exists. I am not certain how that is possible."

"Do you have any idea what this 'secret' is?"

"The extent of my knowledge from having spent years interrogating powerful people and sticking my nose into places I shouldn't have yielded no less grandiose a conclusion than that this 'secret' is important enough that entire generations have been dedicated to keeping it hidden from the world. Be extraordinarily careful looking into this, Xanem Nuremar, for the next person you talk to could be a member of the cabal dedicated to keeping this secret. The only groups I know have some involvement in this are those I mentioned earlier – the government of Nakisho, the historical guilds, the church, Huerogrand, and the Academy City. Beware of any involved in those especially, for there may be smiles on their faces but there will be knives in their hands."

Reldon's mind raced. It was a lot for any single mind to comprehend. "How can any secret be so important that half of Lärim could be involved in keeping it safe?"

Tycheronius stared back at him and Reldon knew it was too vague a question to ask. Whatever this 'secret' was, it had to be something which could change the course of the war. *But why are so many people so scared it could come out? If it is something that could help us destroy the Churai, then we have to find out what it is. Without asking anyone about it. Or even mentioning it. How is this going to be possible? Grandma might be our only way, but if what Tycheronius is saying is true, that could be the most dangerous option.*

"Thank you Tycheronius. Thank you for trusting me. I promise I will get to the bottom of whatever this secret is."

He nodded. "Go and bring peace to Rim. There has been something fetid about all this for far too long, and it would be well to see it resolved. I wish you and your Ilewa the favor of fortune."

The room rushed back to him at the same time he felt another frigidly cold burst of air.

Alira!

Chapter XXIV

As it turned out, against the amazing expectations of some people, horses were also at the complete mercy of the terrible storm which sought to leave Lärim in a total mess of ice and white.

The snow drifts along the main road away from the house had grown so high that Ethilia could no longer see her horse's legs beneath them, and she had to pull her own legs up to avoid losing a boot in the awful stuff. She couldn't help but feel bad for the poor thing. Thick clouds of visible breath escaped its mouth as it powered onward, determined to make it through. She gave it a cursory stroke every once in a while to show her appreciation.

It was such an incredibly ill-thought-out plan, Ethilia was certain they were both going to die out in this frozen wasteland. The snowflakes, which were more like tiny solid ice particles, were carried by the wind with such force that they were more akin to being pelted by glass, and it would be a miracle if she made it back to the house without a hundred tiny cuts on her cheeks. Even though the horses were strong, it would only be a matter of time until their energy ran out and they would be stranded, snow piling up to their eyeballs. *How in the world that Korrainian girl can stay so cheerful and confident in all this is simply beyond my comprehension. I think if a Churai burst from the snow and set upon us she would still have that insufferable grin on her face.*

"This is ludicrous! We should go back now!" Ethilia shouted for the fourth time.

It was nearly impossible to hear over the howling wind, but she could hear the laugh of her raspy, heavily-accented voice. "This is our destiny, Miss Ethilia! Trust in the spirits and we will make it through!"

Ethilia lowered her head to shield it from the flurry. *Any sane person would not be out here.*

Luckily some spots of the road had endured such constant wind that none of the snow had any chance to settle. They tended to be in more open spaces, so even though the path was much easier for the horses, the wind became intolerable and the horses whinnied in protest as they were (at least in their imagining) being bitten by a thousand tiny flies. The final quarter mile of road leading to the checkpoint happened to be largely clear, but no less treacherous as a result, and their poor horses sped to a gallop just to get out of the wicked weather.

Finally after what was probably no more than a half an hour of drudgery, they reached the first checkpoint, which was a small wooden shack on the near side of a bridge which would have spanned over a small river at any other time of the year. Now it was just snow. Endless ridiculous snow.

There was a closed gate barring passage across the bridge – or at least Ethilia was fairly sure there was somewhere underneath the snow piles. She saw spokes of metal poking out from the tops. What was most surprising was the lack of light from within the shack.

They dismounted and stood uneasily before the door, which was partially inaccessible and hadn't been cleared recently.

"Something is very wrong," Ethilia said in a quivering voice.

The Korrainian princess pulled on the door until it freed just a few inches of space before sticking her foot in and pushing it further with her shoulder. She held it open wide enough for Ethilia to slip in before she did.

Inside it was completely dark as the only window, one which faced the bridge, was rendered opaque by yet another snow pile outside. Something smelled awful, forcing Ethilia to clap a hand to her face. Somehow she already knew what the smell was.

"I…uh…might have something to make a torch here somewhere…" Kiera said, fumbling around, "Can you not make light with that magical symbol on your arm like Alira?"

"I'm a Golden Magician. We don't have Keinume."

"But your magic produces light."

"When I use it, yes. I'm not a light magician, so snapping my fingers and producing a ball of light isn't exactly my forte. When I heal, it produces light."

She heard Kiera sliding her hands around the wall until she heard the clattering of a wooden object.

"Here you are."

Clack. Sparks flew. *Clack. Clack. Clack.*

At last a small flame flickered into existence in the head of the torch, in which she had put some dried grass and perhaps some sort of cloth.

"How did you keep those dry with all of this?" Ethilia waved about.

"Have you never heard of a tinder box?" she asked cheerfully, "It is very important for surviving in the wild."

Kiera stoked the flame with a blow, and it blossomed into a much brighter light.

However, what they saw in the partial darkness made them wish they hadn't lit anything at all.

Bodies lay strewn about. Five of them, their limbs twisted about in grotesque positions, and a good portion of their blood having been emptied onto the floor. The men were scarcely recognizable, save for what scraps of their white uniforms still remained. The lone table had been destroyed as one of the men's bodies had been thrown through it, and virtually all other furniture had met a similar state or been knocked over.

"What in…what happened here?" Kiera gasped, "They look like they were mauled by a bear!"

Ethilia shook her head as she knelt to survey their injuries. "Worse. Come look."

The lacerations were unmistakable – deep and surgical. The unfortunate reality was that these men, with all of their shattered bones and mangled innards likely died slowly from blood loss.

"What could have done this, Ethilia?" Kiera asked, her raspy voice getting very quiet.

"Nothing else does this. It was a Churai."

Kiera shuffled back as she started to hyperventilate. "No. No, no no, we must get out of here. Not one of those things!"

"Calm down. Losing our heads isn't going to get us anywhere," she rebuked.

"Ethilia, we cannot fight one of them! If it's still around, we are going to get killed!" She began to edge towards the door.

"You can smell the bodies, and you can see the bloating. This happened days ago and they're likely long gone by now. What happened to all of that Korrainian courage all of a sudden?"

The light wavered as her hand shook terribly. "This is not something to be courageous about! I am terrified of fighting something which I cannot put an arrow into and kill. You should be too!"

"Do *not* tell me how I ought to be. Right now you are scared of a shadow, a specter, something which poses no immediate threat to us. There is nothing we can do for these men now."

There was a powerful fear and hesitation to the huntresses' voice. "Then w-what do we do now? We must warn someone! Maybe someone at the next checkpoint could be in danger."

"Do you not even listen to yourself? You're terrified at the possibility of running into the Churai, but then in the next thought you want to go gallivanting off to the other checkpoints in hopes of helping them and possibly even running into the blasted thing. You said it yourself, we *cannot* kill it."

"But we could *warn* them if it hasn't attacked yet and they could get to safety!"

"It's too late for that now! We could spend hours and hours freezing to death, trudging through endless snow, in the hopes of maybe finding a handful of guards that haven't been torn apart yet, and what would we gain?"

"It is not about gaining anything, it is the moral course of action. It is our duty as people to act in the best interest of our fellow men and women. The spirits say-"

"Enough about the spirits!" Ethilia shouted. "There *are no spirits!* If we really were surrounded by all these good spirits, do you really think they would be allowing *this* to happen?" She jutted a finger towards the bodies. She knew she was saying far too much already, but her annoyance had grown to anger several days ago after being cooped up with this Korrainian girl for far too long. "And I would love to follow along with your beliefs on doing what's best for other people if you weren't from an entire country that does exactly the opposite to each other every day. So do *not* give me moral lessons. I've had enough of this freezing out in the cold, and I'm going back to the house. Follow me or don't, I care not."

She stormed over to the door and pushed it as open as it would go. As she left, she heard a small, uncertain voice, stained with hurt.

"You really believe all of those things, Ethilia?"

Ethilia didn't answer, and slammed the door behind her. Within a few tense seconds she was on her white horse and heading back north.

Her anger took a good long while to cool, even with the freezing ice tearing up her cheeks again. She was so upset that she could feel her eyes filling as she rode onwards. Ethilia cursed her nature to cry when she was angry.

The first two hundred yards were somewhat of a blur. All her conscious mind could focus on was how much the Korrainian girl really got under her skin. *Her little 'innocent act' is so incredibly frustrating. I will not be the one who stands by, trusting anyone with big eyes and a sad story, while they plot our very destruction. Korrainians don't change. They never change. They will always want nothing more than to see Nakisho razed to the ground.*

It was infuriating, how much the others were so trusting. They never questioned her motives, not once. Reldon probably didn't ask a single question before giving the girl a horse and riding off to parts unknown with her in tow. *If a wolf showed up one day wearing a mask and told them it was there to help them defeat the Churai, I swear they would let it eat them.*

She had every intention of returning to the house and telling the rest of them that Kiera went off on some silly quest to find survivors and she hadn't been able to talk her out of it. It would get her out of the snow and the miserable cold. She would finally be able to change clothes after sitting on a drenched, frigid saddle.

It would be so easy.

And yet, she still issued the command for the horse to slow to a stop.

Looking up into the gray nothingness that was the sky, her equally icy blue eyes fought to stay dry.

Ethilia took a long breath.

Why are you being like this, Ethilia? She thought to herself as her conscience's disappointment in her decision was enough to make her run away and hide from the scrutiny. *That girl hasn't spoken one ill word to you since she met you. She doesn't deserve this. You're abandoning her.*

She let out a frustrated groan through gritted teeth.

Her horse wheeled around at her slightest command, hooves crunching loudly as it sped to a gallop.

In just a few short minutes Ethilia saw the shack approaching, and Kiera's horse still stood outside. She hadn't left yet.

A piercing scream lit up every signal in her brain. It was Kiera.

She never completely halted her horse, her fear driving her to leap off and roll to safety before prying the door open once more. "Kiera!"

Inside the torch had fallen onto the floor along with its owner. Kiera lay on her back, screaming in fear as a dark figure loomed over her, menacing her with the point of a blade.

Every instinct told Ethilia to run for her life. If she didn't, this would be it. This would be her final day. And yet her feet remained planted where they were.

The figure stood up straighter, its shadow of a face slowly turning to address her with its glowing red eyes.

Her heart pounded and her whole body trembled.

It lowered its sword before speaking, its voice sounding like a man's voice, but with a timbre much lower than anyone was capable of producing naturally, and in an accent she had never heard before.

"I see you. You fear me."

158

Ethilia couldn't even respond she was so terrified.

"Give me the information I need and you will not die. Tell me where the Xanem Nuremar and Ilewa Nuremil are housed."

Kiera suddenly and frantically scrambled out from the range of the figure's sword, a move which Ethilia was certain was going to get her killed, but for whatever reason the figure was fixated on the other half of his dialogue and didn't even flinch.

Her voice came out as more of croak. "W-why do you want to know that?"

"That is unimportant to you. You will answer or you will die."

She knew that if she told it that she didn't know, she was going to die anyway. And she was certainly not going to tell this barbaric creature where Reldon and Alira were. Not to mention it would be placing the royal children in danger. So she gathered up what courage she could find within her trembling heart.

"I will tell nothing to you, Churai."

"Then you will die."

There was an immediate spike in magical energy, one which seemed instantly familiar.

Pain exploded from her arm as it felt as if a blade had sliced it open. She shrieked. Magic flooded into her fingers at her command, forming a golden harness around her arm. It had been a nasty gash, and she hastily rebuilt the damaged muscular structure and stemmed the bleeding in just a few seconds.

The Churai had stopped its attack and looked on with curiosity as she worked to close her wound.

Death Magic. It feels so strangely similar to Golden Magic. Like a brother and sister.

Ethilia whispered under her breath, blinked, and opened her now golden eyes.

The figure was most certainly a Churai. It was like looking into eternal blackness, a void which even put the darkness of night to shame. Surrounding it were tendrils of writhing black magic which slithered around Ethilia, awaiting the command to kill.

She held out her arms and supercharged her magical power to surround her entire body in a modified golden harness which formed a sort of interlacing globe which she expanded to encompass Kiera as well.

"Your tricks will not stop your death."

A tendril lashed out at her at lightning speed, but instead of finding its target, it struck her harness. A resonance shook the room as it attempted to worm its way through, but the two opposing forces could not overcome each other until Ethilia sent a jolt of Golden Magic through the thread which it touched. With a flash of light it was repelled.

The Churai cocked its head. Whether it was confusion or bemusement, it did not matter, as it then proceeded to rain down an assault of dozens of tendrils at once.

Ethilia felt the sudden draw of energy from her body as each one was repelled. It was enough to nearly take her breath away, but she knew she absolutely could not betray as much to the Churai.

She stood as firmly as she could, moving her hand about to assist in the dispatching of the foul magic. Ten, twenty, even thirty strikes assailed her makeshift shield to no avail.

At long last the attacks stopped and the tentacles of power withdrew. Ethilia's head was spinning from the drop in magical energy.

"What is this power you possess? None may refuse death."

"You cannot hurt us," Ethilia said confidently, "You might as well go find someone else to torment."

"You *will* die."

The Churai raised its sword. Her heart dropped as she realized she had no way of stopping that.

Its speed was incredible. It closed the distance between them in a split second, its feet barely touching the floor. It was everything she could do to simply dive out of the way, crashing to the floor, to avoid being skewered on the spot. She never even had the chance to scream. With a pivot, it brought its sword up for the killing blow.

Mid-attack, it lurched as if struck in the back. Slowly it craned its neck and rotated to reveal an arrow sticking out from its spine, emerging from its black light armor.

Kiera cowered in the corner, her bow in her hand. As it turned to face her with its fearsome red eyes, she screamed and scrambled across the floor to her feet, leaping over a chair just before it was hewn in two. She felt around desperately for something to throw and managed to get a hand on one of the guards' swords. With a cry, she hurled it at the figure. The blade found its body and rightfully should have done serious damage, but the Churai simply looked down as it clattered to the floor, no sign of pain or consternation at all.

Ethilia then saw the tendrils.

Kiera wasn't protected.

"No!" Ethilia screamed, sprinting across the room and leaping from the broken table. It had been a knee-jerk reaction. Her last thought before leaping on top of the creature was that she couldn't believe she was doing this for a Korrainian.

There was no time for slip-ups. Either this would work or they would both die.

With a thud she landed on top of the Churai and she placed a hand against its head, feeling coarse hair.

With a pulse of Golden Magic, she saw.

Many people's bodies had she seen with her magic throughout her relatively short life. Old bodies, young bodies, ones which were missing limbs, missing organs, and most of them just simply corpses. Humans had a predictable structure and didn't differ much from person to person, at least not in ways that mattered greatly.

This creature was most certainly not human in any way.

There were no organs that she could identify. Blood did not run through its veins. In a sense, this was not a fully corporeal creature. She saw into the depths of this void and did not see anything which even closely resembled human thought, emotions, or attachments. What replaced all of those was a singular drive, a purpose for existence – what that was, she could not derive, but it was overwhelming. It was like looking into the mind of a hammer. Where a hammer would want only to pound nails, this Churai had another isolated purpose she could not understand.

Beneath that was a hole of death. The feeling of death was peculiar – tantalizing, almost liberating, yet horrifying. It felt so similar in many ways to her Golden Magic that it made her sick.

All of this was imparted to her in a fraction of a second before she took every ounce of gleaming magical energy she had left and jammed it into the void.

A major resonance instantly nearly shattered their hearing. The Churai only had a second to scream, a dread shriek of which neither Kiera nor Ethilia had ever heard in their lives. Its red eyes momentarily shone bright gold as they went wide with revulsion before going dim altogether.

With Ethilia still atop it, the Churai faded to nothing before their eyes and she toppled to the floor.

"Ethilia!" she heard Kiera shouting as the world faded in and out. "Ethilia, are you all right? We did it, we killed a Churai!"

She weakly raised a hand and Kiera took it. "You were...so brave..."

"Do not die, Ethilia!" she cried in that stupid accent of hers.

"I'm not...dying, you..." She coughed. "I just...overdid it. Now is the part where I...fall unconscious and have...strange dreams...and wake up with a splitting headache..."

"I will keep you safe, Miss Vendimar."

Ethilia let out a breath and gave a weak smile. For all her posturing about being a Golden Magician, this Korrainian girl had more of a heart of gold than she ever had.

"I'm sorry...for what I said."

There was a flash of hurt in her eyes, before she waved a hand. "Think nothing of it. I understand why you said those words. I am sorry I pushed so hard for you to believe in the spirits."

There was movement in the peripheries of their vision, and Ethilia rotated her head to see a crow standing atop the broken table, watching them silently.

Ethilia sighed as Kiera's eyes went wide.

"Wonderful. I'll never live this one down."

"Ethilia, look! It is a-"

"A sign. I know."

She rolled her head to the side again and saw her otherwise flawless golden hair drenched in one of the pools of blood on the floor. Touching it with a finger, she looked back at the ceiling again.

"Lovely. I'm ready to fall unconscious now."

Chapter XXV

Alira pushed the heavy front doors open with some difficulty, her complexion nearly as white as the snow from the exertion of having carefully melted snow for nearly an hour.

The job still wasn't done. As far as she knew, Reldon, Sillida, and Bryle were still working on freeing the serving men without bringing the entire roof on their heads, but thanks to her own efforts, she figured that wouldn't be a problem.

She sighed heavily and her lungs worked reluctantly, a slight pain in her chest. *Just a few days ago I had all the magical energy in the world, and now I seem to be back to normal. Or...at least I think this is normal.*

Alira unraveled the scarf from around her face, large pieces of ice still adhering to it. The rest of her warmer gear she couldn't get off fast enough – the transition from staying alive in the miserable cold to trying to cool down afterwards in a warm house was making her body cry out for relief. Slipping up the stairs and into the girls' quarters, she lay down on her bed for just a few minutes while her body worked on regulating her temperature.

How did it go? Reldon's voice sounded.

It was...a lot of work. It's a very large roof, so by the time I had finished clearing off one quarter of it, another quarter was starting to fill in with snow again.

Like trying to bail out a ship with a hole in it.

Exactly. How are the serving men?

They're a great help. We should have them free soon enough, and they will likely be able to repair this faster than we can. There was still a giddiness to his voice and she couldn't help but smile exasperatingly.

You're still very excited.

Of course I am! It's a key, a clue to the solution to all of this. Tycheronius said it himself – there is something wrong with this world as we see it, and there is some sort of massive secret being kept by a few that could change everything!

That sounds like a good story, but do you really believe that, Reldon?

His voice was almost indignant. *But of course I do! Why would Tycheronius lie?*

She rolled onto one side, nuzzling her pillow. *It just seems so...outlandish. I mean, Grandma as Tycheronius's master? All of Lärim's powerful people working together to make sure no one knows some truth they hid hundreds of years ago? It just sounds a bit more like a storybook than a history book.*

That's the point. He even said the history books are wrong.

In what way?

There was a considered pause.

I...don't know. Something to do with this Secret.

And how would we find out what this Secret is? She definitely felt like she was doing nothing more than playing along. It was all so strange, so fantastical, and all she really wanted to do was dismiss it as just silly talk. Yet Reldon believed in it wholeheartedly and she couldn't dismiss him so easily.

Not even Tycheronius could do that, but he said when the time came, we could ask Grandma and she would reveal it to us.

Just like that?

He said it would be extremely dangerous.

But there is no other way.

Unless you can find someone else, like maybe the head of the Church of the Omniscient One who might know and convince him to tell you everything, Grandma might be our only option.

Just how old is Grandma?

Old enough that Tycheronius knew her well. And I think he lived...Actually, I don't know how long ago he lived. Centuries ago, I suppose.

She closed her eyes as a bead of sweat ran across her forehead. *So even if we can find Grandma and get her to tell us about this Secret, how does that help us in our fight against the Churai?*

I'm not sure yet, but if it's something this big, maybe it could be something that helps us turn the tables.

*But Reldon...*She was doing her very best to be polite. *We have a very real enemy trying to kill all of us. You know that, you have fought them. I understand maybe trying to find some way we can get an advantage, but this whole... 'Secret' idea isn't really a plan. There are too many unknowns.*

You're right, we do have a very real threat ahead of us. And you're right that I've fought them. I nearly died, and Lendir did die. There could be hundreds of them out there, and we are horribly outmatched by them. I don't know how to kill them any other way than blasting them until they disappear, and that's also not a strategy. As we are now, we cannot defeat them. We would die trying. And that's why I want to follow any leads I can find that might give us victory. Even if it means straying from our path for a while.

We might not have that much time, Reldon. You heard the High King, that army we fought was not their main force. They could attack with greater numbers and more Churai at any time.

Then all the better we find a way of defeating them quickly, because if they attack after this storm, we will most certainly-

There was a high, raspy voice shouting over the noise of the wind, and they both heard it.

Alira leapt out of bed and met Reldon at the top of the grand staircase as he approached from the opposite corridor.

It was Kiera entering the house, her arm supporting Ethilia who looked paler than usual.

Two guardsman helped escort Ethilia to one of the velvet chairs in the foyer. Kiera grinned at Alira and Reldon as they descended the staircase.

"You both mirrored each other. That was cute."

"Kiera, what happened to Ethilia?" Reldon said urgently.

"She is all right. We had a bit of a run-in with a-"

"...a Churai," Ethilia finished her sentence.

Reldon and Alira both sputtered as their hearts sunk.

"Churai? Here? W-what happened?!" he demanded.

Ethilia attempted, in her usual way, to straighten her posture as she sat, but ended up slumping lazily due to lack of energy.

"We rode out to the checkpoint and discovered nothing but bodies there. We were shortly..." she cast a look at Kiera, "...ambushed by the Churai who was lying in wait."

Alira was overcome with emotion at the thought of her friends having to fight one of those evil creatures. She embraced Kiera and Ethilia in turn, repeating, "I'm so happy you're both all right."

"I...I don't understand," Reldon struggled, "How *did* you fight it off? They are nearly impossible to kill."

Ethilia gave a wry smile. "Maybe for you, o savior, but not for a Vendimar. He didn't seem to understand Golden Magic. If you could believe it, he actually demanded I tell him what power I possess – the absolute nerve of some monsters."

"But how did you stop it from cutting you to ribbons where you stood?" Reldon pressed.

"My Golden Magic was its antithesis. No, maybe not so. Perhaps it would suffice to say that Golden Magic and Death Magic are akin to two fraternal twins – very different, but share much. I do not know how else to describe it. I was able to halt his attacks, and it confused him enough that it gave me an opening. With some help, of course."

Kiera nodded with her child-like grin.

She continued. "I was able to touch him with my Golden Magic, to reach inside and see what abominable composition made these creatures function."

"What did you see?" Alira asked.

Her response was as if recalling a bitter memory. "It was appalling. Like a deep pit of nothing but blackness and purpose. In case any of you were wondering, they are not human and are not living beings in the sense that we understand it. It is not the usual bits of life which fuel them – not blood nor air, not love nor compassion. They are death. They are purpose. There was little else to see."

"What purpose do they have?" Reldon asked.

"I do not know, but for the moment they must be looking for you. He was insistent on finding out where you two are. For some reason they are not able to follow the road to the house."

Kiera laughed. "What road?"

"Point taken," Ethilia said with a smile.

"They are far too close. Somehow they know we are in this area," Reldon said.

"It is my studious opinion that they are able to sense the magical discharges coming from this small portion of Lärim. It would make sense to me that once Miss Ayuru ceased her war against the snow, they had no compass to which they could follow," Ethilia surmised, her attention unable to ignore her blood-soaked hair and wet clothes.

"Then we should stop using all forms of magic or Phyrim until the storm is over."

"Are you sure you will be able to do that, Reldon? To live like the commoners must be like severing an arm for you," Kiera said with a teasing grin.

"I lived more years as a normal boy than I have as a Spellsword. I'll manage."

"Yes, well, if any of you need me, I will be soaking in a bath for the next several days," Ethilia said, pushing herself to her feet, which only shakily held her up. She paused. "On second thought, don't disturb me. Even if you need me."

After three stairs she began to sway, prompting Kiera to catch her and guide her upstairs.

"Alira, you must be exhausted. Would you like a bath as well?" Kiera asked.

"You are very kind – I do not feel tired at all, actually. But I would love a bath. I feel so sweaty."

Ethilia scoffed as Alira surpassed them on the stairs. "You are… such a show-off, Miss Ayuru. An hour of blasting snow and you are as glowing as a grape, but I kill a single Churai and suddenly my body forgets how to walk."

"Killing a Churai is no small feat, Ethilia. You should be proud of what you did."

As they reached the top of the stairs, Reldon stopped them. "How exactly did you *kill* it though?"

"Golden Magic to the brain. Or whatever void fills their empty heads. I put every ounce of power I had into that creature's skull, and by some divine grace it worked."

Reldon drew in breath. "So Tycheronius was right. Golden Magic is the best way to kill them. He never found any way to weaponize it though."

"Maybe a blast directly into the squishy bits between their ears is a weapon unto itself?" Kiera laughed.

"It's not a very good weapon if Ethilia has to get into harm's way to make it work."

"Aren't you *Spellsword*, Mister Reldon? Getting into harm's way is your entire strategy," Ethilia said with a dim look.

"Right, I have a sword. You don't."

Alira snapped her fingers. "Is there a way to imbue Golden Magic into a weapon? Like a sword or an arrow?"

Ethilia shook her head. "None that I am aware of. In general, imbuing magic into weapons can only be done between Ilewa. I have no Ilewa."

Alira hummed to herself. "I wonder if Elly has one…"

"She wouldn't know for a few years. In *any case*, it is bath time. I refuse to stand here with soldiers' blood in my hair for another minute." And with that, Kiera led Ethilia away down the hall. Alira exchanged a look with Reldon before shrugging and following them.

The damage to the roof had been extensive in the spot where it had caved in, but the surrounding structure was largely untouched. By the time he had gone upstairs to check on their progress, all of the serving men had managed to squeeze through an opening in the rubble that Bryle and Sillida had freed for them, and had been working on repairing the damage. Watching them work was like magic in its own right. He had seen furniture or windows break a few times around the house and even a single serving man worked with incredible efficiency to repair it – and this time all four of them working in tandem made the mountainous task seem like just another day's work. *Wherever the High King hired these four from, they are truly the best at what they do.*

It couldn't have taken them more than a few hours to at least return the corridor and the connecting rooms to a livable state. Randolfus, the serving man who had helped Reldon through his nightmares, laughed as he remarked that it, "may look like an ugly blemish on the face of the house from the outside, but by the Omniscient One it will hold for the rest of the storm."

That was the question in Reldon's mind: how long was this storm going to last?

They were about to enter their sixth day of the storm and there were no clear skies in sight.

He peered out the window in the foyer, watching snow accumulate nearly to the lower pane itself. For some reason his thoughts turned to Sterling. He was somewhere out there in all that cold and ice – there was no doubt in his mind at all that the old Spellsword was still alive. *You never were going to answer my questions, were you? You promised that you would answer them after we were done, but you knew when the storm would strike and you fled before I had the chance to pry it out of you.*

Secrets were the natural state of life in Lärim, or maybe even the whole world, and he hated it. After what Tycheronius had said, there was no way he could completely trust them again – not Sterling, not Grandma, not even the High King. Niuro had been a man who had walked the same path as Reldon: in fact, they had in many places stepped on the same floors and saw the same things. It was this parallel he couldn't ignore. They were separated by hundreds of years, but still somehow he felt like he knew him.

It was like knowing himself.

And that was why, despite Alira's protests, he could never dismiss what the old hero had to say, about anything. He had a strong suspicion that what Tycheronius and Giavere found out about the Secret had something to do with their deaths, and they were reaching through time to warn him not to make the same mistakes.

It makes so little sense that they would be telling me to go to Grandma for answers, even if they're telling me to be careful of her. What if she had something to do with their deaths? I suppose they wouldn't know that at that point in their lives.

It had become the only secret that mattered anymore. Sterling could keep his secrets, and so could the High King. All that mattered was unearthing the one true Secret, the one that could mean that difference between finally ridding the world of the Churai or being buried in the bones of the dead in their wake.

He breathed hard onto the window, fogging it up.

Once the storm ends we will have to make some decisions about where to go and what to do next, and I don't think Alira and I will agree. I don't understand why she refuses to believe anything I say about Tycheronius or the Secret. She still thinks it has something to do with Lendir. Soon enough she's not going to be able to keep ignoring this.

Scratching his head, he stretched his arms. Maybe he was overthinking it all. Besides, there was nothing he, nor any of them, could do until the storm was over.

You're too stressed, old boy, he thought to himself, *Just try to relax while you can.*

It was nearly dinner time, but he figured he would see if anyone was willing to share any good times they were having. Heading down the stairs to the lower floor, he opened the door to the game room, expecting perhaps to see Kiera or Bryle enjoying a hand of cards or dice, but instead there was only a single person in the room.

She sat alone in front of the crackling flames of the hearthfire, her knees drawn up to her chest, hugging them tightly. Her dark eyes flitted up at him as he entered.

"Sillida? Are you all right? What are you doing down here by yourself?" Reldon asked, shutting the door behind him.

Her face returned to her knees. "Nothing." It sounded as if she were fighting tears.

Reldon approached her, pulling up a velvet chair beside her. "Come now, Sillida, I can see you're troubled. We've been friends for how long?"

There was a pause as her mind processed it all, and she finally let her knees down and crossed her hands in her lap. Her eyes were red and puffy from crying.

"You have to promise you won't interfere," she said weakly.

"I can't promise you that. If it's something I can help with, I will."

Sillida pressed her lips together, but relaxed, breathing deeply.

"It's about Bryle."

"I had a feeling."

"So you...know?"

"Everyone does, Sillida. It's not a secret. You fancy him."

She nodded sadly.

"So you told him?"

Another nod.

"Did you tell him while you were digging out the serving men? That might have been a bad time."

"No, it was after that. We were just finishing up, and he told me he was going to go rest, and I followed him and asked him if I could ask him something...I told him how much I liked being his partner, and that we make a good team. In Errum, Ferrela, and especially here in Lärim. And so...I asked him...if he wanted to be my partner...you know...all the time. My heart was beating so fast I could hardly stand it."

Reldon leaned in closer, his voice gentle. "And what did he say?"

A new stream of tears worked its way down her face. "He said no, Reldon. He said he wasn't ready for that. And that he needed some time to think. Whatever that means. He's so *stupid* sometimes!"

She buried her face in her hands as her sobs came anew, and Reldon pulled her close, giving any semblance of comfort to her aching heart.

Dammit, Bryle.

It took time for her to find a place of peace from the pain, but once he figured she would be all right, he stood to leave.

"Where are you going?" she asked, sniffling.

"I'm going to have a word with Bryle."

He had been precisely where Reldon had figured him to be. He found his old friend sitting in his plush chair in front of the fireplace in the brandy room, sitting quietly without any brandy in sight.

"Ah, good to see you, Reldon. Come and join me. I have something I want to talk to you about."

"I know what it's about, Bryle. I talked to her first."

"Oh."

Reldon did not sit in his usual chair, but instead stood with his arms crossed just a few feet away.

"I take it you're upset with me," Bryle surmised.

"I just don't understand it, Bryle. We live in a world where almost everyone wants to kill us, and you turn your nose up at the one person who thinks you're great enough to be your partner."

Bryle shook his sandy head. "It's not that simple, Reldon. I…I panicked. I didn't know what to say. She…she ambushed me!"

"Oh don't be so dramatic. You weren't ready because you never wanted to be ready. You've been coming up with every reason in the book why you shouldn't be together and couldn't find a single one."

"But I…what if I'm not ready, Reldon? We've got so many other bigger matters to see to!"

"It's not a small matter to her, though Bryle. To her, you are everything – you are the world. The Churai could invade tomorrow and it would all be worth it to her to have one day together with you."

He blinked. "What is with you getting all sappy all of a sudden?"

"Take it from someone who understands where she's coming from."

His longtime friend scratched his head in his usual way that said that he understood the point but was still too stubborn to follow along. "I don't know, Reldon…"

"Stand up."

Bryle narrowed his eyes. "What?"

"Stand up," Reldon repeated.

Bryle slid off his chair and stood before his friend, who appraised him with a stern expression.

"I'm going to ask you very plainly. Do you fancy her?"

His eyes cast about the room. "Reldon, I…"

"Yes or no?"

That further gave him consternation to see how serious Reldon was about this. Their relationship had always been bolstered by their love of humor and horsing around, but in this moment Reldon looked on him with a deadly seriousness that he hadn't given him since the Battle of Nakisho. Bryle's eyes searched his face for any sign that it might be another sick attempt at a joke, but realized quickly that he would not be able to worm his way out of it.

After a moment, he gave a curt nod. "Yes."

"Good. Then come with me."

Reldon grabbed his wrist and pulled him toward the door.

"Oi, where are we going now?"

"To where you need to be."

"Reldon, no! I'll fight you!"

He shot a nasty look back at Bryle as the air around him shimmered and vibrated from Phyrimic release.

Bryle's eyes went wide and he became much more pliant. "All right, all right, I get it! I'll come quietly!"

There were no further instances of rebelliousness on their way down to the parlor. He walked right past Kiera who stood in the foyer and watched with silent alarm as they stormed by her.

Reldon threw the door open and pulled Bryle into the room where Sillida sat by herself. She immediately perked up as they entered, standing and flattening the skirts of her simple dress.

"R-Reldon, what are you doing?" she asked.

"What needs to be done. Come here, Sillida." His voice didn't hold any ferocity, but he made sure it was known that he was done being subtle about this.

He released Bryle as they stood before each other. "If you try to run, I will turn your stockings to glass."

Bryle swallowed hard.

"Now, you both know why you're standing here. This has gone on long enough and you're making all of our hearts hurt for having to watch it. Now, I have been both of your friends for nearly as long as any of us can remember, so I'm doing this because I care about your happiness, and because I know you very well. Bryle, I know you like to run away from problems you can't face head on with a sword. Sillida, I know that when you're not trying to be tough, you're too shy to tell anyone your true feelings. So I'm going to make this very simple for you. Sillida, do you fancy Bryle? Do you want to be his partner for as long as you can, possibly even for your whole life?"

She went redder than Reldon had ever seen her before. He couldn't even see her freckles anymore.

With an emphatic nod, she responded, "Yes, I do."

"Bryle," he continued, "Do you fancy Sillida? Do you want to protect her and make her happy?"

"I... uh..."

Reldon glared at him.

"Yes, all right? Yes, I do."

If there was a look that told that Sillida's heart was visibly fluttering, she was showing it. Her fingers trembled at her side, her dark eyes wide and genuine with joy.

"Then as far as I'm concerned, you're together. As partners, as a couple. Clear?"

Sillida nodded jubilantly.

Bryle nodded, less enthusiastically.

Reldon looked him in the eye again. "Then kiss her."

It was his turn to go completely red. At first he couldn't make eye contact with his new partner, but Reldon knew he wouldn't be able to avoid her loving gaze forever. Finally, slowly, he took a step towards her and poked out his face awkwardly like the amateur he was.

Sillida didn't seem to care how silly he looked and practically jumped on him, giving him the biggest, most heartfelt kiss she had ever given him, her hands locked behind his head, preventing him from breaking away.

"Perfect. Now I'm sure you both have a lot to talk about." Reldon grinned as he made his way to the door. By the time Bryle had managed to take in a breath, Sillida was either crying or laughing – possibly both at the same time.

Reldon closed the door behind him, took a long breath, and smiled broadly.

"That was a very kind thing for you to do," came a girl's voice from the corridor to his right. Peeking out from around the corner was a grinning Kiera. She leaned against the stone wall, rocking her weight back and forth on her heels.

He shrugged, her pleased look contagious. "I only did what needed to be done. I'm sure if I didn't do it, someone else was going to. Those two are insufferable."

"You know it is about to get much worse. Until now she has been a fawn following around her love, but in the coming days she is going to be a love-struck puppy."

Reldon nodded. "Might as well give them this time while we still can. Who knows what will happen after the storm?"

Kiera could have been nearly as joyous as Sillida had been. "You are a good friend to have, Reldon of Errum. I am certain they will not forget it."

"They had better not," he laughed as she joined him walking back up the stairs. "They should probably name their first child after me."

"Tell me, though, Reldon, you pursue their happiness like a huntress would pursue her prey, but you do not do such for your own happiness? What of Miss Ayuru? Do you love each other?"

It would have otherwise been an impertinent question, but he figured Korrainians were much more open about love. "I certainly care for her. We have talked about it. I am giving her time and space. She is dealing with a lot these days."

Kiera nodded, her violet eyes pensive for a moment before curling into an evil grin.

"Perhaps someday I will have to intervene for you!"

"That would be unwise, princess," he responded with his own evil grin, "because if it doesn't work, you would have the two most powerful people in the world upset at you."

She laughed nervously. "Perhaps patience would be best then."

They rounded the top of the stairs and strode into the foyer to the salutes of several guards. "And what about *you*, Kiera? Is a princess allowed to fancy anyone?"

Kiera guffawed. "T'would not matter whether or not I was 'allowed'. I do not have a love of my own at this moment, but it does not bother me. A huntress often needs to be alone. Besides, I had far too many suitors before…well, before you rescued me, and they were enough to make me want to be by myself for a while."

"Were they all that bad?" Reldon asked.

"Well you know about the most recent suitor – he was at least two decades older than me. And as for the others…I have had a great many suitors since I was a small child, and they were not selected because they were handsome, or brave, or intelligent. Either their fathers had land, money, power, or a combination thereof. Even those who were my age were distasteful at best."

Reldon smiled and raised an eyebrow as they made their way towards the dining room. "Come now, surely they weren't *so* bad?"

She gave him a bemusedly even look. "When I was eleven, one of them would not stop sniffing my hair, and when my father rejected him as a suitor, he did not ask me for a lock of my hair as he left – he asked me for all of it!"

Reldon couldn't help but howl in laughter.

"Sometimes Korrainian men are strange! Or perhaps it is that all men are strange. Either way, I am not looking for a man until I am ready."

"That's not what you said the other night," came a smug voice from the study which connected to the dining room. Ethilia grinned evilly, garbed in a thick golden robe with an embroidered fabric towel securing her wet hair.

"Ethilia, what is said in the drawing room is to stay in the drawing room!" Kiera cried.

"And what was said in the drawing room?" Reldon prodded.

Ethilia shrugged. "Slipped my mind."

"I don't believe you for a moment."

"Ooh how cynical of you, Master Spellsword."

The three went together into the dining room, which was attended by Randolfus, Tavia, her two children, Elly, and Alira. A pot of hot, thin soup filled with a variety of vegetables and veal presently steamed at the center of the table.

"Ah, good to see you three – I shall be back with more bowls. I do so apologize, in our short time following the repairs, this soup is all I have been able to put together," Randolfus said, scurrying back to the serving kitchen.

"It looks wonderful, dear serving man, worry not," Kiera responded kindly, taking a seat next to Alira.

Reldon sat across the table from Ethilia, who sat next to Kiera.

Tavia's daughter was working very hard at ensuring every drop of her soup made it onto the floor, while her brother sat quietly, swirling his spoon about in his bowl. Tavia rubbed her temples and gave them a courteous smile as they sat. "Are our guests Bryle and Sillida to attend?"

"For the moment they are indisposed. They should be by shortly," Reldon said as Randolfus returned to place a porcelain bowl before him.

Kiera snorted as she held back laughter, warranting a disdainful look from Ethilia. Tavia's eyes cast about curiously and one side of her lips curled into a wry grin, but she did not respond.

What did you do? Alira's thoughts came.

Only what needed to be done.

You got in the middle, didn't you?

Sillida was upset, I had no choice.

If there were such a concept as a mental sigh, she was doing it. *How did it go?*

It went great, they're a happy couple together now.

Bryle fought you, didn't he?

Every step of the way.

So you really didn't have any choice at all then. He was never going to do anything.

Sillida would have been waiting until the grave for him. Poor girl.

Tavia spoke up again after clearing her throat, "Miss Vendimar has filled me in on the situation with the Churai – do you believe we are adequately concealed here against their advances?"

Reldon nodded. "As Ethilia mentioned, they do not seem to be able to find us here for the moment unless we use magic or Phyrim to draw them to us. For now we are no easier for them to find in the blizzard than any other human would be able to."

"And if they should chance upon us, we have methods of dealing with them?" There was a hint of anxiety in her voice that was otherwise completely understandable.

"Do not worry, if another one comes to visit, Ethilia and I can dispatch of it again!" Kiera said enthusiastically.

"Speaking of which; Ethilia, I wanted to speak with you about how you had killed that Churai," Reldon said. Her icy blue eyes peered up at him, impassive. "As you know, Alira and my destiny is to destroy the Churai and rid them from this world forever. I believe your power may be the key to doing so."

She took a sip of her soup broth before responding. "Excellent. I humbly accept your designation as the new Ilewa Nuremil."

"Not quite. Now that we know that Golden Magic can be used in theory to kill them much easier than simply overpowering them, it is important that we use this to our advantage. Ethilia, how many magicians are a part of your sisterhood?"

Her eyes narrowed. "You are not funny."

"I wasn't joking. We are going to need all the help we can get."

The healer screwed up her face, peering around the table before answering, embarrassed. "There are three, all right?"

"Why is that so hard to admit?"

"Because I could not convince the others to join. It is not amongst my prouder failures."

"Who are the current members?"

"Myself, Elly, and a woman named Nuremia, the court healer for King Obrim in Atheria. In case you were wondering, and I know you all are, her name means 'masterful' in the old tongue. She is rather powerful in the ways of Golden Magic."

Reldon nodded emphatically. "Perfect. And what other Golden Magicians do you know of?"

She set her spoon down and laced her fingers together in thought. "There is obviously Miss Ayuru, who can utilize Golden Magic. Each court within the Lärimite kingdoms has its own court healer, except for the Sjard. For some obstinately outrageous reason, they do not like using Golden Magic. The court healer in Darum is a woman named Civilia Greenwood, an impossibly stubborn old Darumite magician who views everything not 'traditional' as near heresy. The court healer in Teraxella is Xari Temblence, a middle aged woman who has been blessed with the gift but has not been so blessed as to be supremely talented with it. She also did not like the idea of a sisterhood with so few members, which naturally is a self-defeating statement. I'm sure Princess Itholos could enlighten you on the Korrainian healer."

"No need to be so formal, call me Kiera!" she said for what was probably the twentieth time, not realizing that Ethilia always did it on purpose, "I knew the court healer quite well. After my mother died, she was one of the courtly women who helped raise me. She is a kind woman, very wise and in tune with the spirits' will. If you intend to find her, her name is Aila Sethatendrikos. I would so love to see her again."

Reldon, who had been jotting the names down on a small piece of parchment, paused with a snicker. "Should I even attempt to spell that family name?"

"It is not so strange in Korraine. I once knew a man whose name was Pariaki Darakenmoriisekenpilothroalinamolokolithros."

Everyone erupted in laughter, Kiera included.

"Do you know of any other Golden Magicians?" Reldon prodded.

"Occasionally rumors of more surface, but to little substance. Last year I travelled all the way to Thirin Keep on nothing more than a whisper that a girl was able to miraculously heal using naught but her bare hands. By the time I arrived several days later, no one could locate her. Though I do not doubt for a moment that other Golden Magicians walk this country, I have found it fruitless to attempt to search for them without harder evidence," Ethilia said with annoyance.

"Ethilia, could I ask of you a favor?"

She blinked slowly, the impatience in her eyes obvious.

"Would you be able to convene with the other Golden Magicians and have them meet in Nakisho? We shall need their help."

Ethilia rolled her eyes. "That is not possible. We court healers have important duties to attend to and cannot be interrupted on the whim of just anyone."

"How fortuitous it is that he is not just anyone!" Kiera poked.

She ignored the Korrainian girl. "My time is very precious to the High King. I am certain he would not want me pursuing other such endeavors whilst under his employ."

"Oh I am certain we can make arrangements with him," Tavia interjected, her words seemingly coming down from on high to Reldon's rescue, "This is, after all, for the good of the realm, is it not?"

Her eyes searched the room for something and it was difficult to read what she felt about this plan. "Why yes, Your Grace, I suppose it would be."

"Ethilia, I don't understand. I thought this was your dream, to unite all Golden Magicians together. Why are you so reluctant?" Reldon finally asked. The table went silent.

Her icy blue eyes looked like they were about to freeze him solid.

"I have travelled this path before, Xanem Nuremar. Many times. I wish this sisterhood would become a reality – it truly would be a dream come true – but I must live in reality and not expect the world to hand me what I want. I have many other duties I should be attending to once I return – my dear sister desperately needs training, and I worry for her every day in this cold."

"She could not be safer than in Nakisho Castle, sweet healer," Tavia said in gentle reassurance.

"And this is more than some far-off dream now, Ethilia," Reldon continued, "This sisterhood that you want so much could mean the difference in this war against the Churai. You've proven that they can be defeated – they have a weakness. Now, it makes sense to bring the brightest minds that the Golden Magicians have to offer together to come up with a way we can use this. And you're the brightest of them all, Ethilia. I know you can do this. You don't even have to do it for the realm – do it for yourself."

Ethilia had been watching him with a cold regard, but her chilled demeanor was beginning to melt and he could see her trying to blink tears from her eyes. She peered about the room before muttering, "But it's nothing but a stupid dream."

"It's not stupid. I will join your sisterhood, Ethilia!" Elly rang out.

It caught her by complete surprise. "You would…" she began, her red eyes wide.

"And I will too," Alira said with a broad smile, "I am part Golden Magician after all."

Reldon held out a hand. "There you have it. Your sisterhood grows by the day. It's not just a stupid dream. Maybe it's your calling in this world. And if you want it bad enough, never give up on it."

Ethilia struggled to maintain her composure, wiping the tears from her eyes and finally giving a weak smile. "All right. You win, Xanem Nuremar."

"Good. Because if you don't do this, we're all going to die," he ribbed her.

She threw a napkin across the table at him to raucous laughter. Just as she did so, Bryle and Sillida walked in the door looking very sheepish as all eyes bore holes in them.

"So, uh, what did we miss?"

Chapter XXVI

Apprehension filled his being as he stood on the outskirts of the military encampment, pockets of smoke billowing to the heavens between the larger tents and more permanent structures. Or, Kex figured, it *would* have been filling him if he could feel even an iota of his frozen body.

The blasted snow had been falling for several days and he cursed his initial lack of urgency when he decided to travel out from Nakisho all the way to the Academy City. Exactly how many days of the rippling winds and swirling clouds he needed to signify there was an oncoming storm he wasn't certain – but apparently more than his mind had taken into consideration.

Traveling had been a miserable mess, and he regretted ever leaving one of smaller towns outside of Nakisho where at least he could sit near the fire, sing songs, and drink ale. *Oh they warned me, yes they did. 'Don't be goin' out there lad! Unless you want to freeze your limbs off and drink like a dog from then on!' Rightly I should have listened.*

Yet this was somehow more important.

His black horse, which had been far more cooperative than it probably ought to have been, shook its head and grunted as he climbed back on the saddle.

"Yes, I know, I'm sorry. I dislike the snow as well. What I wouldn't give to be able to breathe fire in times like this. It's only a little further, come on now. Ha!"

Kex snapped the reigns and the horse reluctantly lurched forward into the snowbanks that used to be roads.

It would otherwise be extraordinarily difficult to find who he was looking for, but he knew her well enough to know where she would be stationed. Though it had never been her intention to actually be helpful, her assistance was greatly appreciated and desperately needed.

Their special bonding time on the way back to Lärim from Errum was anything but. There had been a firmness, a fiery disposition in how she dealt with him that he had not seen from her before, and he knew exactly what it was: she was hurt. The pain he saw in her eyes after having to yank his rear-end out of the flames by his crimson hair for the umpteenth time was about more than he could handle. Her words had stung, but he knew he deserved them. He never attempted to explain himself further for the duration of their travels, because it wouldn't have done any good. She was upset, and she had a right to be. By the time they had found themselves standing outside the Nakisho city gates, she had been fully intent on not saying a word to him as he left, but he wasn't going to let it end that way.

"Listen, I'm sorry," he had said as earnestly as his personality would allow.

She had stopped and craned her neck around at him, analyzing him with those pained eyes of hers. "I don't think you are, Kun. You won't stop this until you're dead. There are still people who worry about you, and I don't think you even care anymore."

A younger Kex would have argued, maybe even pressed his views just a bit further, but he had learned in the last ten years that many fights existed which served no purpose other than to be avoided. She would not see his perspective, and he couldn't possibly have faulted her for that.

"I do care, Kaia. If I could change the past, I would. All I can ask now is for your forgiveness. I will change, I promise."

She had shaken her head mournfully, looking at him squarely. "No. I can't. There has been a great deal of pain in our past that you are going to have to address before we can break bread together again. It is not me you should be apologizing to, for the transgressions which have hurt me pale in comparison to what you have done to the others. If they can find it in their hearts to forgive you, then maybe I will let this all go. Until then, Kun...Just...don't come back."

It had been a spear to the heart, but he knew much more was coming if he was to face the others again.

"Where can I find them?"

"The wasteland of fire and steel that used to be the Academy City grounds. Either you will find peace or more pain...but then you're used to that by now."

Her words still knocked around in his empty skull as if he needed further reminder why he was out in this abysmal weather travelling into a battleground.

All of the fighting seemed to have stopped for the duration of the storm. The colossal towers of smoke which had risen from the Academy City itself had long since drifted into the gray sky, and a series of damaged structures remained to mar the skyline. The central spire had great holes in many places, and the dormitories had been blackened by severe flames. Once upon a time there had been seas of green grass surrounding the Academy City and the small merchant city which encompassed it, but what wasn't completely encased in snow at this point was rendered a no-man's-land filled with charred craters. Somewhere around a half-mile outside of the city proper was the military encampment which housed the legions of rebel magicians who saw no recourse from Brina's old policies than to fight their sisters to the death.

And here everyone thought for a gleaming moment that the Kuru invasion would bring an end to the civil war. All it did was give them a common enemy for a time, a worthless truce that only lasted long enough to expel the invaders before getting at each other's throats again.

As much as he wished he would regret the services he had rendered under her employment, he still could not bring himself to care. The money had been good, and the job kept him from further forms of self-harm or worse at the hands of the Churai. Brina had been a cold, megalomaniacal witch and her ultimate goal was one wheel short of a carriage as far as Kex was concerned, but there was a sort of order about her that he appreciated. He was always paid on time. The missions were always clearly defined. And for that, as a client, he didn't mind her terribly. *It's the fact that on a moral level she didn't scare the hell out of me is what actually scares the hell out of me.*

The camp was large enough that he knew searching it would take days, not to mention if any of them caught wind of who he was, they would roast him over a spit. Instead he decided to use a technique which they had utilized since their days adventuring together.

Kex had no Ilewa, but as he learned early on, the ability to speak mind-to-mind was not limited to strictly Ilewa bonds. Any two beings who possessed Phyrim or magic could communicate telepathically, but it was a great deal weaker and harder to maintain. In fact, while testing its capabilities as a late teen, he discovered that the link became completely broken at around two-hundred yards of distance between the two involved. What was more important was that a link could not be created unless within just a few feet of each other initially.

Since their link had been established many years ago, he did not need to stand directly before her in order to communicate with her – Kex only needed to be within two-hundred yards.

Dismounting from his horse behind one of the tents furthest from the command building, he swallowed hard before projecting his thoughts outward in that old unused channel.

Celia. Are you here? It's me, Kunarus. Please come and speak to me.

Snow and wind whipped his face. Seconds passed, followed by minutes.

He shivered terribly and breathed hard into his hands.

Either she wasn't in range, or she wasn't going to answer.

Kex slipped onto his belly to lift the bottom edge of the tent's Phyrim-reinforced fabric, and to his surprise no one was inside. *At least while my hood is up, no one should know immediately who I am.*

It was a tight squeeze, but he managed to slip in between the steel poles holding the fabric in place and rolled to a standing position. It wasn't as warm as he would otherwise have liked, but there was no snow immediately crushing him so that was definitely a plus.

A small, cold fire pit rested in the center of the tent, and he fished out his flint and steel to get it going again. After a few *clicks* it was at least producing enough heat so he wouldn't lose his limbs and have to drink like a dog.

Movement.

The flap of the tent opened, and he had no time to react.

A woman entered, and as soon as her gorgeous blue eyes locked on his, he knew it was her. She was so short, by comparison of course, and only a couple of worry lines on her forehead marked the years that had passed since they last spoke.

"Celia!"

She watched him for a moment, a sense of disbelief coming over her. Slowly she lowered her hood and her raven hair came free. "Kunarus? Is it really you?"

He did the same in kind, the firelight revealing his stark red hair and ugly scar. "It's me, Celia. It's been a while. Keeping warm?"

Kex was uncertain exactly what he saw in her eyes, but he was pretty certain it wasn't awe or joy.

"Is that all you have to say, Kun?" she asked, tears reflecting the flickering firelight, "After all of this time…After everything…"

"I'm here to say I'm sorry, Clouds."

She thrust a finger out angrily. "Don't you use that name. That's what Kunarus used to call me. The kind, gentle Kunarus, the one who wanted to help people and spend every waking moment with his friends. The Kunarus I knew stood for something."

"It's still me – and I haven't changed as much as you think I have."

"No." She shook her head. "All I see in front of me is Kex the Ravager."

"Will you please listen to me? I'm trying to tell you that I would make amends, and whether you forgive me or not is up to you, but I will be heard. Please, at least give me a chance to clear the air?"

"To wipe the slate clean, you mean. I don't think that is going to happen, Kun. You abandoned us, and abandoned everything that meant anything to you. And for what, glory? Coin?"

"For *meaning*," he emphasized, "I did what I did because I could see what we were doing was nothing but bronze pieces compared to what was happening out west, not to mention the impossible amount of corruption bleeding from Huerogrand. I loved our lives. I loved all three of you with all my heart, but there was a niggling problem weighing on me everywhere we went. Especially in Teraxella, everyone knew someone who was killed after some Kuru incursion or a Churai slaughter, and no amount of errand-running was going to fix that."

"Is that how you saw it? We were doing nothing but errand-running?"

"What I'm trying to say is that we did a lot of good helping people, but the real fight to help the most people was going on near that damned wall, and no matter how delicately or forcefully I put it, no one would even come part-way to trying to understand."

The wind gusted overhead and the tent trembled.

"We were little more than *children* at the time, Kun! We may have had adult bodies but we weren't ready for open warfare, and the academy knew it better than we did! There were *reasons* we couldn't simply ride out onto the battlefield, magic ablaze – namely among them that we would have been killed!"

Kex crossed his arms. "And yet they flipped that exact policy the moment the Nurems were spotted, in which case they were far too eager to dispatch children who were still eating their own mucus."

"That's why I'm here, Kun," she pointed downward, "I disagreed with it then and I disagree with it now. The Academy under Brina was a tyranny. And word has reached our ears of your testimony at the Nurems' trial. You were her lapdog. *Why?*"

He threw out his hands. "Because I was desperate! After years of fighting, I had *nothing* to show for it. Everyone likes to tell you on the front lines that you're a hero – that you're doing it for all the right reasons, but that doesn't put food in your belly or pay for the medicine to heal your damaged body. Taraxella can scarcely pay its own troops, much less some Ravager who wanders into the no-man's-land with a fire in his heart but mud for brains. After I retired from the war to catch my breath, I realized there was nothing to come back to. Nothing at all. My friends hated me, my peers avoided me, and I was a wanted man for being a Ravager. I gasped for whatever air I could get."

"But you did all of that to yourself!" she cried, "We *begged* you not to go. We told you this was only going to lead to more pain and sadness, but you wouldn't listen. All you cared about at the time-"

The flap to the tent flew aside once more, and both Celia and Kex flinched. In stepped a man, nearly as tall as Kex, with scruffy hair atop a well-sculpted head attached to a powerful physique. His light-blue eyes gave away nothing but fury as he saw who stood before him. The sturdy chin gave away who it was.

"Dantus, I-"

He hadn't even gotten out the second word, and his former friend had already torn his hammer from the Infinity Scabbard and was on him.

Ripping his own hand-and-a-half sword from its holding, he shifted his stance just in time so that the hammer glanced off of his blade.

"Stop it! Dantus, stop!" Celia pleaded.

Dantus sent a blow at Kex's face with a mailed gauntlet, and Kex wasn't able to catch it in time before the metal tore at his lip and chin. By pure instinctual reaction, he wrapped his own arm around Dantus's to restrain him and jammed the pommel of his sword against his forehead.

It had the desired effect, as Dantus staggered backwards holding his head and groaning. Celia leapt in between them with her arms outstretched.

"That's enough, both of you!"

"You're a traitor!" Dantus shouted in his lion's voice.

"I have betrayed no one." Kex wiped the blood off of his lip which was now dripping down his front. "Except for myself."

"You are a man without convictions. You are nothing more than a hedonistic pig who spews lies and bows before demons so that they might toss you coin! You are pathetic!" He continued to scream.

"I did not come here to fight with you, Dantus. I know you are both upset with me and I don't know if I would be able to forgive me either. I had to at least try to make amends."

"We are done with you. You can go back to whatever hole you crawled out of," Dantus cursed.

"That's enough," Celia snapped at him, before turning back to Kex, "Kun, we worried about you for a long time – years even. We hoped against all hope that you would come back and see the error of what you had done, but you never did. We thought you had died. For a good long time we mourned, but it wasn't a complete mourning – we had no body, no news, no nothing. Your memory was blessed and painful to us. And then we heard who you had consorted with, and the terrible deeds you had had a part in, and every ounce of that sorrow we held in our breasts turned to hurt and shortly to anger."

She paused to brush the streams of liquid sadness from her cheeks.

"It's only been months since that, Kun. *Months.* We're not ready to reconcile yet, and right now I don't know if we ever will be."

Kex could only stare back at her, his words finally having failed him.

"You need to go. Maybe someday we will find you. Until then...just go."

He stared at her for a good long while as his heart gradually broke in two. It had been too early, the wound was still fresh. Nothing he said would make any difference now.

With nothing but a slow nod, he left the tent. He never remembered the cold, nor the first hour or so of riding. Everything was a blur, and all he ever remembered from that point forward was his solution.

Chapter XXVII

The storm was finally starting to let up.

Eight days after the first snowflakes fell, the wind gradually subsided, transitioning from a deafening howl to intermittent swirls of activity. Snow continued to fall throughout the day, but instead of whipping projectiles of ice, they more peacefully drifted to the immense mounds below.

Still, the storm's change of heart was no less troubling in regards to the amount of snow that was still piling up. In fact, some of the gardens were covered in at least three or four feet of snow, and in some places much more. By the time the biting cold had been muzzled for the season, all of the young inhabitants of the illustrious estate ventured outside to survey the damage and found the landscape completely altered. Entire trees had been buried, resembling icy stalagmites jutting to the sky with nary a branch to be seen. Babbling brooks, flower gardens, and any last remnants of another season were entirely erased. The road was simply impassable for the time being, as no horse was going to be willing to trudge through nearly four feet of snow. The sun had yet to show its much-needed brilliance and warmth, but the previously opaque sheet of gray snow clouds was starting to thin out and occasional speckles of light would flicker through for a fleeting second.

"It looks like a wonderland!" Elly shouted, prancing about in the courtyard, which was currently the only part of the estate that had been shoveled.

"What's so wondrous about all this snow?" Bryle said.

"Nature is very powerful. It is incredible to look on its work," Kiera marveled.

"All of that 'work' is currently impeding our path back to civilization," Ethilia said sourly.

"Ha!" Kiera responded with a scoff, "Civilization. I'll stay right here."

"In the snow? You Korrainians are a special breed," Bryle quipped.

She giggled in return. "Wait until you meet the Sjard. They are more obsessed with snow than the Spirit of Nature is."

"I have met them," Alira piped in, "They are indeed quite loving of snow, but they have put it to such good use! Their streets are made of ice and their carriages have blades underneath them. Like a sledge!"

"Sounds like fun. Just be careful where you put your toes." Bryle laughed.

"You had to say it, didn't you?" Ethilia asked, completely deadpan, "I believe you are doing your best to make the Golden Magician wriggle."

"How can I not when you make it so fun, Ethilia?"

It had escaped no one's notice that Sillida had been more or less attached to Bryle the last day or so. They were always holding hands and she was constantly watching him for his reaction to everything. If not for the brimming smile on her face, it would have seemed almost slightly neurotic by Reldon's reckoning. Still, it brought him a sense of pride at what he had helped happen, even if it was making Bryle uncomfortable. *Especially* if was making him uncomfortable. *The only one wriggling here is you, my friend, and it is hilarious to watch.*

"So what is to be our next move, everyone?" Reldon asked the question that likely no one had considered for days. "The storm will go away soon, and we will be left with many decisions to make."

There was a silence that came over the group as everyone considered their options, or perhaps the best way to reveal their path.

"Naturally I always have a plan," Ethilia winked, "Even if it wasn't my idea. I shall head to Nakisho to see my dear sister and to write a variety of silver-tongued letters, and from there to Atheria. The sisterhood shall expand in the coming months, you have my word as a Vendimar."

"Sillida and I haven't decided yet," Bryle said, "But we wish to help you in your fight. Any way we can." He tapped the hilt of his sword. "If you need me to carve my initials into some Kuru, just point me to them."

Ethilia laughed. "And what would those initials be, the letter 'B'? Oh how memorable."

"S & B," Sillida said with a shy smile.

Kiera cooed and pinched her cheek. "You are far too adorable for my human heart, young dove."

"Our plans may rest on yours, Reldon," Bryle said, "Including Elly. So I guess the question is, what are *you* going to do next?"

"We haven't discussed it very-" Alira started to say before Reldon cut in.

"We are going to search for Grandma." There was authority in his voice. "As much as we would love to be doing more for the realm, there are many enemies we cannot best yet, even with our power. Out there exists some kind of power or knowledge which could help us defeat the Churai once and for all, and we are going to search for it."

Reldon, we hadn't decided on this, her voice chimed.

"What kind of power? And how do you know? What does it have to do with Grandma?" Bryle asked.

"I know not what power it is. It could be anything. And for the moment I cannot answer all of your questions, I will need you to trust that I know what I know for a reason. And I will need you especially to trust me, Bryle, because where Alira, Elly, and I are going, you cannot follow."

Bryle looked to have been slapped in the face. "What are you talking about?"

"It will be far too dangerous, Bryle. This may not involve fighting Kuru or some well-known enemy with flesh, blood, a shield and sword. It could mean facing depths of magic only Alira and I can handle. I don't want you to get hurt. You or Sillida."

"This is exactly what you said in Nakisho, before going off to the kingdoms, Reldon. When are you going to starting trusting *us*? We're not helpless children, we can help you!"

"Bryle, when it comes to the magic I'm talking about, you *are* helpless children."

"Oh so that's it then. Times got tough and Reldon sent us home. Thanks, mate. I appreciate the confidence."

With that he stormed back into the house with Sillida in tow. Every eye looked back at Reldon.

"I do not understand, Reldon. Does this mean that I may not join you either?" Kiera asked.

Reldon shook his head mournfully. "I don't want you to get hurt either, Kiera."

There was a sadness in her eyes, reflected back at him before she cast the look towards Ethilia, who seemed impassive.

"Don't look to me for help, he's right you know. You and Bryle can't possibly expect to walk into a battle with a magician or Spellsword and expect to leave with all of your limbs and your wits. Not without a fair bit of luck. It is my opinion that despite the seeming callousness of his words, he is being as responsible with your lives as one can be. Kiera, you simply should not be putting yourself into such unneeded danger, and no amount of big violet eyes are going to change that."

"But what of the Churai we fought?" Kiera said in quieter voice, "We fought it together. And Reldon, if you do not want me to come with you, then where ought I go? I cannot go back to Korraine!"

"Kiera, that fight with the Churai was complete dumb luck," Reldon responded, "Even the most powerful magicians and Spellswords die fighting those damn creatures. Lendir was one of them. It would be much safer for you to put your skills to better use protecting someone else for a time."

"Like who, Reldon? Who would I walk with?"

Before Reldon could say anything, Alira spoke up. "I think it would be a good idea to go with Ethilia."

They both stared back at her.

Ethilia spoke first. "You can't be serious."

Alira met her gaze with a determined smile. "You two do work so well together after all. And I think it would be good for the both of you." Her last few words were so pointed she could have cut through armor with them.

For the moment, Kiera looked positively delighted. Her beaming countenance gave Ethilia obvious consternation.

The baffled healer clasped Alira's hand and led her just a few yards away and spoke in a loudly forced whisper.

"My Lady, she is Korrainian! She is going to be eaten alive in the courts of southern Lärim! I've seen diplomats tarred and feathered in western Atheria for being 'too Korrainian'. Besides, I really must protest – I have much work that needs to be attended to and I cannot hope to see to it all with her...being herself," she said, peering back at Kiera. She waved happily in return.

"This is a test for you," Alira started with some authority in her voice, "We talked about how the world can only change when people decide to say no to the old ways. Now is your chance. She is a princess of Korraine, but no one has to know that."

"Her accent will give her away. There will be no hiding her origins."

"Then I trust you will protect her."

It was not a suggestion. Reldon knew that much.

Ethilia screwed up her face and stood up straight, resigned, letting a visible puff of breath from her lips.

"You know, My Lady, if you were anyone but your illustrious self I would tell them to...well, suffice to say I only do this for you."

"That is all I ask. She will be a good friend." Alira gave her a warm smile as they walked back.

Ethilia raised her voice conclusively. "I will go ease the tension with Bryle. If he should be so gentlemanly as to speak with a lady such as I. My Lady. My Lord."

Her shoes tapped as she stepped up each stone stair, and Kiera decided to follow her inside.

Reldon stood alone with Alira, and he could tell by the look she was giving him that this was not about to be an enjoyable conversation.

Reldon, we never talked about this fully. When did we decide we were going after this 'Secret' of yours?

There is little else we can do now, Alira. This is the only path that has been laid before us which may lead to an advantage over the Churai.

How can you know that? Her mind's voice turned agitated as she stomped her foot. *If you really believed this was the only way, then why did you send Ethilia to gather all of the Golden Magicians?*

He set his jaw. *In case this doesn't work. I'm not blind, Alira. I don't know what could be waiting for us on the other end of this tunnel, and you could be right – we might come away with nothing, or worse. I want to be ready in all cases if we can, including the possibility of failure.*

Reldon knew that when Alira got frustrated or upset, her eyes would tear up and each word would become more and more emotional, and this time was no exception.

This could be nothing but chasing ghosts! You're the only person who has spoken with this illusion of Tycheronius and I don't know whether to believe him or not. It could be nonsense for all we know.

He mentioned Grandma by name. And Sterling. It can't possibly be a coincidence.

He...mentioned Sterling as well?

Reldon nodded. *There's no way this is nothing. Or at least it wasn't nothing when he and his Ilewa were alive. Whatever this 'Secret' is, it has persisted for hundreds of years and they are trying to warn us about it. Grandma is the only person who can unlock the Secret. So we have to find her. You were the last among us to speak with her. Did she say anything about where she was going?*

Alira wiped her eyes with the back of her hand. *She was going to Thundercrest Mountain to save Sera. Lynad was with her. I thought I told you about it already.*

Reldon ran a hand through his hair. *And that was the last time anyone spoke with her. That was a very long time ago. She couldn't still be there. Could she?*

She shrugged, putting her chilled hands into the pockets of her longcoat. *Maybe if Sterling knows Grandma, he could help us find her.*

But we would then have to face the problem of finding him. He has been gone since the storm started.

We might have an easier time finding Lynad.

If he wants to be found. After what happened with Sera I wouldn't be surprised if he finally decided to stay at home with her for good.

Alira shivered. "Brr! We can come up with a plan later. Could we go back indoors?"

Reldon nodded, following her towards the giant doors. He grabbed her arm gently, prompting her to pause.

"It's not nothing, Alira. I promise."

Her eyes flitted about for a second before settling on him again. "I believe you, Reldon. But please, don't make decisions for us both again without asking me."

As the otherwise milder day progressed, messengers arrived every few hours, the line of communication finally having been opened long enough to bring letters from Nakisho. Each messenger brought a sack filled with letters, and they formed a mountain of parchment on the dining hall table after just two deliveries. The serving men worked tirelessly to sort through each one, tearing open and inspecting those without specific addressees, while delivering those with.

Most of the letters were for Tavia, but there were some which had no other purpose than to keep everyone informed of the goings-on around Lärim and Errum. Everyone but Bryle and Sillida sat about the table, listening to the reports and helping in any way they could.

"Reports of further Kuru incursions from the remnants of the larger force continue to plague a few countryside estates clustered around Opterus, but extending as far east as Deficinas and Nevo-Kulan. However, these small raiding parties have proved little more than a nuisance for the personal forces of these estates, and should not persist," Tavia read in an almost narrative voice.

"They shouldn't be too much trouble for your family, will they Ethilia?" Alira asked.

Ethilia scoffed with an evil grin. "Of course not. My family has the most fortified house and the largest private force outside of Nakisho. They will hardly notice a difference."

Tavia was handed another letter and she scanned it over before reading.

"Little word has been received from our reclusive brothers to the north, but a Nakisho diplomat returning from The Sjard following the Kuru invasion has reported the kingdom is in a state of mourning after the death of their leader, the High Chieftain Duren Hansjadden and the disappearance of his niece, the well-respected Thyra Hansjadden. Following the attack, it is difficult to estimate the losses, but at least one-third of the population of Tamak was eradicated, including a majority of their warriors and magicians. Damage to the city was incalculable. The High King has deemed it necessary to send several battalions north to ensure The Sjard are not in further danger should another invasion force emerge from the northern sea."

She flipped over the letter and continued.

"It is as of yet unclear how the Kuru have managed, upon two occasions, to mount large scale attacks using bodies of water as methods of travel without the use of naval vessels. Earlier this year, King Dunan of Errum reported a similar tactic must have been employed for the Kuru army to have been able to seemingly circumvent the northwestern Nuru defenses and to begin a siege of Freiad Castle. Magicians, Spellswords, and men of science alike are baffled at how these troop movements could have taken place. Clamor in Naiwa-ki-Shokassen during the storm has been to counter-attack against the Kuru, but the High King urged caution at a time when Lärim's foes do not appear to be playing this game of strategy by the same rules as the rest of civilized society."

"We already knew that last bit," Kiera pointed out.

"Thyra is still missing," Alira said sadly, "When I last saw her, Elly and I were being spirited away from the battle and she told me she was going to return and fight. I…begged her not to go back. I knew the fight was lost. If she's dead, then…"

"Take heart, my dear, the report only presumes her dead," Tavia clarified in a calm manner, "Not a great many weeks have passed since that battle, and the storm has undoubtedly complicated searches. She is likely in hiding to wait out the nastiest of the elements."

Alira nodded with a weak smile. "I hope Sveti is all right too."

Tavia sifted through several more letters, setting a few aside for later consumption. Her attention settled on one and she read it aloud.

"Troop movements have been confirmed on the Errum mainland – a host estimated to consist of around 25,000 able-bodied men and magicians have taken to the fields of the West Errum Plains some six days ago. It is presumed by our tacticians that King Garen has taken the storm in the north as a timely opportunity to move his forces into place at one or several castles in the northwestern quarter of Errum. It is our esteemed opinion that a full-scale Nuru invasion, the likes of which has not been seen in many generations, is decidedly inevitable."

An uncomfortable pause ensued as the gravity of the situation set in.

"Dear spirits, he is actually going to do it," Kiera breathed.

Reldon shook his head in disbelief. "He is really going to invade them. By himself."

"And 25,000 others, to be fair," Ethilia said.

"But no allies, "Alira interjected, "Lärim will not join him, and neither will the Academy City."

"There is even the question as to how much Huerogrand will help," Reldon added.

Kiera stood and leaned against her chair, clenching her fingers and releasing them methodically. "Surely he must know this is folly. The wall is not something to be underestimated, and the Kuru have many men."

"But perhaps they are weakened after their last failed invasion? Maybe now is the best time for King Garen to take to the field, if he cannot be dissuaded," Tavia said.

Reldon tapped his fingers on the table. "If only we had convinced anyone to join, this campaign wouldn't be destined to failure."

"There is no changing that now," Alira said firmly and without consternation, "Only our next path matters."

A serving man handed Kiera a letter and she accepted it with mild confusion. Tearing it open, her eyes viciously tore into its contents when she read the sender's name at the top.

The room went into silent anticipation.

When she finally finished, her violet eyes peered off into the distance, her mind clearly racing.

"What is it, Kiera? Is everything all right?" Alira asked.

She rotated her gaze to look at Alira, rife with conflict. "I have a brother."

No one was certain how to respond, and she continued.

"My father, the King of Korraine, has sired a child with that...that..." She used a Korrainian word that made Tavia's eyes go wide. "This is a kindly letter informing me of how much they wish I would return to see my new half-brother, and also to politely let me know I no longer have any claim to the Korrainian throne. How nice of them to spare the paper to write two letters."

"But he can't…he can't do that! You are his daughter, you will always have a claim to the throne," Reldon asserted.

"That is exactly why. I am his *daughter.* He has a son now, who places higher than I do on the chart of succession. Besides, it would not matter anyway." She pointed at a dark seal on the bottom of the letter. "He has passed a new law declaring children produced from his former marriage illegitimate. As of Korrainian law…I am…I am a bastard now."

Her head sunk to the table with wracking sobs. Her fist closed tightly around the letter, crumpling it and slamming it on the table. Alira hastened to stand so she might comfort the girl, but it was too late.

Kiera shrieked in anger, threw the letter in the fireplace with enough force that she stumbled, and dashed out of the dining hall in a complete hail of bitter tears.

Tavia stood, signaling everyone else to stand. "I shall see to her. Perhaps it would be best if the remainder of the letter opening resumed…in private."

Reldon sat alone in the brandy room, or the parlor as the serving men called it, a roaring fire before him and several thousand thoughts at once threatening to rob him of his very sanity.

If this time away from society in an illustrious mansion was intended to be a time where we could rest, regain our bearings, and allow the stresses of the world to leave us for a time…I think we may have been sent away to the wrong mansion.

He fully expected that Bryle would not be joining him for their nightly chat over a full glass of brandy (which incidentally never emptied), but to his complete surprise, the door to the parlor creaked open after only about ten minutes.

Reldon stood, looking back at the door. "Bryle?"

His sandy-haired, freckled friend raised a hand meekly. "Good evening, sir Reldon. Do you mind if…I uh….join you?"

"Not at all, please," Reldon said, giving a gentle kick to Bryle's chair.

The tension that he feared would follow Bryle around didn't seem to exist. It was like nothing had happened at all – the lad even seemed jovial.

"Am I to pour my *own glass of brandy?*" he asked in faux incredulity.

Reldon sunk back into his plush, high-backed red velvet chair with a grin. "You *did* show up late, after all. The serving men can't be hanging about all night."

Liquid poured from behind him, followed by a *thunk* as the stopper was placed back on top of the crystal decanter. Bryle slid into his chair, setting his amber-liquid-filled glass aside.

"Reldon, I owe you an apology."

"No you don't, Bryle, stop it."

"Yes I do, just listen, mate. I know you said what you said for good reasons. Sometimes when I want to help, I don't think about how dangerous it could be. You're looking out for what's best for us – Sillida and I, and I appreciate it. Really, I do. You want to protect her as much as I do, and I guess I wasn't thinking about that earlier. So I'm sorry."

Reldon waved a hand. "Don't worry about it. I just want to make sure you're both safe. Alira, Elly, and I have a vicious road ahead of us. You know how these things go…Sometimes all we can do is hope we come back from them."

"I didn't mean to make the decision harder. I know everything has been a bit tense in this house lately."

He snickered. "You can say that again. There have just been so many *emotions* lately. It tires you to madness."

Bryle's evil grin returned as she gave an exaggerated shrug. "I suppose that's what we get for travelling around with so many women. They're inconsolable, the whole lot of them!"

Reldon laughed. "I'll never know what Sillida sees in you."

"Same, mate. Same."

"I'm surprised how much your attitude towards her has changed in such a short time," Reldon appraised him with a prying grin of his own.

Bryle's face went momentarily red as he gave a shy smile. "I dunno, yesterday I simply wasn't sure - about anything really, especially her. But spending time with her…looking into those big dark eyes up close…"

"Dear spirits, Bryle, you really have softened. Now you're being poetic. You're going to make me sick."

"Shut it, I know you feel the same about Alira. When they give you that warm smile and they get those little creases near their lips when they're truly happy…I swear I could die, Reldon."

"I haven't had nearly enough brandy to entertain this amount of talk of romance," he said, lifting his glass.

"You 'ent going to drink that and you know it."

Reldon shrugged absently. "Maybe I will. Maybe you should too. This might be one of the last nights we ever spend in our very own brandy room, and if this…stuff…is truly the best of its kind, then maybe someday we will regret not drinking it."

Bryle was quiet, eyeing his glass like a fish watches its prey before snatching it up. "All right, I'll try. But only if you do. And not a small sip, you have to take a gulp."

"Ready when you are."

They both took a simultaneous gulp of the brandy, and they both ended up choking on it as it went down, spilling a fair amount onto the floor. It came as a surprise to neither one of them that the brandy had, in fact, not changed since they attempted to consume it previously, and it still had the taste and affectation similar to that of liquid fire. Bryle had even leapt to his feet, hopping about as it scorched him all the way down.

"Ah, I can't feel my throat!" Bryle croaked. "How can anyone drink this?"

Reldon's reaction hadn't been quite so violent, but as soon as he had swallowed he knew he probably made a mistake. Brandy, and by proxy any other spirits he presumed, would never have the same thirst-quenching effect that water or other kinder drinks might possess, choosing rather to be nothing more than a harsh, sizzling punch in the throat followed by settling into a pit of magma in his chest.

He coughed and his eyes watered. Without much hesitation he set the glass aside.

"I think I will take it slower next time," Reldon laughed again.

Bryle returned to his seat, practically in stitches from the stupidity they had partaken in.

Several deep breaths later, Reldon had largely recovered enough to speak again.

"So what is to be your plan then once we leave the house? Are you and Sillida going to return to life in Nakisho?"

That question caused a change in demeanor in his old friend's face. He looked into the fire as he answered.

"You heard of that letter today about King Garen's invasion, right?"

He nodded in response. "What of it?"

"Sillida and I…we're going to help out. We're going to fight the Kuru."

"What? How are you going to do that? You're only fifteen, the both of you!"

"We know that. But we are not about to go back to living a simple life in Nakisho while you fight Churai and our countrymen battle Kuru to the death. There *must* be somewhere we can help fight. Even if it means attacking from Lärim to…create a distraction or some such plan."

"I understand where you're coming from, Bryle, but did we not just make this decision today to keep you and Sillida *out* of danger? How does this plan make sense if you're wanting to dive into the fray again?"

Bryle cradled his glass, his eyes reflecting firelight in a way that supported the ferocity of his convictions. "Because they're not the same dangers. You were right to keep us out of your fight. Every man has his fight, and yours is too much for us. But Kuru are flesh and blood - people like you and me. The enemy always makes sense to me when you can put a blade in them. I leave the more complicated ones for you and Alira."

"You don't know that you won't run into a Churai. Or a magician or Spellsword."

"I took down Detryn didn't I?"

"You keep bringing that up, but I don't think your next battle will be quite so easy."

"It doesn't matter, don't you see, Reldon? If the world is coming to an end, I want to fight so that there might be a home afterwards for Sillida and I to someday live in. I could go running scared back to Nakisho or even back to Errum, but if we don't put a stop to the Kuru soon, there might not be a home left to go back to. That's why we have to fight. And because I don't know if I could live with myself if something happened to any of you while I was shoveling snow for silver back in Nakisho."

He had made up his mind. *I have already tried once to keep him and Sillida out of further danger, but he is determined to live by the sword. And I suppose if this is a compromise with him…letting him fight the enemy he knows rather than the one he doesn't might just have to do for now.*

"All right," Reldon said with finality.

"'All right'? That's it? You're good with it?"

"I wish I weren't, but it is your decision, Bryle, and Sillida's of course. All I might hope is that you are both ready for what you're planning to do, and I wish you nothing but victory."

Reldon leaned in and offered his forearm. Bryle took it with a tight grin.

"Be careful, mate, and be sure to come back to us. It's a promise."

Bryle nodded happily, reaching over to pick up his glass and raising it.

"For Errum."

Chapter XXVIII

He could only have imagined how it must have scared them.

Day after day, for two weeks, the seasonal blizzards crushed morale and roofs alike, leaving the defending Kuru in a poor state of spirit as they attempted to rebuild and recuperate. Those on the walls had it worst as there was little to protect them from nature's onslaught. Dozens of men had been carted down from their sentry positions, frozen in a meaningless death, only to be replaced by others who would meet the same fate days later. Their jobs meant little as they did everything they could to stay warm. Fires blazed along the bastions, throwing caution to the frigid wind as to revealing their numbers.

The strongest among them languished as such for nearly a week, and when the snows finally abated, their jubilation had been unbridled. They would live to see another season, or so they thought.

On the morning following the ceasing of the snowfall, the sentries had finally taken a cursory look eighty feet down to assess how much snow had actually fallen.

Oh, and they saw snow. But as the sleep faded from their eyes, they saw much more.

King Garen's force had rested during the day at Bythas Castle, and once evening fell, they stole into the silent, cold night with nary a torch aloft, each captain instructed to keep their men quiet.

It had been a precaution that he probably hadn't needed in light of the shoddy defenses the Kuru kept during the storm, but the Nuru king always preferred to leave nothing to fate.

By the time the sentries had noticed, soiled themselves, and promptly began their shrieking, the trebuchets had loosed two dozen flaming boulders simultaneously. Mountains of dust and debris filled the sky, rubble joined boulders as parts of external wall crumbled away. It took until after the third volley of hail-fire that the Kuru finally sounded the alarm, blowing their horns shrilly.

For two hours the bombardment proceeded, and still no Kuru reinforcements emerged onto the walls to assist in repelling the Nuru force.

King Garen had snickered to himself. *They truly did not expect a single soul to be out during the storm.*

Ranks of men eventually piled onto the top ramparts, frantically dipping their arrows in oil and lighting them. Garen could tell there was no formation, no discipline to the way they were defending. It was desperation.

He lifted his hand and his counterattack sounded off. Thirty eight ballistae released their payloads with a brief *woosh* and the creak of massive wooden timbers. Eight-foot long ballista bolts hurdled through the sky in their dozens, having trained their aim towards the crenellations. Many flew high or wide of their mark, smashing against the wall or sailing high over the top, but many found their mark. Before the stunned Kuru archers could release a volley of their own, they were skewered on the spot, unable to even let out a scream.

One of Garen's generals issued the order for the archers to step forward in front of the ballistae, and they nocked arrows with a clean efficiency, not bothering to waste time with lighting them aflame. It would have no additional effect anyway.

Finally the Kuru were able to fire a few ragged shots into the air, but few found a target.

At a shout, the legion of Nuru archers raised their bows in unison, responding with a thunderous shout of their own.

At a nod from Garen, the general lowered his arm and they released a terrible rain of arrows, blotting out the sky for a long moment. There was no sound for a few seconds after the ripple of *plunks* from the bows sounded off. However, if the Kuru hadn't had a chance to scream before, they were certainly doing it now.

From the ground it was impossible to assess the damage the volley had caused, but it was obvious to all present that the Kuru had mounted a haphazard defense of archers in the first place, and after the storm of arrows landed, none lined up at the ramparts again.

Either they are scared or they are dead. It makes no difference to me.

The trebuchets continued to pound for several hours. Occasionally another ragged force would attempt to man the walls, but were slain in short order. It was an understatement to say the Kuru were not prepared for this attack. *Their strongest forces are doubtlessly occupied by the Lärimites to the northeast. It could take them a day or so to reach us, and by then we will be through.*

Volley after volley pounded the stones of the massive wall into a mess of rubble, eventually tearing down enough of its foundations that a section of the upper wall collapsed in upon itself, toppling over the rubble pile. Roars of righteous fury urged the foot soldiers onward, and they rushed the gap with zeal and spear.

Only a few hundred terrified soldiers stood to defend the bottleneck and were cut down in short order, many choosing to rout instead.

Garen snapped his horse's reigns. "After them! You lot, with me!"

His cavalry regiment responded, reaching a gallop behind him within seconds. Climbing over the rubble with the horses was a challenge, but only delayed their charge for a time. There was no way their tiny Kuru legs would carry them far enough to escape Garen's judgment.

Hooves pounded the grass as they reached terra firma, closing the distance so quickly the fleeing soldiers did not know how to respond.

Garen's sword rang out before hewing limbs from bodies. It was exhilarating work. *None may stand before the new Nuru Empire.*

And none did once he returned to his generals.

"Get the men into marching position beyond the wall. I want them moving within the hour. We will strike hard and we will strike swiftly. I will not give them the chance to mobilize."

One of the older generals, a count by the name of Balon, spoke up. "Your Grace, if you wish us to slay the routing troops, you need not engage them yourself – we can issue the orders to the cavalry and they shall do your bidding."

"It needed to be done quickly. They will not be allowed to return to their cities and forts to report our size, our position, and our heading."

"That is well understood, Your Grace," Ser Erethar responded. He was one of the Knights in Remdas-Kuwis, a trainer, a military genius, and quite the contrarian sometimes. *He's one of those Knights that act as guardians for Spellswords and magicians. The magical type. That man could slay each and every one of these generals without blinking an eye.* "However, it is your safety we are concerned about."

"Speak frankly, Erethar. Am I not a knight, strong as any?"

"Absolutely, Your Grace, but you are also a man just as we all are. A stray arrow could fell you, just as it could fell me. Errum needs its king, and your men need its leader."

The Knight leaned forward and spoke quieter into Garen's ear.

"Your Grace, you have no heir. Should anything happen to you, your kingdom would be in chaos. Surely you know this."

Garen put a gauntlet against Erethar's breastplate and pushed him aside as he urged his horse forward.

"This does not concern me. Glory awaits Errum. Death awaits Kuru."

Their concern had been noted, but he would not be prattled at like a mewling kitten. *If I should die in this war, it will be a death in service of my country. A dignified death that any Nuru should be grateful to have. I will raise Errum from the smoldering coals of servitude to the bonfire of power and influence if it kills me.*

Hours passed and the army marched in perfect unison.

Green banners flew high. The men chanted and sang war songs. Kuru villages fell and were looted in short order. It was all so perfect.

It was only once the snow grew far too deep that their progress was finally impeded. Scouts fanned out and scoured the Kuru countryside as the army settled in for the evening. Garen fully expected a counter-attack during the night and instructed large watches in shifts, not to mention the leagues of silent horseman searching the night in plain clothes for any sign of movement.

And yet after a night of baleful sleep, no attack came.

They're lying in wait for an ambush. They must be.

Somehow it was more disconcerting that their march had been completely unimpeded and their armies were nowhere to be found than if they had issued every man in the country to attack.

The next day brought delays – siege weapons were becoming mired in the snow, requiring hours of work to move them a half mile. In the meantime, Garen sent organized raiding parties of horse to surrounding villages to lay them to waste and pillage supplies. They returned, blood on their swords, gold and rations in hand, with no reports of Kuru resistance.

Garen paced about his war tent at night. His generals finally entered, clapping a fist to their chests in his presence.

"You wished to speak with us, Your Grace?" General Balon said.

The king motioned towards the war map atop his table and they gathered around. "Show me where your scouts are searching."

"Yes, My Lord. The first and second divisions are searching here, to the west, among these rivers – around two or three miles out. Third, fourth, and fifth divisions are forging ahead to scout where we have reason to believe there is a city called Isenlis."

"Do you not know for certain, Balon? Has this city moved recently?"

"No, My Lord, but the Kuru have been locked in their self-imposed cage with no contact and no Nuru has seen the city since the War of Shattered Stone, some six hundred years ago when it was being besieged."

"Noted. Do go on about the scouts."

"The remaining scouting divisions are searching to the east and northeast, where it is forested. It was our first suspicion that perhaps the Kuru army was lying in wait for our passage by the great forest, but so far the scouts have found little but snow and silent trees."

Garen slammed his fist on the table, startling all the generals.

"Where *are* they?" he shouted.

"Your Grace," Ser Erethar spoke up, "It is possible their forces are occupied to the east or they have directed all forces to retreat back to the capital. Perhaps after the failed invasion of Lärim, they do not have the men to mount a proper attack."

King Garen watched each of them as he spoke. "If that is the case, then there will be no fight when we reach this city. We will take it, its riches, and its resources. We shall use it as a base to stage our invasion of the capital."

"My Lord, with respect," asked General Acryth, a middle-aged military man who had risen to prominence decades prior with a heroic defense of the Nuru border after a particularly concentrated Kuru attack, "Would it not make more sense to take each major Kuru city, drain them of resources and fighting men, and gradually choke off the capital? If they will not come out to fight, we may be able to avoid a confrontation altogether if we should starve them out."

The very suggestion was asinine.

"No. Do not ever believe the Kuru will go quietly into the waiting arms of a Nuru Empire. Their hatred of our kind has spanned millennia. They will never capitulate, they will fight and they will die. Kuruverrum is the prize. It is the head of the snake. Our armies will drive hard, strike fast, and rip the head from the snake's writhing body. The rest of the war will be a simple cleanup."

He could tell the generals were uneasy. The possibility of missing armies emerging at the worst time scared everyone, and it was to be expected. *However, I will not change my mind on this. The Kuru will pay for their unlawful and savage incursions on our soil over the centuries.*

He continued at their silence. "I want you to move the scouts a mile further out in all directions. There are to be no surprises. By morning we will march on Isenlis, and if fortune should favor us, it will be in Nuru hands by nightfall. Send a small contingent of men to the city and offer the

204

people clemency should they open their gates to us, and death if they do not. If they are truly without protectors, they will not hesitate to acquiesce."

They all clapped fists to their chests again before leaving the tent.

For a moment, he stood in silence. The weight of commanding a nation was far heavier than he had imagined. *How father lived so long is beyond me.*

After a moment, Garen could hear songs rising up over the army's camp, old Nuru folk songs.

He stepped out of his tent to listen in the cold air. Thousands of men all sat together around their fires, their voices in unison reaching up to the heavens.

A niggling fear Garen had before embarking was that the men would not support this war. He was taking these men from their families in the middle of winter when they surely would have preferred to stay home. Morale would always be the driving force of an army, and if the men didn't support what he was doing, there would be no war and no Nuru Empire.

And yet here they were. Morale was soaring.

They've had enough of Kuru attacks, of feeling unsafe in their own towns. Under my father they were told that help would arrive soon to protect them, and even if it did, it was only for a time. The Kuru have always been masters at striking and fleeing, the cowards that they are. As much as he cared, my father would never take that final step towards ending hostilities once and for all.

There was much killing to come in the days ahead. Many of these men would never return home.

My only regret is failing to convince the two most powerful sorcerers in the world to support us. We could use their help. Even appealing to the young man's Nuru sense of nationality hadn't worked. I knew they didn't trust me, so perhaps if they heard the words from someone else, it would carry more weight.

He sighed as the voices lifted him up as well.

Such a waste of a fake letter.

Reldon and Alira packed their possessions with a sense of both relief and sadness at the forefront of their minds. Naturally it was fortunate that they all made it through the storm in one piece, but parting with the beautiful mansion was a somber affair. It had, after all, been a wondrous place to spend the storm, and for better or for worse their experiences would carry with them for years to come.

I still can't believe you actually did it, Alira thought to him with a sense of wonder.

Reldon struggled to force another of his pairs of trousers into his pack, befuddled at how it all had fit when he had originally packed it. *They needed a push. A big push. Off of Uncertainty Cliff and into Romance Ocean.*

Where do you come up with the things you say? Alira laughed from the other room.

I'm not sure. There is a possibility my head was hit by a mace during the Battle of Nakisho.

Her ethereal giggling continued. *I'm glad he's not upset with you.*

Aye, Bryle will be fine. I am worried about them though.

Do you think we should try to stop them?

I already tried. They won't be swayed. Bryle is intent on killing Kuru and Sillida is intent on following him and doing whatsoever he does. It doesn't seem like – Oh! Someone is at the door.

Reldon ceased their communications and answered the door. Tavia smiled back at him, looking as regally prim and proper as usual in gold, silver, and blue gown adorned with yet more flowers which Reldon was sure were out of season.

"I'm sorry to disturb you, Xanem Nuremar. May I come in?"

"Of course, Tavia."

She noticed his mostly-packed bag. "I do so hope you and your Ilewa have found comfort in the house of the High King. It is to my most shameful realization that much has been in tumult since you have arrived."

Reldon shook his head with a grin. "Not at all, Your Majesty. Besides, most of us spent months on the run from bandits, mercenaries, and governments altogether. Tumult might as well be the name of the town in which we now live our lives. How is Kiera? Is she all right?"

"She is understandably morose. Though she informed me it was not her larger concern, she was after all just forcibly removed from her own family."

"Which part of it *does* she care about then?"

"She bears little love for her remaining family, as you well know. Her father the king has chosen to abandon her in return for her deserting her country, or so he sees it. She now has a half-brother, borne of a woman she despises. Above all, however, she finds herself most distraught at her removal from the line of succession of Korraine. In a sense, she no longer belongs to the royal family of Korraine. She is no more than a minor noble – I would need to look into her current title, but I can say for certain she is no higher than a marquess. Undoubtedly this is all hard for her, but no longer being able to call herself 'Princess Kiera', as she has since she was born, must be hardest of all."

Reldon nodded sadly. "What an awful step to take to get revenge on your own daughter. He already has a son who replaces her as the next monarch. He didn't need to do that."

"I'm afraid it is much worse than that," she said, sitting on the neighboring bed to Reldon's, "What the King of Korraine has done is not only petty and repulsive, it is also illegal. It was agreed upon in the Covenant of Kings, the original document which created the High King as a legal entity that reigns over subordinate Lärimite kingdoms, that any and all changes in succession laws or removal of any individual from the legally prescribed chain of succession would be subject to approval by the High King. As far as I am aware, no such request has reached the desk of my husband."

Reldon's eyes went wide. "What is going to happen then?"

"The High King is very patient, and will wait for a time to receive the proper request from the King of Korraine. However, if no request is received within perhaps a month or so, I suspect he will issue a proclamation to Lärim as a whole that Kiera's deposition has no legal backing and shall not be recognized. This would infuriate the King of Korraine, as many of his line have been argumentative about the Covenant for many generations and claim that they were forced to sign it. They greatly dislike having to report to the High King about what they view as internal affairs, irrespective to the fact that my husband and his father have been extremely patient with them over the years."

"This can't be easy for Kiera to be in the middle of."

"Most certainly not. She is a very young woman whose fate may decide the fate of nations should these affairs prove disastrous."

"Do you think they will?"

"I hope not, but I would not rule it out. It is a particularly bad time to be staging further conflicts within our own kingdoms as Kuru attempt to invade from every which direction, but the Korrainians have been needlessly disobedient to our laws in recent decades. The High King may decide enough is enough."

Reldon was subconsciously relaying this information to Alira, who took it all in with silent shock.

"What is to be done for now? Kiera should not go back to Korraine."

"Of that we agree, and the High King would definitely agree as well. I have not been in direct contact with him as of yet, but I imagine he will want her to stay as close to Nakisho as we can convince her to be. Miss Ayuru's plan to have her accompany Miss Vendimar back to Nakisho and to Atheria sounds like a well-suited plan for now, and I doubt the High King will have any objections. The point remains that if she returns to Korraine, her life very well may be in danger."

Before Reldon could even form a response, there was a blood-curdling scream from downstairs, definitely from a young child.

Tavia and Reldon exchanged a brief look before sprinting out and down the broad staircase. They bolted around the corner into the ground floor corridor and found the three youngest children in the nursery room, surrounded by various toys. Antixius was sobbing loudly, Varia confusedly stared at her brother, and the older Elly immediately stood as they entered.

Alira came to a screeching halt in the doorway at almost the same time.

"Elly, what did you do?" she demanded.

"Nothing! I didn't do anything this time, honest!" she responded, holding her arms in an exaggerated shrug.

"Then why is he crying?"

"I don't know!"

Tavia scooped up her child and held him close. This was a different type of crying than usual – he was not upset or needing something, he was completely *terrified*. Reldon painfully remembered hearing children scream like this in Ferrela during the start of the Battle for R'Nal. Elly herself had cried like this when she was to be executed.

"Tell me what happened, Elly," Alira tried to say patiently.

"We were playing with toys and then he kept *staring* at me."

"So you hit him," Reldon accused, crossing his arms.

"No, I didn't hit him! He just kept staring at me and then started screaming!" She waved her hands about frantically.

Tavia bounced the inconsolable boy in her arms and cooed gently to him. "What's wrong, dearest? What has happened?"

For several long moments he would not respond, tears flowing down his face unabated. By the time she was able to calm him down to a point where he was sniffling and hoarse, she tried again to speak to him.

"Whatever is the matter? What made you so scared?"

He pointed at Elly.

"Did she hit you?"

208

He shook his head, to Elly's relief.

"I told you!"

"Then why are you crying?"

"She's…she's…There's something…wrong with her…"

"That's not very nice," Elly said, crossing her own arms.

"Antixius, I don't know what has gotten into you, but I think playtime is over for now. Come, you shall take to your nap early today. Miss Elliana, I am terribly sorry for his ill comments. I shall ensure he is taught some manners."

She stormed off upstairs as her son's crying resumed, leaving the four of them standing in the nursery.

"I *told* you I didn't do anything wrong," Elly repeated.

Reldon's eyes narrowed despite this. "Right, but what did you mean by 'I didn't do anything *this time*?'"

Her eyes darted about the room, before smiling pathetically.

Reldon, did you see his eye?

No, what was wrong with it?

I don't know if it was anything wrong with it, but… It was different.

How different? Besides being red and full of tears.

It looked like his father's eye looks – with that orange sunburst.

Chapter XXIX

Reldon made very sure to savor his final breakfast at the High King's estate – it was likely to be the last high-class meal he was going to have for some time, and he knew the others felt the same way. Except for Ethilia, of course, who always expected gourmet treatment wherever she went.

It was the first time Kiera had left her room since the previous day. Though she put on a good face, it was clear enough that her mind wasn't entirely with them that morning as she swirled her spoon through her porridge. They were all scheduled to take their leave after breakfast, and Reldon assumed no one would see each other for some time, so he had hoped to make their last meal together a good one.

"Have you ever drank brandy, Kiera? Bryle and I have had some and it is…a different experience."

She sort of snapped back to attention. "Oh, no I do not often drink brandy. Korrainian women prefer wine."

"That may just be you, my dear," Ethilia said with a sidelong grin, "What few Korrainian women I have met preferred their liquor as stiff and strong as their personalities."

He knew the entire conversation was going to be silly, along with his next question, but the entire purpose was to get everyone smiling again.

"What about you, Ethilia? Have you ever been drunk?"

It had the intended effect and everyone laughed, Bryle harder than the rest. Everyone laughed except for Ethilia, who was nonplussed.

"T-the nerve! What a bizarre question!"

"That's not an answer."

Her face was crimson and she sputtered terribly. "Of course not! I am a healer, I do not partake in such base pastimes!"

It was working. Kiera was smiling again. Even Tavia seemed mildly amused.

"Come now, Ethilia, even Sillida has had drink before."

"That was one time!" Sillida shouted to more laughter. "I snuck a bottle of wine from one of the nobles and found out that I didn't like it, so I brought it back."

"It doesn't take half the bottle to find out you didn't like it, Sillida."

"That wasn't me! I took one sip and gave the bottle to my mother!"

"I don't see what you're laughing so hard over, *mister* Bryle," Ethilia huffed.

"You girls are so squeamish, it's hilarious!" he responded.

"We are not *squeamish*, it is simply unladylike to speak of such matters."

"Not we true Korrainian ladies!" Kiera jutted a thumb toward her chest. "We talk of any such matters without fear. Women where I'm from could drink any man here under the table!"

Ethilia exhaled. "Again, I think that's just you."

It's working!

What's working?

She wasn't supposed to hear that thought. *Nothing.*

Alira narrowed her blue and green eyes but her grin remained.

You're riling them up on purpose.

He only smiled back, taking a bite of his bread with eggs on top. "Alira, which is your favorite element of magic to use?"

You're the worst. "I…um…I think I should love them all equally."

"There is no need to be so modest in such esteemed company, My Lady," Ethilia said with a warm smile, "There are no other forms of magicians here, so you can say freely how much you love Golden Magic. I will not tell anyone."

Elly's big eyes stared into her master's, wondering at her response. "I…uh…"

Reldon, Bryle, and Kiera cracked into laughter, and Alira hit her Ilewa numerous times.

Tavia smiled. "You are quite the incendiary figure, Xanem Nuremar."

Alira glared at him. "Wait until I set him on fire."

Kiera was by then laughing so hard she could hardly stay in her seat.

"Oh dear spirits! You are all too much! I am going to miss you all so greatly after we leave."

"We will miss you too, Kiera. Do not allow Ethilia's ego to overcome her until next we meet," Reldon said with a wink.

"Hmph!" she harrumphed, "You mistake pride for ego."

The youngest serving man whose name escaped Reldon surprised him by reaching over his shoulder with a small platter bearing a letter with its wax seal broken. He delivered one additionally to Ethilia and another to Tavia.

"My apologies for breaking the seals of your letters – we must ensure your safety from any untoward schemes by way of the mail."

"I understand," Reldon said, flipping it open to read it. Alira huddled in.

> To the Xanem Nuremar and Ilewa Nuremil,
> Do not read this letter aloud and do not reveal its contents to the others. Enemies surround you that would use this information against you if given the chance.
> I cannot reveal to you who I am yet, but rest assured I know what you seek and I desire to assist you in obtaining it. You know by now that you possess two of the four amulets which hold ancient power, and you require one more. Allow me to bring clarity to any doubt you may have – both of the remaining amulets are in the possession of Rizellion, the Churai Master in Drunerakerrum. He has held them for some time, and does not intend on giving them up. They have been far too instrumental in their work.
> Regrettably I know not which is the false idol and which is real, but beyond a doubt I know that you must infiltrate the heart of the Kuru's strength and destroy Rizellion in order to retrieve the one you covet. This is the only way you can ensure ultimate peace as your destiny mandates.
> Counter to what you may believe, there are a number of friends who would see you succeed, and we wait along the way to provide what aid we can. Should you choose to trust me, meet me in Irothrim, the Darumite capitol, at the place where metal and water create their music. I have much to teach you.
>
> A friend.

Alira leaned back into her chair again, working consciously to conceal her bewilderment.

Who do you think it could be? Should we trust him? Or her?

Reldon reread the letter. *It could be a trap.*

Ethilia scoffed at her letter. "My father can be absolutely impossible at times. He will never admit his faults so long as he continues to draw breath."

This person knows us. They know what we're looking for and where to find it.

Right, and there could only be a few people that could be. One of them is Rizellion himself.

That gave her pause.

Can we…truly afford to ignore this letter?

Irothrim is far to the west of here, and whether we choose to trust this person or not, we will likely have to pass through anyway. We must get that amulet.

Could he or she be lying to us about where it is?

I don't think so. Bryle told me about his infiltration of the Chroniclers and they had found the same information, and it wasn't offered freely. It may be scary, but it is real – Rizellion has what we need.

Alira's mind raced and it was difficult for Reldon to keep his own thoughts straight. *I don't understand. This seems so backwards. If we need the amulets to be strong enough to defeat Rizellion, and we have to defeat Rizellion to get the amulets, how could this plan possibly work?*

Reldon shook his head. *This person in the letter believes we need to kill Rizellion to get the amulets. I don't think so. If we were able to somehow sneak in and steal it before he notices, we would have all the power we need to take him down.*

Except that we don't know what these amulets do when they're together.

'Power of limited creation' sounds like it should be enough.

If you believe the priests at the church of the Omniscient One.

I don't understand, Alira, when did you become so cynical?

Her thoughts were volatile. *I very much dislike all of this Reldon. Every plan we have had is founded on faith or part of a story. We never have all the information and there are far too many 'ifs' for my liking. This is going to be the most dangerous plan we've ever followed, and I just want to be double… no, triple sure that it's going to work.*

"I completely understand, Ethilia," Kiera responded with a nod.

Ethilia sighed. "Unfortunately, you shall have to meet him as we head south. He requests me to visit him and to bring my sister with me. I do not believe the latter request is a particularly good idea at this time, but I should deign to pay the family a visit on our way to Atheria. He is my doting father after all."

Alira, I hear what you're saying, but we may never have all of the information. This world is far too full of secrets, and that is why we are doing this – to unlock the greatest secrets of them all. We will find out what the amulets do when they're together. We will unravel this great mystery that Tycheronius talked about, and we will use it all to make ourselves stronger. It won't be easy, but we don't have a choice.

"I will do my best to remain silent as a good Nakisho woman," Kiera snipped.

"That is for the best," Ethilia responded, not noticing her inflection, "He has a particular enmity towards Korrainians, as most Lärimite lords and ladies do. Present company excluded, of course."

Tavia nodded in approval.

But I thought you wanted to find Grandma.

I do. She's the biggest mystery of them all.

So which are we trying to do, find the amulets or find Grandma?

Maybe recovering the amulet will lead us to her.

Her mind deflated. *More maybes.*

"If you might all indulge me for a moment, I have something to say to you all on this day that you leave this haven in the snow," Tavia started, taking to her feet, "It has been a blessed experience and a wonderful time to have spent this year's storm with each and every one of you. I hope you will find it in your hearts to forgive the shortcomings this house has presented in light of the roof partially collapsing and finding danger while under my protection. For this I truly apologize. It is my hope that if fate should look kindly on us in the coming year that perhaps we should find ourselves back here again to enjoy each other's company for the next storm."

"Hear, hear!" Bryle said, raising his glass, eliciting the same response from the rest.

"Go forth on each of your important missions with the blessing of the High King's Consort and of course with that of the High King himself. Be steadfast, be honorable, and above all be safe. To each of your health."

They drank whatever liquids they happened to have to her toast, and it didn't take long thereafter for the meal to end and for everyone to make for the great, blindingly white outdoors.

Sun had broken through in full force, with a few clouds still persisting after their brothers and sisters had moved on. What the life-bringing light revealed was a world of snowbanks, seemingly without end. By then, the serving men had cleared the courtyard of snow and a portion of the road heading south. The otherwise oppressive wind had died down to little more than a nipping breeze.

Each of their horses awaited them on the road, saddled and ready.

Dressed in their heavy snow gear, the group congregated in the courtyard on their way out.

"So this is it," Reldon said with a tone of finality.

"Oh come now, Reldon, don't say it like that. No one is dying here."

"I meant that less so for you, Bryle. Alira, Elly, and I are heading west with you and Sillida. We are going to Darum."

Bryle beamed. "You are? Splendid! Then where?"

"We don't know yet. We will find out when we get there."

"So it is us then that are being left," Kiera said with her typically devilish smile.

Ethilia shrugged. "So be it, we shall have a more civilized time among nobles and kings rather than with those…dirty Darumites."

"I'm beginning to think you just don't like anyone, Ethilia," Bryle said.

"I never said I didn't like them – only that they're dirty."

"How are those not the same for you? Look at you, have you ever even *seen* dirt?"

Reldon spoke up with a laugh. "I believe what Bryle is trying to say is that we are going to miss both of you."

"Likewise," was all Ethilia had to say, giving Bryle the stink eye.

Kiera gave each of them a strong hug, giving the strongest hug to Reldon. She shook his shoulders. "Be strong, Xanem Nuremar. Accept no weakness. If you are ever in peril, think like a Korrainian and trust in the spirits. They have never failed me."

Reldon nodded. "Don't let her tell you what to do, Kiera."

She laughed heartily. "Not even kings can tell me what to do."

Ethilia cleared her throat loudly. "Let's be off then. We shall see you all again in good time. Farewell."

Her goodbye had been as impersonal and catlike as her greeting had been some weeks back, and they all smiled as Kiera rolled her eyes and mounted her horse, kicking up snow as they trotted off towards Nakisho. With one last spirited wave from the former Korrainian princess, they were out of earshot.

Alira was particularly bubbly. "Did you see Ethilia?"

"What do you mean?" Reldon asked.

"She hides it well, but I think she was happy. Oh how it would make my heart sing if her and Kiera became good friends."

Bryle scoffed. "Please. A corpse with a hairlip would make her happy. Relationships aren't her forte."

"How harsh you are, Bryle!" Alira gaped. "You make her sound as if she takes some pleasure in death."

Elly spoke in monotone. "She sings to the bodies sometimes when she's studying them. It's weird."

Reldon climbed onto his horse, signaling the others to follow. "So she takes pride in her work. I fail to see fault in that."

"All right Reldon, I'll cease my teasing, but if you start singing to the Churai we're going to have a problem."

The wind brushed their faces as the partially open road passed beneath their horses' clopping hoof-falls.

"Master, where are we going?" Elly inquired.

"To Irothrim, Elly," she answered, "To the capitol of Darum. I've never been there. I don't believe any of us have."

"Are Varia and Antixius coming too?"

"No, they must stay with their mother. Our path is not theirs."

She quietly looked ahead. "I'm going to miss them."

"You will see them again. I promise."

"You forgave Antixius quickly after what he had said about you, Elly. That was very grown-up of you," Reldon commended her.

"He didn't mean it. He's always saying weird things."

"Oh? Like what?"

She shrugged absently. "I don't know. Things that don't make sense. He wouldn't call me Elly, even though it's my name."

Reldon and Alira exchanged perturbed glances. "What did he call you?" She asked further.

Her eyes got a far away, almost glazed over look.

"Arilia. I remember it from somewhere, but I can't remember where."

"That's a pretty name. I didn't know he was so creative making up names."

"It's NOT made up!"

The outburst left Alira in shock, and Elly did not speak for several hours.

Isenlis burned.

216

To King Garen's surprised bemusement the city garrison had refused to surrender, refused to allow Nuru troops access to the city and its resources in exchange for their lives. A scant two hundred or so men had stood atop the walls, their courage faltering with every forward march of the oncoming Nuru horde. As valiant as they looked standing their ground against a significantly larger force, they routed like any other garrison when pelted with a rainstorm of arrows. None manned the ramparts by the time the battering ram was hauled forward to smash the front gate open.

To his further surprise, somewhere around 2,000 men with pitchforks, hammers, knives, and other improvised weapons awaited them on the other side, screaming like wanton beasts to keep their courage alive.

Admittedly it had given him pause for just a moment. Did these brave men, set on protecting their families from an unknown people, deserve to be hewn where they stood? It was a quandary, to be certain.

One he would not be mired into for long.

All it took was a snap of his fingers and the generals had issued their archers forward. As they pulled back their drawstrings, the full implication of their decision to stand before this army had been realized. The scream of valor quickly became screams of terror as they trampled each other to get out of the way.

The first volley left hundreds dead, and the second maybe a hundred more. A third was not necessary, as the remaining resistance had adequately dispersed. Spearmen bearing their king's green livery marched into the city unopposed, filling every street with Nuru dominance.

"The city is ours," General Balon had told him, "What shall we do with it, Your Grace?"

"Begin the process of converting the larger structures into a temporary base and collect all the city's resources there."

"…All of the resources, Your Grace? You would have us strip the city bare?"

"I do not believe I misspoke, general."

"As you wish, My Lord. And what of the people?"

"Let the men do with them as they wish."

There had been a silence which spoke the man's consternations better than any pathetic words he might have conjured up.

King Garen had turned and put his face intimidatingly close to Balon's. "They were given every opportunity to surrender. To flee. I am not a monstrous king, but I am one without sympathy for those who would seek their own destruction. They had their chance, and they chose death and destruction. Let them now reap what they sow."

Hours later, Isenlis burned.

The portions that were militarily significant or contained precious resources were spared, but most other sectors of the city were in flames after the men had raided them.

He had seen it in their eyes – hatred that could only have been borne of countless Kuru raids putting their families in unrelenting peril for years and years on end. Hatred which had aged like a fine spirit, patiently waiting for its time to return the favor, and when they finally had the chance to make them hurt, *really* hurt, he did not stand in their way. And for that they cheered his name. They killed Kuru in his honor. Isenlis fell in a parade of Nuru nationalistic pride.

That night they had invented new songs to sing – songs that compared the Nuru to a dog who had been kicked one too many times and finally decided to rip the Kuru to shreds.

It all was ecstasy to King Garen's ears. It was finally time.

He strapped on his regalia, his finest armor and made his way towards the building which had become their head of operations during their stay, his boots splashing in pools of Kuru blood with every step.

"Your Grace," General Balon's voice came from behind as he hustled up to match pace with his king, "If I might have a moment, we have a report for you."

"What is it, Balon?" he responded irritably.

"We are experiencing some additional problems with the siege weapons becoming entrenched in the snow outside of the city. It could take several-"

"Do not tell me of problems in my moment of triumph."

"Triumph, sir? I recall Kuruverrum was the prize, not Isenlis."

"It still is, but this is a moment of triumph for the Nuru people. History will be made today."

"I…I don't follow…"

"You never do. Keep your mouth shut and fetch me a ladder."

Though clearly confused, as it was the man's natural state, he acquiesced simply enough. The forward base was housed within a large building that King Garen imagined had originally been used for matters of state, like a town hall. As it was the largest building around, it would do nicely.

The latter creaked as he climbed to the top, the smoke around him being whipped around by the wind. He stood high above his men, who noticed him and cheered, gathering closer to the foot of the town hall to listen to what he had to say.

"My brothers! Our time has finally come! A time when we might finally emerge from the shadows to show the world what we as Nuru are capable of!"

Their cheers shook the foundation of the building itself.

"The powers that exist in this wretched mainland have stood by and watched the Kuru murder your fathers and sons, rape your mothers and daughters, and bring fear to the hearts of millions of Nuru for too long! If there is one lesson I have learned from my father's reign, it is that we cannot, and *will not*, continue to rely on disgusting bureaucrats in Lärim to bring security to our children. It is time that the Nuru stood on our own. From this day forward we will fight our own battles, and we will win on the backs of strong Nuru men and women. In no way shall we be inferior to any other people ever again!"

He clapped an iron fist to his chest.

"The role of a king no longer suits the needs of this realm and our people. The Lärimites call their leaders kings, but they are held in check by one who calls himself the High King. I will *never* allow any to believe themselves our betters, starting with him. And that is why you shall all be the first to hear this proclamation. From this day forward, the Nuru Kingdom of Errum is no more."

Confused chattering erupted, but only for a second.

"In its place, a new country will rise from its ashes. Men! As of this day, you are the valiant soldiers of the great Nuru Empire! And I shall lead you all unto victory as your first Emperor!"

The cacophonous reaction was so loud that some buildings which were already in a bad way collapsed to the ground.

Emperor Garen reached into a sack which had been tied to his belt and retrieved a new crown, one of black gold set with emeralds on each of its imperial spikes. As he rested it on his head at last, the chants came high over the ruins of this Kuru stronghold.

Hail the emperor! Hail the emperor! Hail the emperor!

"And as my first decree as Emperor of the Nuru, I hereby dissolve all alliances and treaties with all other nations, including our so-called allies in Lärim, as their treaties are worth less than the parchment they're written on. They honor no treaties, they obey no alliances, and so there shall be no friendship again until we are treated with the respect we deserve! Drunerakerrum will fall, and only the Nuru Empire will stand to gain. From this day forward we will forge into the new age as Nuru, proud and victorious!"

He fully expected apprehension or even silence. It was a complete departure from all of his father's policies which had been unbearably moderate, bordering on subservient. In the hours of raiding and pillaging he had considered introducing his new diplomatic policies incrementally, but finally decided that glory waited for no man, much less the new emperor of the Nuru. The very first, in fact.

The men did not return his words with silence, however. Their screams of approval left him with an elation he had never felt in his years playing the sycophantic prince silenced by his father at court.

This world will tremble before my ambition. There is no longer room for any more gray. The other nations and people of this world will either stand with us or be cut down.

Chapter XXX

"I'll be playing one minstrel face up and two paupers behind. See if you can't weasel your way around that, you little cretin."

Detryn knew it was the man's tell – he would sling insults when he knew he had no hand to back it up. Not that he would take the risk of not knowing for certain.

He 'ent got nothin', Detryn. He drew a priest and a ranger, Gihan sounded off in his mind from across the room.

Isn't it amazing how his false confidence grows as his chances of winning die?

"And what is your bet, good sir?"

"Four copper," the Korrainian miner said, tossing the coins into the pile.

"Tsk tsk! Not feeling confident?"

"Shut up and make your move."

Detryn laughed to himself and placed an assassin card face down, followed by five coppers.

"That's it? That's your winning move?"

"That would depend on *your* next move, my friend. Do draw."

The man glared back at him as his ripped a card from atop his own deck.

It's a shield-maiden, Det. He's gonna put it face down.

"One card face down. You make the move to end the game. If you've got the stones."

"Oh the suspense is simply killing me. Very well."

There were only two cards which could defeat the shield maiden and win the round, and those were the assassin and the lover. However, the danger was attacking a face-down card if one did not know what it was. If he attacked with the wrong card, he could lose all the money for the round.

But I leave nothing to chance.

He had three face down cards, and he flipped all of them face up. He simply couldn't help himself not to make a theatrical end to the game.

"I've got a knight, a duke, and an assassin. Now, I wonder which shall I attack with?"

"Make a decision so you can lose already, you piss-ant."

"Oh very well. Assassin to face-down card."

The man leapt from his chair, picking up the card and tossing it at Detryn. "You little bastard! You're a cheat! It's impossible that you always know everything I'm putting down! I want this man arrested!"

Detryn got to his feet as well. "I resent those remarks, Korrainian. I always play fair and square. Perhaps you should blame your own lack of strategical intellect for your consistent losses?"

"Why you-"

A Korrainian guard with heavy lamellar armor and a pointed helmet stomped over to the table from the other end of the tavern with a hand placed on his curved saber-like sword at his hip.

"What is the problem here? You had best not be engaging in violence!"

"It's him! He's a cheat! He's stealing people's money!" the man ranted.

"All right, that is more than enough. Do you have any evidence to present? Any at all?"

"Have a look at his deck. Make sure it's legitimate."

Detryn rolled his eyes. "Oh what a graceful way to lose."

The guard flipped through his deck three times, and shook his head. "There is nothing suspicious about these cards. You need to pay him his money and leave. If I catch you being violent again I will throw you in the gaol."

The miserable loser threw a few more copper onto the table and stormed out of the tavern, creating much more of a scene than necessary.

"Thank you for upholding the law, dear guardsman," Detryn said cheerfully. He handed him a small handful of copper pieces under the table.

"I only do my duty for the king. I will be watching."

As the guard returned to his corner, Detryn smiled broadly at his pile of winnings.

That's the third fighter this week. Are you sure people aren't catching onto us?

They can catch on all they want, they have no proof and the law is on my side.

But what if they just stop playing and then we 'ent got the money to pay the guard?

Then we move to the next town. I thought I explained this to you already.

It doesn't make no sense to me, but you keep winning more coin so I just do my job. How much have we made tonight?

222

With this bit in mind, we're looking at around...thirteen silver.

That 'ent as much as last night.

This pond is just about dried up methinks. Perhaps one more night and then we'll be off again.

All right, but when are we planning on finding Reldon and the others? We came to Korraine to get away from the soldiers in Nakisho and to wait out the storm, but now the storm is over.

It was a conversation Detryn hadn't looked forward to confronting. From the freezing plunge they had taken in Nakisho to barely surviving each night due to the cold or having no food or money, for a time he had just been happy to still be breathing. Soldiers had indeed been pursuing them for a while and they only managed to escape due to Gihan's Phyrimic specialization, but by the time they reached the Korrainian border they all but gave up the search. One didn't have to be a local to figure out that kingsmen weren't welcome in this prickly country.

For the entirety of the accursed storm they had loitered about in taverns, making money for a room with Detryn's tricks like the old days, drinking the nights away and trying to stay warm around the fireplaces. It was a perfect environment for a good con, as it was a completely captive audience – the storm prevented any of them from leaving, so many decided to play with Detryn out of sheer boredom. After a while they did have to migrate to another nearby tavern once or twice as the captive audience became more like a caged wolf and decided that they didn't like losing money to someone who miraculously never seemed to lose.

Let's take a walk. I could use a little fresh air.

Leaving the warm of the tavern for the wretched cold outside was not his idea of fun, but he knew he was going to have to have this conversation away from eavesdroppers.

They walked in silence down the quiet, snowy Korrainian street of a town he had never heard of. A few lights dotted a few of the tightly compacted houses made of sandy colored bricks. Elsewise there were distant cliffs and pebbly fields – none of which ever inspired Detryn to anything close to an "emotional reaction".

"So what's the plan, Det?" Gihan said in his big fat voice, "When are we going after Reldon?"

"I hadn't planned out that far. Haven't given it that much thought."

"That 'ent true and you know it. You always think of everything. What are we still doing here?"

Detryn ran a hand through his absurdly long, slicked back hair.

"What's the point of going after them?"

Gihan's enormous cheeks practically quivered with confusion. Not that that was difficult to elicit.

He went on before the big lug could form a coherent thought. "The life we've been living here may not be as… glorious as I would like, but we have had everything we need: food, drink, a roof, women, and fairly good company. Not to mention the coin. What more could you want?"

His caterpillar eyebrows stitched together. "None o' that means nothin' if our brothers are dying out there. There's more to life than coin."

"Weren't you at least partially responsible for Harbin's death? I'm starting to wonder if you don't like Reldon because you're not fond of the competition."

He jutted a massive finger into Detryn's chest. "I told you before, I didn't kill him. Unlike Reldon, I would never murder one of my brothers."

"What if Huerogrand told you to?"

That gave him a potent cause for consideration. Detryn could practically smell the smoke.

"I would want to know why. I might do it."

"Exactly." Detryn crossed his arms. "You would have your reasons to do it, and he might have had his."

"Then I want to hear those reasons. From him. And why are you defendin' him? What's happened to you all of a sudden? A couple weeks ago you wanted revenge and now you just want to hide here in Korraine?"

A cold wind caressed his face, gently reminding him of his recent brush with the inevitable. "Close calls with death have a way of readjusting one's priorities."

"So you get a bit cold and now you want to curl up by the fire forever and forget the rest of the world?"

Detryn forcibly lifted his coat and shirt to reveal the nasty gashes across his entire torso, at least a dozen in all, mostly healed but leaving his body looking like a pockmarked warzone. "Do you see this?! I've been this way before! This is what you end up with if you're lucky. There's no glorious revenge at the end of the road. Reldon is the most powerful Spellsword who ever lived, and his Ilewa is a firestorm waiting to explode. If you keep going down this path, I promise they will roast you alive. I was fortunate to just have the little rat girl create a bunch of new holes in my body. I learn from the past, Gihan."

"That might have been what happened to you, but I 'ent gonna go down that easy. Maybe he will have some good reasons, and I wanna hear what they are. But if he 'ent got good enough reasons, there's no way I'm lettin' him get away with it. I'll catch him without his Ilewa. I'll fight him one on one like we used to, but this time it 'ent with sticks and I 'ent gonna let him go free when it's all done."

This idiot is going to get himself killed faster than if he jumped off one of these Korrainian cliffs.

"You do that. I'm warning you that it won't work. You and I aren't at the top of their priorities with all the Kuru and Churai running amok. They will sweep you out of the way like an oddly human shaped dust bunny."

"They will try. I'm leaving tomorrow morning. Are you coming with me or not?" Gihan asked with an air of finality.

Detryn breathed in long and hard, releasing a cloud of warm air into the frigid night sky. *There's not going to be any convincing him not to keep pursuing this. Going with him will be fraught with danger but staying here will likely be bad for my health as well. If he starts doing something incredibly stupid, I --*

Footsteps that he had heard approaching were now coming far too close to be a passerby.

Stepping into his peripheral vision were a man and woman. The man was absurdly tall – several heads higher than both Gihan and Detryn. He looked to be perhaps just past the prime of his life, but extremely dangerous in his full set of plate armor with a longsword at his side.

The woman, with her shoulder-length red hair, near-perfect complexion, and fierce eyes, was painfully familiar. *Come to think of it, I've seen both of them before.*

She spoke first. "You came quite a way to escape justice, boys."

Gihan answered smugly. "And who might you two be? A couple of bandits?"

His intellectual deficiencies never cease to amaze.

"Oh! It's my favorite yipping lapdog from Nakisho. Good to see they've promoted you from kicking homeless vagrants to hunting them down outside the city walls to kick them. Real yeoman's work."

"As you can tell, I have the noble following of seeking out pathetic criminals like you and either bringing you back to prison where you belong or leaving you a blackened husk if you refuse. Please, I do so hope you resist. It's my favorite part of the job."

"Who are you two?" Gihan asked.

Oh dear spirits.

"They're a fire magician and a Knight from Nakisho and they're here to take us in. We already established that."

"Not too bright, that one," the fire magician laughed, "But since you and I are practically old chums now, I'll do you the honor of telling you my name so you know what to beg. I'm Vecilia. Now start begging."

"You know, Vecilia, there doesn't have to be violence. We can enjoy each other's company tonight and return to Nakisho with you in the morning like civilized men and women of sorcerous origins."

Her eyes narrowed. "You are repugnant. We shall not be enjoying each other's *company* on any night. You are to decide now – are you coming *quietly*, or shall we go with the burned husk plan?"

"Perhaps there is a misunderstanding. We were simply-"

"Burned husk it is."

Before Detryn could even react, she had already produced two handfuls of bright flame, hurling them at Gihan and himself in turn. They both hastily threw up a force field and they exploded in a wave of heat that incinerated the snow beneath them instantly.

The Knight drew his longsword and rushed Gihan, who also ripped his own short blade from the Infinity Scabbard just in time to block the oncoming attack in a shower of sparks.

Immediately Detryn knew that this was not going to be like any other fight he had been in before. This woman began by shrieking at the top of her lungs – a wild, horrible screech not unlike that of a wounded animal or someone who had utterly lost their mind in grief or pain. It caught him so off guard that he stumbled backwards onto his rump. As she unleashed her banshee-like wail, her red hair and eyes flared and a storm of flames encircled her body as if she were donning a cloak of pure inferno.

Her screams continued and the tower of fire grew in size and intensity.

I think I might have bit off a bit much with this one.

When silence abruptly pervaded, she lashed out.

Wicked balls of scorching flame assailed Detryn in the dozens, and his instincts told him to flee and leave Gihan behind, and he was not one to ignore his instincts. He managed to block a few with his force field, and the rest exploded against the stone streets below, melting entire block's worth of snow with a huge *hiss!*

It was everything he could do just to stay alive. It was, in a literal sense, raining death. This woman's power outmatched his own by several magnitudes. He weaved about in serpentine motions, explosions erupting to his left and right, singeing off his eyebrows and numerous times setting his coat aflame.

Detryn dove behind a building and forced his shoulder into a snowbank to put out the fire that had started. She would be on him again in seconds. He had to think.

This woman is not going to be willing to kill civilians in order to kill me. I can use that.

Something in his peripheral vision caught his attention. A sort of oil was flowing across the stones beneath him and over what remained of the snow toward him, and it stopped about a foot from where he was catching his breath.

Well damn.

The flames moved at incredible speed along the oil and found him in seconds. Once again he dove out of the way just in time to avoid the explosion which left the entire side of the house charred. Detryn's ears rang as he pushed himself to his feet. By now he could hear the screams of locals as they noticed the beacon of walking destruction stalking its way through their town.

Making a mad dash towards one of the few houses he saw with light in its windows, he slammed his shoulder against the door in an attempt to gain unwarranted entrance, but it was locked. Placing a hand on the wood of the door, he sent a powerful jolt of Phyrim into it and the force snapped it in half as it fell inward. Bolting inside, there was a Korrainian family of five cowering against the far wall of their tiny house, a mother, a father, a son, and two daughters. They screamed in terror as he broke in, and without skipping a beat he leapt over their table and stood next to them as his inevitable judgment approached.

She stepped inside with her flames subsided, her visage no more impassive than it had been before the battle. Her eyes had been fixed on Detryn's terrified face before flitting to the family who cowered beneath him and back.

"Step away from them. Now."

"You don't really expect me to follow that order, do you?"

"Step away from them or I will make you."

"Vecilia, stop, stop, stop, we can talk about this!" he pleaded with his hands in the air. "No one has to die today!"

"You had your chance to come quietly and you refused. Now you must die."

"What, no trial or anything? How is this justice?!"

"Your death warrant was signed the moment you fled prison. I am simply the executioner if necessary. And it is. Now move, or I will burn you to death slowly."

She made a menacing step forward with her hand outstretched, and Detryn made a decision without thinking, which had turned out poorly every time he had ever done it.

He reached down and grabbed the male child by his neck and pulled him in front of himself. The boy screamed and his parents jabbered at him frantically in Korrainian. Detryn put a finger on the boy's temple.

"Don't come any closer or I turn his brains into jelly!"

Vecilia stopped, and her eyes flared again with anger.

"This is a new disgusting low for you. Hiding behind children? You sick bastard."

"You're not giving me much choice here, Vecilia."

"You don't get a choice," she said angrily, flames igniting again within her enclosed fists, "You either let that boy go or I will roast you one appendage at a time."

"I'm willing to entertain the idea of coming quietly now, if we can learn to forgive and forget," Detryn said with a smirk, "I don't think this is going to go well for you when you return to Nakisho. Your superiors aren't going to be thrilled at the idea that a simple execution turned into a hostage situation, possibly with the deaths of a few locals."

"Accidental deaths are a part of the job. And I don't negotiate with the likes of you."

"If either of those statements were true, we wouldn't be having this lovely conversation. Like it or not, there is only one outcome here in which you don't end up just as wanted as I am. You will let me go, appendages in their current un-roasted state, and you may feel free to pursue me again shortly."

"You lie. You are nothing but a criminal."

"A criminal with nothing to lose. If I'm going to die here, why should I not cause a little damage first?" He pushed his finger into the boy's temple hard enough that he started to cry again.

It was clear he had her trapped. There was nothing she could do other than let him go, and she knew it. Her fists were clenched so tightly that liquid flame dripped onto the floor and sizzled on contact.

"You don't have to give me an answer. I'm taking this boy with me outside and you will stay here. I will let him go and start running. After that – good luck finding me. The hunt is on."

And he did precisely that. He rotated around the fuming executioner magician in the center of the room with the boy held firmly with one arm. She made no move to stop him as he backed out of the door. Her jaws were so tightly clenched together he thought her teeth might shatter.

"When I find you I am going to kill you oh so slowly."

"Aw, don't worry, I find you attractive too. See you shortly, Firetop."

Detryn picked up the boy, who was not particularly heavy, and increased his speed to a fast jog across several streets before letting him go and descending into a dead sprint.

He whirled around buildings at incredible speed, knowing that in a few seconds that walking harbinger of death and destruction with red hair would be putting the miles past her to find him.

It was going to be now or never for their fail-safe. If he returned to the square behind the tavern to find no one there, he was as good as roasting over a spit already.

To his incredible luck, Gihan was there waiting atop a horse with another waiting.

You beautiful brute! Oh thank the spirits there is still hope!

"Come on Det, we have to go now!" he shouted, pointing into the distance.

A light of incredible intensity was approaching at a rapid pace.

Detryn scrambled into the saddle. *Where is the Knight?*

I knocked him out for the moment, but she 'ent gonna stop! Let's go!

By the time she came close enough to see them, Gihan condensed immense amounts of Phyrim into a tiny nexus of energy and held it in his hand. They both kicked their horses onward to a quick gallop and he tossed it behind him.

The detonation was huge. Gihan had told Detryn weeks ago that it was one of the abilities they had taught him as an Infiltrator. It did not cause a lot of damage, as it was not intended to. It was nothing more than a rapidly expanding pocket of Phyrim that would upset all debris in a wide area and send it high into the air.

The effect was an explosive cloud of dirt and sand that extended possibly thousands of feet in all directions and persisted long enough to provide their escape cover for at least a few minutes.

It would be all they needed. At full gallop they would not catch up.

What took you so long? I had to improvise back there! Detryn chastised him.

That Knight was a lot tougher than I thought he would be. Just be happy I got to where we planned to be if everything went wrong.

It definitely went wrong, all right. We should probably ride for a while if we're to lose her.

He snorted, which was disturbing through his thoughts. *Still think it's a good idea to stay here?*

Point taken, Gihan. Point taken. Please, lead the way.

Chapter XXXI

Two minds swirled with uncertainty as they approached the ancient city of Naiwa-ki-Shokassen.

Both rang with the specters of their past, the age-old distrust and hatred having been drilled into them from a young age.

Ethilia had been only six when the cruel realities of the world were brought to her otherwise flighty attention. Opterus was a city that had primarily been home to several of the great noble families in Lärim, but like any other city it needed a strong working class to act as a backbone to its very weighty head.

As a girl of noble birth, it was considered acceptable to interact with those of means or even of relative means – those in the middle of society. However, she found out quickly that not everyone who wasn't a noble fit into that echelon.

It had been an early spring day, when most of the snow was gone but a few wet piles here and there persisted, usually just off the roads or underneath trees where the leaves had shielded the snow from the sun's rays. She ran about the streets with her friends, a few other girls her age from the higher society of Opterus. Most of them were not born of magic, so she always felt a little different, but her friends never teased her or made her feel like she was strange. In fact, she was especially useful to have around when it came to climbing trees or wrestling around, because if any bruises or cuts occurred, she could heal them without too much problem.

That day hadn't been any different, as they had decided to ball up the remaining snow into their hands as tightly as they possibly could and throw them at each other. It was all good fun until someone was hit in the face and started to cry, the snow having left a nasty blemish on their otherwise perfect noble skin. And as was her nature, Ethilia was always the one to jump in and say, "Don't worry, I'll fix it!" and return it to normal in just a minute or so. They were always so grateful. Of course, she learned years later that using her Golden Magic so repeatedly for such small, cosmetic injuries was probably going to give them *magicanum toxicosis* over time, but they abandoned her the moment she gained a royal position in Nakisho anyway, so in hindsight she thought, *What's a little magic poisoning between friends?*

After that incident, a few more girls showed up that Ethilia had never seen before. They didn't wear quite as nice clothing, and they talked a bit differently, but they still seemed like nice girls. What had been important in her six-year-old mind was that they were ready to play, and they loved throwing snowballs just as much as Ethilia's other friends. It had been great fun until teatime, when Ethilia had to return to her family's mansion.

Normally a servant was there waiting for her to walk her to see her parents upstairs, but that day her father had been waiting for her in the foyer.

"Hello father!" she called to him cheerfully.

He had not immediately responded, his scornful gaze flitting between her and the doorway behind her.

"Were you playing with some new girls today, Ethilia?" he asked her pointedly.

She nodded with glee. "They were a lot of fun."

"And do you know precisely who they were?"

Her smile faded as she shook her head.

"Those were peasant girls, my daughter, and Korrainian ones at that. Undoubtedly from the Korrainian quarter of Lower Opterus. Did you know that you were making a mistake by playing with them, Ethilia?"

Her blue eyes got big. "No father! Why was it a mistake?"

"It is obscene for a girl of your stature, being a daughter of a major noble family such ours, to be seen cavorting about with those at the bottom rungs of society. You're old enough to know the ways of the world now, and you will come to understand that appearances are *everything* to a family of means."

She cocked her head and narrowed her eyes in confusion, but he continued.

He crossed his monstrous arms. "Moreover, you are not to associate with those Korrainians anymore. You shall know them by their speech, by the bizarre beads and charms they carry on their persons, and by their superstitious ways. They do not love the High King as we do, Ethilia. We believe in this great kingdom and its culture, its people, and the preeminence of the royal family. Korrainians do not believe in any such ideals, and spit in the face of our High King. Now you wouldn't like that much, would you Ethilia?"

Her attention sank to the floor as her hands fiddled with her frilly gold dress. "No, father."

"No you wouldn't. They are different, my love. They are not the same as us."

"But father," she said, looking back into his face several feet higher, "I use my magic on them, just like my other friends. I can see inside their bodies when I fix their hurts. All the bones and…even their hearts…they're all the same. I don't understand, father."

He knelt down and looked into her eyes as she looked for guidance.

"It is not relevant that their bodies are similar, my daughter. Everyone is born with eyes, a nose, a mouth, and ears. Everyone has a heart. It is what is inside that heart that matters most."

"So I need to look inside their hearts," she said with determination.

"No, that's not what I meant. What I'm saying to you is that those girls may seem the same as you, but they are not – not in ways you can see with your eyes or your magic. In their minds and in their hearts they do not share the love for the High King that we do. They do not believe in bringing prosperity and growth to our kingdom. Their parents would see it destroyed and a Korrainian society in its place, and those same parents will teach those children to hate our kingdom every night before they go to sleep, just as I teach you the opposite. To put it simply, my darling daughter…they are incompatible with you. With us. With our family. And that is why you are forbidden to play with them anymore. You will be doing yourself a service by avoiding them. Continue to play with your friends from the other houses, they are good girls. Am I understood?"

At that time she could think of no other response than "Yes father."

That conversation had shaped her view of the world as she knew it for next ten years. And in her view, her father wasn't entirely wrong.

Kiera, however, had had a very different experience that pounded against the wall surrounding her heart as they entered the city and proceeded to Nakisho castle. She remembered the nights her mother would sit with her in her quarters before the fire. From a similar age or perhaps a bit older, she would sit upon her stool in the warm glow of the flames as her beloved mother would brush her hair, which had been significantly longer in those days.

She had had the conversation one night after meeting a boy who had come with a royal envoy earlier that day. Kiera never fully understood what the purpose had been in bringing him along for such important business, but he had been polite and quiet throughout the proceedings. As they had stood silently at court, listening to the courtiers argue with each other, she had looked at him straight in the eye and he had looked back. Shyly they exchanged smiles. He was a handsome boy, with perfect blond

233

hair and freckles. After the proceedings they had led him away and she had waved goodbye to him, which he reciprocated.

Later that night when her mother had been brushing her hair, she had inquired after him.

"Mother," she asked, "What was that boy's name? Today at court."

"That was one of the Atherian duke's boys. A cute little thing. I saw you making eyes at him."

"I did not, mother."

"Ah, my mistake. After all, what young boy could possibly resist such beautiful violet eyes such as yours?"

"Do you think so, mother? Do you think he was enamored?" she asked excitedly.

She laughed. "You are too young to know that word, my dear. Yet still you know better than to fancy Kingsmen. Your father the king would be very upset."

Kiera's shoulders had slumped as her feelings wilted.

"Princesses should not be slouching, my dear."

"But mother, I do not understand what is so wrong about these men who come to visit."

Her mother pulled her brush through the ends of her long hair and ran her hand down its soft length. "Kiera, if this were a perfect world we live in, you would be free to love as you wish. Nothing would make your mother happier than to see you happy with the perfect husband who gives you joy unparalleled. In the world we live in, however, old hatreds run deep in our veins. A great many wrongs were done to our people long ago by Kingsmen, and our people would rather die than see their princess with one of them."

"That doesn't make any sense, mother. What if a Kingsman makes me happy?"

Her mother wrapped her arms around her daughter and hugged her tightly. "Then it would make your mother just as happy. But it would make the kingdom sad."

"Maybe the kingdom is stupid."

"Perhaps you are right. Yet still your father is the divine head of that kingdom, and he would see its glory outshine any Kingsman. My Kiera..."

There was regret in her voice as she trailed off.

"Yes, mother?"

"You are old enough to know that they will never stop hating you, these Kingsmen. Some of them may be kind, and will love you, but the old ways cloud the judgment of even the sharpest minds. If ever you leave this country, they will see your charms, hear your voice, and they will hate you because you are different. They will, at times, treat you worse than a peasant, even though you are a princess. The cruelty in the eyes of some men and women is enough to make your mother wish she could tear them apart with her bare hands, but that would solve nothing. Korrainians and Kingsmen have been doing this for too long. Above all, my Kiera, promise me something?"

"Anything, mother."

"Promise me you will always be kind. Even as they spit at you. Even as they tear the charms from around your neck and curse your name. Do not curse them in kind. Do not become the animal they see you as. Show them kindness, and perhaps then they will finally understand."

Kiera never forgot that promise. As her fellow countrymen had descended into base lechery, thievery, and murder, she continued to embody that promise. After her mother died, her words were emblazoned into her brain forever as she was determined to live up to the ideals of a woman who only wished the world to be a kinder, gentler place. As she was young and impetuous at times, she struggled to take attacks at her people with anything but a dour face, but every day she tried to be just a little bit better. Everyday a little kinder. For her mother.

So even as she received narrow-eyed looks from guards and merchants alike on the streets of Nakisho, she smiled and waved to them all the same. She would never allow them to create another monster.

The cobbled roads in Naiwa-ki-Shokassen had largely been cleared of impediments by the time they had arrived, so their brisk walk up to the castle was without issue. Ethilia walked with such confidence that it bordered on irritation anytime she was stopped by a guard.

Finally they reached the massive iron gates which stood before the entrance to Nakisho Castle, and soldier in a long white coat and a curled brown wig with a wide brimmed hat stepped forward to greet them, crossbow in hand.

"Ah, welcome back, Lady Healer. I hope you have found yourself returned in good health?" the kindly young soldier chatted.

"Well enough, perhaps slightly chilled. I would warm up in my room if you would be so kind as to open the gate," Ethilia said, trying not to make too much of a show of her wrapping her arms around her middle in an attempt to withhold body heat.

"I'll be happy to do that right away. And who is your friend?"

"I'm Kiera. A pleasure to meet you!" she said cheerfully.

The man was quiet as he was lost in thought. After a moment he fished about in his pockets for a piece of parchment and read it silently before snorting in laughter.

"It says here I'm supposed to bring you in on charges of murder from the last time you were in Korraine, but I think given your help during the invasion no one will object if I happened to lose this," he said, tearing up the parchment.

"Except the Korrainians," Ethilia pointed out.

He shrugged. "Doesn't bother me none." He made a signal to the soldiers atop the walls and the gate creaked loudly as it grinded open.

"Thank you, good soldier," Kiera said.

"Ehm, just a moment, miss. I will have to take your weapons while you're in the castle. For security reasons."

Ethilia and Kiera exchanged a look. Kiera pulled her bow from around her shoulders and unsheathed her long hunting knife (which was more akin to a short sword) and several smaller knives and handed them off. To Kiera's shock, Ethilia knelt and retrieved a decorated knife from what must have been a sheath strapped to her leg.

"Ah, that won't be necessary, your ladyship."

Ethilia cocked her head. "You said we weren't allowed to be armed."

"Well, she can't be. You're different."

"Why am I different?" she responded with growing agitation in her voice.

"You are the Court Healer, your ladyship. You are well respected and trusted in the castle. She is...well..."

"Korrainian. You can say it."

"That's not at all what I meant..."

Ethilia poked the handle of her dagger towards him more insistently. "Take it or your superiors will hear about it."

Wordlessly and with a pale face, he took all of their weapons. Ethilia stormed off towards the castle with Kiera in tow.

"Ethilia, I don't know what to say!" she sputtered, trying to keep up with her blistering walking pace.

"It's best to put them in their place early and often. Lest they forget who their betters are."

The castle was just as Kiera remembered from just before the Battle of Nakisho. Compared to the castle she was accustomed to, this one had more of a terrifyingly robust air about it. From the bladed shield-spikes lining its dark, sullen walls to its *flamtuxellum* keeping watch from insurmountably high towers at all times, it gave off a feeling that it was ready to forge yet again into war at any time.

Companies of soldiers marched in formation about the grounds before the castle proper, stopping long enough to give a salute to Ethilia, who strode by them without a further glance.

In short order they made their way up to Ethilia's quarters, which Kiera had never been to before.

It was far larger than any room Kiera had been given – large enough for her to stable several horses in, should she have had the desire and means to. At least four armoires, a massive mahogany desk, a standing golden mirror, four maroon velvet chairs, two matching mahogany coffee tables, and a tea hutch occupied the bulk of the room, and a divider separated off what Kiera assumed to be where the beds were. Several marble busts of men unknown to her Korrainian recollection rested atop matching columns, with sunlight illuminating their every feature as it flooded in through windows several times her own height. There were crystalline chandeliers, a white marble fireplace with a roaring flame inside, dozens of paintings on the walls, and two flags just above the mantle – the white and gold one of Nakisho and the checkered sky blue and white one of House Vendimar.

She hadn't prevented herself from being frozen in place as she entered, in awe of such splendor, but Ethilia paid her no mind. A small girl who had been sitting before the fireplace got to her feet and curtsied as they entered.

"Sister! It is good to see you!" she squeaked. Kiera was a bad judge of age, but she guessed the girl was around…ten or so? To no one's surprise, she looked like a younger Ethilia, with her pristine shoulder-length blond hair and crystal blue eyes that had a brightness, a vivacity about them that Ethilia's only showed rarely.

Her older sister smiled and embraced her. "It is most fortunate to see you well, Tessalia. Dear sister, this is Kiera Itholos, Princess of Korraine. She is accompanying me on my way to Inderi-Xenus."

There was a significant amount of hesitation to her greeting, her eyes passing back and forth before saying anything.

"Pleased to meet you, Princess Kiera Itholos. I am Tessalia Vendimar."

It was such a rigid introduction that Kiera knew she had spoken similar words a hundred times.

Kiera waved a hand before giving the girl an unexpected hug. "No need to be so formal with me. Please, just call me Kiera."

"A-as you wish, Miss Kiera."

"If you will both excuse me, I simply must change into another set of riding clothes," Ethilia said, retrieving them from an armoire and disappearing behind the divider, "Do tell me, Tessalia, how your training has been coming along. I regret that my absence may have impeded your progress."

Kiera and Tessalia sat across from each other in front of the fireplace.

"Not at all, Ethilia. In fact, I've been coming along very well."

"Has Master Melossi been instructing you?"

"Sometimes. But mostly I teach myself."

"Noble, albeit difficult. I do hope you have not become discouraged."

"Ethilia, I can do so many things I could never do before. It has been so exciting! Before, cups would break or candles would go out without me making them, and it was scary. Now, I can *tell* the magic what to do."

"How free you must feel, dearest younger sister. It brings me joy to see you are no longer miserable."

Kiera interjected. "Why were you miserable, Tessalia?"

Ethilia answered at first. "I shall have to inform you on the road to Opterus."

Tessalia spoke next. "I was not allowed to be the magician I was born as."

"Speaking of which, I assume that you have received a letter from father as well?"

There was a pause as the young girl's features drooped. "Yes."

"You do not have to return if you do not wish it."

She grabbed a handful of the skirt of her dress and stiffened her jaw. "I...I do not want to go back."

Ethilia finally emerged from behind the divider, dressed in yet more immaculately white and gold travelling gear that Kiera knew would never actually protect her from the elements.

She placed a hand on her sister's blond head and gave her a warm smile. "Then you do not have to. I will speak to father. I am displeased with him anyway."

"What are you going to say to him?"

"Something to the effect that he is a dreadful father for what he did to you, that he should be ashamed of his behavior, and that he has brought dishonor upon our house. Perhaps with a few more colorful words for emphasis."

Tessalia covered her mouth in a gasp. "Ethilia, you cannot speak that way to father!"

"I can and I will. What is he going to do, lock me in my room? I have a lifetime contract to serve the High King here. I go where he pleases and any who impede me are followed up shortly by troops."

There was a knock at the door, and the person on the other side did not wait to be let in. It was a woman, perhaps in her thirties, with longer wavy brown hair and sizable…features. She wore otherwise simple clothing, no more than a dark blue dress bearing the High King's crest embroidered on the upper left chest.

"Ethilia!" she exclaimed, "You have little idea how happy I am to see you safe!"

"Master, what *ever* are you wearing?"

"Never mind that! I heard about what you faced during your stay to the north. We were all terrified that you were hurt, or worse."

"As you can see, master, we are very far from death's quiet whisper."

The woman turned to appraise Kiera. "You must be Princess Kiera. It's a pleasure – my name is Kaia Melossi, Court Magician to the High King."

Kiera smiled without standing. "Call me Kiera. You are Ethilia's master?"

"Officially. Though I'm certain Ethilia would prefer to be without one."

"Oh, not at all, master. I would be completely lost without your guidance and direction," Ethilia responded with dripping sarcasm.

Master Melossi ignored it, handing her charge a rolled up piece of parchment.

"The High King has approved this venture of yours. I don't know what good it will do, but clearly the wisest among us believe that some difference can be made."

"Your confidence in me is noted, master." Ethilia scanned over the letter. "We are to be accompanied by armed guard. How splendid."

"Did you really expect him to leave you two unprotected? No offense to you, Princess Kiera, but neither of you have any form of magic with which you could competently defend yourselves."

Kiera shifted forward in her chair and unslung her bow from her back, holding it in a standing position on the wood floor. "I have this, and I can use it well."

"That is well, but will do you little good against even an apprentice magician or Spellsword. The High King will have you accompanied by a few members of the 1st Regiment of Foot and one of the court magicians under my tutelage. She is an earth magician named Otomia. A little stubborn as with most earth magicians, but she is highly skilled."

There was yet another knock on the already open door, and Kaia shuffled aside to allow line of sight. In the doorway stood a middle-aged couple. The woman was not quite as tall as Kaia, but was certainly her elder by at least a decade, with worry lines visible on her forehead and around her mouth. She had otherwise long clove-colored hair brought up in a complicated series of overlapping braids secured by a green ribbon, and she sported a black woolen dress and a white overcoat. The man next to her was undoubtedly the largest, most powerfully built person in the room had it not been for his pronounced slouch, unmistakably from an injury.

Kiera did not recognize either of them, but Ethilia knew them instantly. Telmar, Reldon's father, was looking like a ghost of his previously vibrant self, but it was good to see him up and walking. He looked like he had lost a significant amount of weight since his initial brush with Brina, and the stress had aged his face and hair several years. The gray hairs were now winning the battle over his head. He wore a simple winter robe, as he was, by Ethilia's reckoning, not ready to don armor quite yet.

"Ah, Melina and Telmar. Do come in, it is a pleasure to see you well," Ethilia said, getting to her feet.

"As well as can be expected," Telmar chuckled gruffly.

"We received word that you had returned, and we had to catch you before you were off again," Melina stated.

"We've only been in Nakisho for maybe an hour. How-?" Kiera let the question trail off.

"Word travels at hawk's speed in this castle – it has to in order to protect the High King. Which is precisely why I do not recommend doing anything embarrassing. Everyone will know within a few minutes and they will never forget," Ethilia explained sourly.

"Ethilia, you were a very small girl. Everyone understands," Kaia said gently.

"We're not speaking of this now, Kaia. Or ever. How may I assist you this *fine* day, Melina?"

She blinked. "I had heard that you spent this year's storm with our son. If you would be so generous as to calm this worrying mother's mind, I would ask how he fares? It has been some time since we have seen him."

"He and his Ilewa are well – or at least as well as my position allows me to delve into their business. As usual they are preoccupied with matters which greatly exceed the importance of our own, but I should be happy to report that they are in good health and sound state of mind. So says their loving Golden Magician."

Melina and Telmar smiled broadly. "That is most kind of you to report. I'm sure you hear this very often, but you are a very precocious young magician, Miss Vendimar."

"Often enough I have considered adding the word to my official title. 'The Precocious Miss Vendimar, Golden Magician to the High King and Nakisho.' I thought perhaps it would be a bit too self-aggrandizing."

Kiera's look was of a bemused confusion and she directed it towards Tessalia. "Has she always spoken like this?"

The girl nodded with a shy smile. "Since I've been alive."

Ethilia returned to Melina to avoid becoming too much of a public marvel. "If you should like to see your son, he is headed hence to Irothrim with Bryle, Sillida, Elly, and his Ilewa. You may be able to get a message to them through the messenger magicians."

"That will not be necessary, it is good to hear that they are well. We are being recalled to Errum, so it saddens me to know we will likely not see him again for some time."

"And when shall you be returning to us?" Kaia asked.

"That is the difficult part. We will not be."

Everyone's ears perked up and there was deafening silence.

She continued. "You may or may not have heard, but word has reached us that King Garen has declared that our kingdom is now the

Empire of Errum, and he is emperor. His first decree was that we shall no longer have diplomatic ties of any kind with other nations. We've been ordered to return to Remdas-Kuwis and await instruction. Until he wills otherwise…I doubt we shall return."

There was nothing but shocked silence followed by sputtering attempts to vocalize the confusion.

"The 'Empire of Errum'?" What in the world is he thinking?"

"He can't do this!"

"You can't leave us forever!"

Melina put up her hands to calm the fervor. "It is my hope that we shall not have to leave for long. Cooler heads will prevail, as no nation, except Drunerakerrum, can exist forever without diplomacy. These policies are untenable and he will come to realize it soon enough. Until then, we shall just have to be patient. We will write often."

"Oh please do, Melina," Kaia said with genuine sadness in her voice, "These corridors will be several shades less bright without you both here."

There came yet another knock at the door. It was a man Ethilia had seen at least a thousand times – the court page.

"I'm terribly sorry to interrupt," the young man whimpered.

"You might as well come in, half the kingdom is already in here," Ethilia stung sarcastically.

"My most sincere apologies, Miss Vendimar. The High King has requested your presence at your earliest convenience. And he has requested Princess Kiera Itholos to attend as well."

They sucked in air at the same time.

Ethilia and Kiera both knew that the High King of Lärim did not request audiences with just anyone for any reason. Though they knew that Reldon and Alira had met with him on a few occasions, the Nurems' level of importance greatly dwarfed their own.

The page noticed their nonplussed reaction and pointed down the corridor. "I'll…uh…wait to take you to the High King when you're ready."

Melina smiled and crossed her arms. "It sounds like you have both caught the eye of important people. I wish you the best of luck, and Telmar and I hope to see all of you healthy and bright-eyed as soon as possible."

"Travel well, dear diplomats. Do try to speak some sense into that 'emperor' of yours," Kaia said to laughter. She turned and swung the doors inwardly as she left. "Good luck you two."

The doors shut with little noise and Tessalia only watched the two teens with eyes eager for answers.

"Well, let us be off then," Kiera stood to leave.

Ethilia let out a squeak of disdain. "Wha-! Where do you think you're going?"

"Going to see the High King. Didn't you hear?"

"Dressed like *that?*"

"What's wrong with it?" she responded, rotating and eyeing her clothes, which were mostly leather and fur travelling clothes fitting tightly to her figure, along with her bead necklaces and a sash around her middle with all manner of designs.

"They're *riding leathers!*"

"But they are very nice riding leathers."

"I don't give three halves of a cracker how nice they are! One does not step before the High King in anything less than full regalia!" Ethilia said, slamming open one of her many wardrobes and fishing through its contents.

"And by regalia you mean…a dress?"

Ethilia stopped, slapping her lap and whirling around to face her. "Are you or are you not a princess?"

Her eyes drooped very slightly. "Not anymore."

"Only in the mind of miserable useless men many miles from here. In this castle you are a princess, and shall dress accordingly. Here, try this on."

Kiera snatched the clothing out of the air, giving it a suspicious glance. "You surely cannot be serious."

"Come now, Kiera. We mustn't keep the High King waiting."

"Tell him I'm sick."

"One does not shirk a meeting with his Gloriousness. You are beautiful, do not be afraid."

"I feel silly, Ethilia."

"It's all in your head. Let your princess heart come alive."

Kiera groaned and stepped out of the room and into the corridor.

Offsetting her extremely red face was her gorgeous flowing white and blue silk dress with a tight bodice encompassing her entire middle, puffed sleeves secured at the elbow by blue ribbon, a sapphire broach at her chest affixing a blue and gold shawl wrapping around her upper bodice and exposing her bony shoulders and collarbones, and on her head she wore another blue ribbon with a matching pansy atop it which held her now shoulder-length dark hair.

"It really brings out your violet eyes. Though I wish you had worn the necklace that went with it," Ethilia complained.

Instead Kiera had her mess of beads. "These are not negotiable."

The court healer sighed. "Fine. Let's be off then."

Kiera thought Ethilia pulled off the regalia much more gracefully than she did. Naturally she was wearing a dress that was completely, immaculately white, with gold lace down the back and a gold shawl around her bust. She had definitely been more creative with her jewelry, as she was draped in a golden pendant, two golden bangles, and a diadem on her perfect golden hair. Everything about her was tinged with the most opulent gold and white Kiera had ever seen.

"Ethilia, have you…ever worn anything but those colors?"

She paused with a slight huff as they walked. "Never."

"Not once?"

"Not a single time."

"You're teasing me."

"Am I?"

Kiera's eyes narrowed playfully. "I think you're lying."

The court page pushed open the broad double doors to a small entertaining room where those who would meet with the High King could wait in relative comfort. It was every bit as lavish as the rest of the castle, with plush white velvet couches, paintings, and marble busts of previous High Kings.

"I shall see if the High King is ready. Just a moment," the page said, bowing and entering the solar.

The wait was killing Kiera. To be seen in such clothes would be an embarrassment in Korraine.

"Stop fidgeting," Ethilia whispered sharply.

"I cannot help it. This accursed thing is squeezing my middle and I can hardly breathe."

"I swear, if you adjust it in the presence of the High King…"

"I must breathe somehow!"

The page reemerged by poking his head through the door. "The High King is ready to speak to you."

The High King's solar was smaller than either of them imagined, but it was highly comfortable. Several of the same white velvet chairs sat around a marble table, just next to a roaring fireplace. Bookcases lined the walls that weren't encompassed in their entirety by towering windows that lent a spectacular view of the bleached countryside for many miles, with distant snow-capped mountains in the distance giving it an air of power and majesty.

The man himself stood on the opposite side of the table, quietly watching them enter. He was as Ethilia remembered, but stood as more of a symbol to Kiera – a symbol she had always been told was tantamount to a slave master. He was silent, calculating, tall, and handsome, with long curly brown hair that fell to chest level. Today he wore no hat upon his head, but made up for it by donning an interesting silver and purple slashed doublet that was not loose or puffy as was the typical fashion, but instead was tight fitting. Over the top he bore a sort of open overcoat, black and silver, with a frilled collar and silver brooch clasped to a matching black and silver cape. Only his breeches were looser, giving way to his black boots with silver buckles.

Kiera was not a terribly short girl for her age – she even stood a few inches taller than Ethilia – but the High King simply towered over them. He fully had the capacity to look terrifying, and by all rights she should have been scared, but he gave off an aura of...calm authority that fear was the last emotion she was feeling once she stepped into the room.

Ethilia gave a low curtsy and gave Kiera a severe look to urge her to do the same. "Your Grace."

He gave them a slight nod. "Thank you both for coming. I would be most understanding had you been too spent to attend. The journey can be long and treacherous in this season."

There was another man in the corner of the solar, and they both noticed simultaneously. He was very large, standing perhaps a few inches shorter than the High King, but was grossly overweight. Multiple chins were bulging out from beneath his wired collar, looking somewhat like a leafed stem atop a tomato. His clothes were obviously rich as well, but contained so much fabric that it could have been made into clothing for at least two smaller men. With a bulbous nose and long, greasy, curly hair, he was quite a sight to behold, but from his complexion he looked much younger than expected.

"I apologize for not meeting with you alone. I was finishing important business as you arrived. This is the Lord Mayor High Prince Calmarian Shoka-Dathrim of Naiwa-ki-Shokassen, my younger brother and uncle to my son the next High King."

Kiera was trying not to laugh, and Ethilia elbowed her inconspicuously.

"It is our most distinct pleasure to meet you, My Lord," Ethilia said with another curtsy, not quite as deep this time.

The fat man appraised them. "I hope you fare well. You are both so beautiful that it would have been a shame should the elements have claimed you."

The High King gave him a sidelong glance. "Is there anything I can have my serving girl fetch for you? Tea?"

"You are most gracious, Your Grace, but we are well sated," Ethilia responded.

"Then let us sit and discuss issues of import. My good brother, I give you leave."

"Is this one Korrainian?" the huge mayor said, pointing at Kiera, "Why have you brought her kind into your castle, brother? Have you learned-"

The entire atmosphere of the room shifted as the High King repeated himself.

"I said I give you leave, brother."

His gaze could not have been described as anything but even, but the inflection it gave was more impactful than if he had slapped him in the face. Calmarian sputtered for a moment before turning and waddling out.

"My most sincere apologies for his impertinence. He does not often think before opening up his thoughts to the world around him."

The apology was directed at Kiera, but she merely sat up straight in her chair and nodded nervously.

Ethilia broke the silence. "It's quite all right, Your Grace, there was no harm."

His orange sunburst eyes did not stray from Kiera's violet ones, even as Ethilia spoke. His gaze was soft, understanding.

"Do you fear me, Princess Kiera?"

Her eyes darted about searching for an apt answer to that question. "No, My Lord."

"But you do not trust me."

Kiera's eyes sunk to the floor to avoid further eye contact. "No, My Lord."

Ethilia sharply inhaled, but the High King held up a hand. "It's quite all right, Miss Vendimar. I am not in the business of punishing dissent. I completely understand why you might not wish to put trust in the leader of your people's enemies."

Kiera looked at him again with sadness in her eyes. "Your people hate mine."

"Some do. Of that there is no doubt, and if it were in my power to change their minds, I would not hesitate to do so. The old hatreds which have tainted our two peoples for many centuries are a plague with little cure, I'm afraid. Perhaps time and understanding will be the best remedy. And it is this understanding that I hope to gain from you here today. I invited you to my solar so we might speak of your kin, and of your place among them. It is most regretful what your father has done to you, and I would hear you speak of it with me if you are willing."

Kiera fidgeted again. "Am I still to be a princess, My Lord?"

Even his eyes were tinged with sadness. "According to the law, yes. And given that I embody the laws of this beautiful kingdom, I shall always see you as such, dear Princess Kiera Itholos. However, among your old peers, your name in the days to come shall bring little but disdain. The title of princess shall not preface your name on their lips until the day they return to the spirits to which they pray. This does not necessarily speak to the will of the people, as it would turn out. Little time has passed since this decision, and it has already reached mine ears that some discontent among the Korrainian populace has resulted from it. Your people still call you princess, Kiera."

Her spirits were visibly lifted. "Th-they do?"

"As it would seem," he responded with a very warm smile.

"But…" she considered, "What are they going to do about it? They aren't going to rise up are they?"

The High King laced his fingers together on the table. "I cannot say. But I should warn you, if you are concerned for your father's safety, the armies of Lärim will not come to his aid. If it were a rebellion in regards to most other decisions, Nakisho would be honor-bound to send troops to assist, but given that this was an illegal act to change his succession, any repercussions that have already been set in motion shall not be impeded by any action taken by this administration."

Kiera bit her lip. "I hope they do not think to install me as Queen."

"It would not be without precedent, but I find that unlikely. It was the change of succession that has invoked their ire – it would be most logical if they should want it reversed and little more."

She was practically gnawing on her lip, and the High King noticed.

"Is there something you would like to tell me? Something that is bringing you tribulation?"

Kiera exchanged a look with Ethilia, who gave her widened eye look that said *whatever it is, go on, tell him!*

"I…" She played with a ribbon on her dress idly. As soon as she looked back up at his face, she knew she had to tell him. "I have been approached, My Lord."

"By whom? Who has approached you?"

"Garen. Of Errum."

"Oh? And what did our good friend the emperor say to you?" he asked with a wry smile, which also transferred to Ethilia's nervous face.

"He…wanted me to usurp my father."

Ethilia gasped and covered her mouth. "He what?!"

High King Julius merely cocked his head. "And why would he want such a thing?"

"I do not know. He told me I deserved to be on the throne and that the old ways needed to die."

What was otherwise the type of allegation that would have brought entire courts to stunned silence had no obvious visceral effect on the most powerful king in Lärim. If anything, he appeared pensive.

"Such sentiments would be consistent with his most recent proclamations as emperor. Though it is perplexing why he would remove all diplomatic ties with foreign nations only to attempt to overthrow nations abroad in order to expand his influence. Curious indeed."

"Your Grace, what is to be done about Emperor Garen? Surely he is not in his right mind," Ethilia said.

"It is not my place to say. Whether he is of sound mind is not known, but he believes his convictions and so do his followers. That is all that matters for now. He is otherwise preoccupied with bringing a sudden and bloody end to the Kuru, which gives us time to consider our options, but I shall regard him as Lärim has always done. You see, Lärim is the father to all nations, and the Nuru and Kuru are two of its many children. Sometimes children rebel against their father as they grow – it is a most natural progression."

The High King leaned in, his eagle eyes watching Kiera's every movement.

"It would seem that powers that exist in this world have taken a keen interest in you, Princess Kiera. Now if I may be so bold as to ask, what is to be your next move?

He wants to know if I'm going to try to take over my father's throne, she thought warily.

"I am…conflicted, My Lord. My father has wounded me so by his actions, but he is still my father. There is so much happening with me in the middle…I wish I could go hunting again and forget all of this."

His reaction was sympathetic. "All who have destiny thrust upon them most certainly wish for simpler times – your friends the Nurems were no different. You and I are not dissimilar in this respect. The weight of responsibility that the illustrious title of High King brings is not something most could withstand. I would not wish to persuade you towards one end or another, but I understand the gravity of the situation you find yourself embroiled."

"I…do not feel safe, My Lord. My father might try to have me killed to take the decision away. And being Korrainian and…wearing these beads…in the rest of Lärim makes me more like prey than a huntress. I have so few choices available that make me happy."

His features grew stern. "Of that I can promise you – no harm shall befall you whilst you are in my kingdom. Regardless of your father's act of succession change, you are still royalty and shall be regarded as such by all my subjects, both king and peasant. For now all I can tell you is how the administration of the High King shall respond to these happenings and it shall be your prerogative to act accordingly. I shall be keeping a constant vigil on your home land and will not allow any further transgressions against the rule of law. In the meantime, I understand you are both on a mission of your own?"

This time the question was directed at Ethilia.

She perked up as if she'd been poked. "Y-yes, Your Grace. Reldon and Alira have tasked us with bringing together the court healers and other Golden Magicians from around Lärim in a single place."

His eyebrows raised. "How ambitious! And to what end?"

"To consider a strategy to use Golden Magic to destroy the Churai. We discovered in our time with the High- well, *your* consort, that Churai have an aversion to Golden Magic, which I suppose would make sense as they are the embodiment of death."

He leaned back and narrowed his eyes in deep thought. "I struggle to recall, but I believe I had heard this theory before."

"Undoubtedly your Lordship has heard of it in all his learning. It has been known for some time, but there has never been a way to turn it into a weapon. And that is the purpose for our meeting."

"Ah, this seems suitable. Very well, as you have been told it is my decision to grant this request, Miss Vendimar. However, I cannot force the other court healers to take leave from their positions – that will need to be achieved of your own charm and wile." He traded another smile with Ethilia before looking back at Kiera. "Consider what I have said carefully before making a decision which could alter the face of a country. You shall both be safe under my protection in this heart of Lärim, but I will not be able to extend such protection to Korraine."

Kiera swallowed. "You are very kind. Much more than my kin would have me believe. I thought you would be angry with me when I told you about these schemes to make me Queen."

He shook his head, taking to his feet. "As I said, in light of events reaching mine ears from Korraine, this administration is largely indifferent to the fate of the Korrainian throne so long as a legitimate ruler sits upon it. The rest is all politics."

Kiera and Ethilia took the cue and also got to their feet with another curtsy.

"You have our eternal thanks for this meeting, Your Grace."

The High King nodded with a small smile. "Go well in peace. We shall meet again soon."

His page opened the door to allow them exit, and at the last second Kiera turned and spoke once more to the High King who had sat down to review some parchment.

"Oh, Tavia wishes you well and good health, My Lord."

For a long moment he looked lost, staring off into the air before blinking. "Ah. Yes. Thank you for relaying that."

Dear spirits he has no idea who I am talking about.

Chapter XXXII

Darum was a country with little aesthetically to recommend it, other than the snowy mountains looming to the north. There were some plains to the south, but they were not the same as the plains in Errum or southern Lärim; instead, the entirety of the terrain was much more similar to that of Korraine – rocky, sandy in some places, utterly inhospitable and all the while covered in at least two feet of snow. Unlike large portions of Korraine, however, Darum did have some small forests and ponds, with much more wildlife.

As they had travelled, Reldon, Alira, Bryle, Sillida, and Elly had noticed the primary focus of the country through what they saw dotting the landscape on either side of the road for miles: mines. Black stone buildings poked up from the rocks to mark the placement of each mine in relative silence, as all of the pertinent action was taking place below. They passed multitudes of carts on their way to Irothrim, each practically overflowing with various metal ores like iron, tin, and in some cases gold.

All of these roads and carts led to Irothrim, the capital city, which anyone could see from many miles away, but not due to any buildings or colossal walls. It was the smoke that gave away the city's position to any who might search for it. Enormous plumes of black smoke billowed into the air at all times, causing the air surrounding the city to smell strongly of something none of them could identify. Reldon thought the smell was similar to the smell of a forge, like his father had had in Freiad.

Gaining entrance to Irothrim was harder than any city they had yet been to. The guards were all dressed in full military attire, complete with breastplates, iron and leather boots, metal lobster gauntlets, and sturdy black plumed helmets which covered almost their entire faces, save for their eyes and mouth. They asked an incredible number of questions: "Who are you?" "Why are you in Darum?" "How long are you planning on staying?" "What nationality are you?" "How much money did you bring with you?" It seemed to both Bryle and Alira that they were asking these questions to ensure they weren't some sort of rebels. In fact, they were told they had no choice but to leave their horses in a stable outside the city to prevent them causing any trouble with them.

Inside the city, the smoke was significantly worse, and with it the smell was oppressive. All of the houses, workshops, forges, smiths, and fortifications were made from a combination of stone and iron, lending everything a dark grey appearance, which wasn't helped by the black banners they hung everywhere.

Strangest of all were the people.

Everyone, from the warriors to the midwives to even the children running about on the cobble-and-iron streets were donned in some form of armor. The entire Darumite population looked as if they were in the final stages of preparing for war at all times. Though the younger children were the exception, all able bodied young or old adults also carried some form of weapon, be it a spear in their hand, a sword at their hip, or an axe strapped to their back. In short order, everyone but Bryle, clad in his own armor, was beginning to feel a bit naked.

How peculiar! Don't you think it would be tiresome and not comfortable at all to be wearing armor and weapons at all times? Alira asked. *I think I just saw a little girl with a mace!*

It isn't much different than how we have to be armed and ready all the time, and we're not much older than some of these boys and girls.

But they act like they're under invasion.

Not too long ago, that fear wasn't too far off.

They were most certainly garnering attention as they made their way through the streets. Ruddy-faced men with long unkempt hair and shirts of chain watched them with something between caution and disdain as they passed. Women made no secret of shooing their young ones away from the visitors.

The sound of hammers on anvils was nearly deafening as hundreds of them sounded off every minute.

"This is a strange place," Elly said over the noise, holding Alira's hand tighter.

"Where did you say you were meeting your person, Reldon?" Bryle shouted.

Reldon unfurled the letter again, reading aloud, "'At the place where the metal and water make their music'. Any idea where that might be?"

"Hard to tell in all this mess. Let's find somewhere quiet."

Occasionally they would see someone pass by who was clearly a Knight, a Spellsword, or a magician, as they were the ones dressed in the heaviest or most elaborate armor. A magician and Knight team that walked by put them on their nerve's edge, as the Knight was weighed down by so much plate armor that not a single part of his actual body could be seen. As for the magician, she bore a type of tempered iron armor on her whole arms, legs, and torso that was form fitting enough to allow easier movement. Over top she wore crimson livery with a wicked orange symbol of flame, and her head was covered in a red hood.

As they walked by, they clearly detected their Phyrimic or magical presence and their attention snapped up to observe them. For a moment Reldon and Alira were certain they were going to say something, but were astonished as they allowed them to pass without a word.

"Let's go to that inn and get off the road. These people don't trust us," Bryle said, ushering them inside. It was a large, nearly windowless inn with a sign over the door with just the words *The Cursed Wagon.*

Inside most of the light was provided by two roaring fireplaces flanking both long walls of the rectangular shaped building. Two dozen dark wood tables made up the center of the hall, and a bar on the far end with several massive barrels made up the downstairs – relatively standard fare for an inn, as they assumed there were rooms above.

However, few of the chairs were filled, as the patrons were crowded around someone standing on a wooden crate in the corner of the room. She was a short young woman with long straight black hair and fair skin, wearing a silken gown or robe that neither Reldon nor Alira had ever seen before. It was a long robe with flowing depictions of fantastical creatures in vibrant reds and yellows on a deep blue background, with bells and ribbons dangling from her sleeves.

She waved at them as they entered, and her crowd turned to look at the newcomers.

"You! Do come quickly! You don't want to miss this!"

They all exchanged quizzical looks but joined the rest of the armored crowd.

"Welcome to all of you, to experience the wonders and mysteries of the magical realm. Many of you see me here from week to week, performing acts of magical miracles beyond your wildest comprehensions, but today I have something to reveal to you all. Little have you known that all this time you have been in the presence of magician royalty, as I, the wondrous Nova Castermark, am a user of all the elements! That's right, I am one of the long foretold practitioners who can harness all of the latent powers of this world and use them for good!"

The crowd cheered and urged her onward. Reldon shot Alira a look, whose eyes were wide with confusion.

That's not possible!

"Now observe! Legend is at hand! And behold the power of the elements!"

She extended a hand into the air, directed overhead of the crowd and with a burst of heat she let loose a jet of flame that almost reached the top floor of the building. Her loving patrons clapped and further cheered. With her other hand she mirrored the same action, and instead of fire a powerful stream of water emitted from her hands to splash noisily on the floor behind the crowd.

"I'll clean that up!" she shouted after she realized what she did.

The barkeep sighed and shook his head.

Next she clasped both hands over her head and from within she produced a light brilliant enough to force all observers to shield their eyes. Within a second, it was gone and she was on to the next element, which she brought to bear by using a complicated series of hand gestures before punching the wooden floor beneath her. At first nothing happened, but gradually their footing grew unsure as the floor vibrated and then shook violently.

This was enough for the crowd to become unruly in their cheering as they wrestled their way forward to drop coins into the young woman's jar. Further cries of "Bless you Ilewa Nuremil!" and "Please help us kill the Kuru!" only served to broaden the smile that was on her face. She raised her hands and calmed her new fans/disciples.

"Rest assured, I will do everything I can to use my powers to rid this world of all of its ills, including the dastardly Kuru to the west. In fact, I shall be leaving to head there tomorrow, so you can all expect good news to grace your ears! Many great miracles can I achieve, but I cannot do it without you. Being a heroine does not always pay for a room at the inn, so your coin is ever appreciated! I love you all, and I bear you good tidings!"

More coins clinked into her jar and many men offered to buy her drinks, but she politely refused, stating she needed to "keep a clear mind".

Alira was dumbfounded. If Reldon didn't know any better, the feeling he was getting in copious quantities from their mind link was pure jealousy.

Once the men had moseyed back to their tables, leaving her clean up the watery mess she had made, Alira stomped up to her. Nova looked up with a smile.

"Well hello! You're a cute one. Did you enjoy seeing the fire and water and such?"

Alira's eyes narrowed and she got her pouty look. "You are *not* the Ilewa Nuremil." Reldon could tell she was scanning her with her magical vision. "You're not even a magician!"

"Woah, what feistiness from one so small! Did you not see the flames? Who are you anyway, with your outlandish clothing and Atherian accent?"

Her eyes immediately began to glow a threatening red.

"I'm the *real* Ilewa Nuremil," she growled.

Fear drenched the woman's face as her eyes went as wide as they could go. "T-there's no way. You're just an ordinary magician! Here to stop me from making my living and helping people!"

Alira yanked her sleeve up her arm and forced enough magic into her Keinume that the silver rose emerged with a bright ferocity that would have shaken the entire building if she had continued.

"The silver rose! Oh dear spirits! I'm sorry! I'm so sorry! Please, I meant nothing by it, just trying to make a living! Please don't tell everyone!" she exclaimed in a loud whisper.

A few people had craned their heads around to see what the ruckus was, but Alira pushed her sleeve down again to prevent from making a scene. "We need to talk."

"Yes, talk! Thank you, thank you! Just over here, let us speak."

They walked to the furthest corner of the room which was vacant and reserved for her various items and bags, far enough from earshot so long as no one got *too* heated.

"You must be...um...Miss Alira Ayuru," the woman tried to say cordially.

"Yes," Alira responded with a complete lack of cordiality, "How long have you been pretending to be me?"

"Oh, not pretending to *be* you, Miss Ayuru. I never claimed to be you. I only said I was also a user of all elements, that's all!"

"But you're not. You're not even a magician. How did you do it?"

There was a great hesitation as the woman's dark eyes considered her options. Alira's flashed red again to help make up her mind.

She fished into her pockets to retrieve what they all initially thought were baubles. Upon closer inspection they appeared to be some kind of black metal with small leather straps affixed to them.

"What are these?" Bryle asked.

"Artifacts of incredible worth. This one produced the flame, this one creates water, and this one becomes very bright when activated. As for the earthquake, it's a series of mechanisms in the basement of this building operated by-"

Suddenly a dark-eyed young man with shaggy black hair jogged up with a grin on his face. What was striking about this young man was that he seemed to be carrying at least a dozen different weapons on his person. "How did the show go today, my dear? I...." He spotted the bits of metal and leather in her hand. "That's not good."

Nova's eyes went wide and her lips drew together. "Why hello my love, this is Miss Alira Ayuru and her friends. Isn't it nice to see them?"

He froze. "Alira Ayuru. The real Ilewa Nuremil. Definitely uh...definitely not good."

"This is Xaetius Alsmith, my beloved and assistant. We make a wonderful team together."

The man, who was likely about the same age as Nova, bowed with a series of clanks. "Pleasure to meet you all. Please have mercy on us."

"Those aren't your real names, are they?" Reldon asked cynically.

"They could be," Xaetius replied.

"But they're not."

"What if they are?"

Elly chimed in. "Then they're silly names."

Nova huffed. "You are correct, they are stage names. I'm not even Darumite. I don't even know where I come from. I never knew my parents, spent years on the road as an assistant to a travelling charlatan before joining the academy in Nakisho. That's when I discovered my passion for finding rare artifacts from lost civilizations. Does that suffice as an explanation?"

"Hardly," Sillida spat.

"You forgot to tell them the part about being expelled from the academy!" Xaetius added joyfully until he got a cold stare from Nova.

"I'm going to guess they didn't like you using ancient artifacts to procure more coin," Bryle presumed.

"We had some professional disagreements," she stated simply, "I felt my talents would be better used elsewhere."

"How many places have you claimed to be the Ilewa Nuremil?" Alira asked pointedly.

"This is the first. I've always claimed previously to be a magician. I've wished my entire life I could be a magician, ever since I was a small girl. I saw how gallant they are, roaming the countryside helping to save lives...I wanted that. But you can't change your blood or your birth circumstances. I'm as average and uninteresting as the next girl and I always hated it. So when I found my first artifact that could actually make me feel like a real magician, I knew what I had to do."

"Become a fraud?" Bryle snickered.

"No! Even if for the occasional moment I could see the awe and wonder in people's eyes as they looked at me the same way I looked at the real magicians…then it would be worth it. The coin was just so I could keep doing it."

Alira took the young woman's hand gently. "Nova…I understand what it's like to want to be something different. For a long time I wanted the opposite – to be normal like you. Being a magician isn't all glory and saving people. Everyone makes mistakes, but when you're bringing magical elements into the situation, one little mistake could hurt or even kill someone. It's an incredible responsibility. For all of the good that we do, there are a lot of people who hate us because of the mistakes we have made. I wouldn't wish that on you, Nova. Or…whatever your real name is."

"You are very kind, Miss Ayuru, but I am ready for this responsibility. With these artifacts I plan to help a lot of people. I'm going to stop doing this show soon enough, once I have saved up the coin to continue to experiment on them."

"What do you mean?" Reldon asked.

"Well…you see, there are some major drawbacks to these artifacts. For whatever reason they need time to…rest. Real magicians can hurl fire around for a while, but this one for example can only release a single jet of flame for around three or four seconds before having to rest for as little as two hours and as long as six. If I can't reliably use them consistently, then I will never be of use to anyone, so I've begun tinkering with them in the hopes of figuring out why they need to rest for so long."

"You may end up breaking them, you know," Bryle mentioned.

"That is a risk I am willing to take."

"I've never heard of such powerful little artifacts. Where did you find them?" Alira asked.

"There are a series of ruins in northeast Lärim, otherwise the far eastern portion of The Sjard, where scholars are just now unearthing what they believe to be an entire ancient city. When they found these, we were convinced that they possessed power that may have outstripped our own, with exception to magicians and Spellswords, of course."

"Wait, you said *they* found those? They let you keep them?" Reldon inquired.

She pressed her lips together again and peered around the room. "Dear spirits, you stole them!"

"I only took them on my way out! I was a part of the team that discovered them, so they're essentially mine anyway."

"If they're so valuable, they are going to hunt you!"

She waved a hand towards Xaetius. "That's what I have him for."

He smiled broadly and nodded with vigor.

Bryle scanned the man's weapons. "That's a lot of iron you're carrying."

From what they could see, the man was wielding a short sword at each hip, at least four daggers around his belt, a longsword and spear on the bulk of his back, a mace and flail strapped to the small of his back, and pointed blades were affixed to his knees, elbows, and boots. He was like a walking weapon rack.

"Oh thank you, I figured I would travel a little lighter today so I could move around."

"*Lighter?* How are you not crushed under all of that?"

He thought about it for a moment before shrugging. "Doesn't feel that heavy to me. I would think your armor would be heavier."

Nova clasped Alira's hand with both of her own. "I'm sorry for impersonating an Ilewa Nuremil. It won't happen again. I'm begging you not to tell anyone that I'm not a real magician."

Alira thought for a moment. "Have you ever heard of a place in Irothrim where the metal and water make their music?"

She nodded enthusiastically. "Of course! Why do you ask?"

"Take us to it, and I promise we won't tell anyone."

"Deal. Come along, Xaetius, we're off to show them Irothrim's prized attraction."

The inner city was a labyrinth of choking smog, grid-like streets that often ended abruptly and without reason, and entire mobs of people moving from task to task with what looked like military efficiency. Everyone looked as if they were on a defining mission, and no one took any time to stop and talk. It was all like one massive factory, focused entirely on production and discipline.

It was such a culture shock that Alira couldn't help but to inquire.

"So…what do people do here for fun? They…do have fun, right?"

"Of course they do," Nova responded casually, "It usually involves drinking, contests of strength or endurance, and occasionally even real combat."

"You mean they fight in an arena?" Bryle asked.

"Oh absolutely, but some fights are for honor and are not as formal as a gladiatorial bout. Duels are a way of life around here, so don't go dishonoring some man's daughter or he may run you through. All completely legal by the way."

"If fighting and drinking are all they do here, do they not have any art or academies?" Reldon asked next.

"Academies? Certainly not. Between us, these people are more likely to use a book as a stein coaster than actually read it. If I continued my life as a scholar, this would be the last place I'd want to be, what with it being essentially a desert of intellectual thought. The only learning they care about around here is how to make and use a better weapon or armor."

"If you're not so fond of them, then why choose Irothrim to befraud?" Bryle asked without irony.

Her eyes shut with strained patience before letting it go. "We haven't been here terribly long, and we go everywhere. The culture here is severely lacking in, well… culture, but their coin is good. We'll be gone soon enough."

Bryle had been eyeing the young man carrying so many weapons, perhaps out of a sense of wary caution. "You don't say very much, do you Xaetius?"

He seemed surprised by the question and he smiled awkwardly. "Nova does all the talking for me. I do not need to."

"Master, look!" Elly pointed ahead.

Standing near the middle of the city was the only dab of color within miles – from the outside it looked to be an untamed forest, green and plentiful, but as they approached they realized it was not wild foliage, but carefully planned greenery in a massive circular formation. A circle of various trees and bushes dotted the outer ring, creating a wall from the winds and noise from without. The middle ring was nothing but well-kept grass, unblemished by any structures or even weeds. (Although many sheep and goats grazed on it) The innermost ring was a cobbled road with two connecting roads bisecting the whole circle leading back to the dreary city. There were bubbling fountains around the innermost ring that were somehow not frozen in the midst of winter. In fact, the entire park was a complete mystery, as it was a splotch of impossible greenery that could not have been growing at this time of year.

In the very center of all the circles was a colossal standing contraption that neither Reldon nor Alira would have been able to aptly describe. It appeared to be a series of metal tubes emerging from within the earth, twisting and writhing around one another like a nest of snakes or worms, and finally resolving into thirty-two straight, slitted, capped tubes jutting into the cool air at graduated heights. Each tube, except perhaps the smaller ones, were large enough to fit a person through.

"Here we are!" Nova exclaimed.

Almost everyone else was nonplussed.

Reldon stammered. "W-what is this place? How is all of this possible?"

Nova shrugged, pushing the hair out of her eyes. "I couldn't tell you all of the details, but I do know one part of it. Put your hand on the dirt under the grass."

They all obeyed and incredibly the dirt was warm to the touch.

"There is some kind of geothermal vent below all of this. Nothing ever freezes. And if I'm not mistaken there is an aquifer that provides the hot water for all of this." She waved a hand at the enormous contraption.

"So what *is* it?" Alira inquired further.

"The locals call it the Grand Firehorns, even though they are not horns and there is no fire involved, but we won't get into that. I'm not completely sure how it works, but it seems to use that same hot water from below to create steam, forcing it through each of these tubes to make sound."

"How exciting!" Alira beamed.

"But it's not working," Elly pointed out.

"I've only ever heard it from across the city, and only a few times. It has a…haunting sound to it, but I suppose that depends on what song is being played on it. I couldn't tell you how to make it work."

"Maybe it only works on certain days?" Sillida posited.

"Or maybe someone has a key to use it," Bryle said.

Alira walked closer to it, staring up at the gleaming metal whistles at the top.

"Or maybe it just takes magic."

She held a hand out and felt the latent energies within her welling up to be ordered. Her Keinume focused this power, and reached out to the heat and water below. It felt familiar, two halves of a whole. Water and fire – opposites, but on this day they would become one.

With a twist of her hand, she felt a surge of powerful steam erupt from within the ground beneath, and within a split second it worked its way through the maze of tubes and through the whistles at the top.

The noise was deafening, and shook the ground. Steam billowed out of all of the whistles at once creating a cacophony of metallic sound she had never heard before. It was not a good sound, it was a burst of incredible noise that cast its relentless pride across the entire city.

Everyone, including several onlookers, had nearly fallen to the ground from the surprise and covered their ears just a bit too late.

"I don't think that was how it was supposed to be played," Bryle said, picking at his ear.

"It's harder than it looks, Bryle."

Several passersby watched her to see if she was going to do it again. One older woman approached Alira and stood beside her as she peered up at the mess of metal.

"Try funneling the steam through the tubes one at a time. See which sounds you like together."

Alira appraised the old woman for a second before trying again.

At first it was difficult like the previous time, as steam had a tendency to rapidly expand and didn't like being controlled. A similar sound as before, chaotic and dissonant, squeaked through, but she quickly learned to control it. After a few seconds, she had funneled the steam into one of the lower whistles, producing a rich basso. Then she took a little bit of that steam and siphoned it into one of the mid-range whistles. It was still dissonant, so she tried an adjacent one and it created an almost perfect harmony. One by one she added sounds by trial and error, until she had an otherwise pleasant chord surging through the pipes.

It wasn't terribly taxing on her, just difficult to control. She stopped and looked back at the old woman, who grinned back at her.

"Well done, Miss Ayuru. Well done indeed."

Alira's own smile dropped instantly. "How do you know who I am?"

The old woman was short, dressed in simple garments and with her long white hair tied back in a single braid. Her gnarled, bronze complexion was still a soft one, and she looked up at Alira with kindly dark eyes.

"I know a great deal about you and your Ilewa. My name is Yapoti. Thank you for coming to see me. You must have many questions."

"A few." Alira laughed nervously.

The woman turned and beckoned. "Come, we must talk."

She's the woman we're looking for! Alira shot the thought over to Reldon.

Reldon relayed the message to the rest as Alira walked away with Yapoti.

"Oh, look at the sun, I think we have another show to prepare for. I'm glad we were able to help you find what you were looking for!" Nova said with an incredible amount of faux glee.

"You're not going to be pretending to be Alira again are you?"

"I would never. Or, at least, never again."

Reldon gave her an untrusting look and she took Xaetius's hand and walked back towards the grime of the smoky city.

"There is much to do, my love! Off we go!"

Bryle shook his head. "They're absolutely going to go swindle more people aren't they?"

"Without a doubt."

Yapoti led Reldon, Alira, Bryle, and Sillida over to sit next to one of the trees in the park, and again as they settled onto the grass, the world felt warm beneath them – a peculiar feeling not often felt outside of a particularly sunny day, much less a cloudy one in winter.

"Thank you all for coming to see me. I realize it must have been anything but easy travels," Yapoti started.

"It could have been worse. We could have been hunted the whole way," Bryle joked.

Yapoti smiled at him. "And how do you know that you weren't?"

At first Bryle must have figured it was an addition to his joke, but she continued to look expectantly at him. "I…uh…never saw anyone. Never heard anything."

"Does that mean they do not exist?"

"I…suppose not."

"Then how can you be so certain you were not followed?"

Bryle did nothing but shrug, perplexed.

Her attention returned to Alira and Reldon. "You may know little about me, and it would not be remiss of you not to trust me, but today it is my hope to teach you about the world – how it works, how to see it, how to analyze it. Once you have learned to do this, only then will you be ready for what comes next."

Reldon responded, "That all sounds valuable, Yapoti, but surely you must see from our eyes that we know so little about you that we don't know why you're doing this. There was another man who taught us as well, and we knew just as little about him. For everything we're taught, we feel further in the dark. Would you be willing to tell us at least who you are before we get started?"

"I have told you that. I am Yapoti."

"But who *are* you? Where are you from? Why are you doing this?"

"An inquisitive mind is something to be cherished, young Spellsword. Allow me to propose a deal then. A series of questions for a series of questions."

"But why? Why should I?" Reldon asked impatiently.

"Because at the end, I can tell you where the amulets are."

Alira flinched. "Can you not simply tell us? Many lives are at stake!"

She chuckled. "Much impatience in you two. Believe me when I tell you that many more will stand to perish should you not learn the lessons I have to teach you today."

She's not going to give up.

Alira sighed. *I hope this won't take too long.*

"All right, Yapoti. Ask your first question."

She paused and appraised both of them with her ancient eyes, searching for something. Perhaps it was understanding she was looking for? Or weakness?

"Young Reldon, this first question is for you. Why does the bee endear the flower?"

It was a completely arbitrary question, and Reldon's face scrunched up with confusion.

"Why do bees like flowers? Well they don't eat them. My mother told me that they carry flower dust to other flowers so they can grow and make more flowers."

"And do you believe your mother is correct?"

"I don't see why not. It sounds logical to me."

"And why do you believe bees do this?"

Her questions were pointed, but so kindly delivered that it didn't feel like needling. At least not yet.

"I would imagine they would want there to be more flowers, so they do it happily."

"Why would they want more flowers? Would that not be the procreation of flowers for the sake of procreation?"

"Maybe they do eat a part of the flower or bring it back to their hive."

"What tells the bee to do this?"

Reldon thought for a moment before shaking his head. "I suppose I don't know. They're just made that way."

"So you believe they were created? By what?"

"The spirits? The Omniscient One? I do not know."

"But either way you believe. You believe it so you know it is true. And why do you believe what you believe about bees?"

He could tell she was coming to an actual conclusion, so he followed along. "Because I believe what my mother told me."

She nodded. "So would you say it is accurate that your entire belief in bee behavior is based on what someone told you?"

Reldon nodded in return. "Yes."

"And how do you know she was telling the truth?"

"Because my mother would never lie to me."

"Precisely. Faith is what you have in your mother. Faith is what you have in what she taught you about bees, among many other topics. Much of what we all do is guided by faith in one source or another – be it the spirits, fate, each other, and even our own instincts. Even what I'm telling you right now you will need to take on faith to believe. After all, I could be lying to you."

"Are you?" Reldon asked with a smirk.

"You will have to reflect on that, otherwise you shall never know," she said with a playful expression, "You may now ask a question."

Alira and Reldon conferred quietly before he asked his question.

"Where are you from, Yapoti? You do not speak or look like any we have seen. We thought you were Sjard at first."

"I hail from a tribe long since rendered extinct. I no longer have kinsmen or kinswomen who might share in my background or my experiences. The name of my people you would not recognize but suffice to say I hailed from a once-proud people who used to live on this very spot."

"What happened to them?"

She gave a very weak smile. "I would prefer not to say. It is not a good history."

"I'm sorry to hear that," Alira replied with a frown.

Yapoti veered the direction of the conversation like a master navigator. "Now it is your turn to answer a question, Miss Ayuru. If you heard a desperate pounding at your door and they pleaded with you to let them in or they would be dead in seconds, and you only had time for a single question, what would that question be?"

Alira was taken aback by the question. *Your question was about bees!*

Reldon laughed internally. *Go on, answer the life or death question.*

"I would ask them who they are."

"Hm!" Yapoti hummed. "Would the answer to that question determine whether or not you opened the door?"

"Perhaps not, but what if it was one of my friends? Or worse, one of my enemies?"

"Would your familiarity with this person, for better or worse, be the deciding factor as to whether they lived or died?"

Alira hesitated from the intensity of the questioning. "It might help me decide if they were lying about being in danger or not."

"Ahh, quite an interesting take indeed. If they said they were someone you love, would you let them in?"

"Of course I would."

"Even if they provided no evidence that they were who they claimed to be?"

"There wouldn't be time for that. If they were going to die in seconds, it would be best to allow them entry and figure out the rest afterwards. I'm not too afraid someone is going to hurt me anymore."

"Then why bother asking who it was in the first place?"

Alira bit her lip, knowing she was being outmaneuvered. "Because I had to ask something. That's what you said."

She cocked her head. "Did I? I said you could ask one question. I did not say you had to." Alira wasn't certain how to respond, and luckily Yapoti went on. "This is the lesson. You do not have to accept the premise of my scenario as I lead you to it. To think outside of the realm of this situation and to make the decision not to ask any question at all would, in effect, create another perhaps more favorable scenario. Do not allow yourself to be dragged into a hole created by others. Think for yourself, my dear."

Alira nodded, thinking to her Ilewa. *This is a lot to take in. It's very hard debating with her.*

I don't like it. I don't know if I'm learning anything, and I want to tell her to stop.

But we need the information she has.

Unfortunately.

"Very good. Now proceed with your next question," she said, placing her hands in her lap.

After conferring again, Reldon and Alira initially wanted to ask her why she was doing this, but considered with her being an expert at debating and choosing her words extraordinarily carefully, she would have likely responded by telling them she was doing it to teach them important lessons for the future and not the *real* reason why. Instead they elected a question that they already at least partially knew the answer to.

"Do you know Grandma? The ambitious old magician woman?"

Her impassive stare only gave up a hint of a smile, a look of being entertained. "Why yes, I do know the woman you refer to as 'Grandma'." It was the expected answer.

"How old is she?"

Yapoti's head slowly inclined until she was watching the clouds pensively, searching for an answer.

"I will admit I do not know. It has been so many years I have lost track. The world has changed so much since I was young. Or when she was young, I'm sure."

"What sorts of things do you remember from when you were young?" Alira asked.

She chuckled again. "Precious little, to be frank. I recall it being a difficult time for our race of men. Many changes were taking place, whole peoples rebelling against their kings. Much more was understood about magic in those times."

"Much *more*? You mean we're losing our knowledge of magic over time?" Alira pressed further.

"Oh yes, and by choice for some. It is my personal hope that you will be able to change that, Miss Ayuru." She shifted and raised her eyebrows. "I can see you using your magical vision, young lady. You could simply have asked if I was a magician. As you have discovered, I am in fact a magician, but I am potentially the worst magician of any peoples in such an advanced age, as I have not used it in a great many years. It lies dormant within me, ever-ready in case I should need it, but I will not wield it."

"Why not, Yapoti? What if you're in danger?"

"Then I shall accept my fate and become one with the spirits. I have lived far too long, done perhaps too many deeds. And above all I have spent much of my life seeing the world as it is meant to be seen, and nothing can take that away from me now."

Reldon and Alira exchanged another quizzical look.

"It was to be among my next lessons. Shall we begin?"

"You mean we're not...debating anymore?" Alira asked to Bryle's laughter.

"There will always be much more time for debate, if you should like," she said with a broad crooked-toothed smile.

"I am all right with moving on, actually."

For the next hour or so, she had Reldon and Alira sit in silence in a meditative state, listening to the world around them. In the distance they still heard the metallic chorus of hammers on anvils, among other noises of the city. Especially for Reldon it was difficult to stay quiet and clear his mind of everything when so much was going on. His wouldn't cease its screaming at him that he needed to get moving and that time was running out. Eventually, however, he was able to calm his mind enough to be receptive to Yapoti's words.

She had them reach out with the thinnest of strands of magic or Phyrim to perceive the world around them without the use of their eyes, to see the life that surrounded them. With some concentration, they could sense the insects in the grass which had survived the winter by remaining in the warmth from the heat below. There was even a family of gophers living somewhere near the colossal steam music machine.

The rustling of leaves became like a symphony, and the minute chittering of creatures began to sound like real conversation. The world around them was alive with a vibrancy they had never felt before. Or at least Alira felt it. Reldon struggled to sense anything beyond surface readings of energy from living creatures.

This is incredible, Reldon, Alira had thought to him after over an hour of silence.

I have no doubt of that.

Are you not sensing it? All of this...nature?

Not really. But perhaps you can send it to me through our link.

That's not how it works. You have to quiet your mind so you can feel it too.

There is so much to do and to think about that it is impossible. For me, at least.

Yapoti spoke to them, her eyes still firmly shut. "See the world as it always has been, long before any man or woman tread upon the land or even before any birds navigated its skies or fish its seas. Irilitia is its own living, breathing entity with a most decided will of its own. All in life exists

267

in the image of the spirits and of this planet. A great many truths will always exist – fundamental truths that will never change. All things follow the same patterns. Your heart beats and rests. The tides come in and then recede. We are born and then we die. Not only do all living creatures live this way, but all of existence operates on a singular, unmitigated rule, that everything that has a beginning has an end. Just as you wake, live your life, and sleep, so do even the spirits. Someday it shall all come to an end, and nothing we do today or in one thousand years will change that."

Reldon and Alira heard nothing for a long moment, and when they opened their eyes, Yapoti's were open as well, looking at them with concern.

"Danger approaches and we will have to cut this shorter than I would have liked. Remember the lessons I have taught you today, for if you don't, you will shortly meet with a fate worse than death. It was a pleasure meeting all of you, even if three of you are…asleep."

Bryle, Sillida, and Elly had indeed taken the time to catch up on their beauty rest, nestled together next to a tree.

Reldon got to his feet and Alira followed suit. "Please, tell us where to go from here. Tell us where we might find the amulet we need."

"It is an answer you will not like, but it will help. The amulet is in the possession of the Churai Master among the Kuru. Kuruverrum, the Kuru capital, is where you must go. Much fire and death pervade the air surrounding that city in the days to come, and now may be the only time you will be able to gain entrance undetected. The Churai Master keeps the amulet in a secure location known to only a few. There is not time to explain how, but I can tell you it is within the Kuru king's treasury, in a vault labelled with the old numerals "XIII". Retrieve it and return safely. The entire race of men depends on it."

Before they could inquire further, there were some frantic footsteps against stone approaching them from behind.

"Nova? What are you-?" Alira started before being interrupted by the panicked young charlatan.

She was breathing so hard she was in danger of collapse. "I…uh…hello, you all! I just needed to…uh…ask you for some help. Again. Please?"

A panting Xaetius caught up a few seconds later. "They'll be on us in less than a minute."

Bryle, Sillida, and Elly leapt to action from their slumber.

"Who will be? Nova, Xaetius, tell us what's going on!" Reldon exclaimed.

"Ok, here's the truth," Nova began, waving her arms around dramatically, "We went off to start our next act, like we've done hundreds of times. I'm thinking…someone must have…I don't know, taken offense to our new material…"

Xaetius cut in. "She pretended to be an Ilewa Nuremil again and now soldiers are after us."

Nova punched his arm repeatedly. "Xaetius! How could you!"

Alira stomped her foot menacingly towards her. "How could *you*? We had a deal!" The air around her seethed with intense heat.

She held her hands up defensively. "Now, now, I'm sure there will be plenty of time for blame and punishment later, but for right now we need your help. Just tell them that we're not the real heroes!"

"That wouldn't explain why you ran away," Sillida said.

"Speaking of which, I think we should keep running," Xaetius insisted, tugging on Nova's long sleeve.

"And go where? Leave through the city gates? There's nowhere left to run. Please, please, you *must* help us clear our names or we won't see the light of day again!" Nova pleaded.

Bryle crossed his arms. "Maybe that's what you deserve for tricking all of these people. Now the law is finally catching up with you."

The sound of a legion of heavy boots stomping on the metalled roads finally entered the park, and they could see at least two dozen heavily armored soldiers making haste towards them, including a magician-Knight pair, also covered from head to toe in gleaming armor.

"Last chance to run…" Xaetius continued to insist.

"No. It's time we sorted this out," Reldon answered, walking towards the center circle where they would see him easier. The rest nervously followed suit.

In only a few moments the soldiers had them surrounded, long spears menacing at their inert subjects.

The magician stepped through the line of soldiers with her Knight in tow. Every inch of her body was covered in either powerful, well-polished metal armor or her yellow-colored livery. Once she was a few feet before Reldon, she stopped and reached up, removing the helmet which had previously swallowed all of her head.

Underneath was a woman with a stern look, probably around Kaia's age, with dark, wavy, shoulder-length hair, almond eyes, thick eyebrows, and thin lips tied into her fierce expression.

"Hello, young man. Worry not, we are not here for you or your little friends – just those criminals whom you have made contact with. We will not hurt you. Step aside."

"There has been a misunderstanding," Reldon responded, "They are not who you believe them to be."

Her smile was of strained patience. "I was there when they proclaimed themselves the heroes of legend. They will be taken in for questioning, even if it is unverified."

"You can save the time it would take. I am the real Xanem Nuremar. And this is Alira, the real Ilewa Nuremil. Those two are nothing other than actors. If you are in search of the heroes of legend, we are they."

The magician gave him a skeptical look. "Step aside, kid. Enough of your games."

Alira spoke up. "If you don't believe us, use your magic-sensing vision. You will see."

She breathed impatiently, but blinked slowly, her eyes flashing purple for a moment. She nearly fell to the ground she was so shocked by the sheer amount of immense energy they gave off.

"You are the…"

"As I told you." Reldon smirked.

"You will come quietly for questioning."

Reldon shrugged and shook his head. "Why not ask your questions here? We're cooperating after all. Why are you hunting the Xanem Nuremar and Ilewa Nuremil?"

She stepped back and spoke a few words in private with her Knight.

"Wait here. The King would speak with you."

That took them all by surprise. This was in no way intended to be an apprehension on petty crime.

They must have some kind of rule in this city against us. I don't think the King wants us here, Reldon thought.

Or maybe he does *want us here. To control us.*

I would see him try. We are strong enough to slay entire armies.

Be careful of that pride of yours, Reldon! We aren't looking for a fight.

I'm also not backing down if they start one.

In the period of time it took the king to arrive, some fifteen minutes, the air was tense as the soldiers did not lower their guard for even a moment. Bryle even took the time to take his helmet out of his bag and secure it to his head. Sillida used a whetstone on her sharpest knife. Whether or not it made them uneasy or not was unclear, but Reldon noticed a few of their spears held less steady, which was a moral victory in his eyes.

The king finally arrived with an escort of six more magicians, three Spellswords, two Knights, and around 50 more soldiers. It was most certainly a show of strength.

He was King Zarminius Ecthelia Ironmaw, a monstrously tall man with long greasy hair, a beard to match, and fiercely scarred features that spoke to many battles or duels, though it was difficult to tell whether he won or lost them. On his chest was a suit of brigandine armor, while studded leather armor covered the rest of his body – comparatively, he was much more lightly armored than his subjects surrounding him. All that separated him from the others was a massive six-foot sword on his back and a rugged iron crown on his head.

Reldon and Alira remembered seeing him at their trial. Though he had never spoken a word, they knew that the angry rebuke that had been delivered via the Darumite general had been approved by this man.

All of the Darumites present fell to one knee in reverence.

The magician woman scowled at Reldon and Alira. "Bow before your king."

"You will forgive us, but we bow to none," Reldon said firmly.

That seemed to inflame a few passions, as some of the troops shouted curses, only to be shortly silenced by the king. He stepped into the inner circle with his entourage behind him and faced them down from twenty feet away.

His voice was impossibly rough, like metal through gravel.

"I will admit myself surprised to see you here in Darum, Xanem Nuremar."

"If we are not welcome, we were just about to leave, your majesty," Reldon responded coolly.

"On the contrary. Stay for a moment and let us speak. It is not every day this city bears witness to legend. Tell me what you are doing in Irothrim, and perhaps we may have common cause."

"We were merely stopping here on our way to the Kuru border. Men die as we speak, and we believe we shall soon have the means to end it," Reldon said with confidence. It was not entirely true, but he didn't think it a good idea to try to explain how they were searching for trinkets.

"Oh? This is favorable news. And when shall you be heading west?"

"Now, if we're…allowed," Reldon said, motioning towards the legion of troops surrounding them.

"Don't mind them, just a simple assurance that regicide does not take place."

A wave of unease pervaded the congregation.

"You really believe we would do such a thing?" Reldon shouted back.

"Though not a king, Brina was the rightful leader of the Academy City. And we have heard of your threats against the Korrainian king. We are no friends to the Korrainians, but such behavior towards royalty is a blatant disregard to the Lärimite way of life, and especially to us Darumites. Life is conflict, and conflict is war. Only the strongest can hope to lead into battle, and there has never, nor will there ever be, a weak Darumite king. Even in my advanced age, Kuru fear me."

The king approached them, waving off his guard. The closer he got, the more Reldon could see every one of his scars on his face, crisscrossing his features. Reldon could only speculate at how many covered the rest of his body.

"You do not fear me. You do not respect me. It is overconfidence borne of youthful pride, but you will be taught respect this day."

And with that, he threw his leather gauntlet to the ground in front of Reldon and his soldiers pounded on their shields, cheering loudly.

No, Reldon, don't accept! Alira begged him.

"We are important people after all," the king continued, "Duel to first blood, none of that magic rot. Are you a man or a Kuru?"

The jeering from the soldiers overwhelmed his senses. Alira's disapproval was obvious. Bryle pushed his way to Reldon and told him, "Reldon, you don't have to do this – let me do it in your stead."

Conflict tore at him. Was he truly a man? Would he be able to hide behind Bryle and still live with himself? Did he dare deny a king?

For a moment, his defiant gaze held strong against Zarminius's foul smirk, and they said nothing.

Then Reldon knelt and picked up the gauntlet, and the crowd roared.

"I hope you know what you're doing," Bryle had said to him as the legions cleared space for the duel. Those words threatened to unnerve him more than anything, but Reldon knew he would need to stay focused. Without Phyrim, he was no more than a competent young swordsman against a man forged in steel his entire lifetime.

The king slowly drew his immense blade, a sword so huge it even dwarfed Reldon's. The cross-guards splayed out into two jagged spikes that looked perfect for hooking opponent's blades. He held it aloft before digging its point in the ground, idly stroking his mustache.

"If you think to cheat and use magic, my magicians will immediately know."

Reldon tore his own sword from the Infinity Scabbard in all its splendor, the gold hilt and beautiful crystalline pommel glittering in the fragments of sunlight that broke through the cloud coverage. He whirled it overhead and between his fingers before settling into his stance, squeezing the red leather firmly.

"I won't need it," he said smugly to raucous laughter.

His opponent chuckled. "Let us begin then. To first blood."

You can do this, Reldon!

With a roar, the king charged. Reldon knew from his training with Lendir that the biggest mistake would be to alter his formation or try to dance around his charge, which is what instincts would normally dictate. Instead, he merely lowered his sword to hip-height and waited.

King Zarminius's sword came down with incredible force and speed, just far enough away that he couldn't be undercut, but just close enough that if Reldon did nothing his skull would be split by the tip of the blade. Reldon took a passing step forward and brought his own blade up into an inverted cross and let his cross-guard take the punishment.

The impact was jolting, and he knew that if it were an ordinary sword, it could have broken the guard. In one swift motion, Reldon shoved his opponent's blade to the side and windmilled his blade to strike with the other edge. It was a tactic that would almost always work on lowly soldiers, but the king reacted instantly and recovered quickly enough to lock blades horizontally. With a jarring thrust, the man pushed forward and caught Reldon's blade in his own cross-guard.

In an instant he knew he would have to free his blade or he would lose. Luckily his choice to take a full step backward and pull his blade did manage to achieve this, and he circled cautiously around his opponent, who circled in kind. It had been a tactical retreat, but would be necessary, he knew.

Changing tactics, Reldon lowered the tip of his blade to touch the ground behind him. It was a stance which feigned an opening, but he knew he could easily counterattack.

His opponent took the bait and took a hard two steps forward, using his reach to his advantage and thrusting from a full four feet away. It would be too easy. Reldon rainbowed his sword over his middle, and with powerful downward force, drove the king's sword into the ground and followed up with a passing step and a strike which had nothing defending against it.

It would have been the end of the duel, had it been a less experienced opponent.

Incredibly the middle aged man arched his back so far back that Reldon's attack did little but graze his beard on its way past him.

Reldon's guard was down. He felt the rap on his shin, like a punch that knocked him off his feet.

There was a silence as Reldon smarted and rolled away. A magician rushed in to assess the damage. Somehow he had managed to strike one of the few areas protected by his greaves.

"No blood. Fight on," the magician called.

His confidence faltered. Even some of his best maneuvers were being countered like they were but child's play.

"You've got some skill, I'll give you that, boy. But you haven't got a chance against a real warrior."

Without even waiting for a response, the king immediately resumed his attacks with a series of diagonal strikes, and Reldon shifted on his bruised leg painfully to parry them.

I'm going to have to get creative without using magic, or I'm not walking away bloodless from this one.

An idea struck him as he riposted another blow. He would engage him in a bind.

Twisting his hands to deflect an attack, he purposely pushed the king's blade into the ground along with his own, and locked their cross-guards, so neither could disengage hastily. Bringing an elbow down with as much force as he could, he pounded on the king's hand.

It did not have the desired effect. His hands were massive and very strong, and his grip did not lessen in the slightest. Reldon panicked and leapt to swing for his face, landing a blow against his cheek. The king barely flinched, but Reldon's hand cried out in pain from the impact.

His opponent roared with laughter, breaking the bind and shoving Reldon hard enough that he tumbled backwards.

I'm running out of ideas. He's so much bigger and stronger that there's not much I can do to defeat him.

The gargantuan king had a smug look on his face as he stepped closer, winding up for another powerful blow. Jeers from the soldiers and desperate encouragements from his friends filled his ears. In theory, combat always sounded so straight-forward. If they strike this way, counter that way. It seems so easy when you're hitting a wooden post or even sparring with someone, but once you're actually in a situation, you never account for the factors that might give them a major advantage, like his size, strength, or experience. Nor does one consider fear.

Though it was a fight to first blood, one mistake could still cost him his life. As Reldon pushed himself to his feet, his forearms trembled trying to hold up his sword despite the urge to flee.

Look for an opening. He's big and swings hard. He should be leaving openings.

Finally the big strike came and Reldon had to roll out of the way to avoid it. The massive sword struck the stones with enough force to dislodge a few and crack a few others.

Before he could look for an opening, another swing nearly decapitated him and he ducked in the nick of time. Reldon tried flailing his blade forward at his legs, but his own sword didn't have the same reach. It had been a sloppy counterattack and they both knew it.

With a stomp, the king smashed Reldon's sword to the ground, wrenching it from his grasp – it disappeared into nothingness instantly. He was defenseless.

When the finishing attack came around, Reldon had shut his eyes instinctively.

Once he opened them, the point of blade was at his face. The old king smiled.

With barely a movement, the tip nicked his cheek and blood came down his face.

"Winner!" the magician shouted to a roaring crowd of soldiers, holding her king's arm as high as she could, given the fact she was nearly two feet shorter than him.

Elly and Alira rushed to Reldon's side.

"Let me heal you, Reldon!" Elly said, holding her hand out.

The Xanem Nuremar held out a hand, not looking away from his opponent.

Once the jubilation had died down, the huge man stepped up to Reldon again, looking down from his head's towering perch.

"Let this be a lesson to you, boy. Confidence is a boon, but arrogance will get you killed. No matter what you do, there will always be someone stronger out there. I saw you sitting at that trial, thinking you deserved to get let free. You were nothin' but a pup. I still think that's what you are, but this little slice of humility will help you grow."

He knelt down to look at him face to face, leaning in so the rest couldn't hear.

"It took iron to accept this duel. You have honor. You have heart. Don't lose that, no matter what no one says. Despite what we said at the trial, I want you to succeed in killing all the Churai. When the time comes and you need us to charge in with you and hew some Kuru heads, you know where we'll be. And we'll be ready."

Reldon nodded. "And I'll be looking for a rematch."

The king's face was beaming as he gave Reldon a shove. "And you'll have it! Men, the warriors of legend are leaving us to fight the Kuru. Show them respect!"

They all pounded their fists twice against their shields and shouted, "Hail the Xanem Nuremar!"

"Now get out of my city."

Chapter XXXIII

After resting in their fancy room at the strange high-class inn for an hour in otherwise complete silence, Kiera finally puckered up the courage to say something.

"Ethilia, I think that was a kind act you did today," she told her sheepishly.

She did not look up from her book. "It was nothing. Abuses must be pointed out and denounced wheresoever they appear."

Kiera peered over at the magician Otomia, a woman of perhaps thirty with an obstinate disposition and plain features, who shrugged dispassionately.

Two days had passed since their initial departure from Nakisho, and naturally Ethilia had had some business to attend to in Opterus, the city of her birth and childhood. However, as it would turn out it was not a joyous homecoming, but more of a familial confrontation.

At first her family had been happy to see her, but their jubilance quickly soured once they realized why she was actually there.

"I am here to deliver this to you, father. And you as well, mother," Ethilia had said loudly and clearly, handing them a sky-blue-wax sealed envelope. Standing in that grand foyer, their voices echoing around, returned to her old feelings of home, but they were not the same as they once were. Too much had changed.

"What is this, Ethilia? Are you not going to embrace your loving mother?" her mother Sathiria had asked her, taking the envelope.

"No. I am here on behalf of not only my own determination, but also that of my dear youngest sister Tessalia."

"I sent her a letter asking her to come home," Ethilia's father Tebrius grumbled, "Why has she disobeyed me?"

"She does not currently, nor will she in the near future, see fit to return to the treatment in which she was being held prisoner. What you are holding is an organized list of grievances which she and I have agreed upon to commit to record such that there shall be no confusion as to why she refuses to leave my care."

Tebrius tore open the envelope and poured over it with near-frantic speed.

"This is all far too oversimplified, and she could never possibly hope to understand-"

"Understand what, father? Why you convinced her for two years that she wasn't a magician despite the fact that she clearly was? Why you then ignored this fact and told her to never use or develop her abilities for the following year knowing full well that this was not possible to control? Why you then refused to get her the direction she needed and kept her locked in this house? Why you never allowed her to have any friends? Father, I must be blunt, your actions in regard to her care have been nothing short of unconscionable, and I will not stand by and be silent while you continue to attempt to harm my sister."

"Do not speak to me this way! What I did was for the betterment of the family!" he shouted, his face beet-red.

"I shall never understand your concept of bettering the family whilst ensuring one of its member's destruction. And *you*, mother. I find your complete lack of conscience and better judgment in this case completely abhorrent. Did you never think for even one moment about what was best for Tessalia? That not only might this plot of yours backfire and deliver to the family shame beyond compare, but that you would be sacrificing the life and happiness of your youngest daughter in the process? How could you, as a self-respecting magician, knowing in detail how magical development works, *possibly* do this to her in a sound mind?"

Kiera by this point had been so shocked at her righteous indignation that she thought it possible Ethilia might decide to just attack them. *That's how it likely would have happened in Korraine.* She could tell her friend was fighting tears with all of her might, but it was a slowly losing battle. Kiera also noticed, peering at the balconies of the grand foyer, a young man and woman watched with horror at what was occurring.

Her mother's response was measured, but testy. "Someday you will understand what it is like to be a mother and have to also consider the best future for both the family and House Vendimar. For now, you cannot understand. Life is different in Nakisho Castle than it is here. Every noble family is looking to devour the others, and we will not allow that to happen to one of Lärim's most esteemed houses."

"So to save the house, sacrifice the family, or at least its members," Ethilia spat, "We will never agree that what transpired here over the past four years has been but damaging to both Tessalia and to our family name. We are all stupidly lucky that word of this has not escaped as of yet, and I have, out of love for my family, sworn my guards and magician to secrecy on this matter."

Her slender white-hose laden leg took a step forward before her hulking father. Tears were rolling down Ethilia's face.

"Word of Tessalia's treatment shall henceforth not escape my lips, but if I am to be entirely plain, someday I hope it does get out so this is never allowed to happen again. You can rest assured that until Tessalia receives a *very* heartfelt apology, you shall not see either of us again in these halls."

Ethilia's parents were nonplussed as she turned to leave.

"And if I should ever hear of anything like this happening again, I will have no choice but renounce the Vendimar name."

And with that, she walked straight out the doors and into the cold again with her guard in tow, with nary a word from her family. Once they had reached beyond eyeshot of the mansion, Ethilia finally let her tears flow for a good portion of the trip south. Kiera's heart broke for her friend.

Where it comes to her family, Ethilia is one of the proudest people I know. It must have been extremely painful to threaten to renounce her own name.

At the end of the day they had found high-class lodging in a town just north of Inderi-Xenus and unceremoniously retired for the day. This was the first Ethilia had spoken to anyone since Opterus.

"If it helps, I know what you are going through. I might have gone a bit further and become wanted in my own country, and my family name has left me rather than the other way around, but…"

Ethilia closed her book and rolled over on her bed to face away from Kiera.

"I know what you're trying to say, but I do not wish to speak of this any further. Good night."

And that was that.

The next day, she was in better spirits. Not perfect, mind you, just better.

Riding to Inderi-Xenus was quiet and relatively peaceful. On the horizon, distant plumes of smoke persisted from Academy City to the west. The air was cold, but not unbearably so.

"Atheria is so different than Korraine," Kiera mentioned at some point as they crested a series of rolling hills.

"Is this your first time?" Otomia asked.

"No, I had passed through on our way to Errum for the stately funeral before the storm, but before that I never had much experience outside of my country."

"What's so different about it?"

"Everything is so..." she peered around, "...so squishy."

Ethilia snorted in an attempt to conceal laughter. "What does *that* mean?"

"I do not know if that's the right word to use, but the ground is so soft. There's snow and underneath the snow is soft earth. And there are bushes and trees. When it's wet, it's all so...squishy. It's different from Korraine. It's nothing but rock, sand, and scrub – so much tougher."

Otomia smiled to herself. "Yes, I suppose you would consider Atheria 'squishy' then."

As they entered the city of Inderi-Xenus, Kiera couldn't help but sate her curiosity by pointing about and inquiring about nearly everything.

"That neighborhood looks different than the others. Who do you reckon lives there?" Kiera asked excitedly.

Otomia shrugged. "Probably the artisan-class. They've got a little more coin than the laborers. They stay somewhat close to their workshops."

"Ooh, look at that ship, Ethilia! That one is bigger and has more ballistae. The other one must be a trade ship. What would you say, twenty-man crew?"

"Sure," Ethilia responded irritably.

Kiera went on. "I would very much like to explore the forests to the west. Seeing it in its entirety as we crested the northern hills was breathtaking. I imagine the hunting must be splendid. I wonder if this city has a hunting lodge – I hope they are accepting huntresses!"

"You are a ball of energy today, Your Royal Highness," Otomia said with a small amount of bemusement.

Kiera either disregarded the statement or didn't hear it. "There are so many sailors here! Do you think they live here in town or do they even...live on their ships?"

Ethilia had finally had enough and groaned loudly. "Kiera, *must* you do this? I think you won't be satisfied until you've talked both of our ears off. And besides, how can this *possibly* all be new to you? You're from a *city* for spirits' sake!"

Usually it would wilt the otherwise perky flower that was Kiera, but today was not that day. "Nevo-Kulan is a very different city. It has no wharves, no ships, no sailors. It really doesn't even have different neighborhoods and sectors like this one does. To my sadness, Nevo-Kulan is more like one giant slum."

"I can see how proper cities like this one and Nakisho would excite you," Otomia said.

"Don't encourage her," Ethilia responded.

At least two hundred generalized questions and observations later, they had made it through to the castle without having been hassled even a single time on their journey. To Ethilia and Otomia, it was yet another castle housing another king who demanded respect. To Kiera it was like an entirely new experience, despite the fact, Ethilia pointed out, that she spent most of her life living in the castle.

The sun had long since reached its zenith and was beginning to cast an orange light through the pockets of clouds. They were led through the gates, past the snow-laden courtyard, and into the keep without much ceremony. In Ethilia's recollection, it had never really been King Obrim's nature to be overblown about pomp and circumstance.

King Obrim was precisely where all the courtiers had surmised him to be at this hour: enjoying a large feast of roast boar, ale, a pot full of cooked onions, wine, boiled beets, and a bottle of spirits. He sat at the head of his long banquet table with his two head magicians at either side of him, taking small bites using utensils while he gripped an entire boar's leg in his massive hands and ripped the meat off with his teeth.

As they entered, the young ward who had led them through the castle called out in his nasally voice, "Here to visit Your Grace, the Court Healer to the High King, Miss Ethilia Vendimar and Her Royal Highness, Princess Kiera Itholos! Escorted by Otomia Freimark, earth magician in the service of the High King."

The King, a beast of a man standing taller than nearly any man they had ever seen, with a bushy dark beard and little beady eyes, dropped his shank of boar, jumping to his feet with a broad smile that even made Ethilia reflect it.

"By the spirits, well met lasses!" he thundered happily, stomping around the table to greet them face-to-face, "I didn't know you lot were coming, or I would have had the fancy plates prepared! And probably done up the privies a bit."

The magicians sitting at the table were visibly embarrassed at their king for what was probably the thousandth time, putting their faces in their hands.

"You are too kind," Ethilia said in her cordial voice, bowing deeply. This time Kiera did the same without having to be prompted.

281

"Look at you," he said in an adoring voice, "Look how much you've grown, Miss Vendimar! You're as beautiful as ever! I saw you at the trial but I never got a real chance to say hello. I remember when you were just a wee lass, no higher than my knee. Such a shy little thing you were, all dressed up like a healer. You were the talk of Nakisho castle back then for a few reasons!"

"Ah, I…Have you met Princess Kiera yet? She has been eager to meet you, Your Majesty," she said, swiftly changing topics.

"You were on the boat headed to the funeral, but I never introduced myself! King Obrim Naraxenus at your service, Your Highness." He bowed and kissed her hand once offered. "Terrible what your father is doing to you. You will always be a princess in Atheria, I can tell you that with confidence. You can stay here in the castle if you want! We have plenty of rooms. Can't stay in the wine cellar though, that's where I like to stay."

"You are too kind, Your Grace," Kiera said with a beaming smile.

"Come join us for dinner. There's a roast boar, or at least what's left of one, plenty of onions…I think I saw a turnip here somewhere," he rumbled happily, sitting himself back down at his chair.

"That sounds splendid-" Kiera started.

Ethilia grabbed her by the sleeve. "Must you be so provincial!" she whispered sharply, before turning back to his lordship. "We are well sated, thank you for your hospitality, your majesty."

"Suit yourselves. Either way, come sit down! Have you met my court magicians? This is Tara and this is Mirya. Hm? The other way around? Don't be givin' me that, I heard you call her Tara just yesterday! Well either way. This beautiful fire magician is called Mirya Dedrik, and this brilliant water magician is Tara Cayleigh. But I swear to the spirits, do *not* start callin' them by their last names or they won't bloody stop."

Mirya Dedrik was a blond woman in form-fitting crimson robes with powerful high cheek bones and pointed chin, blue eyes and aged in her thirties. Tara was a bit younger, probably in her late twenties or thereabouts with long, straight dark hair, fair skin with freckles, walnut eyes, and garbed in a flowing blue robe dotted with silver stars.

They stood before bowing low before the princess and noblewoman. "At your service, my ladies," they responded in near-perfect unison.

"A pleasure to meet you both," Kiera said with a quick curtsy before sitting next to Mirya. Ethilia sat across the table next to Tara.

"All right now, remind me again what your purpose was here? I've already forgotten," King Obrim asked intently.

"It was our hope to see Nuremia, your court healer," Ethilia explained, "It has been very long since we last spoke, and there are matters of great import we must discuss with her."

King Obrim stared off for a moment as if he had no idea who she was talking about until he suddenly flinched with understanding.

"Ah, right! The healer magician. She fixed me right up after my last bout – bit of a nasty one, that. Way over in the hills a few weeks ago, west of the city there were some lads spoutin' rot about yours truly while I was checkin' up on garrisons. Can't have that, lasses, can't have that. Ol' King Obrim had to show them who's the ruler here, and oh how they squealed like hogs as I walloped 'em! One got a lucky shot to ma face and actually drew blood. As you all know, that's a capital crime in our good lands – you should've seen his puffy lil' vulture face when I told him I'd have his head removed from the rest of his bird body. And he *cried* and *cried* like a wee girl, no offense intended, until I laughed and told him he would only have to spend a few days in the stocks. Come to think of it, I think he might still be out there. Oi, ponce-hat, go check on him, will ye'? If he's still there, clean up the bones."

Ethilia could tell by her wide eyes that Kiera had absolutely no idea how to react to King Obrim. Through what little experience she had, Ethilia knew that the man liked to traipse about in different topics, going on tangents and stories, and one had no choice but to let him finish. Interrupting him was a guaranteed method of invoking his ire.

The pristine healer cleared her throat as politely as she could, garnering his attention back to the conversation. "By Your Grace's leave, may we speak with Nuremia? It is very important."

"Eh? Oh, of course, of course lass. I'm sure she's around here somewhere seeing to her 'studies' or whatever you magicians do," he said coarsely taking a massive swig of ale, "What is the cause for haste, Miss Vendimar?"

She sat up straighter. "On the orders of the High King we are investigating a potential advantage we might be able to gain against the Churai using Golden Magic. It may require the collaborative effort of all Golden Magicians across Lärim to turn it into some sort of weapon we may use."

He nodded approvingly. "Aye, that sounds like a good cause for haste. Well, my court healer and the resources of this castle are at your disposal. Except for the oak spirits I keep in my chamber, those are twenty years old. You can have all the wine you like though! Tara, would you be so kind as to show our guests to…wherever Nuremia is?"

Tara stood immediately and gave a deep bow. "Yes, Your Majesty."

King Obrim rolled his eyes, but for once decided not to say anything further. Kiera and Ethilia also stood with a low curtsy, saying "By your leave," in unison. Tara then turned and led them out of the chamber and through a series of corridors lined with small arched windows to let in the sun's rays without allowing the cold in as well.

Ethilia had shot Kiera a look, and the Korrainian girl frowned. "What? What is it?"

"*Must* you embarrass me everywhere we go?"

Tara snickered.

"How did I embarrass you? I do not understand."

"A proper lady always turns down an offer of food if she arrives after the meal has been served. It is basic etiquette, princess."

Kiera's doe-eyes were lost in confusion. "Is that the custom here?"

"Of course it is, otherwise you risk insulting the host – in this case the King of Atheria!"

Tara spoke up with a giggle, her voice sweet. "I can promise you, dear healer, that His Lordship the King does not pay much heed to etiquette. You could have sat and eaten three plates and he wouldn't have batted an eye."

Kiera slapped her hands against her side. "That is good to know now. I was hungry, Ethilia. We haven't eaten since early morning."

Ethilia sighed. "Kiera, a lady does not offer up such information publicly. If she becomes famished, she can issue a servant to fetch her some small…" she searched for the word.

"Nibbles," Kiera finished for her.

Ethilia huffed. "You can't use a word like 'nibbles' in serious conversation."

"It is well that this is most spirited conversation then!" Kiera said, giving the healer a playful shove.

Tara laughed. "You two argue terribly so! You are otherwise correct, Miss Ethilia, but as I said, much formal etiquette is lost here. Mirya and I have been heavily trained in the ways of propriety, but it has been a wee useless since our service began in this castle."

"Does he ever frighten you?" Kiera inquired.

She smiled and shook her head. "Never so, I am more wont to be frightened to embarrassment of what he might say or do next. His Grace may look like a big bear, but I can promise you he is the gentlest and kindest of any lord you might meet, and he has a terrible soft spot for ladies. We all know how hard it is for you, dear princess, to be banished from your own homeland, but should you elect to live here with us, you would be made most welcome."

"You are all very kind," Kiera beamed, "I like Atherians very much. Is Nuremia nice as well?"

Tara laughed nervously, and after a pause proclaimed, "Not always."

And she was not incorrect.

Nuremia was a woman in probably her forties, tall, lanky, with weathered features and bad posture, her upper back hunching her over. Her eyes were steely and her thinning long hair wavy blond and streaked with gray. As soon as she saw Kiera and Ethilia enter, it was not the joy of seeing a long-lost friend that took her, but more of a dry bemusement.

"Ah, Ethilia. I might have known it was you. What scheme do you bring to me today?" she said with her crackly voice, grinding up ingredients in a mortar and pestle.

Ethilia still embraced the woman and kissed her cheeks. "It is good to see you, Nuremia. This is Kiera Itholos, Princess of Korraine."

"Estranged princess from what I hear."

Kiera shrunk, but Ethilia continued.

"Yes, it has been a difficult time for her, but she is here to assist us this day. We are here on the behest of the High King and the Nurems."

Her eyebrows raised again as she mixed some herbs together in a bowl. "My goodness, that does sound serious."

"And only something the Golden Magician Sisterhood can solve. We are at a stalemate in our fight against the Churai until the Nurems can gain the power they need to finish them off. Lärim…nay, humankind needs a weapon to turn the tides. I believe we are that weapon."

Nuremia lowered her utensils and appraised Ethilia with a skeptical stare. "A coiffured girl and a cranky old woman? Forgive me for being cynical, but I can't imagine the Churai are shaking in their boots."

"Not just us, but Golden Magic as a whole. We need to gather all of the Golden Magicians for this monumental task that lies before us – the greatest work we will achieve. Our power can destroy the brutes and it is up to us to find a way to turn it into a weapon."

She finally set down her flask and mortar and put a hand on her hip. "And you believe that we have the ability to destroy Churai when not even the strongest warriors and magicians can?"

"I do not just believe it, I have done it."

Her eyes lowered. "*You* killed a Churai? What did you do, talk it to death?"

"Golden Magic, my dear Nuremia. If enough is injected directly into their heads, they cease to live - If that's even the right word to use."

"Rubbish," she dismissed, continuing her alchemical work.

"It is not, as I said, I have done it myself. Reldon, the Xanem Nuremar, also backs this up through the experience of Tycheronius Niuro, who had allegedly killed several Churai. He theorized that Golden Magic would be our most potent weapon against them, but he could not figure out a way to turn it into a weapon. That is where we come in, Nuremia. We ladies of healing made a vow to always fight pestilence, injury, and death. These beings personify all of them, and it is our solemn duty to assist in their eradication."

The woman sighed heavily. "All right, I see where you are coming from, Miss Vendimar, but it will be no small task to unite the court healers. Politics are involved. Not many lords would be willing to part with their healer for weeks or months at a time."

"Even if they make use of messenger magicians, this must be done. The alternative, doing nothing, is much too grave an option."

"Remember that we are not warriors. Many of us Golden Magicians haven't been so spry as to even use a weapon in many years."

Kiera pounded a hand to her chest. "I will help be your strength then."

Nuremia scanned the princess but couldn't help but smile at her declaration. "Fine. I said yes once before to join this little sisterhood of yours, and I suppose it won't hurt to give it purpose, even a wayward one. Let's get started."

Chapter XXXIV

Weeks passed, and the siege of Kuruverrum dragged on without interruption. Minor skirmishes erupted in places, but the city largely refused to acknowledge any defeat nor admit surrender. It was known to most that the Kuru had retreated their massive forces to within the walls of the city to defend it, making assaults on the fortress-city impractical. Naturally the drawback to this action was that the city would be quicker to starve out, but there also did not seem to be any evidence of that either. With other cities the Nuru had starved out, they had thrown their starved dead over the walls to rid themselves of the stink and disease, and in most cases had resorted to eating everything short of each other. A few cities, despite their rancor towards the Nuru, did surrender their homes in exchange for clemency and food, which had been provided graciously.

Kuruverrum displayed none of these symptoms however. There was no evidence that anyone inside the walls were starving, nor were they even fearful of the horde of Nuru with their waving green banners.

Reports continued, however, to emerge of Kuru marauders raiding Taraxellan settlements between their fortresses and some even took to the Sea of Whispers to attack targets as far away as Atheria. It was unknown where these bands were originating from, but they did not strike with the desperation one would expect of a rabid, starving force of brigands. Instead they were as organized as ever, hitting settlements, even those with small forts, with enough precision to loot them of food, valuables, and occasionally women, before disappearing faster than they'd arrive.

Teraxellan forces were already spread thin enough that each major castle or fortress city was only at one-fifth of their normal garrisons. In an attempt to stop the raids, several contingents of light archer cavalry had been dispatched to key settlements in the hopes they might predict where the next attack might come, but the invaders still remained elusive.

What hampered the Teraxellan efforts the most, however, was a war fund that had slowed to a trickle. Since many hundreds of years ago, an accord had been struck between all of the Lärimite kingdoms to pay a portion of their tax revenue to Teraxella in times of war such that they may be better equipped to deal with Kuru armies. There had been times that some countries had deigned instead to send troops to aid in the defense instead of taxes, and previous High Kings had reluctantly and only temporarily allowed it, but the gold coming in from their Lärimite brethren had largely kept Teraxella strong for its whole history.

Now, unfortunately, there was enough turmoil in Lärim that the shipments of coin had stopped coming.

Atheria, Naiwa-ki-Shokassen, and Darum still faithfully paid their share. Korraine had always been difficult to collect from, but now they sent only fractions of what was due, claiming political unrest as their reason. The Academy City posited much the same, as their civil war resumed, albeit much less violently, and no one could agree as to who was in charge of the Academy coffers. Attempts to aid The Sjard by means of troops were underway, as little word had been received from them since the initial Kuru invasion.

The High King had his hands completely full trying to rectify this situation, dispatching emissaries to the Academy City to broker a truce or at least to aid in establishing a more cogent chain of command amidst the chaos. As far as anyone was aware, it had not met with great success, and allegedly no contingent had been sent to Korraine, and it was rumored that the High King didn't see the point in trying. Talk was abound that the Korrainian king had fallen far out of favor with High King Julius and that if there were to be a civil war in Korraine, he wouldn't do anything to stop the violence.

All of this Reldon and Alira had learned on their way through Teraxella, as political talk seemed to be all anyone talked about. It was only natural, they reasoned, given that political happenings played a crucial role in whether or not Teraxellan families would live another day. Every inn they stayed at seemed more like a local government congregation, as collective conversations included everyone from the drunks throwing dice to even the barmaids that worked there. Most of the time it remained civil, but once or twice tempers got a little too heated and they were sent off to cool down.

General opinion in Teraxella towards the High King was positive. Most realized that the High King was the governing force that compelled the other kingdoms to provide the coin, their lifeblood, that they needed to repel the threats. They held the Darumites in high regard for their martial prowess, their commitment to the fight, and for providing the most coin, arms, and experienced generals and officers of any kingdom. There was a natural brotherhood between the two that could only have been forged in the heat of battle. They were largely neutral towards the rest of their sister-states but had always seemed to have particularly nasty things to say about the Korrainians, as they had never been faithful in holding up their end of the bargain.

And annoyingly, they were approached on countless occasions while in Teraxella by women asking where their parents were, and they simply couldn't understand how they could be travelling alone. In fact, the entire idea mortified them and a couple of times they shouted about demanding to know who was letting their children out alone. Reldon had to tell them reluctantly that they were the Xanem Nuremar and Nuremil and that they were in fact on an important mission and wanted their presence to remain a secret, to which they responded, "That's nice, dear," and continued the fruitless search. They learned later that it was because Taraxellan streets were so dangerous with all the incursions that children would go missing in only a second's notice, and so mothers especially had banded together to ensure no children remained alone out in public. It was an encouraging display of human kindness, Reldon thought later, but less than helpful when they were in a hurry.

It was at a crossroads heading west or north, nearing the Kuru border that they had all plaintively stopped to say their good-byes, and even though no one admitted to it, they all knew it could be for the last time. Elly had flat-out broken into tears at the thought of Bryle and Sillida going off on their own, knowing that they meant to go to war.

"It's going to be all right, Elly. I promise we'll be back. There are just some Kuru heads we need to knock together first," Bryle had said, ruffling up her blond hair.

Reldon had looked at his friends mournfully, his voice wavering. "I suppose there would be no sense in telling you to be back by a certain day?"

They had shaken their heads in unison. "We can't promise that, Reldon," Sillida had concluded.

"In case anyone was wondering, we're heading south towards Gurendras-Namu," Nova had butted in, "There are some people down there that we really must see. What? You don't have to look at me like that, I didn't mean people to *swindle*, I am speaking purely of some researchers that may have some clues as to how my artifacts work. And if they can't help us, then we're heading back east. We know a few scholars that aren't *completely* out to get us."

"Out to get you, you mean," Xaetius laughed.

She had scowled at him. "You're simply delectable my dear, but do you have to smile all the time? You say the most serious things as if you were telling a joke."

He had appeared to ponder for a moment before nodding with a huge grin. "That sounds like me!"

Alira had taken both Sillida and Nova each by a hand. "We will not part today having said goodbye as if we would not meet again. Instead, let us leave each other by saying 'good luck'. Until next we do meet. I am happy to be friends with you all."

Nova had nodded uncomfortably, rearing her horse and uttering "Uh, yes, until next time. Let us go, Xaetius. Destiny awaits!"

With that Bryle had echoed her with a laugh, and a pull at his reigns, "That's right, Sillida, destiny awaits! I hope you're ready to not bathe for a while!"

"You're disgusting," she had said as their voices trailed off towards the distant military camps.

After that it was back to the three of them – Reldon, Alira, and the tiny healer Elly accompanying them. It was so quiet for much of the ride north that had it not been for the rhythmic beating of their horses' hooves, the silence would have threatened to envelop them entirely.

By nightfall they had stopped in yet another Taraxellan town with a small inn, and like usual they attempted, to their best ability, to keep as low a profile as they could.

This was not one of their better days.

It started off when they entered the inn and attempted to pay for a room. The innkeeper gave them a strange look, which was common, and obligingly handed them the key. However, as they made their way towards the stairs there was at least one comment made towards Alira that wasn't particularly appropriate by some of the patrons. It hadn't been the first time, and it would undoubtedly not be the last, so they usually ignored it, but one man made a comment so vile that Reldon snapped.

The man had at least a foot on Reldon height-wise, but still he got as close to his face as he could.

"Say it one more time and I'll rip your tongue out!" Reldon screamed at him. The man's ugly face contorted into a smile.

"I'll say it ten more times, you little shit, and then I'm gonna do it just like I-"

The room vibrated with Phyrimic energy as the man was yanked clear off the ground, his feet wildly kicking as he was suspended by his throat. Reldon held out a hand which practically glowed with the power he was releasing. The other patrons screamed and knocked chairs over attempting to get out of the inn.

He wriggled around like worm in all the confusion, and Reldon held up his other hand.

With another spike of energy, the man began clawing at his throat and mouth, shrieking in either pain or terror.

"Reldon, stop, that's enough!" Alira shouted.

He continued to hold him aloft for a long moment before letting him drop to the floor with crash, smashing through a chair on his way. Without further ado the vile man spat blood and sprinted out the door and into the cold.

The innkeeper instantly had a fit, his face beet red. "What in blazes have you done?! What the hell are you?!"

"Sorry, sir. I can fix this." Reldon set about lifting a few chairs to hover about in the air as their constituent pieces reassembled themselves in the correct positions and he used Phyrim to seamlessly reform them into a single piece, so there would never even be evidence of having been broken.

"Nevermind the chairs! You've scared away all my cursed customers! Get out! And take your money with you!"

That was how they found themselves back out on the road again, tired, grumpy, and looking for a new place to stay.

It took an additional hour of riding to find the next town, and luckily word had yet to spread of what had happened in the previous one.

This time they managed to get up the stairs of the inn and into their room without causing any sort of mass chaos, which was certainly a nice change of pace.

"You didn't *have* to do that, Reldon. Those men are awful and they can say whatever they want. I don't have to listen to them," Alira scolded him.

Reldon lay on his bed with his eyes closed and hands over his eyes. "I was not going to let him insult your honor. You deserve better and he deserves to be tongueless."

"Look, I can do a handstand!" Elly shouted happily, running across the small room, planting her hands on the ground, throwing her legs in the air, and promptly toppling over with a loud thud. She groaned and held both hands on the back of her head.

How is she not *bothered by all of this?* Alira thought.

She's seen it all, I guess. What happened tonight wasn't even enough to stick in her mind for more than an hour.

There was a small fluctuation in magic and Alira sprang into action and grabbed Elly's hand. "Elly, we've talked about this – you can't use Golden Magic every time you hurt yourself."

"But my head hurts," she whined.

"Don't be doing anymore handstands then, silly. Come on, let's go walk down the hall."

Alira took her by the hand and led her out.

"Master, where is your amulet?"

They froze.

"*What?!*"

She padded at her neck frantically, looking around in a panic. She saw a man scurrying down the hall and into a room and Alira immediately gave chase only to find the room locked.

Alira slammed hard on the door. "Give it back!"

"No, I found it, I keep it! Thems the rules!" the muffled voice called back.

"You bring it out here right now or else!"

"Or else what? You gonna shout at me? Go on and play with your dollies little girl."

Reldon turned the corner to see his Ilewa's face scrunched up in a look of fury. She slammed an open hand on the door and held it there. Suddenly he felt a massive spike in magical power like he hadn't felt since she had exploded an entire hill back at the High King's mansion.

"Keep on slammin' the door, it won't do you any... any... Dear spirits why is it so... It's so hot. So hot! Dear spirits! Let me out!"

Reldon bolted over to her. She whipped her head around towards him with a narrow-eyed look that could kill.

Lock it.

Alira, no! I can't do that, you'll kill him!

"I'm roastin' alive! Let me out!"

Finally she opened the door and the man, shirtless, scrambled out and collapsed on the floor unconscious. His skin had begun to turn red along his entire body – Reldon wouldn't have been surprised to see steam coming off him.

Alira had nonchalantly walked over and plucked her amulet from his hand, reattached it around her neck and went back in the room, despite now shocked onlookers gathering on the stairs.

Reldon shut the three of them back into their room, his heart beating hard.

"How hot were you making that room? You almost cooked him alive!"

Alira sank into her bed, the literal heat of the moment having subsided and her expression downright ashamed. "Maybe as hot as a bread oven. Maybe a little more."

"Dear spirits," Reldon sighed, sinking to the floor.

"He had my mother's amulet. I couldn't..."

All three of them sat in silence for a moment as they considered what had happened that night.

"Maybe we're all overusing our abilities a bit," Reldon posited.

Alira nodded regretfully. "Are we... growing too overconfident in them?"

"We certainly do rely on them a lot."

Elly climbed onto the bed next to Reldon and reached towards Reldon's face and toward the cut that had scabbed over on his cheek.

"I want to heal that cut, Reldon. Please?"

Reldon sighed. "No, Elly. Did you hear what I said? Besides, at this point maybe I should let this cut become a scar to remind me that I'm not invincible. Sometimes I forget that – it's hard not to believe it when you can tear just about anyone apart with Phyrim without a second thought."

"Agreed," his Ilewa replied, "Let us try to avoid using magic or Phyrim unless it's absolutely necessary."

By about the afternoon the next day they stood before the Wall of Isolation, which stood immensely taller than they had ever dreamed. They had been to major cities like Nakisho and seen the towering temples and imposing castle, but this wall dwarfed them all in size. Reldon had never understood any form of height measurement beyond the size of a person, but he figured the wall had to be at least over one hundred standard foot-lengths tall. It wasn't like the Nakisho walls with spiked, bladed shields, dark as night, and crawling with sentries and ballistae; rather, it was clearly a wall which had stood much longer, used brick-laying materials and techniques that were different than any other building they had seen before. While the Nakisho walls or even those in Remdas-Kuwis were composed of larger, flat-cut bricks, the Wall of Isolation was made of more crudely cut slate stones, ranging from some as small as Reldon's fist to as large as a cart, all held firmly in place by a hard cement mixture.

Lining the length of the wall were countless round towers, constructed at the bottom with massive granite blocks. There were some type of support wedges also constructed out of harder stone that separated each tower and extended at least a dozen paces outwards. It seemed strange to have the supports on the opposing side of the wall, but Reldon guessed there were probably more supports, probably bigger ones, on the other side. Arrow slits had been built in rows along the entire length of the wall and all the way up the towers and given that there were three rows of arrow slits up the wall meant there were probably three floors within.

They expected some kind of resistance, or at least to be watched carefully by some remaining sentries, but given the situation with the Nuru invasion, not a single soul harried them as they appraised the colossal structure. It was a silent, hulking marvel of a structure that stood as a testament to nothing more than Kuru hatred.

The three only stared up at its splendor for a long moment before Reldon finally said, "Can we...make an exception for this one?"

"Yes please," Alira responded.

"Hold on tight. I'll be back for Elly in a moment."

Reldon wrapped his arms around Alira and felt the usual jolt of power as their energy pools merged. It felt so nice to hold her, his Ilewa, in his protective embrace. In many ways he felt at his strongest when he was close to her.

He released a powerful jet of Phyrim underneath them to counteract the downward force of gravity and lift them gradually to the battlements atop the wall. Jumping back down and using a similar technique to soften his fall, he picked Elly up into his arms and repeated the process.

Just out of caution, Alira had flared up her Keinume, ready to defend if they were assailed, but there was truly no one around. A month prior it had probably been teeming with men, but now not a single person remained.

Reldon waved them over to one of the stone staircases that went to one of the inner floors within the wall and they found long wooden floors that stretched for miles, pocked with cold, lifeless braziers, weapon racks, barrels of supplies, and cast-iron arrow stands. What was the most shocking was that a very large portion of the supplies had been left behind. As he pried open some barrels, the strong smell of vinegar escaped and filling the container were a variety of pickled foods. Bows still hung on the weapon racks, and hundreds of arrows filled their stands.

It was as if they had all left in a hurry and were told to only carry what they had on them.

Fingering through the selection of bows, Reldon eventually pulled a small one down. It was only a couple of feet long and had a very pronounced recurve, made of a very pliable wood like ash or yew.

He held it out for Elly. "Would you like your very own bow?"

Both Elly and Alira eyed him inquisitively as the small girl took it.

"It's a small bow intended for use on horseback, but it's a perfect size for you. After all, you need something to protect yourself."

"But I have magic," she responded skeptically.

"And how many magical bolts can you fire in a row?"

She thought about it. "...Maybe twenty?"

"Wouldn't it be nice to have a bow that you can also use if you get tired? The string isn't very hard to pull."

She nodded, a rare form of acceptance on her face. "Maybe you're right, Reldon."

"Perfect, let's go practice!"

They returned to the cold, windy battlements above where only the sun aided in the frigidness. Traversing to the other side of the wall, Reldon lifted up Elly so they could all look for the first time upon the land that was Drunerakerrum.

As the sun illuminated the land before them, from the vantage point of the wall they could see the Kuru lands stretch for many miles, complete with forests, lakes, and two fairly large cities far to the north and south, all coated in a gleaming white layer of snow. They could see some small herds of deer moving about the trees, and some snow falling further north.

"Wow..." Alira said, "It's... different than I expected."

"How do you mean?"

"With all of the stories they tell you about the Kuru, I didn't expect their country to look so... normal. It looks just like Lärim."

Reldon smiled. "What did you expect it to look like?"

She shrugged. "If everything I had been told since birth were true, I was expecting to see big rocky mountains and volcanos with terrifying creatures everywhere. Something like a nightmare. But it looks kind of like Atheria, actually."

He pulled an arrow from a small quiver he had found for Elly. "Here, try to shoot that boulder way down there at the bottom of the wall.

You nock the arrow on the bowstring like this and then pull back as hard as you can. Now, release!"

She let go and with a *twang!* it fired the arrow down into Kuru air, tossed around by the high winds and missing its target by a ways.

"Congratulations, Elly. You've fired your first arrow. And it was on Kuru soil, so I'm fairly sure that's an act of war. Now you've done it."

She was shocked for a second, but realized it was a joke and giggled.

"All right, who's ready to go behind enemy lines?"

The cavernous cell resonated as the Magician of Justice slammed down a heavy book on the table before her. Ripping the cover open and flipping through a few hundred pages, she finally settled on a set of records and began pacing the cell. She was of a tantalizingly beautiful age, with red hair, fiery red eyes, and perfect skin on her slightly longer face. Somewhere in the darkness on the opposite end of the cell sat her Knight, the massive lump of muscle that he was.

"You eluded us for some time, Mr. Kex. We have many cases against you that we may or may not be able to prove, but we know you did them. It would be easiest if you just admit to them so we can get on with the fun part of all of this."

Kex leaned back in his chair. "Please, by all means, take your time, Snapdragon. The fun part for me is just watching you pace."

"Silence!" she shouted, slamming a hand on the book. "Charge one: Impersonating a soldier of his royal High King's army in an attempt to flee the country. Do you deny it?"

"I was less intelligent and not as subtle in my formative years. I don't deny sneaking into the army, but it was not an attempt to flee the country. I wanted to fight."

"Then why did you not enlist?"

"I…uh…wasn't old enough."

She scribbled in the book, saying to herself loud enough for Kex to hear, "One count of falsifying identity".

Kex shrugged. "You already knew that one."

"Charge two: Bearing false testimony to the crimes of one Taro Minrath."

He snickered. "You must be digging deep in the book to find these. That was an age ago."

It served to further rile up her temper.

"Charge three: Swindling the fisherman of Quilias Arterum, Atheria into believing you had caught a nine foot-length long snapping fish, complete with false corpse, in order to sell them your secret bait recipe, which, in fact, turned out to be nothing more than earthworms fried in mushroom oil."

Kex couldn't help but smile, but she continued without giving him a chance to respond.

"Charge four: Falsely convincing the entire town of Ilimdras, Teraxella that you were the deceased husband of one Jania Mudathrim, risen from the dead, after violating his gravesite to steal his clothing, valuables, and other personal effects."

"She was mourning! She needed one last night with her husband!"

"You are NOT her husband! Charge five! Impersonating a member of the royal court in order to mandate to the citizenry of Coteryx, Atheria that under the king's authority all towns must make their fountains flow with beer, their priests must use the phrase 'as the birds say' in every sentence, and must build a statue of a turnip in the town square and no one was allowed to speak of it to anyone on pain of death."

The Knight in the darkness finally couldn't take it and burst into laughter.

"It is *not funny!* These are serious crimes!"

Kex chuckled as well. "I had forgotten about that one."

"That's enough! Next charges: Extortion, assault, destruction of private property, jailbreaking, and murder! Laugh at those if you dare!" She slammed the book shut and leaned on the table with both hands. "I have enough credible evidence here to get you sentenced to death in the High King's court. You had better start begging soon, or I might just walk out of this cell and straight to the bailiff."

He crossed his arms. "I helped save this city from the Kuru invasion. I fought alongside the Nurems. Surely that must count for something."

"It *might* have, had you not immediately decided to re-enter your old life as murderer-for-hire. How long exactly were you planning on doing that for? Hm? Did you think someone wouldn't have noticed you, especially after your grand entrance at the Nurems Trials?"

He had no answers and she continued whether he had them or not.

"You are in a precarious situation and you had best tread carefully. The High King and any juries do not look kindly on murderers. But since I am a forgiving Magician of Justice, I might just be willing to help you out if you help the state. As it turns out we need someone of your…disposition…for a job."

"Ha!" he guffawed, "The state doesn't like murder so long as it's not their idea."

"You are not being asked to murder. There are two men of interest that we require recaptured for their crimes, and they are nearly as heinous as yours. If you value your life, you will work with us to capture them."

Kex scowled. "Nice try, but I know you'll simply bring me in on the same charges as soon as they've been recaptured."

She shook her head and put a hand over her heart. "On my honor, you shall not be retried for these same crimes. Do this, and I will personally burn this book to embers myself. You will be a free man."

This doesn't make any sense. They're willing to forgive and forget all of my crimes in exchange for helping them capture two men with lesser crimes? That would be complete nonsense, unless…

He smiled.

They have nothing. They know they can't prove almost anything in court. This way they don't get embarrassed in front of the High King and set me free anyway – instead they trade the weak case for the strong ones. I could go free either way, but if I don't get them to burn that book, they're only going to keep arresting me for the same charges. Might as well play along for now.

"I'll do it."

"Excellent. I knew you would see reason. Their names are Detryn and Gihan, both young Nuru men. You will assist us in capturing them, but if they resist too fervently, you are authorized to execute them."

"Does that mean we'll be hunting them together, Snapdragon?"

She turned her back to him. "Yes. And my name is Vecilia. Do not think to try anything or I will roast you on a spit until your skin is as red as your hair."

Distant rumbles and the heavy smell of smoke would have been enough to unnerve any Kuru citizen or even to bring panic to their otherwise pathetic lives, but the wafting feelings of dread threatened more to bring the Churai Master to feelings of ecstasy, if such an equivalent existed in the black hole of his being.

Rizellion sat in his dark, cold throne room away from the light of the public, tapping on the arms of his stone chair with a long claw-like fingernail as he awaited the underling to bring him whatever useless bit of complaining he was wont to bring.

Living in a dungeon beneath the Kuru stronghold was nothing more than a strategic move, regardless of how disappointing the amenities were. The Churai would be able to attend to their own business in complete silent privacy, devising strategies without the pointless groans of the Kuru military officers. Little did they understand that their protestations were irrelevant, and that death would find them all one day. It was the natural order.

Rizellion knew, however, that even though the Churai power was great, he knew that their numbers were small for now, and that revealing the extent of their influence to the public would result in distrust of the monarchy at best and a full-scale revolution at worst. There was little these groveling worms could do to fight the Churai should it come down to it, but wholesale slaughter was not part of the mission. Not yet at least.

So for now, the Churai Master bided his time, entertaining the transient and rather shortsighted thoughts of emissaries from the surface.

One such man finally emerged into the endless, dimly lit cavern, stepping down the long central lane gingerly. He knew that at least fifty sets of red eyes watched him from the darkness flanking him on both sides, as only the lane he walked was lit with a few torches.

"Welcome again to my domain, emissary to the king. You may speak." His fear was delectable.

The skinny thing with an unkempt beard and bizarrely over-stuffed clothing spoke in stuttering bursts. "Y-your Churai lordship...The king w-would like to know... W-what your plan is to be... in r-regards to the Nuru force outside our w-walls. They pound our....our defenses daily, and if it were not for subterranean food supply chains, they w-would have.... would have starved us out long ago. Our m-men grow restless and anxious..."

Without adjustment to his foul expression, the Churai Master scoffed. "It is fascinating how the Kuru people have managed to survive this long. Without our intervention you all would have been conquered centuries ago. You flaunt your strength when raiding villages with no garrisons, killing suckling children, but when they finally grow tired of your impudence and fight back you cower in your castles and beg us to save you. Pathetic creatures."

The emissary slowly and deliberately sank to a knee, stammering more insistently. "You have my sincerest apologies, My Lord. If I m-might speak for the king... he is willing and able to dispatch men...he only wishes to know if you should deign to assist in the b-battle to come... It would g-greatly affect the strategy involved-"

"Yes, yes, I shall dispatch death upon them. You should know full well by now that their leader is among their troops. King, emperor...it means little to an agent of death. He is the true prize in the battle to come – and the only reason why I have deigned to grant the Kuru aid in this at all. A Nuru king has not come so willingly into the waiting claws of the Churai in my recollection, and it is a mistake I intend to allow him to make. Without him the country will be in chaos and the forces gathered outside your walls will be lost and simple to remove, even for your simpleton soldiers."

"I u-understand, My Lord. The king thanks you for your assistance... When shall your..." he paused as he desperately searched for the right word, "...death...be dispatched?"

"When the time is right and the opportunity better presents itself. For now you will just have to continue wallowing. It's what you do best."

"Y-yes... M-my Lord. I shall go tell the king now."

He practically sprinted from the dungeon to Rizellion's amusement.

Female Churai Nithilion approached to retrieve the Word.

"Acquiescence?" she inquired in a hiss.

"When I give the order. Dispatch two murders. Target Nuru King. Retrieve head as proof. Obey."

"Obey," they all responded in unison.

Chapter XXXV

Conditions in Nevo-Kulan had worsened by the day until it was a city Nimia no longer even recognized.

As a lady-in-waiting for Princess Kiera, or just Lady Kiera now, she had witnessed several minor rebellions that had sprang into being in the Korrainian capital, her lifetime home, but never before had the level of anger equaled the amount of moral degradation on the streets. In a truly ironic fashion, the safest places in the city were wherever the massive crowds had gathered to shout, throw rocks, and protest, due to the fact that at least there was justice of the masses wherever they congregated. In the quieter parts of the city was where the real danger presented itself – robbers, rapists, and murderers ran rampant in the unguarded portions as the rest of the king's garrison had retreated to the castle to ensure none entered.

Nimia had not been permitted to leave the castle in over three weeks. It was beginning to feel more like a siege. Every day was nerve-wracking as she had no choice but stand as prettily and quietly as possible in court and listen to the men argue and posture at each other. There were days when it felt no safer than in the streets, as the king had struck her on more than one occasion because she was being too slow in fetching them food, or sometimes for no reason at all. He had been very cruel since he blamed Kiera's escape on her.

I've been subjected to this humiliation and pain before, but never this often. The king has lost control of the situation and everyone knows it. But I daren't say anything for fear of losing my head!

"Surely word will reach him soon, Your Grace," one of the lords from the north told the king enthusiastically, "The letter was dispatched nigh on two weeks ago."

"It was clearly intercepted at this point, you dolt. The common rabble are behaving in treasonous fashion, and if I had the forces I would have them all clapped in irons and they would each be losing a finger or two for even gathering like this. I am the King of Korraine, their shepherd, their rightful ruler. I will not forget this." He sat atop his throne, slumped to one side with a hand to his face. Frustration had gotten the better of him long ago and all tact and reason had left him shortly thereafter.

"Your Grace," another lord that Nimia thought came from the west near the border, probably a duke, said with some pent-up consternation, "With respect, we should not be known to the world as the eight-fingered kingdom. It was the opinion of the present council two weeks ago that the letter sent to Lord Patogina would be a contingency should this situation not rectify itself. You all said they would disperse, but they haven't. With further respect, Your Grace, it is time to consider revoking this succession law. It serves little purpose and it has enflamed the passions of the people more than any law passed in my lifetime."

The woman who had for so long been joined at the arm with the king, Lady Sophia Itholos, his new wife, finally stood to speak. She was a woman of perhaps thirty years old with beautiful long dark curls, angular face, piercing blue eyes, and voluptuous hips that undoubtedly had been the source of the king's interest in her.

Nimia and Kiera had both known her for many years as the king's mistress, and she had been at his side since shortly after the previous queen had died. The King had made no secret of their affair and dared any to challenge him on it, and only Kiera ever did. Sophia and Kiera hated each other – Kiera for seeing her as a lying, cheating charlatan after the power of being queen and trying to replace her mother, and Sophia for viewing the girl as nothing more than an upstart, ill-behaved teenager needing to be put in her place. The new queen couldn't have been more joyous after Kiera had fled and brought disgrace to her name.

"Lady Kiera has shown her true colors by abandoning this kingdom and fleeing into the waiting arms of kingsmen. Without this law, she is not only a pretender to the throne, but a pretender who echoes the dogma of the High King. Would you like to have her as your ruler?"

"Of course not, My Lady…"

"This law has brought a stable line of succession to the Kingdom of Korraine and given it an heir worthy of its splendor. A girl of such questionable moral character cannot and will not be considered a viable candidate to rule this country and its people. I would sooner die," she spat, sitting back down in a huff.

"At this point, your ladyship," the man rebutted, "whether the law stands or not, there is nothing standing in Lady Kiera's way now if she should decide to take the kingdom by force. Our armies are unreachable. The populace is livid and would support her. And now we know that the High King is furious with these developments and has refused us aid unless we revoke the law. The pressure is mounting, Your Grace, and soon we will have little choice but to concede."

Another of the lords, this one Nimia did not know, leapt to his feet angrily, "You speak near-treason! Such an action would bring untold embarrassment to this court that we should never recover! I will not stand for our king to look weak in the face of true justice!"

They don't understand. The king already looks weak and insecure for having declared Kiera illegitimate in the first place. The people don't like kingsmen either, but what they saw was the king force her out of Korraine and to the kingsmen – most would agree she had no choice.

Several raps erupted from the window covers as rocks bounded off of them. It had been fortunate that this had taken place in the winter – if it had been summer, they would not have been able to keep the windows closed for days on end.

The crier, a boy about twelve, made his way across the courtroom and knelt before the king.

"Speak."

"By your leave, the king's court magician," he said without looking up.

"Excellent, she may enter."

He retreated out of the large iron-and-wooden doors and was replaced by a woman in simple black robes, not dissimilar to a monk's. She had wavy dark hair that was chopped even at her shoulders. Typical to many Korrainians she had a longer chin and nose, with bright skin, unfortunately marred by a large burn scar across her chin and the right side of her face. Nimia had spoken to her on a few occasions and found her to be kind in reasonable circumstances, but firm and relentless when her king ordered her to be. Without much knowledge of magic, Nimia never fully understood what exactly she could do as court magician, but she did hear from another of the lesser magicians that her black robes pointed to her use of Shadow Magic.

She also knelt before him and spoke with her scratchy voice. "Ceriina Hezimuth, court magician, ready for orders, Your Grace."

"Our previous attempts to reach Lord Patogina have failed by normal means, and I can only assume that our letters and best couriers were intercepted. I shall need to make use of your talents to ensure this letter is received by him as quickly as possible."

Nimia did not wait for him to signal her and took a step up to hand her the letter.

"It will be done, My Lord."

"Have you also readied the others?"

"Yes, My Lord."

"How many do you have available?"

"One experienced fire magician and two unexperienced, along with one experienced earth magician and an unexperienced shadow magician, my apprentice."

"Good. Do you put your trust in your apprentice's skills, Mistress Hezimuth?"

She looked up at him, impassive. "I trained her myself, so she is skilled but untested."

"Have her deliver the letter to Patogina then. I have another mission for you and the other magicians."

"My Lord?"

"Have your fire magicians disperse the crowds starting tomorrow morning. Ensure they do not congregate near the castle again."

Ceriina's eyes momentarily widened. "Yes, My Lord, but they are many and we are few. They will only be able to keep them at bay for so long without hurting anyone."

"Then if you have to burn a few, so be it."

There was a long, hesitant pause before she finally dipped her head again. "Understood."

"As for you, you may approach."

Her head snapped back up again as she followed his instruction, stepping up the stone steps and kneeling again.

The king leaned in and began to whisper to her.

There were only four souls in the room that heard what he was saying to her: Sophia, Ceriina, the king himself, and Nimia, as she always stood only a few feet away in case he needed anything.

It was difficult to hear the entirety of his order, but Nimia heard enough.

He was ordering his court magician to kill Kiera.

A terrible, cold shiver worked its way down her spine as she continued to stand as straight as possible, not giving away any indication that she had heard anything at all.

Dear spirits, no! How could he do this to his own daughter? He just wants her out of the way!

She knew she just had to breathe, but the room was suddenly feeling very hot.

Do not cry, Nimia, do not cry. Be strong for Kiera.

Ceriina retreated slowly back down the steps and bowed.

"You have my leave. Go."

She turned and took the long walk out of the court room.

"Court is adjourned for now. I need rest. I will see you all here tomorrow for more unproductive talks."

Everyone bowed and shuffled out of the room and into the stone corridors amidst the continuous roars of the crowd outside.

Nimia wasted no time. She only had an hour or so until her evening duties would be expected to be done, so she had to hurry. Making it back to her quarters three staircases later, she grabbed some parchment and quill dipped in ink and went to the privy where she would be safe from prying eyes.

Her handwriting was atrocious in her speed, but she knew she would be forgiven for it. In just a few minutes she was done and wrapped a long strip of leather around it to bind it closed, finally slipping it into her smock and heading for the staircase again.

To her shock, she nearly ran into someone climbing the staircase at the same time in her haste.

To her further shock, it was the king.

She had managed to stop in time and not touch him, but he was still dismayed.

"Watch where you're going, girl!" he shouted, slapping her hard across the face.

She nearly lost her balance and leaned against the stone wall of the staircase.

Her heart was pumping harder than she could comprehend.

"Begging your most gracious pardon, Your Grace. I am but a stupid, clumsy girl."

"Where are you off to in such a hurry?" he demanded.

"Off to fetch the wash, My Lord. I had forgotten it until now, my sincerest apologies."

He leaned in close to her, his scraggly beard nearly touching her face.

"Useless. Get on with it then." He stomped away up the stairs leaving her gasping for breath thereafter.

I'm alive. Dear spirits I'm alive.

She raced down into the understory of the castle, to where she knew the postern door was. Few in the castle besides the king and the marshal knew where it was, but she had stumbled upon it a few months ago.

Watching for any onlookers, she gingerly eased the door open to the outside.

It only took a few seconds until her contacts from the populace scurried over and began whispering to her through the crack of an opening.

"What word? Tell us, what does the king plan?"

She shoved the parchment into their hands and pleaded with them, "Please, please have your fastest rider get this to Princess Kiera, wherever she is. You must hurry! The king plans to have her killed!"

Their eyes were all wide. "No! He cannot! We will deliver this letter and warn her!"

"And you must be careful yourselves, my friends, the king plans to sic his magicians on you all tomorrow. Fire magicians, earth…he's going to kill you if you don't leave the square!"

The man who spoke nodded quickly. "Thank you for telling us. Bless you. You will find ultimate peace in the arms of the good spirits. Go, Nimia. Be safe! Before anyone comes!"

Nimia slid the door shut and locked it once more, taking a long heavy breath. It was all she would be able to do – Kiera's life would be in her own hands now.

Just when she thought she was safe, however, she heard the thunderous sound of boots and chain moving down the staircase into the understory. She panicked and wanted to hide, but there were nothing but empty meat hooks and wine racks – she would be caught regardless.

Several guards emerged from the staircase, ripping swords from their sheaths and advancing towards her. "Stop, traitor! Do not move!"

Chapter XXXVI

Over the several days Reldon, Alira, and Elly traversed the Kuru countryside, there was a general fear of being discovered, but they realized quickly that there was simply no one to discover them.

Avoiding cities was the easy part, as the Kuru did have established cobblestone roads that winded around landforms and population centers, and well-worn dirt roads that carried on through forests and fields, so staying out of the way of traffic would have been a minor problem had their been any traffic. Only on rare occasions would they hear the distant *clack* of hoofs on the road, and it would give them more than enough time to get off the road and hide so the rider could pass – not that they were ever going slow enough to notice.

Reldon had noticed that everything from the massive Wall of Isolation to the dilapidated roads to what intermittent ruins they passed on their way were all of a very old construction. All he had to compare it to were some of the older structures that had made up the castle in Freiad – ones that looked like they had been pieced together over a period of time with varying types of stone and mortar. Without entering any of the cities he had no way of knowing if such methods of antiquity comprised most of their urban composition as well, but from what he had seen, Drunerakerrum looked to be a country that hadn't evolved much in hundreds of years.

Gradually as they approached the western capital, they could smell the smoke even from miles away. Pangs of anxiety wracked them, knowing that this was about to be the most dangerous feat they'd ever attempted.

Still, the capital was to be another half-day's travel further west, and the sun had long since waned, leaving twilight to take its shift over the land.

Um...Reldon? Alira's voice chimed into his head.
Hm?
Are you... are you scared?
He nodded. *I would be lying if I said I wasn't.*
This is the furthest we've ever been from home and from any help and we're about to go right into the enemy's lair. I'm trying not to shake or Elly will notice.
I'm honestly surprised that she's not scared.

She is – I can sense it, she responded, squeezing Elly's hand comfortingly, *but she's being strong about it. I'm not sure why now of all times she is trying so hard to be brave.*

Reldon slowed to a stop.

Do you...see that?

Yes, I was just going to ask you the same thing.

There was a partially hidden light, glowing orange like fire, in the small forest of the trees off to the left of the road.

Best we keep moving –

Looking back at the road, however, revealed a figure standing still in the middle of the path, maybe one hundred yards from where they stood.

"Ready, ready, ready," Reldon repeated. It was their signal to ready for battle.

Alira pulled Rytzermion from her pack, and Elly pulled her bow out and worked on nocking an arrow as they had practiced.

Typically they would have ducked into a ditch or behind some trees, but the figure was clearly looking straight at them. Luckily Reldon did not see any glowing red eyes or else their strategy would have been drastically different.

Reldon took the front while Alira followed ten paces behind, followed immediately by Elly, all of them slowly approaching.

"Oi!" Reldon shouted in the near darkness, "Who goes there?"

The figure only held up a hand and beckoned them to follow. It rotated and walked silently towards the woods where the fire was.

I'm going to catch up with it before it leads us into the forest. It could be planning an ambush there.

He picked up speed and met the figure in short order as it made no attempt to outrun him.

"Who are you? Where are you taking us?"

It stopped, turning again to face Reldon. Though difficult to make out features, it looked to be an elderly woman, around as tall as Alira.

"I know of you and your quest, Xanem Nuremar. Come, sit with me. We have much to discuss."

This conversation feels very familiar.

Is it safe? Alira asked cautiously, holding Elly back.

I...think so.

"You must be hungry. I should be able to fix that," she continued, stepping into her campsite. There was a cooking pot suspended over the fire and several small tents set up surrounding it.

Reldon, Alira, and Elly entered the campsite, not taking their eyes off of the woman as she entered the firelight. She took off her hood to reveal coarse features marred by far too many years and scars. With a round face and bulbous nose, deep creases and shriveled ears, she was a sight to behold but not for good reasons. Time had aged this woman about as well as it would a cup of milk. Wispy gray hair pointed in all directions after removing her hood and she looked at them with dark eyes.

"I am Hanea. Welcome to Drunerakerrum, dear Nurems," she croaked.

They exchanged looks.

Alira, that was one of the names Tycheronius warned me about. This must be another of Grandma's friends.

"You were expecting us," Reldon stated.

"Why yes. I knew you would pass this way. Having a nice fire and good company is welcome on a cold Kuru night, is it not?" she said with a gnarled smile.

I think we can trust her, Alira thought to him, sinking onto one of the stumps she had placed for seats.

"Yes, this is much appreciated, Hanea. I'm Alira, it's a pleasure to meet you."

The old woman beamed. "What nice manners you have! Here I was afraid all of that power might have gone to your heads. I made hare stew, eat up."

Reldon took one of the wooden bowls when offered. "I don't mean to be rude, Hanea, but how much exactly *do* you know about us?"

"I know you've been spending time in each of the Lärimite kingdoms over the past four or five months or so attempting to convince them to be anything but themselves. I know you recently lost a friend and mentor. I know you spent the storm in the company of royalty in northern Atheria, followed by a trip to both Darum and Teraxella on your way here. You caused quite some trouble in the latter, my dears."

They further exchanged looks of awe, but Reldon returned with, "You probably heard a lot of that from the others. Your friends we met on the way here."

"Ah, but I also know that you struggle with nightmares. Both of you do. You, young man, require direction, a strong hand to guide you where to go. You, young lady, seek trust above all else. Both of you fail to see this in the other, or fail to acknowledge it. Doubt besets both of your minds. You live in fear of both what you might become and what you have already become."

Alira and Reldon were speechless.

"And if I had to guess, you'll probably be leaving the *concea* root at the bottom of your bowl because you don't like the texture but don't want to be rude by tossing it into the snow."

Reldon put his bowl down and shook his head. "All right, this is too strange. How do you know all of these things about us? The first ones I figured you would all know by now, but how could you possibly know how I'm *feeling?*"

She chuckled. "I have been around people for a long time, young Spellsword. A long time. And when you study them as long as I have, you start noticing trends. Eventually they cease to be trends and become rules, and from rules to predictable behaviors. You two may be legendary warriors, but you're still no different than any other adolescents I've met. I can tell by the way you're sitting, lad, that you're interested in the girl. And similarly for you, girl, I can see you're uncertain if you feel the same. No, that's not right. You're afraid. Afraid of your own feelings. Of what you might do."

"I'm sorry, Hanea, but could you stop that, please? It's like you're…reading my thoughts and I don't know if I like it," Alira asserted as politely as she could.

"I understand, dear. But I assure you there's no magic being used – just ages of wisdom."

"So why are you really here, Hanea? The others had something that they wanted to teach us or do to help us. You're not here just to make us stew and make us feel embarrassed."

She laughed openly. "Right you are, those are just an added benefit! You are about to head into the most dangerous situation you have ever encountered, and you must be ready. I trust you have already been given the location of that which you seek?"

"Yes," Reldon responded, fishing out a piece of parchment from his pack that he had scribbled down the directions on.

"Good. Now there is something else that you must know. Much is going to go wrong in the battle to come, and there is only so much you can do to change it. You will need to make a choice."

She tossed Reldon a small object, which he caught and rotated between his fingers. It was a cylindrical piece of solid, reflective metal about as long as his hand, with a few long perfectly straight lines running along its length. Strange inscriptions covered both circular ends. Any practitioner of magic could tell that it emanated a powerful magical energy.

"It is a device of ancient origin, a relic if you will. A battle is about to take place that will be a defining moment in the history of Rim, and it will be up to you to decide how it goes. On your way through the castle, following the directions you were given, you will at some point spot a dark room with a metal tube protruding from the floor. It leads to a vast series of tunnels beneath the city that are being used for everything from smuggling food to moving troops. The tube has been for delivering messages."

She leaned in closer and her voice took on a serious edge.

"If you should so choose, you may drop this relic into that tube after charging it with magical power. Should you so decide to do this, the tunnels, the understructure of the city, and much of the assailing Kuru forces will be destroyed. This will win the battle for the Nuru and save your friends' lives."

"Our friends? Do you mean Bryle and Sillida?" Reldon exclaimed.

Hanea did not immediately react. "Possibly."

"Then we must do it, surely," Reldon stated to an affirming nod from Alira.

"Understand that while this will likely save your friends' lives, it will also likely doom your own. The magical signal that you give off on activation of this device will be like a beacon to every Churai in the city, and they will find you."

"But if we don't do it, the Nuru army and our friends could die."

The old woman nodded mournfully. "When the time comes, you must choose."

Reldon shook his head. "How can you possibly ask us to make that decision? Our lives or our friends'? There has to be a third option!"

"If you are clever enough to come up with a third option, then by all means," she ruminated, "If it helps your decision, I will be waiting for you exactly one mile from the city to the east, next to a lone oak tree. If you can make it to me, you will be safe."

"Why can't you simply come with us? If you have the power to save everyone, why not do it?" Reldon demanded.

"I do not have such a power, unfortunately. And the salvation I offer cannot be used inside that castle. The old oak is the closest I may get."

"I have so many questions, Hanea," Alira joined in, "What is this device? Where did it come from?"

"That is not important now. Perhaps some day you will know, but not now."

Reldon asked his question, knowing the response he would receive. "What exactly are you and your friends planning? We're expected to follow along, but no one will tell us why!"

"I know this is not the answer you are looking for, young Spellsword, but what we are doing is helping you in your destiny, but we cannot tell you why."

"Because if you do we might refuse to cooperate?"

Her look was even. "Because if we do, you will not understand until we show you. If you can be patient, all will be revealed." She pointed to the device in Reldon's hand. "Focus on this first. Get into that castle, get the amulet, and come back to me alive, and all will make sense. I promise. In the meantime, spoon over those roots, they're nutritious and I like 'em more than you do."

Ethilia had lost track of the number of days she had spent in the Atherian castle with the chipper, fallen princess Kiera and the curmudgeonly, unenthusiastic court healer Nuremia. She found that between the two of them she had to take regular walks out in the filthy snow just to keep from tearing her own flawless hair out.

Since beginning the process of gathering the Golden Magicians, either through Ilewa mediums or physically, Kiera had been predictably useless in the endeavor. After all, she did not have any magic and had no way to assist in any meaningful way short of fetching food and drink from the kitchens. In fact, she spent more time befriending King Obrim than anything else – Ethilia could practically hear their unmitigated laughter from the other end of the castle every evening during dinner.

Nuremia had been more of a boon, but not by much. Each time Ethilia asked her to try reaching the same person more than once, she would respond with, "I just don't see the point..." Kiera's bubbly nature was a minor annoyance, but Nuremia's dedication to obstruction was becoming a problem unto itself.

"Let's run through the list again so we have a fresh understanding of where we are at," Ethilia said, reading through the parchment.

"Listing it off again won't get nothing done," Nuremia muttered.

She ignored her for the hundredth time. Today.

"Alira and Elliana are obviously off fighting the Churai, so they're unavailable to render assistance. Yesterday we received a letter from Civilia Greenwood of Darum informing us that she would be travelling here herself and would *not* be utilizing the services of a Messenger Magician. 'Not proper', she said."

"I swear that woman has put ten years on her life wasting time doing things all 'proper'," Nuremia commented, attempting to channel her Golden Magic into a small strip of flesh, "She's got nothing better to do."

"Since she sent the letter a few days ago and the courier reached us yesterday, she should arrive... tomorrow, I believe," Ethilia thought out loud, "Xari Temblance you spoke to earlier through a Messenger."

Nuremia grunted in affirmation as her golden harness held a solid structure over the scrap of meat. "That airhead isn't going to be of much help, but she should be here in three or four days."

"Every Golden Magician is valuable, dear Nuremia, and Ms. Temblance may be able to assist us in ways others might not. We may only achieve this together as sisters of Golden Magic."

"Look, girlie, I may have decided to join your little sisterhood to keep you from bothering me about it, but that doesn't mean I'm about to be playing nice and friendly with all the kings' ladies. Especially that last one you're about to read off."

"So far we've been unable to reach Aila Sethatendrikos of Korraine. Letters have not made it through to her."

"Good. Let's hope it stays that way."

Ethilia was quickly beginning to lose her patience.

"Miss Nuremia I am surprised at you. Why must you behave thus?"

The middle-aged woman gave her a look that could kill. "You haven't been around as long as I have. I've watched these people squabble and kick and scream every time there was even a mention of working together on anything. Those Korrainians are the worst of 'em all. Why we didn't just send them back into the ocean where they belong all those years ago I'll never know."

"Is that what you think of my friend Princess Kiera then as well?" Ethilia responded with narrowed eyes.

"Nah, she seems like a good enough kid, but we'll see. Since I came here from Errum decades ago I've learned a few hard lessons about Lärimites. They don't know who they are, they don't know what they want, and they protect their own first. Those are hard rules as far as I'm concerned. No one here is an exception."

"You must believe Nuru are so different?"

"We're at least smart enough to mind our own business. Or at least we were, before Emperor Whoever took power."

"Nuremia, surely you can see the direness of the threat we face and why we must all swallow our pride and forget our national origins for just a short time to come up with a solution. This may be the only time this ever happens. Why not enjoy it if you hate those divisions so much?"

"I just ain't got the faith for it anymore, blondie. If you don't think the other Golden Magicians haven't looked sideways at me all these years for being Nuru, you've got a hard lesson to learn yourself in the next few days. These women are gonna find every reason they can to not work with you or me or each other. There's a reason we've stayed in our corners of the country for this long."

Ethilia waved a hand over the harness and it dissipated into nothing, garnering the woman's full attention.

"Promise me that you'll at least try. That you will give this, and the others, a chance. If I'm wrong you can rub it in my face for the rest of our professional careers, but please. Just this once."

She spent a long moment with her old, jaded eyes locked on the young upstart's expressive, icy blue ones.

"I won't promise anything, but you do have my word that I'll be cooperative. I want to get this done as much as you do."

It wasn't a full victory, but it was something.

"Thank you. Since there's no one left to contact for the moment, I'll be at dinner. Will you join us?"

She laughed sarcastically. "I haven't eaten dinner with that king in five years. Not about to start now."

Ethilia suppressed a sigh as she headed off towards the dining hall.

That woman is simply impossible sometimes. Though she is speaking to me more honestly than she did a few years ago, that honesty is still soured with her bitterness. How is it that someone who devotes so much of her life to preserving the vivacity in others has so little herself?

It was the otherwise saddening state of the sisterhood that brought her the most consternation, however. Not the affiliation that she had created, but the overall state of Golden Magicians as a whole.

Our numbers are so few and yet there is such an unwillingness to cooperate or even treat each other with any kind of bond. No one knows when the next Golden Magician will turn up, and for all we know there may not even be another in our lifetimes, as random as it seems. When I found Elliana, I wrote to all the others expecting an excited response, but instead received silence. I don't understand it. Why am I the only Golden Magician with this zeal in my chest, this pride for what we are?

For the umpteenth time, she heard uncivilized amounts of laughter as she approached the dining hall, finally entering to spirited conversation and an obscene amount of food.

As she stepped into sight, Kiera was the first to wave happily to her. "Oh, Ethilia! I am so glad you decided to join us this evening!"

"How lovely to see you, lass, pull up a chair and rip out a turkey leg!" the king shouted, his beaming face contagious enough to make even Ethilia grin, "Actually one leg is hers and the other mine, so... Oi, Mirya, remind me to find out if there's a three-legged turkey. We need a few."

Otomia was there as well, sitting beside the other magicians, forming a line of fire, water, and earth magicians on one side of the table, Kiera and Ethilia on the other.

It had not escaped Ethilia's notice that Kiera had a fair amount of food on her plate and was most certainly not eating in a supremely dignified fashion. Not that the Korrainian girl even noticed, she was too busy giving her that big stupid smile.

"How's your wee project coming along, Miss Vendimar?" the king asked her, taking another swig of ale.

"Fruitfully, Your Majesty. We shall soon have the assistance of all known Golden Magicians." She waited until one of the serving girls came by with a plate of food rather than simply taking it like a barbarian.

He chuckled. "Well if I drink a tad too much I'll have all the help in the world it would seem!"

Don't you start too.

"Now where was I..." he asked semi-rhetorically.

"You were just about to tell us what you thought of Errum when you visited," Kiera reminded him with a flourishing hand signal.

"Aye, that's right. I do quite love the people of Errum – good hardy folk who love a good game, a good ale, and a good fight when it comes down to it. That's why the last place in Errum I'd like to visit is that capital o' theirs, Remdas-Kuwis. I've been to Tigrem and Celimar, good Nuru cities with right scrappers and hardworking farmers, miners, wha' have you. The capital is a wholly different creature. Too many old men arguing about old things that no one has cared about for... well, ever!"

315

Can't stand the bickering old men. That's why, my dears, King Obrim hasn't gotten a single old man at his court. It's a point of pride I'll have you know. I see you snickering over there, earth lass! You think ol' King Obrim is old! I'll have ye' know I've plucked every gray hair from both me head and beard. Completely stops the aging. I feel as good as I did twenty years ago!"

Kiera giggled. "And have you ever been to Korraine?"

"'Fraid not. I've met with your father a few times, but they don't appreciate the likes of us Atherians over there. I'm sure it's a lovely place, lass, and if you were queen I would visit all the time. We really should look into tha'. You deserve the throne more than that half-brother of yours! The thought of it all just brings my blood to a quick boil! Oi, ponce-hat! Where are my armies? Go marshal them! We ride at dawn!"

The boy was clearly frightened. "Tell the…armies to prepare to… march?"

"Tha's what I said, lad, off you go!"

Kiera and Ethilia shot terrified looks at each other but were quickly assuaged by a dismissive wave and a smile from both court magicians.

A courier dressed in riding leathers strode into the hall without announcement and dropped to a knee. "My apologies for this interruption, My Liege, but I have an important message."

Ethilia stood. "Aren't you the one we sent to Korraine to attempt to deliver another message?"

"Aye, Lady Vendimar. I met a Korrainian riding at a breakneck pace halfway there who asked if I knew where to find Princess Kiera. He gave me this."

Kiera stood and took the parcel from the man. "Thank the spirits for your haste. Go in peace."

He bowed his head before standing.

"Go on. Good work," the king dismissed him.

For a long, tense moment, Kiera read through the parchment, the previously jovial expression long gone from her face.

Ethilia stepped closer and reached a hand to touch her shoulder as if she were approaching a dangerous animal. "What is it, Kiera? Who is it from?"

"This handwriting…It's from Nimia! Oh dear spirits, she's alive and well! I was so scared father would have beaten her senseless after I fled. She says she had to smuggle this message out of the castle, as the situation has grown… much worse in Nevo-Kulan. The people have begun to rise up –

316

they chant my name in the streets! Father and the other courtiers have been holed up in the castle for many weeks, afraid for their lives if they try to flee and the king cannot get word out to his vassals for them to send aid…”

She trailed off, reading further. It was the most silence there had likely ever been in the dining hall of King Obrim of Atheria.

“Oh no. Oh dear spirits no. Father intends to attack the people who are gathered! And he… Oh…”

Her knees buckled beneath her and Ethilia helped lower her to the floor as she began to cry.

“What is it? What does he plan to do?” Ethilia demanded.

All Kiera could do was hand her the letter.

“It’s…in Korrainian.”

“It says he sent the court magician to *kill me!*”

The entire hall erupted into furious chaos. King Obrim especially flung curses and obscenities to the heavens before roaring in anger.

“I’ll have his guts! You mark my words! He thinks himself strong trying to assassinate a girl, well let’s see how he fares against a real man! I’ll kill him myself!” he thundered.

“Such utter barbaric…despicable…” Ethilia sputtered.

Kiera rose to her wobbly feet and strode to the other end of the hall, swiping up her bow and placing it on her back before reaching for her quiver.

“What are you doing?!” Ethilia exclaimed.

“I have to go. He’s going to destroy the country. I have to… I have to…”

Otomia rushed over to her as well. “Please, your ladyship, stay here where it’s safe. No assassin will get to you while under the king’s banner. I cannot promise I can save you out there.”

“She’s right, Kiera, you can’t be travelling the country now that you know someone is out to kill you. It’s simply far too dangerous,” Ethilia added.

Undeterred, she tightened her quiver onto her belt and swung her bow onto her back.

“I must do this, friends. I will not hide here while he angers the spirits by issuing orders of death upon his own daughter. He is going to bring war to Korraine again, and much blood will be shed. I will not allow him to hurt the people.”

Ethilia took her by the arm. “This unrest is going to happen whether you’re there or not. You can’t stop it now.”

"Then they need a leader," Kiera responded, her violet eyes exuding a fierce determination.

Ethilia took a step back. "Then you've decided."

"I have. I cannot keep waiting for someone else to stand up to my father's lunacy. The greatest change of my life came from Reldon standing before him and refusing to give an inch. I think that is what I need to do now. The way has been cleared for a new order in Korraine – the High King will not come to his aid and neither will his people. He is finished. But if I'm not there to pick up those pieces, some other pretender will. It is my duty, Ethilia. I can't turn my back on my country."

There was a steely stubbornness behind her eyes that reminded Ethilia far too much of herself.

The zeal in my chest.

The court healer nodded somberly. "Take Otomia with you. I cannot follow where you travel, but don't worry. We'll be safe here."

King Obrim's quaking voice spoke up as well. "Take Mirya too. If it's a magic fight they want, by hell she'll give 'em one! Make me proud lass!"

Mirya bowed, and with one last "Yes, your majesty", joined Kiera.

"And you let King Obrim know if there's any other way I can help you retake your country. I can't overtly declare war, but I can head there with a few men and give 'em a right trouncing they won't forget!"

"Ride hard, Kiera," Ethilia said with a sniff, "and do be sure to bring an extra pair of riding leathers, those are a bit dirty."

"Oh you are so wonderful when you care – you are even crying!" Kiera, of course, had to point out. They wrapped their arms around each other in a warm, shaky embrace.

"Be safe," Ethilia whispered.

"Remember to smile."

That made her laugh for the first time in forever. "Now go on before I really get emotional and embarrass myself in public."

She nodded, and waved to her magician bodyguards who followed silently.

As to the door creaked to a close behind her, Ethilia was left standing in the hall with King Obrim at a loss for words.

She's walking into a battle that will decide the fate of Korraine. And she is doing it with that stupid grin on her face. How can she do that? She had better come back safely or I'll kill her myself.

"She's a good lass. She'll figure it out. One day very soon she'll be queen and life will be very different. I've never gotten drunk with a queen before!" he laughed heartily.

The small page skittered back into the hall with a salute.

"The armies have been alerted and are readying to march, Your Grace."

The king stared at him for a long disbelieving moment. "You wha'?"

"The...armies, Your Grace? They are... ready to march on your orders. The general has been alerted."

"The general?! Ooh lad, what have you done now?"

The page's face went very red and his mouth hung agape.

"Raising the armies? Good spirits, you're trying to go to war! You're a right maniac! Go tell 'em to stand down at once!"

Without another word, he fled from the hall after exchanging a perplexed look with Ethilia, who gazed over at Tara who gave them both a knowing smile that said, "I told you so."

Chapter XXXVII

The time had come and the smell of smoke and death filled the air.

Bryle and Sillida never realized when they snuck in the wake of the Teraxella relief force that they weren't going to be walking into a wide open field of battle with Kuru to slay. There was little blood on the dark Kuru plains, only the ominous sense of foreboding coming from the Kuru capital, towers of smoke bleeding from its walls and inner buildings. Unlike many Nuru cities, the entirety of the keep and village were locked behind immense stone walls rather than the village fending for themselves from without.

The Nuru army was a sight to behold, and it brought an incredible swelling sense of pride within both of their chests. With green and silver banners flying, trebuchets launching flaming balls of rock, and legions of cheering soldiers in the thousands, it was enough to make them punch their fists into the air and cheer how good a day it was to be Nuru.

Still, however, there was little for them to do. They expected their brethren to need them in combat, but it looked like the battle was already well in hand. The Kuru had lasted a very long time under the siege, but their outer walls were crumbling to huge piles of rubble, and soon there would be nothing keeping the invading army out.

"This isn't exactly what I imagined Drunerakerrum would look like. It looks too much like home," Bryle ruminated, standing atop a small outcropping of basalt rock, far from the siege.

Sillida sat near the bottom, her thousand-yard stare gazing off towards Kuruverrum. "It is what I imagined. I dreamed of watching their city burn. Just like Freiad. They deserve this."

Bryle nodded but didn't immediately respond.

"We're going to join in the attack, right?" she followed up.

"When it happens, aye, we will."

"How long will that take?"

Bryle shrugged. "Shouldn't be too much longer. Their walls are barely standing anymore."

She drove her knife into the snow, standing it up by its blade.

Sillida truly believes that this is going to bring an end to all of her nightmares, somehow make it all worth it. She thinks driving that blade into a Kuru is going to bring Freiad or her mother back. Revenge is all she thinks about,

320

and now that we're here... I just hope after all this is over... she'll still be the same girl.

A cold droplet soaked into Bryle's hair, and then another. He looked down at his palm and three more raindrops pooled in the center. In short order the rain clattered off of his armor. Sillida stood up, confused at the sudden weather change.

"But... it's winter. Why is it raining?"

Circling around the reverse side of the city walls of Kuruverrum had been much easier than expected, as a majority of the sentries were focused on the massive army to the south. Yapoti had been right – this would likely be the only time sneaking into such a well-fortified city would have been possible. The cover of the ensuing twilight would also serve them well.

Alira had to comfort Elly every few minutes as they approached the city – the smells, the explosions, the screams... it was a lot for one child to take in and be brave.

"Do not cry, my Elly. It will all be well soon. Remember we passed the big tree on the way here? It's not too far away, and we just need to make it there afterwards to be safe. That won't be too hard, right?"

She would nod, but she could tell the fear was always there and that there was nothing she could do about it.

We will have to be very careful about how we do this. Using magic or Phyrim could give us away.

How do we get in?

Indeed, the portcullises were all closed and no postern gates could be seen anywhere – just solid stone wall.

Maybe if I'm really careful I can use a little Phyrim on these outer stones.

But you just said that would be too dangerous.

He inspected the stones and how they were held together. The fact that they were of such an ancient construction could be a real boon.

Look at the way this mortar was used originally to build up this wall. It's not as good as the material that was used to make Freiad castle, or Nakisho. I think if I take it very slowly and control the amount of Phyrim I'm releasing, I could alter this mortar until we can just slide a few of these stones right out.

I can meditate and tell you if you're releasing too much.

He nodded. Placing both of his hands on one of the stones, he slowly turned the spigot on his Phyrimic power and injected it into the mortar holding the stone to the others.

Alira warned him at the start to keep it down, and he responded. At first he was able to keep the Phyrimic disturbance to a minimal level that was even difficult for her to detect sitting right next to him. However, as he began to make changes to the mortar, little spikes in energy emerged and she had to pinch him to get him to slow down.

This is so difficult to do without making any 'noise'. I can see the tiny openings between the particles and all I need to do is get them moving between those spaces, but I have to give them energy.

Keep going, I can already see it changing!

After around five minutes, the mortar surrounding the large stone had turned into a sort of slurry rather than a rock-hard adhesive substance.

Reldon opened his eyes and slid his fingers in around the rock. *Give me a hand.*

With Alira's help, the stone slid out from the wall to reveal further stones on the back side of it, and they had only freed up around two feet of space, not nearly big enough for anyone to fit through.

They both sat back.

This is going to take forever, Alira.

Sitting in what seemed like defeat, the Nurems wracked their brains trying to come up with a better solution that would not take hours.

There isn't a rush, though. This siege has been going on for a long time.

The longer we're here, the better chance someone will notice us. It would be best to-

A few rain droplets landed on their coats, halting their conversation.

Rain?

Reldon looked wide-eyed over at Alira.

Suddenly there were pulses of magic and Phyrim, massive ones, emanating from the army. A cacophonous collective scream rose high above, not of a battle charge, but of abject terror.

I don't know what's happened, but let's go, now! We have the cover!

Reldon finally let the spigot release a large amount of Phyrim as he placed his hands inside the hole in the wall, and he rapidly rearranged the structures of the stone and mortar until one after another the stones fell from their perches. Light shone from the other side of the wall and Reldon placed a hand on the top of the passage he created to reinforce it so it wouldn't collapse.

"Quickly, let's go," Reldon said sharply.

Elly and Alira scurried ahead inside the wall and found themselves inside the lower floor, wooden boards beneath their feet, torches lighting the way up the stone stairs, and not a guard to be seen.

I'm going to see how to get into the castle, his inner voice let Alira know.

Reldon snuck up the stairs, peeking his head over to look at the battlements. Seeing no immediate resistance, he crept up next to one of the crenellations and gazed over the cityscape to see the castle. As it turned out, the walls had been constructed in a large rectangular format and at the northern, shorter, edge of the rectangle it connected with the castle internally. Likely this was for quick mobilization of sentries, but he could only guess.

Good news, Alira. This wall is connected with the castle. Let's follow it that way, he told her, pointing west.

She nodded, and they proceeded west inside the wall, the torches leading the way.

What was the castle like?

Maybe as big as Freiad's castle keep. Like everything else it looks old. From what Hanea said, there's probably more underground than above.

The inner structure of the wall had a cold humidity to it, and there were places were small amounts of water had pooled and frozen between the stones in the walls, especially facing the city. A dull roar of the events outside could be faintly heard, but was muffled to a degree that kept Elly from growing too frightened. However, the structure beneath their feet was still occasionally shaken by another explosion and dust would be dislodged and fall around them.

Reldon's anxiety bled through their link again, and Alira took his hand to reassure him.

I'm worried about Bryle and Sillida, he admitted.

Me too. They might be out there in all that fighting. I hope they're all right.

You heard what Hanea said. They will only be all right if we decide to save them by dooming ourselves. But I can't just leave them out there to die.

The Nuru army might be able to protect them.

They finally reached the winding stone staircase that led up into the castle and they followed the uneven steps higher and higher. It felt like they were climbing a tower, but it was only leading them into the lower levels of the castle proper.

It opened into a dimly lit corridor that led east, south, and west. Distant scuffling of feet from the east prompted them to go west. It continued for some time until reaching another winding staircase or a turn leading south.

I... don't know where the treasury would be, Reldon thought to Alira.

Wouldn't it be in the lower levels of the castle? Maybe we should head that way?

Maybe we should split up. Just for a minute. Go both ways and see what it-

No. I won't do that now. Not here.

Her mind was resolute enough that he didn't push it. *All right. Let's go that way then.*

Heading south, there was a branching corridor with a series of wooden doors lining it – perhaps sleeping quarters? The main path still led further around the west edge of the castle keep, and a larger door finally presented itself on their left side, which they assumed would gain further entrance into the heart of the castle.

Alira flicked her vision back and forth and did not detect magic immediately ahead, so they pushed the doors open and stole inside the hall.

It opened out to the balcony level of a massive foyer lit by hundreds of chandeliers of flickering flames. The hall was not made of marble or any other more opulent building material, but a dark, gloomy stone that was likely more plentiful hundreds of years ago. Down below there were several military officers gathered around a central table, probably discussing battle strategy in less than amiable terms.

Sticking closer to the wall than the balcony railings, they worked their way around the outer edge of the foyer, locating another door of equal size and weight to the previous one.

Inside it seemed like a sort of lounge or nicer barracks. There were plenty of places to sit, tables to play cards or dice on, and even a life-size statue of a Kuru soldier, likely an admiral or general.

As they slid inside, however, they didn't realize at first that there were two people sitting in the far right corner of the room.

It appeared to be a young man and woman, and their vision snapped up as they entered.

Reldon, Alira, and Elly froze, staring fearfully at them, waiting for their next move.

The woman was definitely a few years older than Alira, with thin, raptor eyes, pinched mouth, and a more athletically powerful build than most women. She wore a dark robe with a few flecks of blue at the shoulders, elbows, and wrist, and she wore one half of her dark hair up. The man was probably of a similar age, and was clearly a smaller man than most, making him about the same size as the woman. His curly dark hair, hazel eyes, and pale skin lent him a different appearance than most Lärimites – exotic, but not too far removed. Both were very easily characterized differently from Lärimites by their very dark eyes and nearly snow-white skin.

Swiftly they got to their feet and carefully took a few steps towards the strangers.

At first when they spoke, it was in a language only they understood – Kuru. When they did not receive a response, they tried again in Lärimite, which came out in a very shaky, strange accent.

"Who are you? What are you doing here? Answer," the woman demanded.

Reldon, what do we do, attack them? Alira's voice chimed in frantically.

Reldon put out his hands non-threateningly. "We're not here to hurt you."

"You do not answer question. Who are you?"

"My name is Reldon. What's yours?"

She seemed perplexed at his question. "You do not ask question."

The man cocked his head towards her and they seemed to exchange a silent conversation.

"Are you Ilewa?" Alira asked with a hint of excitement.

He nodded and spoke in a similar accent. "We are mind partners. You are magicians as well." It was a statement rather than a question.

"Yes, we are. Just like you," Reldon responded.

Alira immediately realized what the woman was doing when she shut her eyes and opened them again with a different color glossing over what had previously been brown. The Kuru woman gasped and stammered in Kuru, nearly falling backwards.

"T-the…You are the…"

"Yes, we are. But we do not wish to harm you, only to talk," Reldon coaxed them.

She went from fearful to angry quickly. "Y-you should not be here! You are Lärim scum!"

The man seemed to plead with her in Kuru which only made her more upset.

"We know we not defeat you, and you will kill us if we alarm. We will not attack. What are you here for?"

His rationality was different from his Ilewa, who was furious at the situation and made clear of it by nearly bursting into tears.

"We're not even here to hurt any Kuru. We're just looking for something and then we will leave," Reldon said.

"What is look for?"

"We're looking for something in the treasury. Would you be able to tell us where that is?" Alira finished for him.

The woman gave her Ilewa a severe look, and made it clear she was *not* willing to help. He was somewhat undeterred, however, and returned a look of skepticism to the intruders.

"You are look for treasure?"

"Not any treasure – we're not looking to steal Kuru gold. We need to take something from the Churai."

They both recoiled at the mention of their dreadful castle companions.

"Why steal from Churai?"

"We have to stop them. That is our purpose, and the Churai are evil killers. This item is not theirs, but it could help us defeat them," Reldon explained as simply as he could. The language barrier was making it difficult to avoid confusion.

Every word seemed to baffle them further.

"You wish to… defeat Churai?"

Reldon nodded emphatically. "Yes, that is what we do. That is our purpose."

The man gave his Ilewa a cheerfully longing look, as if someone had dropped one thousand silver in their lap. She grinned momentarily as well, but her caution was self-evident.

He struggled to piece the sentence together.

"Strange. Kuru are told…you purpose is to…murder Kuru family. Families. But you no wish to kill Kuru families. This is right?"

Reldon nodded again. "Yes, that's right. We don't want to kill anyone. Except the Churai."

The welling of emotions nearly brought the man to tears. "We help you! If you kill Churai, Kuru will be free!"

His Ilewa's arms were still crossed and her eyes narrowed. "What if this is trick?"

More explosions outside rocked the castle.

"Then you can try to kill us later, but that isn't going to help you with the Churai!" Reldon pleaded, "We are the only ones powerful enough to stop them. And we need your help. Just lead us to the treasury and we'll take everything from there."

There was obvious conflict in both of their eyes as they conversed within the confines of their minds, but the Spellsword responded first. "Yes. We will bring you. Come, we are wrong side of castle. Must be careful not be seen."

"Thank you so much," Reldon said happily turning to follow them out. "You never told us what your names are."

"I am Bradek, nice meeting you."

There was a pause where the magician girl was supposed to say something, but she was clearly not in the mood.

"Her name is Adenakia. Aki is nickname."

"A pleasure to meet you both," Alira responded, "Our names are Alira and Reldon, and this little one is Elly."

Bradek creaked the door open and looked out first before waving them forward. "She is cute," he said with a smile.

"I am *not*," Elly responded indignantly.

Alira, can you believe they're helping us? These are Kuru!

They must hate the Churai more than they hate us!

The corridors were endless labyrinths with a few soldiers here and there, but their progress was much faster with a guide. The difficulty was going to be finding their way back out again.

Reldon whispered to Bradek as they backtracked to the southeastern corner of the castle.

"What did you mean when you said the Kuru will be free? Free of the Churai? I thought you worked together?"

His expression soured. "Churai are monsters. Kuru do not know, but king is hostage to Churai. Churai make all decision. We are slaves. When Churai become angry, kill Kuru."

"They kill your people? Then… why has no one done anything?"

"Too strong, and Kuru too scare. Aki and Bradek are powerful, but weak… against Churai. Kuru are no free here."

"But the Kuru people don't know that. They think the king is still in charge," Reldon clarified.

"Right."

They reached a more direct staircase heading down into a lower level at a precipitous pace and they stopped.

"Here treasury. We wait here."

Reldon put a hand on his arm. "Bradek, we *will* free your people. I swear it. Even if we're the only ones fighting, we will not give up."

The man clenched his jaw as his eyes reddened. A broad smile graced his face. It must have been like witnessing a messiah in person. "Thank you. We help all we can. Go. Get your item."

They nodded, and quickly descended the long staircase into the cold below.

I believe we may have promised at this time to free every people in the world, Alira giggled.

It's what heroes like us do.

Is that what we are?

Are we not?

I'm sure some wouldn't think so. Some call me the 'Black Rose'.

Well then we won't save those people.

Reldon.

I was only joking!

At the bottom was a long, rectangular room, flanked on both sides by dozens of doors, each marked with very old iron symbols on them – the old Lärimite numerals. They were difficult to see at first, as there was virtually no light in the room. Alira summoned a tiny ball of light to lead their way.

"XIII is the door we're looking for," Reldon said aloud.

Given that they were in numerical order, it had been easy to find.

The door was made almost entirely of iron, with the numerals stamped at the top center. The heavy padlock would have been deterrent to any normal man who would think to enter, but not for the Nurems.

It only took a few seconds of Phyrimic maneuvering to affix all the tumblers into place, and the lock opened with a click before falling to the floor.

Inside was a simple stone dais in the middle of a tiny room no larger than a prison cell. Atop that dais was an absolutely gorgeous amulet. The metal brooch was of a bronze hue, weaved into the shape of the sun, its enormous gemstone a brilliant topaz yellow, each of its dozens of facets reflecting the white light to look like stars in the night sky.

Reldon reached a hand out to take it, but Alira stopped him with a tug.

"Wait. Remember, one of the amulets here is a fake and will kill any who touch it. Remember the legend?"

He shrugged. "Then we won't touch it."

"Master, be careful," Elly chided.

Reldon pulled a dagger from his belt and slid it off of the dais and into Alira's waiting bag that she held open. Pausing for a moment, they half expected something to happen, some trap to trigger, but nothing happened.

"Easy. Now let's get out of here," Reldon said.

Making it back up the stairs with an incredible sense of accomplishment, their new Kuru compatriots looked at them expectantly.

"You has?" Bradek asked.

Alira nodded with a confident grin.

"Good! Come, we lead you—"

Without warning, from outside the castle windows rose a terrifying collective shriek so piercing, so blood-curdling it could only be from a fear of imminent death. Not the shouts of battle, nor the cries of the wounded, but the sound of a helpless creature being hunted by terrifying predator – except there were thousands of the screams simultaneously.

Something horrible was happening.

They all ran to the south-facing window in a nearby room to see what was happening, and they immediately saw why. Reldon had tried to warn them. But they didn't listen.

Chapter XVIII

The shrieks had risen up first from the men near the front with the siege engines while those from other parts of the army saw nothing but moving shades that could have been shadows and light playing tricks. After the first man fell, then the third, then the tenth in a matter of seconds, the rest of the Nuru charges panicked.

Mists of blood sprayed into existence as limbs and heads were severed from every corner of the force. Formations broke immediately as every man sought any refuge they could. Within but a brief moment, brothers in arms were trampling each other to death like cattle escaping the coming wolves. Commanders and captains cried out in vain to keep order, only to be cut off without warning.

Emperor Garen looked down on his flock with fear and fury.

The word poisoned his ears as his accompanying magicians and Spellswords shouted with terror.

"Churai! It's the Churai, my emperor!"

He could do nothing but stand and watch the carnage. Some tried to fight the monsters and were literally torn apart.

"My liege! W-what do we do?!" they pleaded.

His answer did not escape his lips with the level of confidence they had come to expect.

"Fight. Go."

The woman's eyes were wide with a terror he had seldom seen before, but with tears in her eyes she nodded.

"Magic unit, on me!"

One of the Huerogrand commanders also shouted to his men, "Spellswords, we fight!"

They were only eighteen men and women. He could not see how many Churai tore their way through the battlefield, but they were hopelessly outmatched until the generals could get the rout under control.

As the numbers fanned out to the west and east to escape the onslaught, he noticed that the Churai were ignoring them. They were not pursuing the men who fled. The fell shades were pushing south, and only striking those who stood in that direction.

They were coming for him.

The urge to flee was becoming overwhelming. He had a horse. He knew he could mount up now while the magical divisions held them at bay and he might be able to escape deep into the night.

It tortured him.

They're too fast. And I will be damned if I will be known as the emperor who ran away when death faced him. If I am to die this day I will die with blade in hand.

The emperor took up his sword, put his black, green-plumed helmet on his head, and stepped out of his tent to the unimpeded roar of the battlefield.

Percussions popped his ears from the magicians and Spellswords attempting to stop the Churai. Flames lit up the night sky. Bright bursts of energy rippled into the darkness and exploded on contact. A torrent of water encased a Churai, pinning it down long enough to be stabbed at least a dozen times, only to break free and continue to rip into limbs as if nothing happened.

In the end only two of the Churai had been defeated, and to the best of his ability Garen had counted nine or ten of them taking to the field. They were simply too strong, too fast. Spellswords with expert sword skills were outmaneuvered and slain by the blade and the magicians were torn asunder after their barriers failed and their energy with it.

Not a single one remained.

The eight Churai that remained turned their sets of red eyes in Garen's direction as they finished their slaughter.

Fear of death took him, but in a most incredible act of courage that even he himself did not understand, he held his sword aloft and shouted to his Nuru brethren.

"They are few and we are many! We are Nuru! This day we kill death itself!"

And with that, he tore down the hill towards the oncoming Churai, his life already forfeit. It was but a final satisfaction to see his men rally and charge in with him.

Alira cried out and fell to the floor in terrible sobs as they witnessed the emperor's end. Reldon's knees also failed him as they sank together to the stones.

Their Kuru friends looked on, completely at a loss as to what to do.

"Shhh…" Aki cooed, kneeling to Alira's side, "I am very sorry. You must be quiet. Others will hear!"

Reldon punched the stones until his fist hurt too much. "I warned them. I warned them! Why?!"

Elly also began to cry even though she had not seen out the window.

The cheers from the Kuru below who lined up to enter the fray were deafening.

"We have to stop this," Alira choked out, "Bryle and Sillida are down there. We have to stop it."

Reldon peered up and realized the tube that Hanea had described was but a few feet away, protruding from the floor.

It was like destiny.

"Alira," he said, nudging her.

She looked up and saw it.

There was a moment where Kuru and Nuru met their gazes and there was silence.

"I do not understand," Bradek uttered.

Alira got to her feet and reached into her pack to retrieve the long, cylindrical metal device, staring intently at the pipe."

"What is?" Bradek asked more insistently.

Her gaze met Reldon's. *I-I don't know what to do. Tell me what to do!*

I don't know either! We have to stop this, but we could die after everything we've done so far!

Aki blinked again and gasped. "Magic! Is put in pipe?!"

"What is it do?!" Bradek demanded, trying to push his way towards Alira, to be held in check by Reldon.

"Bradek, stop, you don't understand!"

"You are kill Kuru!?" he exclaimed.

Alira was frozen, her large blue and green eyes wide with fear, not knowing what to say to him.

"No! Trusted you!" he shouted, wrestling with Reldon.

Alira could sense Aki gathering up magical energy as her anger grew.

Time slowed nearly to a stop as she considered. The tube was a few inches to her right. All she had to do was charge it and let it drop and the Kuru army would be defeated, saving Bryle and Sillida, not to mention thousands of Nuru. In her pack was also a legendary item that could mean the end of the Churai if they were able to escape with it.

Five feet in front of her were two Kuru that they had convinced they would save from their captors. They had promised to free their country from oppression. And if she dropped this device into the tube, Reldon and her would have no choice but to kill them.

No matter what, someone would die.

Time stood still.

It was a decision no one could make.

No one but her.

But she wouldn't make it. Not today.

"No."

They all faced her at her utterance.

Alira put the device back into her pack.

"Alira…what are you doing?" Reldon asked, releasing Bradek.

"I won't do it. There will not be any more death. Not Kuru, not Nuru."

"But Alira, how?"

"Do you remember what Yapoti told us back in Darum? Well I refuse. I refuse to accept this premise. There are always more than just these choices."

Reldon was dumbfounded but stood up a little straighter. "What do we do, then?"

She thought for a second and looked up at Bradek.

"Where do the Churai stay? Where is Rizellion?"

"They are below. Why-"

"Can you please lead us to them? Right away."

He nodded with a slight reserve clear in his eyes. "You not kill Kuru?"

"No, we will not. No one else will die today if my plan works. Let's go, hurry!"

It was almost like she was speaking from a voice not her own – it was a commanding voice she did not recognize, but she could swear it was one she had heard before. It almost sounded like…her mother's. Or what she could recall of it.

They raced through the corridors and down a set of stairs, circling around a corner and into the foyer, which now only had a handful of soldiers now that command was attending to the troops. They stood immediately but Bradek shouted to them in Kuru and they stepped aside, clearly confused but not questioning the Spellsword.

Through the foyer it led to a large banquet hall with three elongated tables and hundreds of chairs, a roaring hearth on the eastern wall. They dashed past it all into another corridor that led to a staircase which led down into an almost oppressive darkness.

That was where the Kuru stopped in their tracks.

"We do not go."

Alira did not stop, but ran down the staircase at full speed. "That is all right, thank you for your help!"

Down and down the staircase led. Reldon carried Elly because they were going so fast. The further down they went, the more the small girl's fear built.

"Master, I don't like this," she whined.

"I know, Elly," Alira breathed, "But we have to do this. We will all be ok, I promise."

With each flight, Alira mentally relayed her plan to Reldon. She could tell he thought it was crazy, but he did not question it. She was glad that this time he didn't.

Finally the stairs opened out to a massive subterranean dungeon chamber of a depth they could not tell, as the light was so dim it was impossible to see anything but the pathway ahead.

Reldon set Elly down and they stepped forward along the path.

Elly immediately screamed as she looked around and saw dozens of sets of red eyes watching them from beyond the dim candlelight.

Alira blazed her Keinume to life, the bright silver rose encompassing her entire arm. Without warning she injected it with so much magical energy that the droning sound became a loud roar as it bounced around in the cavernous hall. Light filled the room and revealed the Churai flanking the edges of the room. They flinched momentarily from the light.

"Rizellion! Where are you!?" she demanded. All of her effort had to go into making her body and voice not tremble.

A single set of glowing red eyes further down the hall gazed back at them, and after the deafening show of strength subsided, there came a voice.

It was a voice they had heard before.

"Ah, if it isn't the Xanem Nuremar and Ilewa Nuremil, my dearest of friends. I have been so waiting for this day for a long time. Welcome to my home! Though I wish I could be more accommodating, I am naturally a guest in this house."

Alira, the first part of your plan is working. The Churai from outside are coming down to investigate. The troops outside are safe for the moment.

"Do not lie to us! We know you are the one pulling the strings behind the kingdom!"

He stood up from his throne with a broad smile as he stepped into the light. His sickly gray skin and red eyes, jet black hair, and muscular build were all Churai enough, but it was that knowing smile that set him apart from his minions.

Rizellion towered over them, even standing fifteen feet away.

"Mmm…It sounds like someone in this castle has loose lips. I shall have to see to that."

"Call off your troops!" Alira demanded.

His grin turned into a chuckle.

"So rude, little one! And so quick to business! Why can we not simply talk? It has been so long after all."

"Because our kinfolk are dying on that field, and we want it to end," Reldon responded.

The Churai Master's eyes narrowed slightly. "Ah, but they did elect to invade us, did they not? Does it not make sense that when one country invades another that there shall be…casualties? Why should I call off the Kuru army and allow this silly siege to continue?"

"The siege will end. You already killed Emperor Garen. The Nuru army will leave because they know they can't take the city now," Reldon explained, "His vision of a Nuru Empire is over. This battle, this war is over."

"One cannot simply allow these transgressions to go unpunished, wise Reldon. Your kin have slain a great many Kuru and they want blood. Why not allow them to finish this on their own terms? On the field of battle? It is all they understand."

"That will only result in more death."

His smile was terrifying. "Precisely."

Alira took the device out of her pack.

"That's enough! It's time all of this ended! Call off your troops and your Churai now, or I charge this device and fulfill our destiny, right here!"

That pompous grin did not disappear, but he did take a moment to scan the item in her hand.

"I will kill all of us. You, us, and your Churai. There will be none left and our story together will be over. You know it is powerful enough to do it." She had no idea if it was powerful enough to do it.

Alira could tell when the Churai Master did not hold all of the cards when he got very quiet, that analytical (brain?) of his looking for a way to triumph in the face of defeat. The fact that he was so conflicted about her ultimatum gave her further confirmation that this device was in fact powerful enough to kill all of them.

"You would give up your legendary lives to kill me without a proper fight? That doesn't seem very honorable to me, dear Nurems," was his goading answer.

"You do not have any honor, Rizellion. I saw those dead captives of Rinelle's, hundreds of years ago. You always lie."

He chuckled in response. "Oh how very much you sound like your mother now. All that fire and love for life. Sickening, but remarkable."

It was the second time he had ever mentioned her mother, and it had the same effect as the first time. As her heart sank and she could feel the fight within her slipping away, Reldon stepped in.

"Do not speak of her. It's time you decided. Call off your troops or this castle becomes rubble with all of us ashes beneath it."

Rizellion took another few steps into the light, revealing his wardrobe – not the black and navy plate armor he had previously worn, but a matching set of red velvet trousers and doublet with gold buttons, and a long black coat over top. Jewelry adorned his neck, namely of which was an amulet set with a deep purple gem and dark silver, almost iron-colored, brooch in the shape of a moon. Seeing him wearing clothes fitting a king was all too telling of his real station in Drunerakerrum.

The Churai Master's grin had vanished as he glared at Reldon with his abysmal red eyes.

"You are a fool to believe I do not know the true reason you are here, Xanem Nuremar. You have come for the amulets, their immortal power clearly far too enticing for even the pure, innocent children of legend. Allow me to make you a deal that should be beneficial to both of us. You put that nasty device away, and I let you choose one of the two amulets to take with you. No strings attached. You may choose to trade me for the one I possess," he said, putting a gloved hand to the amulet at his chest, "or you can leave with the one you already have. Now we're all intelligent creatures here, so we are all well aware that one of the two will kill you the instant you try to use it, or even touch it. You do have to touch it with your bare hands to use it, love."

"But naturally you won't tell us which is the real one," Reldon presumed.

He laughed. "That's not part of the game."

"We have no reason to trust you will allow us to leave. If we choose the right one you will just try to kill us."

Rizellion gave them a pouty face. "Am I so hard to believe? I'll even sweeten the deal – as a gesture of good faith, I will call back all of the Kuru armies and bring this battle to an immediate halt."

He motioned to one of the Churai, who nodded and raced up the staircase to deliver the orders.

"The screaming should stop momentarily."

Reldon, I don't like this. I hate the idea of making a deal with him.

Me neither, but it may be the only way we leave alive. Ours is just a bluff, but even if that device is strong enough, we would still die.

Which should we choose? If we choose wrong, then we've lost. We would have to come back all over again.

Also…we wouldn't know until we tried to use it.

She hesitated. *Surely the right one must be the one around his neck. He wouldn't wear something that dangerous.*

Unless he knew we would think that and tricked us by placing the real one in such an easy-to-get place.

Maybe he knew we would say, 'that was easy, this can't be the real one.' But then why offer us so easy a trade?

Ugh, Alira, this is an impossible decision. We will only get one shot at this, and there's no way to tell the difference.

Looking at it with my magical vision, they look identical. Do the think the sun means it's the good one? Or do you think it's like a poisonous snake with bright colors?

There's no way to know. The legends didn't speak of which one was the real one – that would defeat the purpose.

We're just going to have to pick one and hope it's right.

He nodded. *That's all we can do.*

Finally the screaming ceased and rumbling took its place from above, probably marching armies. The Churai that had acted as messenger stole silently down the stairs and retook its position near Rizellion.

"There, as promised, the war is over. So…do we have a deal?"

"Yes. Deal," Reldon acquiesced.

"Excellent. Now, would you like to leave with what you have, or trade for this one?"

Reldon took one of the deepest breaths he had ever taken.

"We will take the one we have and leave in peace."

Rizellion's smile took on nearly epic proportions, a broad, evil, self-assured grin that only someone who had won the ultimate gamble could possibly hope to emulate.

"So be it!" he said with a sickly sweetness, "I shall offer you safety until you are outside the walls of this castle – of course I cannot ensure your protection beyond that. I'm sure you understand."

They nodded with a sinking feeling.

I don't think we picked the right one.

Either way, we need to leave. Now.

"It was a pleasure doing business with you both, and I thank you very much for visiting. We shall meet again very soon."

Rizellion turned and ascended to his throne once again as the Nurems scurried out.

His smile was a terrible bitter-sweetness, but once the children were completely out of sight up the stairs, it soured to a scowl.

"Once they leave the castle, dispatch all murders. Kill. Obey."

"*Obey,*" they repeated.

Alira, Reldon, Elly, and their new Kuru friends made it to the castle gate, which was being slowly cranked open.

"Thank for not kill Kuru," Bradek said to them with a small smile, offering his forearm, "Maybe Nuru not so bad."

Reldon took it. "I think there has been a lot of old hatreds spread between our peoples that have made people kill and do heinous things for hundreds of years without reason. I suspect the Churai are the reason for that. I'm sorry we couldn't rid you of the Churai today, but some day your people will be free again and I hope to be among the diplomats sent to make peace. I hope you'll be there too."

Aki was much cagier and more averse to any contact with Nuru, but she did give Alira a salute. The Atherian girl giggled and returned in kind.

"I will be. Go in peace, Xanem Nuremar. Will see you soon."

The portcullis locked into its open position, and the three stepped out and over the drawbridge onto the Kuru snow, heading directly towards the lone tree they could see on the horizon.

I sure hope we made the right decision, Alira thought with some anxiety.

Either way, we have one of the amulets, we're all alive, and we saved a lot of Nuru and Kuru today.

I'm very surprised he was so honorable to allow us to just leave. I would have thought-

Incredible amounts of magical disturbance approached at a rapid pace.

"MASTER!" Elly shrieked, pointing back at the castle.

Dozens of shadowy creatures leapt between buildings and over the walls at an incredible speed, making their way towards them.

"Oh spirits! Alira, Elly, hold on to me!" Reldon barked. "Alira, shield us!"

Alira issued a powerful, sparkling barrier around them and without warning, Reldon used enough Phyrim to blast a small crater in the ground and sent them hurtling hundreds of feet into the air, angling towards the tree.

With Alira's barrier up, it was an incredibly peculiar feeling soaring over so much land below, the wind coursing around the invisible shield and to hear nothing but its muffled roar. Gravity, however, was still affecting them, and as they fell after traversing a portion of the countryside, their stomachs felt like they were in their chests.

Screaming from the precipitous fall and the approaching earth, they struck with a lot of force – enough that probably would have killed them had it not been for the barrier. Still, as they made impact, her barrier phased out of existence and they tumbled out over the snow, largely unhurt, but time running out.

The Churai were so fast, that as they landed, they had crossed that same distance in almost as much time. Countless red eyes were but maybe one hundred yards away.

It was still so far away. The tree was closer, but it would take at least one or two more jumps to get there.

"Come on, we have to go! Now!"

Alira stumbled to her feet and lifted Elly before latching onto Reldon and producing another barrier.

Once again they were in the air, the sheer amount of Phyrimic energy Reldon was spending creating a potential problem with his reserves. The force required to get them all into the air was taxing his body. He was strong, but since the incident in Teraxella with the young fire magician girl, his confidence hadn't been good enough to recover.

SMASH.

And again they made impact. Elly cried out as she tumbled, blood streaming from her nose.

"I'm really sorry, Elly!" Alira shouted, lifting her again. She had landed harder on her face than she had intended. "Be strong, one more time and we're there!"

For a third time, Reldon blasted them into the cloudy evening air, the last remnants of the sun disappearing. The tree was going to be but a few hundred feet from where they would land and he tried to inject small amounts of Phyrim behind them to direct them further.

He coughed and blood ran out of his mouth.

"Brace! We're just about-"

The ground met them one last time, and Alira's barrier did better to hold, so the impact was lessened on poor Elly. As she shakily got to her feet, she cried and pumped Golden Magic into her face.

"Elly, no time! We have to go!"

"Hurry, hurry!" the voice of Hanea shouted out. "Everyone hold each other's hands!"

Reldon, Alira, and Elly raced up the hill towards the tree as quickly as their failing legs would take them.

Alira turned her head and saw the Churai closing quickly. They weren't going to make it at this rate. She had to do something.

Slipping the device from her pack, she charged it with a jolt of magical energy and screamed as she hurled it towards the swarm of Churai as hard as she could.

That seemed to give them just enough of a pause that their incredible haste was stopped for a moment. It was all the time they needed. The Churai scrambled to get away from the device, but they clearly had no idea how wide the blast radius was going to be.

Hanea stood next to the tree trunk, arms outstretched as far as she could, her feet fixed to the spot.

Reldon and Alira both took Elly's hands and then took Hanea's.

As the world went white from the explosion, everything else disappeared as their bodies became something other than matter.

Chapter XXXIX

All that was, was darkness as Alira, Reldon, and Elly regained their sense of self again and their legs gave out. They fell upon snow – cold, but a welcome break to their fall.

As his eyes adjusted, Reldon could see his Ilewa laying on her back in a snowbank, breathing heavily. Elly had done the same, but had sat up to use Golden Magic on her nose, which was continuing to bleed. With her small threads of magic, it lit up the night air and revealed Hanea standing before them. She had a broad smile on her face.

"Well done, little ones. We are so proud of you."

Reldon tried to speak, but choked on blood coated in his throat.

Alira rolled onto her knees and crawled over to her Ilewa, wrapping her arms around him.

We did it. Oh spirits, we made it. We're safe.

He squeezed her with what strength he had.

I can't believe that worked. They were just so fast.

Alira channeled her own magic through her Keinume, which turned a shimmering gold. Placing her left hand on his chest, he could feel the tightness and the pain from his overexertion lessening.

That's all I can do. You will still need to rest.

"Master, does my nose look right?" Elly asked, scrunching up her nose after having repaired it.

Elly smiled, conjuring a small ball of light to assess her injury. Surprisingly she did a thorough job, and her face looked the same as always, except with blood on it.

Alira rubbed some snow into her palm to melt it and then used it wipe away the blood. "You look as perfect as ever, Elly."

Reldon got to his feet. It was difficult to see, but it looked like they were standing near some sort of massive monolith beneath a mountain.

"Hanea, where…are we?" he asked.

There was no answer.

"Hanea?"

Only the wind returned a response.

Reldon crunched through the snow over to Alira and Elly, with little but the occasional beams of moonlight guiding his steps.

Elly tugged on Alira's coat. "Master, look."

There was a hooded figure standing in front of the monolith, silent.

Reldon took a step towards it. "Grandma."

"It is good to see you have kept your promise to keep dear Elliana safe," her old, deep, rich, unmistakable voice came from the beneath the figure's hood, "I owe you many thanks."

"Grandma!" Elly exclaimed happily, tumbling over the snowbank to get to her.

Grandma held up a hand and the girl stopped.

"It is well to see you here after all this time. A great many years have I toiled such that this day might come to fruition. This is the place where dreams and nightmares lie, ambition and destiny. It is no mistake that you are here now. It has been pre-ordained."

"What…is this place exactly?" Alira asked.

"A monument to vanity, or some have called it. This is the place where it all began and where it shall all end. The birthplace of man and its inevitable betrayal and death. Many lives have been lost to bring these events to bear, and we are at that place that shall always stand as a silent testimony to what man could achieve…and the many more who will die because of their arrogance. This…is the Crux of Civilization."

They couldn't see her face, but her voice was intense. Every word she uttered came from the passionate, jaded heart that had been beating for so many countless years.

Reldon and Alira were uncertain how to respond.

"What are we doing here? And…how did we get here? Was that Hanea's doing?" Reldon asked.

"Here you shall fulfill your true destiny – to bring mankind back to its proper course of progression. Hanea brought you here using a power she acquired long, long ago, just as I have achieved what I have through my own ancient power. We are all here to witness this moment in history. The moment when all would truly be saved."

Reldon peered away from the monolith and spotted three figures standing out of earshot, evenly spaced from each other, completely motionless in the darkness.

"That's…Hanea, Yapoti, and Sterling," Alira noted.

"We are unimportant, merely the heralds of what is to come. It is time to focus on the path that lies ahead. The two of you are the progeny of man's indifference to its own failures, the ones sent to bring correction to mistakes that were made so long ago that few remain who remember. It was by design that the secrets of the past would be buried and forgotten, but we who have persevered have ensured one last thread of hope continued to sound through the ages. That is why *we* are here. You are here, because you have a choice, a question. You know what that question is, and I know the answer. All you need is to ask, and all shall be revealed."

Grandma waited expectantly, her gaze locked on Reldon.

It was the moment Tycheronius had warned them about. His words were burned into his very being.

"...the simple truth of your future is a dilemma. I tell you all of this, because I know sooner or later you will need to know what the secret is, and you will have no choice but to go to her to get it. She is waiting for it. She has always been waiting. For countless lifetimes she has been patiently biding her time for the day in which you demand from her the secret. Once you do, there will be no going back. I only wish to warn you that she will attempt to use you. For reasons unknown to us, she needs you and your Ilewa. I fear that once she has finished what she has started, she will have no further use for you."

Alira was not going to believe what Tycheronius had said about Grandma – she had been stubbornly opposed to the idea. Regardless, they needed to know what the Secret was. Between the constant intervention in their destiny, the amulets, and the prophecy…it was all leading to something. Something that Tycheronius and Giavere died for.

Even though he knew that he would be potentially putting their lives in danger, there was no way around it.

Reldon had to know.

"Grandma," he started with a breath, "Tell us what the Secret is."

There was a moment where no one spoke, but slowly Grandma reached up to lower her hood. She took a step out into a beam of moonlight where her smile could be seen on her wrinkled face – thin as it was.

"I have waited a millennia to hear those words, dear boy. And now all shall be revealed to you. First, however, in order to understand, you must see. Have you brought the amulets?" she asked gently.

Alira removed Grandma's old amulet from her pocket, took her mother's from around her neck, and reached into her pack with a gloved hand to retrieve the last golden one. Advancing a few steps, she placed them on the ground before Grandma.

She nodded again. "Good. Yapoti, step forward."

From deep in the night stepped the old tribeswoman, quietly standing before her.

"You have volunteered to test the third amulet. Please do so with our blessing."

Reldon and Alira's eyes went wide. She was going to die if they picked the wrong one.

"Yapoti, you don't have to do this – do you want to die?" Reldon said.

Without facing him, she responded with a chuckle. "We have spoken of this before, Reldon of Errum. I am ready to die. I have done a great many deeds, and soon it will be my time. Whether now or next year makes little difference when you have lived as long as I."

She knelt down and touched the shining yellow gemstone.

Alira and Elly gasped.

After a long tense moment, Yapoti stood up straight again.

"It is the correct amulet."

Grandma smiled again. "Thank you Yapoti. That will be all."

With a bow, Yapoti disappeared again into the blackness.

"You have all done remarkably well. We have everything we need for you to finally see the truth. The next step, however, will not be dependent on myself or what I can tell you. You will need to pass a trial that has existed since this monolith was created, one that none have ever faced. You must be ready. This will not be a trial that will test your power or your knowledge; rather, it will test you as humans. There are no secrets within. It sees all. The sooner you understand that, the better you will be able to remain sane."

"We're... going inside this...thing?" Reldon inquired.

"It has been closed for so long, it predates many kingdoms. The method to opening it again was thought to be lost to the ages, but that is only because none who lived in those days realized how long us few would live. I have witnessed entire epochs in history to take with me the Secret, and how to reveal it once again after it had been hidden. The culmination of the three amulets and the words to speak through the ages are all that is required to bring the past to the present."

Grandma picked up the three amulets and placed each one against the smooth wall of the monolith. It was impossible to see, but it must have had some kind of metallic surface, because the brooches of the amulets stuck fast to the wall as she placed them. After arranging them in a triangle, she placed her hand in the center.

From her lips escaped long lines of seemingly incoherent babble. If it was a language, it was not one that Reldon nor Alira spoke or understood. For some time she continued, her voice rising steadily as she went. At last, as she spoke the last syllable, she released an intense wave of magic through her hand and into the monolith. She waved them over with her other hand.

"Combine your power and place your hands on mine. You will need nearly all your power to proceed."

Reldon and Alira clasped hands and felt their energies pool together. Alira's dwarfed Reldon's by many magnitudes after their incredible escape, but they hoped it would be enough. As they devoted their strength to Grandma, nearly their entire collective reservoir was gone in an instant. It was enough of a draw in power that it about brought them to their knees.

Still, it worked.

To their shock, the entire structure, looking like nothing more than a two-hundred-foot slab of jagged metal, began to glow intensely enough to light the surrounding area like sunlight.

As if nothing more than an illusion, a human sized rectangle at the bottom of the monolith next to the amulets simply faded out of existence, leaving a clear opening. Even through the bright glow, however, inside was nothing but unforgiving darkness.

Grandma stood next to it and held out a hand.

"If you should wish to truly know how the world functions, or does not, step inside when you are ready. Elliana must stay here with me."

Elly happily trotted over to hug her Grandma.

Alira looked over at her Ilewa, a lump in her throat forming.

Well…are you ready?

No, but I don't think we ever really will be.

I agree.

We can do this, Alira.

Gingerly, they stepped into the opening and into the abyss beyond.

Reldon kept a straight path in what was largely complete emptiness. Occasionally small streaks of red light would pass by, briefly illuminating his path for a fleeting moment and disappearing into the distance.

Voices occasionally would echo about. Most of the time he could not understand what they were saying, or who was saying them, but once he could have sworn he heard someone's familiar voice.

He really wasn't even sure what he was stepping on. The ground was perfectly flat and hard but made no noise as he stepped on it.

Then for some reason, it sounded like he was stepping in water, an inch layer or so. Just in case, he looked down at his feet, but of course, he couldn't see them.

Looking back up everything had changed.

He was standing in a cemetery with looming clouds overhead. There was no wind, and only the distant call of crows to be heard.

Reldon took a laborious breath and looked around. Endless columns of tombstones stretched further than he could see on either side of the cobble path he stood on. Up ahead, there was someone sitting on one of the tombstones, whittling a piece of wood. At first it was an indistinct figure, but as he approached, it became clearer who it was.

"C-Cuthis? Captain Cuthis, is that you?" he stuttered.

The old captain only continued his whittling, not even looking up.

As Reldon approached, the horrifying details came into focus.

This wasn't Cuthis from when he was healthy and jovial. This was Cuthis's corpse – pale, bruised, bloodied, and with broken limbs that functioned as if they weren't broken.

His stomach churned and he stepped back away from the specter. Twisting around, there was a woman standing over another grave. Unlike Cuthis, she stood perfectly still, only moving her head to watch Reldon as he moved. Her identity didn't strike him at first, until he saw her injuries.

From collarbones to stomach, her entire torso had been crushed. Ribs poked out from her skin.

It was the fire magician from Ferrela, from R'Nal. The one they had accidentally killed.

She watched him with a look of judgment.

There were more, so many more.

Every time he turned about, there was another one.

A few soldiers appeared in various states of having been dismembered.

Brina with her lightning-scarred burns stood and watched him.

One by one, so many Ferrelan men, women, and children appeared next to their headstones – some missing limbs and bleeding into the grass, some having been disemboweled, and others having been crushed or burned to a terrifying husk. Hundreds of them, possibly thousands. All leering at him.

"No. No, no, no, you're all dead. None of this is real," Reldon repeated.

Finally, one more person stood by his grave, severe lacerations and a gaping stab wound in his heart, looking at him as if he were less than nothing.

Reldon's heart broke. "No... Lendir...Is that... is that really you?"

Those eyes he had seen so many times, those calculating eyes. They were real, they had to be.

There wasn't a response. Only that cold, accusing stare.

"Lendir, please," Reldon cried, "Please say something."

His former master was as silent as the grave.

Reldon shook his head with tears in his eyes. "What is this... I don't understand..."

Spinning around once more, Cuthis stood in the middle of the path, his eyes fierce.

Cuthis's voice reverberated in his head, every word pointed.

"You be no stranger...to death, boy."

Reldon looked on, unable to make words.

"People...people *die* around you. A fact of life. You are a Spellsword, and it be simply part of your life. Hundreds died... back a' that city, boy... Mos' of them better men than ol' Cuthis...And here you be."

These were the captain's last words. The ones that had cut him so deep. His hands shook.

"People *die* around you, boy. Ol' Cuthis is no exception. A' the end of the day... we who support you...we are freed from the troubles o' this world. We be too weak to... make enough of a difference in your fate. And when we... die...you be all that remains."

Gradually the ghosts of all the hellish souls around him began to fade away.

"In the end you be the one who shoulders the burden. *You* must live with all of our deaths... every death caused in your name...An' that is why your fate be the cruelest curse... You look on ol' Cuthis with pity, boy... but always remember...in his last breaths, Cuthis looked with pity... at you."

Cuthis vanished.

Reldon stood completely alone.

"No...But I... I didn't mean for any of you to die!"

Smoke filled his nostrils.

From one end of the cemetery to the other, the grass lit aflame, spreading quickly until all of the tombstones were completely engulfed.

Only the stone path beneath him remained, and he ran as fast as his legs could take him.

On and on the walls of flame went until the path opened up to a courtyard surrounded by fire.

In the center stood an eleven-year-old girl, her clothes nearly having been burned off.

"I will kill you, Xanem Nuremar."

Alira appeared near his side and held out a hand to her. "Please, let us help you. You can still be our friend."

"I don't believe you. You killed her. You're responsible. You deserve to die!"

"Reldon, don't get involved. I can do this."

He watched her with fear. "No, Alira, she's going to kill you. You can see the flames rising around her!"

"She won't kill me! I can do this! She's just a child!"

Reldon didn't know what to do. Last time he thought… he thought for sure that the girl was going to kill her – maybe he had been wrong?

"All right, Alira. You're right. You can do this."

Alira reached her hand out and clasped the hand of the girl, who grinned that wicked grin.

"Now BURN!"

His Ilewa caught flame.

The screams worked its way into his head like a parasite. He covered his ears and eyes and refused to believe any of it.

As soon as he closed his eyes, it all reappeared again.

"Reldon, don't get involved. I can do this."

Time felt slowed as Alira reached for the girl again.

Not again. Not ever again.

He sent a coursing bolt of pure Phyrim through the girl's chest, and she stood in disbelief.

"Reldon, how could you?!" Alira shrieked.

The girl's eyes filled with tears. "I only wanted a normal life, Reldon. Why did you have to kill me?"

Reldon was virtually sobbing himself. "I didn't mean to! I never meant for it to happen. I'm.. I'm sorry!"

"You always use Phyrim first and ask questions later. Typical," came his mother's voice.

"Don't you understand that you're a plague on this world? You were never sent here to save anyone. You're just another arrogant teenager who thinks he can make a difference, not realizing you're creating more harm than good!" Kex said.

"I should have killed you when I had the chance in Huerogrand," Detryn spat.

Alira appeared before him, hurt clear on her face.

"Why don't you ever trust me?"

"I...I do, Alira!"

"If you don't trust me, then I could never love you."

His heart felt like it was being ripped into pieces.

Lendir appeared last.

"Lendir, please... I miss you. I need your help. Please..."

His master shook his head in disgust.

"You are your own worst enemy, Reldon. But you're also everyone's worst enemy. The less friends you have, the less will die. Maybe when you learn that life has some value will I finally be proud of you. Until then...you're nobody to me."

"No, Lendir...I'm not..."

The voices grew louder.

"Please... just..."

It was deafening. Maddening.

"Just...STOP!"

Elly hugged tight to Grandma.

Normally the nighttime was scary, but she knew when she was with Grandma, she was never in danger.

"Grandma, I missed you," Elly said with a smile.

There was a pause before she answered. "And I you, my dearest Elliana." She must have been distracted.

"We've done so much. We stayed in a huge house and stole the amulet from the Kuru castle, and Reldon...threw us in the air to get to the tree faster. I hurt my nose, but it's all right. I fixed it."

She looked down at her with a weird look that Elly hadn't seen before. "That's good, little one."

Grandma was acting strange. Normally she would kneel down and give her a hug, and she would run her hands through her hair like she always did before. *Did I do something wrong?*

"Grandma, what's wrong? You look so..."

In the pale moonlight, she thought for sure she saw a tear on her face.

The old woman released the girl's hand.

"G-Grandma?"

She lifted her old shaky hand and placed it on Elly's head.

Elly expected her to rub her hair like usual, but she was holding very still.

"Elliana, I want you to listen very closely. You haven't done anything wrong. You never have."

Her voice had never sounded like this before. It was so sad. Grandma was always strong and almost never cried. *Something must be wrong.*

"I...I don't understand."

Grandma held still and said nothing for so long that Elly began to cry. The old familiar matronly figure's eyes were like glass, her lips pinched together, her whole body trembling.

"Grandma you're scaring me," Elly cried.

Gradually her eyes closed, and she took a breath before slowly withdrawing her hand and turning her back to the young girl.

I don't understand, what is wrong with Grandma? Why did she do that?

There was a tortured shout from inside the big metal structure and it sounded like Reldon.

He might be hurt! I have to go in!

She ran inside, and Grandma did not follow, nor did she even move.

Alira's blue and green eyes took a moment to adjust, eventually seeing where the shout had come from – Reldon was in a near-fetal-position on the ground at her feet, and he trembled so greatly that at first when she called his name he did not respond.

Is he...real? Is this the real Reldon or another vision?

She had tried using their link several times to communicate with him inside the monolith while the torrents of memories assaulted her mind, but to no avail. The world suddenly seemed so much more lucid, and if she could reach him, it would prove to her that she had returned to reality.

Reldon...? She thought gently, *Is that really you?*

His eyes shot open and he sat up with a start, his pupils tiny. Heavy, heaving breaths cycled through his lungs as he took inventory of the dark corridor in which they stood.

Alira? I...Where...

It worked. He's the real Reldon.

She knelt down and hugged him.

Are you all right?

I…I'm not sure. I think so. That was just so awful… I couldn't take one more minute of it. I'm not a killer, Alira, honest. I didn't mean it. I didn't mean for any of them to die…

Alira took a look into his hurting eyes. There was a lot of fear, a lot of repentance. Her heart ached for him.

Oh Reldon. I don't know what you saw in there, but it wasn't real. You're a good person. You're not a killer. This place lies to you and hurts you with your worst fears. But it's over now.

What did it show to you?

She didn't have the heart to tell him what it showed her. It didn't sound like it was as terrible as what he saw, but it was sad enough that she could barely even bring herself to think about it without crying.

Just some things I'm scared of – things that make me sad to think about, she thought to him without lying, *Can you walk?*

Aye, he responded, allowing her to help him up. *Let's hurry up and find what's in here. I don't like this place. It knows me too well.*

"Master, where are you?" came a small voice from behind.

"Elly? We're over here! I know it's hard to see," she called back to her, "Follow my voice!"

The healer girl emerged from further back in the corridor, barely visible. "I'm here! Reldon, are you hurt?"

"No, Elly, but thank you for worrying about me. Come on, let's go find what this secret is."

Everything around them was perfectly smooth like glass, though they knew it was a kind of metal. There was no light in the corridor so they could only see where they were going with Alira's small ball of light she created again. It was a long corridor that extended far into the darkness, with no doors, no windows, no features of any kind, but it did slope ever gradually downward.

After they had descended so far down it felt like they were in the middle of the planet, there was light ahead. It was a shimmering sort of light, like the type you would see emitting from all the prisms of a crystal, and it was bright white rather than yellow or orange like torchlight.

As they approached the light, it grew brighter and brighter, opening up to a room larger than any they had ever seen before.

It was a chamber of colossal proportions – large enough to possibly hold half of Nakisho Castle within it. Enormous, cut perfectly square out of the strange metal, it was like being in the world's largest iron crate.

And in the center, the light shone. Once their eyes adjusted, they realized what this place was here for.

It had been constructed for a single purpose.

It was built to house a power so great, few had ever even dreamed of it.

There in the center of the room, stretching almost as high as the ceiling was a gargantuan pile of small glass balls. Thousands, possibly hundreds of thousands of them, stacked haphazardly and with no particular method inside a wooden base hundreds of feet long and wide. The source of light was from somewhere near the center of the base, its light shining through the innumerable glass spheres to create an almost crystalline quality to the assortment.

Reldon, Alira, and Elly stood with their mouths agape.

"What...are they?" Reldon asked, stepping forward to reach for one.

"Oh my goodness. Oh dear spirits!" Alira cried as soon as she was close enough to realize what they were, clapping her hands to her mouth in shock. "They're...they're *Keitas!*"

Reldon turned to her, perplexed. "Keitas? You mean those little glass balls that hold the power of the elements in them?"

She nodded frantically. "Oh dear spirits... This can't be... How can there be this many? The Academy doesn't even have this many! And why are they all down here?" Leaning her face in towards the glittering pile, her eyes were huge. "I don't understand. They don't have any elements in them at all. They have something...*else!*"

"Then what could they possibly have in them?" Reldon asked, taking one and looking into it. "They don't do anything when I pick them up, but maybe..."

His words trailed off, and Alira slowly reached out and picked up one of eyeball sized glass spheres.

As soon as she held it in her palm, she could feel an intense influx in power like she had never felt before.

It overwhelmed her so quickly that she stumbled and fell backwards onto the metallic floor hard on her bottom. The sensation was impossible to describe. It was like she was being infused or filled with magic and some kind of information. Her mind couldn't comprehend it all.

The sensation was so incredibly powerful that her eyes shut tight and she couldn't even elicit a shout.

Her Keinume blazed to life again, her silver rose glowing happily against the dark metal beneath.

Suddenly, it stopped.

Everything was normal.

She opened her eyes to see the worried faces of her Ilewa and her apprentice and they immediately flinched as she did.

"Alira, your eyes!" Reldon exclaimed.

"What, what's wrong with them?" she asked, scared at what she might hear.

"T-they're normal now, but for a moment there, they were pure white!"

"Master, are you sure you're all right?" Elly said, slipping her hand into Alira's.

"Yes, I think so. I-"

Touching Elly's hand sent her into another dimension of sights and sounds.

One moment she was sitting on the floor of that chamber, and the next her conscious mind soared through thousands of flashes of scenes...countless garbled sounds and voices...

In one flash she saw Grandma's cottage in Ferrela, its flowers in bloom.

Lights flickered past and she could see a girl with dark hair playing in the river.

Grandma's voice echoed, "You won't be seeing her for a little while, Zoë."

Disappointment – she felt it.

Images flew past like petals in the wind.

It was Grandma. She had brown hair with some gray. The surroundings were different, but so indistinct she couldn't get any details.

"He will need your power, Mephias. I will help and all will be well."

Magic coursed through the outstretched hand, followed by white.

Alira's perception altered again, revealing a scene that looked to be in Ferrela, but the person that was being spoken to was not Ferrelan, and they were speaking with an accent like Kiera's.

Elly's voice was first, in that strange accent. "I'm sorry, I don't know what you are talking about."

"You cannot be serious," came a man's voice, "We spent a summer greeting each other every day fifteen years ago! Talia, how can you-"

"My name is *Hebe*, I told you!"

The sight disappeared in an instant as more information sailed past her.

It was like she was being pulled back further and further and further, through a tunnel of time. She could feel the end nearing.

The last was just a few grainy images, faint but present. There were brief lights and colors, and there was a face that looked back at her from the water.

She had long blond hair, thin eyebrows, small ears, verdant green eyes, and flawless skin. Her hair was parted such that it concealed half of her face, but she could see the smile on those pink lips. This woman had to be in her twenties or thirties.

A distant, muffled voice spoke to her, some of the words lost to time. "It's time...prepared..."

Her response, in a voice that haunted Alira to her core, was Elly's adult voice saying in a vaguely Lärimite accent, "I've been waiting forever. Let us finish this."

Alira snapped back to her body with a gasp and her arm hurt from Reldon gripping it.

"Alira!"

Her eyes darted between the two. "I'm here, do not worry, I'm all right."

"Your eyes turned white again," Reldon stated.

Alira's wide-eyed attention turned to Elly, the poor girl watching her master intently.

"Dear spirits Elly. You're..."

"So now you see," a voice came from the entrance.

Alira scrambled to her feet to face her from across the room. It was Grandma.

The Ilewa Nuremil raised a terribly shaking hand towards her, channeling fire and causing her Keinume to swell to a deathly red.

"Alira, are you-" Reldon started, but she ignored him.

"W-what did I just see? What have you done? What have you done to Elly?!"

It looked as if the old woman had fully expected this reaction, as she did not raise a hand nor her voice. "Allow me to explain. Please. You asked me to reveal to you the secret, and there is much more you need to know."

Alira's breathing was shallow as the reality of it all gave her a cold sweat. She slowly lowered her arm. "Talk," she said tersely, "And start with what happened to Elly."

"To understand that, you will have to contextualize the past. You have asked me before about my earlier life, and you must understand that it was a different world in that era of history."

Alira cut in. "Tell us how old you really are. How long ago are you talking about?"

Grandma took a short breath. "Over 1,200 years ago."

Her stomach churned so hard she struggled to keep from being sick.

The old woman went on, not waiting for a cue, "In those times, there were far more petty lords and kings. Politics still existed but in a fragmented, defensive sort of way – like dozens of rivals posturing over who had the more secure realm, regardless of how precarious it all really was. Magic was better understood then. Every lord had magicians and the precursors to Spellswords, and each realm had a school to teach magic. However, like everything in Lärim, even something so sanctified as a school for magic was fraught with political undertones. Enrolling in a school, which were funded by the lord, meant required fealty and servitude to that lord. It was a life sentence. And you could not simply avoid instruction."

"Why not? Were there no Ravagers back then?" Reldon asked.

"Ravagers as you understand them were far too dangerous to be allowed to exist in those days, for reasons you see in this very room. These Keitas that have been hidden away here do not contain mere elements, but each is a fragment of being able to control some aspect of the natural or unnatural world around us all. You have discovered one form of magic previously unbeknownst to you – Memory Magic. It was one of many forms of magic that once existed."

"But…" Alira struggled to formulate a question, "Then…why is it all here? When did this happen? All of this magic has been completely unknown to the world!"

"It occurred so long ago that even I struggle to recall exactly when it all happened. Portions of mankind were so enlightened in the ways of magic that they were on the verge of unlocking the secrets of existence. Through these Keitas, hundreds of magicians each possessed a facet of the larger capabilities to manipulate the world around them – take for example Memory Magic. By itself it allows one to delve into the experiences of others, as you have already found. But combined with other forms of magic, one could even manipulate memories. Alter them. Extract them. The possibilities were unlimited."

"That sounds really scary," Alira responded, "Humans were trying to…"

"Play God?" she finished her sentence with a haughty voice, "Did you really believe that story that when the Nurems possessed the amulets they would be granted the Omniscient One's powers of limited creation?" She jutted a finger towards the mountain of glass. "There's your 'limited creation'. But it is not limited. It is only limited by the minds of those who use it. And all those years ago the minds of the few daring enough to stretch the boundaries of human understanding were more inventive and ambitious than any who exist now."

"So what happened then?" Reldon asked, "It had to have stopped somewhere. What made them decide to lock away this secret forever?"

"It was because of the small-minded, short-sighted men that clutched to their precious titles and their deities that began to fear the potential that all this power represented. As magical understanding grew, so did their suspicions that it was all to supplant their authority. I was obviously not a part of those talks, but clearly it was decided that an end would be put to it, and those who spoke against it would be silenced."

"You mean…" Alira trailed off, fearing the next sentence.

"Yes. There was a culling. Practitioners of non-elemental magic were murdered in their sleep. Hundreds of years of progress snuffed out in just a few days. Books burned. Statues crumbled. Histories erased."

It finally struck Reldon. "That's why there are so many alterations to the manuscripts we saw in Lärim! The old ones about magic!"

"You are precisely right. The history you know is not what actually happened."

"So how did you escape?"

"Luckily I had been away on a mission at the time with two of my comrades you have met previously. There were still some loyal to the magicians, and they got word to us in time. We were not the only ones who survived and went into exile, but it was far too easy to lose contact after that."

"Why did they leave the elemental magicians?" Alira inquired.

"I do not know why for certain. I suspected they at least knew in their miniscule brains that magic could not be rendered entirely extinct or mankind would be subject to mass exterminations at the hands of the Churai."

Reldon sat down on the wooden frame. "How could they eliminate so many magicians and expect the fight against the Churai to still be maintained? They had to know it would be an uphill battle."

"The Churai were not perceived as the danger they are today. Similarly to magicians, there were less of them then. They were rarities only to be seen when venturing too far into Kuru lands and did not actively hunt the east like they do today. Understand that the murders of those magicians was devastating to the population of magical bloodlines. Bloodlines branch down family trees in some concentration or another throughout the many years, so magicians and Spellswords are much more plentiful than they were over a millennium ago. There may have been a few hundred magicians in existence and they murdered over half of them. This is why Lärim and Errum have been so ill-suited to combat the Churai threat – it was like burning and salting half of your crop fields before it came time to harvest."

"All right, say we believe all of that," Reldon said, "What does that have to do with Elly?"

Her gaze was like a snake as she spoke. "A great wrong was done to our kind. With the remaining magicians forced into servitude, a vault was made to seal all of the non-elemental Keitas away forever. The magicians of old insisted to the lords that they would seal it in such a way that it could never be opened, but secretly they left a backdoor that would only be accessible through the use of the amulets. The amulets predated all of us. I had never heard of them."

"I don't understand, then why did you need us? Couldn't anyone have collected the amulets, said the words, and gotten all of this back?" Alira said.

"The answer to that is extremely complicated. They knew it was going to need to be impossibly difficult to gain entrance or anyone would do it. If it were done by someone not powerful enough to defend it, the powers that existed might have seen fit to revise the mistake they had made in trusting the magicians to lock it themselves. Therefore the lock was created to require a collective magic level not normally attainable by a single person, or even a small group, and this is all assuming one is able to obtain the amulets and recall the words spoken to lock it in the first place.

And with how ruthless the lords were at that time, it would have been far too much to ask to leave those magicians alive."

Alira slowly sat down as well. "They killed the magicians who sealed it as well?!"

Grandma's nod was slow, with raised eyebrows, as if it were just a fact of life now. "Oh yes. Murdered them as well to ensure none remained who would ever know the words. However, they were not aware of my presence. As I was young at the time, I was able to remain hidden and commit to memory all of the words. It was not a matter of difficulty; it was out of pure necessity. Either I recalled those words or this power remained lost to us forever."

"Couldn't you have written those words down? It would have made it easier to remember."

"I did many times in the latter half of my life. Such an old language is difficult to hold onto during all those years of disuse. But I was not about to commit it all to paper and then die happily, hoping beyond hope that someone would find them and follow through on this age-old mission. No, I was going to see this through myself. So we devised a plan. And it involved her."

Elly hung on her every word, a level of attention she had rarely displayed before.

"We gathered together every willing non-elemental magician we could find. Few remained, and fewer were willing to assist us in our ambitions. In the end we gathered the three you know outside, Elliana's former self, and my daughter, Miria. Our aim was to devise a way for all of us to live long enough that we might see the coming of the Nurems. The legends had stated that they would possess more power than any who would ever live, and we reasoned they were the only ones who might be able to reunite the world with these Keitas."

"Back then it was just a legend," Reldon said, "Did you really believe that much that we would exist?"

"It was the only hope we had left. We were once young and hopeful, starry-eyed dreamers who refused to believe there was nothing we could do to make our friends' deaths anything but meaningless. Even if not the Nurems, we had no choice but to believe some child some day would be born with enough power to do it. We only knew that even with all of us together, we could not hope to open the vault again, and for over a thousand years, even to this day, speaking even in hushed whispers about this vault or the secret it possesses was regarded as heresy. Collaboration on a scale that would be needed proved impossible. So we set about our plan to wait out the centuries."

"How did you do it?" Alira asked.

"This may be difficult to understand, but the form of magic that I wield is called Inverse Magic. Succinctly, it is magic that deals in counteracting forces to lesser, equal, or even greater extents to the energy the force presents. If you fired an arrow at me, I could use this magic to slow it, stop it midair, or even reverse its course. In combat it is largely defensive, but used for more practical applications, it can prove invaluable. We reasoned after some time that if we combined Golden Magic and Inverse Magic and provided it enough pure energy, we may be able to reverse the course of one of the body's natural processes: aging."

"Clearly it worked," Reldon commented.

"Not without much tribulation. At first it was only an idea. But answer me this, young man, what is aging?"

He was befuddled by the question. "How…time affects the body?"

"In a manner of thinking you are correct, but we did not have the ability to manipulate time. We had to figure out over years what exact effects aging had on the body and at what rate so we could include it in our determination of how we could reverse it all at once. After some time we completed our calculations and decided it finally needed to be tested. One person volunteered – one half of the equation. It was her."

Elly didn't know how to handle this news. She only stared back at Grandma, her green eyes lost.

"She volunteered? No matter what happened, she wanted to do it?" Reldon asked, incredulous.

Grandma nodded with a frown. "She was the most zealous of all of us, intrinsically determined to an almost fanatical extent to be young forever. In a sense, she got exactly what she wanted."

Alira and Reldon gazed over at Elly, expecting her to ask one hundred questions, but the girl remained silent, a pensive sadness stamped on her face.

"What was her name? What was she like?" Alira asked for her.

"I remember not her original name, but she fancied going by Eterna. Fitting, given her fate. I do recall she had burning passion in her heart that few in history have ever possessed. Not merely for Golden Magic, but in every venture. She was a person in those years I knew her that would not accept excuses or barriers to what she desired. I swore she spent more late nights awake desperately scraping for a solution than any of us ever did. She was so certain our test was going to be successful, she refused to say goodbye to anyone."

"So the first trial was a success," Reldon presumed.

"It was a complete failure and set us back years. We began reversing the process of aging and at first we weren't certain it was working. By the time we had gone too far, it was too late. She aged backwards before our very eyes, years at a time. A full woman became an adolescent who became a child. Tearing away the connection as quickly as we could, we left her an infant. We were mortified at what we had done."

"Couldn't you change her back and try again?" Alira asked.

The old woman shook her head sadly. "As such natural processes function, my magic can only invert the function, not create an inverse of an inverse. That is not possible. Besides, the primary source of our control over such natural functions of the body was now a year old without any knowledge of magic. There was nothing we could do but try to ascertain where we went wrong and take care of this child until she could use magic again."

"You took care of her for years just so you could try again?"

"Oh dear boy, you know little of the lengths we went to perfect this process. Five years later we tried again and the same happened. Five years over and again we made small progress. It was infuriating. Decades passed and we felt we were no closer to unraveling this enigma. Again and again we tried. Each time the poor girl had no memory of what we had previously done, like a blank slate. We raised her like a daughter countless times, but we still felt as if she were little more than an animal to be symbolically slaughtered over and over.

"I was in my middle years when we had our first breakthrough. I knew not how much exactly we reduced her aging, but when we replicated it on ourselves we could see around five years pass without feeling any older. It was a success, but it would only extend our lives by a century or so, given our natural lives were slowly approaching their twilight years. It wasn't going to be enough. We had to keep going. However, this was during a time of great upheaval in Lärim and the others were drawn away for many years to fight wars, to tend to family…My daughter and I continued our work until we were able to see a century pass and only gain a few gray hairs. She would go no further, though, to my great disappointment. The very idea of what we were doing terrified her and she accused me of trying to deify myself. Regardless of my attempts to dissuade her, she left for the mountains where she would remain for most of her life.

Had she stayed, she would not have already surpassed my natural age to this day."

"How…how many times did you do that to Elly?" Alira asked, scared at what the answer would be.

"Would it assure you to know I lost count? By the time we had reverted her twenty times, was the twenty-first to be any more or less significant? The first time was undoubtedly the hardest, but after that we were so deep in the oceans of our folly that we had no choice but to continue for everyone's sake. Lärim grew tiresome and dangerous, so we left, her and I, to Ceiina hundreds of years ago where we could continue in peace."

"And you never told her. Then how is it that she's the age she is now? Even over hundreds of years she would still·be older, wouldn't she?" Reldon asked, slightly accusatory.

Grandma curled her lips.

"I had no choice but to continuously revert her back to a baby to erase her memories while I devised the next stage of progression."

"I saw it…" Alira said, startled, "The same Elly with a different name, over and over…never being able to see her friends again…being shielded from the world."

"I had little choice. The longer I allowed her to persist in a particular life, the more attachments she formed, and the less willing she was to assist me – not to mention a girl living for hundreds of years would have drawn far too much attention. It was a balancing act so precarious I had no choice but to keep her ignorant of what she existed for, lest she jeopardize everything we had spent epochs working towards," Grandma explained.

Reldon stood up. "How long did you keep this going? Does all this mean that Elly was reverted seven years ago?"

"Actually, no. After all these countless, wretched years even I was beginning to feel time's ravages affecting me as I took care of this child for what would have been numerous lifetimes. I was not going to be able to do it forever, and I knew that. I had succeeded in reducing my aging to a tiny fraction of what it had once been, and I decided it was time to stop. I would only attempt again if I waited long enough that death was imminent. I *had* to live long enough to see this through. In the end I decided to ritard her aging at five years old. That was around 200 years ago."

They all nearly shouted in surprise. "Elly is *two-hundred years old?!*"

"No, she is nearly as old as I am. Her current iteration is about that old, yes."

"Elly, can you…" Alira struggled to ask, "Remember something that happened that long ago?"

The small girl did not understand the question and shook her head. "I remember my friends like Rena and Jaria."

"Rena is a recent friend. Jaria likely died a hundred years ago," Grandma said flatly.

Elly immediately began to cry. Alira comforted her with a scowl towards Grandma.

Reldon glared at her. "How could you do this to her? For this long? Even if she did volunteer 1,200 years ago, she hasn't been the same person all these times you've done it!"

"That was part of the problem," Grandma continued, with little emotion, "I noticed over time she was beginning to remember. Times, places, and people that no one could possibly have been around to witness. There was a source of memories deep within her subconscious that I could not reach. Someday I knew she would remember enough to put a stop to it. So I had to stop. I had to allow her to live as normally as a near-immortal girl could."

"So long as she was still in your clutches," Reldon rebutted.

"I make no excuses for what has been done. The means were regrettable, and we were all aware. Eterna knew what the risks were. The cost of losing all of this forever was far too steep to simply do nothing. Now all of that is over. Elliana may live how she chooses and you, Ilewa Nuremil, are the only person who has ever existed who has the power to use all of these Keitas – to truly transcend the power any mortal might ever hope to wield. I told you many nights ago that there are powers in this world enough to destroy the Churai once and for all, but you would have to be strong enough in mind and body to grasp them. Now is your chance. The power is yours. Take it and fulfill your destiny!"

Reldon turned to Alira. *I don't know about this, Alira. Should any one person have this much power?*

But what happens to all of it if I don't take it? It could be used for evil means.

They aren't going to disappear after you use them – if someone is going to use them for evil means, they're going to whether you use them or not.

Then shouldn't I do it? If I turn all of this down and someone comes by and creates an army of non-elemental magicians, someone should be able to stop them!

"I think we should get some air. This is a lot," Reldon said aloud.

"Elly? Are you all right?" Alira asked the girl.

Her eyes were puffy and she tried several times to say something but couldn't.

"If it helps, my dear," Grandma said gently, "You are still the same person. Nothing has changed."

The young girl stood up and faced the old woman with a look of stubborn resolution.

"I…am not Eterna. My name is Elly. And I don't care about what Eterna wanted. I want to be me from now on."

With that she bolted out and up the long exit. Reldon and Alira went after, knowing that she was going to need a lot of time to come to terms with what she had learned. *Grandma was the only person in her life for so long and she had been lying to her from the beginning. That has to hurt.*

As they rounded the corner out into the night, there was far too much light.

Elly stood frozen in a sea of white light.

There were people, dozens of them, unmoving.

Two figures held long iron poles with bright balls of pure light at the end in a small spherical cage. One of the lightbearers' faces was familiar.

"Kaia, is that you?!" Alira shouted.

She said nothing in return, and only watched them with impassive eyes.

Soldiers formed a semicircle around the entrance, along with what looked like robed magicians.

And out of the darkness stepped a man, dressed in an elaborate doublet, coat, puffed trousers, and hat fit for a man of his station.

"Good evening, Xanem Nuremar and Ilewa Nuremil," came that familiar silky-smooth voice, "I trust you are keeping warm?"

Reldon and Alira froze as deeply as the ice surrounding them.

It was the High King himself.

"I must congratulate you on your ability to unseal this vault after such a long time. After many had long-since considered it to be nothing more than a footnote in history, it would seem the past has been brought to life again. Ah, and I believe I have not yet been acquainted with your accomplice," he said as Grandma stepped out into the light as well.

The light overhead only served to conceal her face further beneath her hood. "You already know of what I represent, young man. You have been taught to fear me. And for good reason."

"I'm certain you have both been told a great many new revelations tonight, friends," the High King said, turning back to Alira and Reldon, "But this woman has, at best, only given you her perspective, and at worst, complete falsehoods. Before anyone takes any rash action, it would be best for you to hear the true reason this vault exists and why she seeks to use it."

"We will listen," Reldon said, "but how did you know we were here or what we're doing?"

"That is not important now, but rest assured that in time you will know all. Of direst concern is that this vault is now open, its primal power released to the world. Do you understand why it was sealed away all those centuries ago?"

"It threatened your ancestors' power," Grandma interjected, "A great many men of good character were reduced to bloodthirsty animals by a power they could not control. I was there. I saw it."

The High King was not fazed. "Though I do not doubt that the minds of some men were corrupt and saw the opportunity to solidify their own position, there was a much graver reason this power was locked away. I do not claim to understand this from experience like the venerable woman does, but it created enough pain and consternation that its effects have reverberated through the years. It was a remarkably simple fact – the power was far too much for mankind to wield without being held in check. What your friend omits in her story is that social order, moral underpinnings, and man's entire sense of self-reliance were being torn down over the course of mere decades. These magicians made promises to the people they knew they could not keep. They offered them endless resources, a cure to all diseases, even to see their deceased loved ones live again. None of it was true, as you could likely surmise, but the hope itself was far too tantalizing for the good people to ignore, and they even took up arms in wars against their lords after the kingdoms revealed these plots to be naught but fantasies. The kingdoms of old struggled mightily to even contain this power, as no mortal soldier could hope to match the strength of a magician that could control the constants of the world around us at will. Shortly stated, the magicians that used this magic were quickly growing beyond control, like a wildfire. They could easily have become tyrants had the old lords not stopped them."

Grandma was clearly dismayed. "The promises that were made were not possible at that time, but if they had been allowed to continue their research, it was an inevitability. Lärimites saw this and rose up to claim the funding themselves. They were not going to be denied."

The High King made a flick of his wrist towards the Nurems. "You can see where the confusion lies. They raised entire revolts which led to wars over obscure ideas that would never come true. The dead cannot live again. There has never been a power in Irilitia that has ever been capable of such, and the magicians knew this. But even had they done none of this, it does not address the matter that they were simply a force of nature unbridled. Many kingdoms attempted to pass laws with the magicians taking part at the negotiations and as the signatories, but the magicians simply refused to attend. When such an unchecked power runs amuck and threatens to depose kings, what other decision are they left with?"

"Regardless of their 'position', murder is never an acceptable solution," Grandma riposted, "Only us few who remain even know of such matters. As it stands now, the Churai threat is greater than the specter of thousand-year-old magicians. If you believe that sealing up this power again would leave the world any safer, you are a fool."

The soldiers and magicians shifted uneasily at her candor towards the High King, but he didn't seem to mind.

"On that I believe we can agree. Now that the vault has been opened again, we do not have the same knowledge and means that our forebears did in locking it again. You are correct – this power would be invaluable in the fight against the Churai, and it should be used as such. However, where we may disagree is that these glass spheres hold enough exotic magical abilities to send our lands once again into chaos. Any reasonable person would not allow this to happen, given the chance to change it, which is why my intention is to allow the Nurems to make use of this power, and train one or two small groups of young non-elemental magicians so the ancient research to improve mankind can resume again. The rest would be carefully controlled by the High King, distributed as needed. Only a handful of magicians would be allowed to exist with these abilities, to prevent what happened a millennia ago."

Grandma breathed out hard. "Do you not see what he is proposing? He is suggesting himself as the sole source of access to the ancient power. *He* alone would control who is allowed to use it. *He* would choose how it is used. *He* would approve of the research projects. That is not progress. That is *tyranny*."

"You speak treason, woman. I am being as reasonable as I believe necessary, but you are crossing a line. I am your High King, and you shall speak to me as such."

"I have bowed to no king in one thousand years, and a welp like you will not be the first."

"That's enough! Stop, please!" Alira shouted at them. "Why can't we talk about this like civilized Lärimites?"

"Like it or not, young lady, you and your Ilewa are the weights on this scale. I am not leaving until he and his minions leave with him. And I will sooner die than give all this up. Not after 1,200 years. And I know a few others who believe the same."

Out of the darkness and to her side stepped Yapoti, Hanea, and the hulking figure of Sterling.

"And we shall not return to Nakisho unless we come to terms that you will not simply hole yourself away here and distribute the power to anyone who asks. She is right. You two are what stands between us. You must help us decide what is to be done. And I trust you will both do the right thing."

There, in the blinding light, Alira turned to her Ilewa, her eyes terrified but full of understanding.

We have to decide.

The decision should be simple, right?

We can't side with the High King.

Wait, why?

Grandma is right – he's going to take all of these Keitas and use them for his own purposes. Whoever controls them could someday control everything. That can't all be in the hands of one person.

It can be in the hands of one person – you! The Churai are the real threat, not the capital. Once we defeat them, free the Kuru, and bring peace to the world, why does it matter if the High King has it? This is incredible power we're talking about. The ability to control every aspect of reality…it's far too much to be allowing everyone to use it.

More knowledge is a good thing, Reldon! The more people who can help, the better the future will be. And what if something happens to me if I'm the only one who can use non-elemental magic? There's no backup plan!

Alira, if all new magicians can use this power, it will only be a matter of a lifetime until there's complete chaos, even if we destroy the Churai.

366

You can't know that, Reldon. Why can't you trust me?

He hesitated. "You know I trust you, Alira. You're the only one I trust with this," he said aloud.

"Then trust that this will be good for the world, not just a few!"

Reldon glanced at both the High King and at Grandma.

Then he remembered what Tycheronius had told him. He was not going to be able to trust any of them, but he especially warned him not to trust Grandma. The others were only looking to keep their own power, which would result in little more than status quo, but Grandma's ambitions were unknown.

As if somehow reading his thoughts, the High King spoke up again.

"Allow me to add one small detail you may find important. Would you like to know how Tycheronius Niuro, the famed Spellsword Master, met his end?" His voice was deadly serious.

Reldon's entire body lit up in alarm. "You...you know how he died?"

He nodded. "It has been kept a secret for a very long time, so it would not damage faith in the Spellswords. As you can probably imagine, he was not killed in battle. He was murdered."

"Please, Your Grace, who killed him?" Reldon begged.

"You may want to ask your elderly friend," was all he said.

Reldon turned slowly to face her, betrayal blackening his heart. She returned his pained expression with an even gaze.

"Grandma...? You... you killed him?"

For a long, strained moment she was silent.

"I had good reason to, but yes. I was given little choice."

His world was darkening around him, despite the flood of light. "How *could you!?*"

"If you listen, I will explain to you precisely why."

"No. No, I'm not listening to any more of your lies!"

The wisest, most righteous Spellsword to ever exist was murdered at her hands.

His anger boiled over. She tricked them. Lied to them. Hurt Elly. He had had enough.

Without warning he swung his arm to attention and released a blast of Phyrim directly towards her chest.

With a flash of movement, however, it was deflected and detonated high in the mountains above.

Alira stood before him, a barrier protecting the entourage behind her.

"Get out of the way, Alira. She murdered him!" he barked.

"Reldon, stop! She must have had a reason, but we won't know what the reason is if you kill her!" Alira exclaimed.

"She said it herself, *murder is never a solution!* Now move!"

She stood tall before him, her stolid eyes firm, but tears running down her cheeks.

"I won't let you answer murder with murder, Reldon. We will figure all of this out. Come with us and it will all be explained!"

"'Us'? You've already made your decision? How can you possibly go with her?!"

"How can you go with *him?* His ideas will lead to corruption, not peace!"

Reldon lowered his arm. "Alira, for once trust *me.* I'm your Ilewa, your best friend…I love you. She is going to use you until she can't, and then she will get rid of you. Just like she did to Tycheronius. Please, listen to me."

Her tears were freely flowing. "I can't, Reldon. I made a promise. I made a promise that I would not allow any lord, king, or even High King control my actions. It's what he does. Once you're in service to him, you can't leave. I'm sorry, Reldon. But I can't follow you. Not this time."

He shook his head mournfully and took a step back towards the High King as she stepped back towards Grandma and her friends. "We will have to disagree then. I'm sorry, Alira."

Alira cried mightily, and Grandma spoke up. "Then we are at an impasse. Let us make this simple. We will have need to discuss this matter further in the days to come, but in the meantime let us choose our most trusted to guard the vault. One each. Agreed?"

The High King almost seemed surprised by her sudden rationality. "We have an accord. Kaia Melossi, my head magician will remain and guard the vault until such a time that we might return and discuss further terms."

"Sterling, would you stay?" Grandma asked him.

He pounded his chest with one massive fist. "I will guard it with my life."

"Then let us go," the High King said simply, "Reldon, I am pleased you elected to see reason. You have chosen wisely."

Reldon did not answer him but watched Alira as they walked away. She looked back at him and they met eyes. Regret, sadness… but mostly hurt. Their trust was more damaged than even before and there was little they could do about it now. He tested their connection and found it closed. For now, at least for this moment, they were not friends, they were not in love…they were not even Ilewa.

Alira sat in front of the wash basin, her tears dripping into the cool, crystal water. The trek to a nearby safehouse Grandma had established some time ago was but a blur to her recollection, her sorrow overtaking her.

Surprisingly, Elly had decided to come with as well. Not for Grandma, she had told her, but because she would always follow her master. It had truly been the silver lining to a very cloudy day. Deep down, though she desperately longed for Reldon's comforting thoughts, she couldn't speak with him now. She was happy that no one had died in that confrontation, but it was only because she wouldn't let him.

I don't even recognize him anymore. From his obsession with Tycheronius to his trust in the High King, he's…just changed so much. I want the old Reldon back.

"How do you fare, young one?" Grandma's gentle voice broke her thoughts.

"I'm fine, thank you."

"It is no simple task to stand up to the ones you care for, dear. You made the right decision. You have earned some rest, and an explanation. Let me know when you are ready, and we will talk."

She squeezed her shoulder and left her alone again.

Well, if I'm going to be talking, I can't be looking like I've been crying for two hours. It brought a thin smile to her face.

Slipping her hands into the basin, she cupped some cold water and splashed it against her face, rubbing away the grime and the tears.

When she looked at herself in the basin again, her eyes were black.

Her heart nearly stopped. *Oh no.*

Oh yes, it responded *I told you I would return.*

She reached quickly for her mother's amulet.

There was no amulet. It was still at the vault.

It let loose a shrieking laugh.

You're mine now, girl.

The face in the basin contorted into a mere caricature of herself, her mouth twisted in an evil, sordid laughter that echoed into the night.

Epilogue

Rizellion tapped his long, claw-like nails on the arm of his throne, his foul mood making the other Churai uneasy.

I will not be outsmarted and outgamed by two children.

"Orders?" she asked him for the hundredth time.

"Silence. I will give you your orders when I am good and ready."

"Acknowledge."

They had snuck in under his nose, stolen the correct amulet, and somehow managed to find a way to escape with their lives. It would be their last mistake, he promised them that.

Rizellion the Churai Master did not lose. He had never lost. They could have their prize. They could have their power. But it would be mightily difficult to use it when there were no magicians left.

A wicked grin peeked out of the corner of his mouth.

"Orders."

His right-hand minion perked up. "Ready."

"Initiate takeover. Obey."

"Obey. Obey! Obey!"

Ethilia walked through the markets with an indignance at having to shop with the common folk.

I merely told Obrim that I was going out to get some fresh air, as I've been working all morning. The nerve of him to suggest I 'fetch the groceries' while out. What a base statement for such a position!

Her basket was filled with all manner of vegetables, and Tara's was filled with several cuts of stinking meats. It was a miracle they were out in the winter, or else the smells might have driven her mad.

She sighed, reading off of the parchment she had been given. "We have nearly everything on here."

"We need a few *tolios* fruit if I'm not mistaken," the magician woman responded.

Her shoulders slumped. "I don't even know what that is. He simply can't expect me to 'fetch his groceries' when he makes up the names of the ingredients. There is no way that is a real fruit."

"It is a real fruit! It grows to the west of here in a-"

She stopped suddenly, and Ethilia turned to appraise her. "Tara? Are you quite all right?"

"Ah...." She groaned, "It's my... head...Something is wrong!"

Ethilia swung about and set her basket down, creating a small golden harness around the magician's head.

"I...don't see anything physically wrong. Can you describe to me-"

She started screaming out in pain.

Several more screams pierced the sky as Ethilia stood up and watched two Magicians of Justice fall to their knees, grasping at their heads.

Crowds stood in confusion, not sure what to do about the screaming women who were clearly in immense pain.

Panic set in. Sprinting over to the other magicians, she encased them in a harness and found nothing wrong with them either.

I don't understand...it's not a physical ailment. It could be mental, but such ailments don't cause such wracking pain as this...

Twisting her hand, she sunk her focus deeper into her conscious mind.

That's when she saw it.

It was a void – a blackness. It was evil incarnate, but as familiar as a brother. She had seen it before, more intimately than anyone else.

She knew exactly what it was.

"Oh spirits no."

Pronunciation Guide

Adenakia: Ah-den-NAH-key-uh

Alira: Uh-LEER-uh

Aila Sethatendrikos: EYE-la seth-ah-TEN-dree-kos

Antixius: an-TICKS-ee-us

Atheria: Uh-THEE-ree-uh

Balon: BAY-lahn

Bradek: BRA-deck

Calderia: call-DARE-ee-uh

Churai: CHOO-rye

Darum: DAH-rum

Detryn: DET-rin

Drunerakerrum: droon-rah-KEH-rum

Dunan: DOO-nahn

Eleqorum: ella-CORE-uhm

Ethilia: Eh-THEE-lee-uh

Ferrela: fur-ELL-uh

Freiad: FRY-ad

Garen: GARE-en

Gihan: jee-HAHN

Huerogrand: HWEAR-oh-grand

Ilewa: ill-OO-uh

Ilisia: ill-EE-see-uh

Inderi-Xenus: in-dare-ee-ZEE-niss

Irilitia: ear-ill-LISH-ee-uh

Keinume: KAY-ee-noo-may

Keitas: KAY-ee-tahs

Kiera: KEE-ruh

Korraine: core-RAIN

Lärim: LAH-rim

Lendir: LEN-deer

Lynad: lin-NOD

Naiwa-ki
Shokassen: nye-wa key show-KAH-sen

Nakisho: NAH-key-show

Phyrim: FEAR-rim

Reldon: REL-din

Remdas-Kuwis: REM-dahs KYOO-is

Rizellion: rye-ZEL-ee-uhn

Rytzermion: rit-ZAIR-me-on

Sera: (Same as Serah)

Sillida: sill-LEED-uh

Tavia: TAH-vee-uh

Tebrias: TEH-bree-us

Teraxella: terra-ZELL-uh

Tessalia: tess-ALL-ee-uh

The Sjard: (replace "j" with a "y")

Tigrem: TEE-gruhm

Varia: VAH-ree-uh

Vecilia: Veh-SEE-lee-uh

Xaetius: ZAY-tee-iss

Xanem: ZAY-nuhm

Zarminius: zar-MIN-ee-us

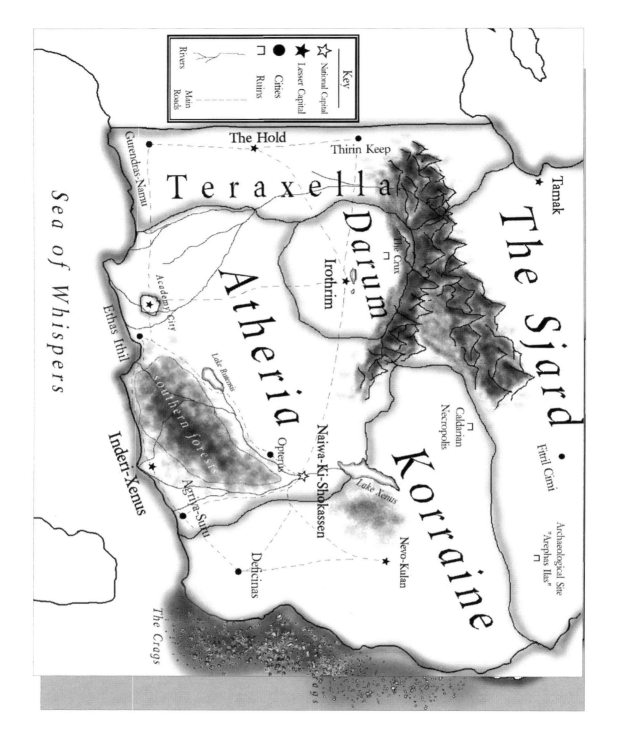

Key

National Capital ☆
Lesser Capital ★
Cities ●
Ruins ⌐
Rivers
Main Roads

Sea of Whispers

The Hold
Thirin Keep
Tamak
Gurendras-Namu

Teraxella

Darum
The Crux
Irothrim

The Sjard

Academy City
Ethas Ithil

Atheria

Lake Rutenis

southern forests

Inderi-Xenus

Agriya-Suhu

Opterux

Naiwa-Ki-Shokassen

Caldarian Necropolis

Lake Xenus

Korraine

Fitril Cimi

Archaeological Site "Arephas Ilas"

Deficinas

Nevo-Kulan

The Crags

Crags

Made in the USA
Columbia, SC
29 July 2022

64148837R00207